An
Assassination
on the
Agenda

AN ASSASSINATION ON THE AGENDA

A Lady Hardcastle Mystery

T E KINSEY

THOMAS & MERCER

Text copyright © 2024 by T E Kinsey
All rights reserved.

Published by Thomas & Mercer, Seattle

www.apub.com

Amazon, the Amazon logo, and Thomas & Mercer are trademarks of Amazon.com, Inc., or its affiliates.

ISBN-13: 9781662512957
eISBN: 9781662512964

Cover design by Tom Sanderson
Cover illustration by Jelly London

Printed in the United States of America

An Assassination on the Agenda

Chapter One

Jenkins the butler, ably assisted by Dewi the footman, was clearing the table after a delicious and highly entertaining lunch at The Grange.

Sir Hector Farley-Stroud had been on particularly fine form. Even though we'd heard most of his stories many times before, his exuberant mood brought new life to even the stalest of them. Meanwhile, Lady Farley-Stroud – who usually cast herself in the role of Voice of Reason and Sensibleness – had been relaxed enough to tell a few stories of her own.

The last of these had ended with an account of her standing on the verandah of their bungalow in India, pointing Sir Hector's rifle at a terrified, and very drunk, British lieutenant who was cowering under a mango tree. His giggling stumblings had awakened the household, and he had been caught trying to paint a regimental crest on one of the Farley-Strouds' goats as part of a game being played in the officers' mess at the nearby army garrison. Just harmless hijinks, he had thought, until he found himself caught in the dim light of the memsahib's lantern, with a loaded Martini-Henry rifle aimed at his head.

'I say, Gertie,' said Lady Hardcastle, clapping her hands with glee. 'Well done you. I take it he legged it?'

'There was a brief pause while he collected his paint pot and voided his bladder,' said Lady Farley-Stroud, 'but, yes – off back to barracks as fast as his soggy breeches could carry him.'

We all laughed.

'The thing m'dear wife always leaves out of this story,' said Sir Hector, 'is that all she was wearin' at the time was her weddin' ring, the locket I gave her for her birthday, and a white silk ribbon in her hair.'

Lady Hardcastle and I laughed again.

'Oh, it was too hot for nightdresses,' said Lady Farley-Stroud, airily. 'Though to this day I've never been sure whether it was the gun or my outfit that frightened the poor boy more.'

The generous lunch and its accompanying ebullient mood were by way of being a celebration of the Farley-Strouds' good fortune. Until very recently, they had been in dire financial straits, and had feared losing their home. But a couple of months earlier, Napoleonic treasure had been discovered in the grounds and Sir Hector had just sold some of it at auction. This had raised enough money to settle all their debts, with enough cash left over to see them comfortably through the next few years in the style to which they had never quite had the opportunity to become accustomed.

'But we're wastin' the sunshine,' said Lady Farley-Stroud. 'Shall we take our coffee on the terrace?'

'I'd better lock up me shotguns, what?' said Sir Hector. 'You know what Gertie's like when she gets out on a verandah.'

'Don't be silly, Hector – we haven't any goats for me to defend. And I'm far too well dressed for shootin'.'

Instructions were given to Jenkins, and we dutifully trooped through the house, across the ballroom, and out of the French doors on to the stone terrace.

We sat at the old wooden table and managed to sigh contentedly in unison, much to Lady Hardcastle's amusement.

As it turned out, fears of wasting the sunshine proved ill-founded. It was still as overcast as it had been when we arrived, though it was certainly warm enough for us to enjoy being in the fresh air. I took in the view across the Severn Valley to Wales while Jenkins fussed with the coffee things.

'Will you be taking a trip to visit Clarissa now you're super-rich?' said Lady Hardcastle.

'We're goin' down there in a few weeks,' said Lady Farley-Stroud, proudly. 'Straight after the summer party. If it ever happens.'

'What do you mean, dear? Might it not happen? We've been so looking forward to it.'

'It's in jeopardy, certainly.'

'Balderdash,' said Sir Hector. 'Lot of fuss about nothin'.'

'We absolutely cannot have a party without suitable entertainment,' insisted Lady Farley-Stroud, 'and our entertainers have failed us. I don't know what we'll do.'

Lady Hardcastle frowned. 'How have they failed you?'

'We booked the Clevedon Pier Orchestra, but their conductor, two viola players, a cellist and a flautist have been arrested for affray and aren't expected to be at liberty on the date in question.'

I suppressed a chuckle.

'But you know plenty of entertainers,' continued Lady Farley-Stroud. 'Actors, musicians and so on. I don't suppose any of your contacts could suggest a light orchestra to play for us? A selection of jolly tunes while we eat, a few waltzes and whatnot for dancin' – you know the sort of thing. A bit of *Merry Widow*, some Strauss.'

'I'll see what I can do. Whatshisname at the Duke's Theatre might know of someone.'

'Adlam,' I said. 'Edwin Adlam.'

'Oh, is he an orchestra leader?' said Lady Farley-Stroud. 'You see? Florence already has the answer.'

I shook my head. 'No, my lady, but he's the theatre manager, so he might know someone.'

'Ah, yes, theatre managers are exactly the sort of chaps who might be able to rustle up a musician or two. It would be an absolute boon if you could find us someone.'

'We'll save the day, Gertie dear,' said Lady Hardcastle. 'The party of the decade will go ahead, complete with musical entertainment of the highest order. You'll see.'

'I hope so,' said Sir Hector. 'Costin' me an absolute pile. Money's wasted if it doesn't go ahead because a few music wallahs got themselves into a scrape.'

'Don't be vulgar, Hector,' said Lady Farley-Stroud. 'One doesn't talk about the cost of these things.'

'Quite right, my little pear drop, quite right. Shouldn't mention it . . . Dashed expensive, though, let me tell you.'

'Well, yes,' said Lady Farley-Stroud. 'Actually it is. But I do so hope it isn't a failure. I have such plans. We shall hold it here' – she waved her hand to indicate the neatly tended lawn – 'where we shall announce the hardship fund we have set up for the villagers, and one or two other local projects we're investin' in. Then, while the chaps from the marquee company dismantle everythin' and restore the grounds to their former glory, we shall be across the Channel and on our way to Bordeaux. We shall arrive in time, I sincerely hope, to be there when our new grandchild comes into the world.'

'How delightful,' said Lady Hardcastle.

'I hope so. I shall be glad to get away by then. Costs notwithstandin', it's a surprisin' amount of work to organize a summer party. The Christmas bean feast more or less runs itself these days, but this . . . well.'

'Is there anything else we can do to help?' I asked.

'Oh, you're too kind, m'dear, but if you can save the entertainment side of things, you'll have done more than enough.'

'We shall make it our top priority,' said Lady Hardcastle. 'We find ourselves between projects at the moment. As a matter of fact, I've been thinking we might go away for a little while ourselves.'

'You have?' I said. 'Somewhere nice?'

'I wondered about a return to Venice. It's years since we last visited. I do so love it there.'

'It'll be even better with no one trying to kill us like last time.'

'Well, quite. So—'

A polite cough drifted across to us from the French doors.

'My apologies for interrupting,' said Jenkins, the owner of the cough. 'There is a telephone call for Lady Hardcastle.'

'For me?' she said. 'Who on earth . . . ?'

'A trunk call from London, my lady. A Mr Featherstonhaugh.'

'Ah, my dear brother.' Lady Hardcastle stood. 'Do excuse me, Gertie dear – I ought to take this. I do hope nothing awful has happened.'

'He asked me to reassure you that all is well with the family,' said Jenkins. 'It's—' He shook his head as though trying to remember the message precisely, but clearly decided it was too important to paraphrase and instead consulted the small piece of notepaper upon which he had recorded Harry's profound words. 'He says, "Tell her it's just work gubbins. She'd probably better bring Strongarm – save her having to explain it to her later." I presume "Strongarm" is Miss Armstrong?'

'It is,' I said. 'A private joke, I'm afraid.'

Harry was notionally our boss in the Secret Service Bureau. I had known him for years and it had become his habit to call me Strongarm. This, I felt, left me no option but to mispronounce his surname as Feather-Stone-Huff instead of Fanshaw. It wouldn't have been worthy of Oscar Wilde, but it amused us.

'Come along then, Flo,' said Lady Hardcastle. 'It's probably nothing but we'd better not keep the silly old fool waiting – a trunk call to Gloucestershire will eat up most of his department's budget on its own.'

We followed Jenkins back through the ballroom and along the corridors to the front hall and the telephone.

◆ ◆ ◆

Lady Hardcastle picked up the earpiece, and with her bending slightly towards me we were able to hold it between us so that we could both hear the call.

'Harry?' she said.

There were a few clicks and crackles.

'Off the line if you please, Operator,' said Harry's voice. 'Government business.'

There was another click and the line became slightly clearer.

'You there, sis?' he said.

'I am, dear,' said Lady Hardcastle. 'Flo, too.'

'What ho, Strongarm.'

'Hello, Mr Feather-Stone-Huff,' I said. 'How are you?'

'Very well indeed, thank you.'

'And Lady Lavinia?'

'In the pink.'

'Little Addie?'

'Little Addie is marvellous. Marauding about the house. Chattering away like a good 'un.'

'Harry?' said Lady Hardcastle.

'Yes, sis?'

'What do you want, dear? You've interrupted a rather convivial lunch with our friends.'

'Flo started it.'

Lady Hardcastle sighed and shook her head. 'Work gubbins, you said.'

6

'Just so, just so. Work, as you so rightly remind me, gubbins. I'm afraid I have to ask you to curtail your luncheon entirely and hie thee to Bristol at once. There's a little matter I need you to look into.'

'What sort of little matter?'

'A murder. Chap's been shot in the Tramway Centre.'

'Nasty place to be shot,' I said. 'I wouldn't want to be shot in the Tramway Centre.'

Harry laughed. 'Well, quite.'

Lady Hardcastle tutted, sighed and shook her head again. 'Surely the local rozzers can deal with that.'

'That's rather the point,' said Harry. 'I'd really prefer they didn't. I need you to get down there sharpish and take over before they get their police-issue size-tens all over it. Find out what you can about the shooting if you're able – you can use the local boys for that, by all means – but the absolute top priority is that they be strongly dissuaded from looking too closely into who the victim might be.'

'One of yours?'

'In a manner of speaking. Can't say too much over the telephone. Just get down there, throw your weight about a bit, and shut the local gendarmes out.'

'I'm flattered by your confidence in the level of influence we have over the Bristol police, dear, but I'm not sure it will be as easy as that.'

'Of course it will. Just take your War Office letters of authority with you and wave them about a bit. Junior officers will wilt before you.'

'And their superiors?'

'They might be a little less liable to swoon in the presence of fancy headed notepaper, it's true, but I'll cable the chief constable and anyone else I can think of to let them know the big boys are taking over. You know a chap there, don't you? Sutherland?'

'Sunderland,' said Lady Hardcastle. 'But he's just an inspector.'

'That's the spirit,' said Harry blithely. 'Knew you could handle it. Call me at home this evening to let me know how you got on.'

'Yes, but—'

'Got to dash, sis. Things to sort out at this end. Everyone's in a frightful flap. Talk to you later. Toodle-oo.'

The line went dead.

'Well, really,' said Lady Hardcastle as she replaced the earpiece. 'What an exasperating man he is.'

'We'd better say our goodbyes, though,' I said. 'Exasperating or not, he did seem rather keen that we not hang about.'

'Teacher's pet.'

It was my turn to sigh and shake my head.

She sighed as well. 'You're right, dear, of course. We'd better get our skates on.'

We said our hurried goodbyes to the Farley-Strouds, and Lady Hardcastle reassured them that she would make every effort to find them a replacement orchestra.

I'd taken only a sip of champagne at lunch to toast our friends' good fortune and continuing good health, so I took the wheel as we drove Lady Hardcastle's Rolls-Royce Silver Ghost Roadster back to the house.

Halfway down the long hill that led back to the village green, we saw my dear friend Daisy Spratt – legendary barmaid and loving butcher's daughter – trudging towards us carrying a canvas satchel. I slowed.

'Hello, you two,' she said. 'You in a hurry?'

'Sort of,' I said. 'What do you need?'

'A lift up this bloomin' 'ill.'

I looked at Lady Hardcastle. She nodded.

'Wait here, Dais,' I said, and drove off down the hill.

Once round the green had me pointing in the right direction, and I drove up to where Daisy was sitting obediently on the grass verge waiting for us.

Lady Hardcastle hopped out. 'I'll wait here, unless you fancy a trip on the luggage rack.'

Daisy clambered gratefully in. 'Thank you, m'lady. I remember what 'appened to Cissy when she rode on the back. Still talks about landin' upside down between you with her drawers on show, she does.'

'Undignified, but hilarious,' I said. 'I take it you're going to The Grange?'

'I am.'

Lady Hardcastle set off down the hill on foot. 'I'll see you at home, unless you catch me up.'

I drove on.

'You been up there yourselves?' asked Daisy.

'For lunch, yes.'

'How were they? They's been all of a pother since they fellas from the orchestra got arrested. Lady Farley-Stroud reckons the whole thing'll be a washout.'

'She's still mildly pothered.'

'Mildly? When I last saw her she was in a right old panic. I can't say I blames her, mind. A party without music i'n't no party at all, is it?'

'It would certainly be a little less lively. But Herself has promised to sort something out, so there was a glimmer of optimism before we were called away.'

'Who'd dare call you away?'

'Harry.'

'Ah. Work, I s'pose.'

'Indeed. But what are you up to? Have you been summoned to the big house?'

'I'm in charge of the drink. Joe delegated it. He says I knows as much as he does about runnin' the pub and it's about time I started takin' on extra responsibilities.'

'Quite right, too. Well done you.'

'I was thinkin' we might supply the wine and champagne, an' all, but I doesn't know so much about that. I'm more of a beer and cider girl. Maybe a brandy or port on special occasions.'

'Herself uses a wine merchant in town – she'll give you an introduction, I'm sure. They'll take good care of a friend of Lady Hardcastle. And I'm certain they'd give favourable rates for a party at the home of the newly rich lord of the manor in Littleton Cotterell, even if you weren't a good friend of one of their most profitable customers.'

'That's very decent of you. But never mind all that, where 'ave you been summoned to? You off to London?'

'Just to Bristol. A murder.'

'What's your top-secret lot got to do with a murder?'

'Who knows?'

'Top secret, eh?'

'So secret they're not even telling us. We've just been told to get to town and make our presence felt.'

'You's good at that, and Lady H is a master of it. If she turns up somewhere, everyone knows about it.'

'Don't they just?'

We had arrived by now at the front door of The Grange.

Daisy clasped the satchel to her chest and got out of the car. 'Wish me luck.'

'You don't need luck, Dais. Just be you. You've got all your proposals and costings there?'

She gripped the satchel even tighter. 'Down to the last farthing.'

'Then you'll be fine.'

'Thanks, Flo.'

'I have to go and get Herself or she'll spend the rest of the afternoon complaining about having to walk home. Let me know how you get on.'

I waved over my shoulder as I drove off.

Lady Hardcastle hadn't made much progress by the time I caught up with her. I parped the horn as I approached and she stopped walking to wait for me.

She clambered wearily in. 'Thank goodness you're back.'

'You've walked all of twenty yards since I left you.'

'Twenty exhausting yards in impractical summer shoes. I couldn't have gone another step.'

'You poor old thing.'

'I *am* a poor old thing,' she said. 'What's Daisy up to?'

'She's in charge of the booze at the Farley-Strouds' summer party.'

'Is she, by crikey? Good for her. It's about time Old Joe started giving her more responsibility.'

'That's exactly what Joe said. I wonder if he's winding down to retirement.'

'Possibly. Mrs Arnold has never been well – I don't think I'd need to take my boots and stockings off to count the number of times we've seen her in the pub. Perhaps they're hoping Fred Spratt will buy the place and give it to daughter Daisy to run. Then they can retire to the country.'

'They live in the country.'

'They live in the country and run a pub, though. Living in the country and not running a pub seems like a much more relaxing proposition.'

'I live in the country and don't run a pub and I almost never relax,' I said.

'That's because you are still young and vigorous, dear. You are a whirring dynamo of energy – you don't need to relax. It would frustrate you and make you melancholy.'

'It would make me extremely happy until I became aware of the mess you were making, then I'd not be able to rest until I'd tidied up after you.'

'Then I provide a valuable service – I'm keeping you young and active. But it's no wonder Old Joe wants to slow down a bit – he must be at least a hundred and four years old.'

'I think he's sixty-two.'

'Even worse, then. Imagine how tough his life must have been to be only sixty-two but to look a hundred and four.'

Back at the house, Edna and Miss Jones had already left for the day, so we had no one to greet us as we hurried in.

Lady Hardcastle changed her impractical summer shoes for more practical summer boots, while I collected whatever I thought might be necessary – most especially our War Office letters in their leather wallet.

With one last look in the mirror to check that we looked suitably professional and imposing, we locked up and set off in the Rolls towards the Gloucester Road and on to Bristol.

◆　◆　◆

'Have you any idea what's going on?' I asked as we motored steadily towards town.

'Not a clue, dear,' said Lady Hardcastle from the passenger seat. 'Not a blessed clue.' She stared out of the side window for a few moments at the passing countryside. 'Harry's been wittering on since late last year about some chaps his Special Branch bully boys have been keeping an eye on – perhaps it's something to do with them.'

'The business with the newspaper advertisements in *The Times*?'

'Exactly that. As part of his continuing efforts to be thoroughly infuriating, though, he's never elaborated, so I'm still none the wiser.'

'Do you have a plan?'

'I'm not sure we have much option but to do as he suggests: waft our credentials under a few people's noses and stake our shaky claim to the case.'

'They're not going to like it.'

'They're going to be livid. I predict a good deal of bombast, chest puffing, and "I don't care if your letters are signed by the King himself".'

I sighed. 'I usually regard not being taken seriously as an advantage in our line of work, but there are times . . .'

'We can only do what we can do,' said Lady Hardcastle. 'More than that we . . . well, you get the picture.'

'You should write that down and send it to the *Bristol News*. They have a column for witty aphorisms.'

She laughed. 'Not my finest work, I grant you, but the sentiment is sound. Harry knew what he was letting himself in for when he sent us up against the massed egos of the Bristol Constabulary – he has only himself to blame if we come away with nothing more than an earful of abuse. I'm not especially keen on the idea of anything being considered to be "men's work", but I do rather think snarling arguments over who's got the most luxuriant chest hair are best left to the boys.'

'You could give them a run for their money if it were chin hair.'

'Don't remind me, dear. I don't know where the blessed things suddenly sprout from. And why are they grey?'

'It's one of the ineffable mysteries of the human body,' I said. 'They might surprise us, though.'

'My chin hairs?'

'One day you're going to do that and—'

'The wind will change and I'll be stuck like it forever?'

'Stuck like an irritating child? I fear that ship has sailed. I was going to say you'll get a smack in the chops . . . but whatever frightens you more, to be honest. Clearly, I meant that the fine men of the Bristol Constabulary might surprise us. They might be grateful to get a troublesome murder off their books.'

'We shall cling to that tiny speck of hope.'

◆　◆　◆

It took us the best part of an hour to get to the middle of Bristol. I had been concerned that we might not find the scene of the crime, nor any biddable constables from whom we could take over control of the investigation, but my fears dissolved as soon as we emerged from Nelson Street on to the north side of the Tramway Centre.

The site of the shooting was made obvious by the presence of a large crowd of gawpers down by the Floating Harbour. As we drew near we could see that a substantial area of road and pavement had been blocked off with heavy wooden trestles. There were three men within the cordon – detectives by the look of them – and the whole thing was guarded by two of the burliest police officers ever seen in the West Country.

I parked as close as I could, being careful to avoid the confusing mesh of tramlines that criss-crossed the Centre. We alighted, straightened our hats, and pushed our way through the crowd.

We encountered a small amount of mulish resistance, but it faded quickly away when it collided with Lady Hardcastle's smilingly calm politeness. Her friendly explanation that 'We need to get through because we need to be at the front' worked wonders and we moved swiftly through the crowd. For reasons unknown, this completely meaningless phrase scattered people before us like the tiny fish who scoot away from your feet when you paddle in the warm water of the Mediterranean Sea or the Indian Ocean.

As we neared the trestles, my heart sank. Our old 'friend' Sergeant Massive Beard had been relieved of his usual antagonizing-the-public-at-the-front-desk duties and drafted in to antagonize the public at the scene of the shooting.

'That's far enough, ladies,' he said as we approached.

Lady Hardcastle smiled her most dazzlingly charming smile. Birds sang in the trees and the very heavens rejoiced to see such warmth and beauty.

'Oh,' said the sergeant, irritably. 'It's you.'

'It is I, indeed,' she said. 'And you know Miss Armstrong, of course – you're old friends, you and she.'

'Clear off, the pair of you. There's nothing to see here.'

'Would that we could, my dear Sergeant. Would that we could. You see, the thing is, we're here on Crown business and I'm afraid I really must insist that you let us through.'

The sergeant let out a dismissive *pfft* and turned his attention to a couple of men to our right, one of whom was armed with a camera.

'You there,' he said. 'Stop right there. No pictures. The press will be fully briefed by the inspector in due course. Until then, you can clear off out of it.'

Meanwhile, I had passed the leather wallet to Lady Hardcastle and she was fishing carefully inside for our War Office letters. The irascible sergeant turned his attention to us once more.

'I thought I told you two to—' he began.

'To clear off, Sergeant?' said Lady Hardcastle. 'Yes, you did. But I told you we were here on Crown business, so I'm afraid we are unable to do as you ask.' She handed him the two letters. 'As you can see, these are signed by His Majesty's Secretary of State for War, and grant us the authority to act on his behalf in matters of national security.'

'I don't care if they're signed by—'

'By the King himself? Wouldn't it be just too glamorous and exciting if they had been? I was at the Coronation, you know. He's a striking fellow, King George. Not as tall as one might imagine – a couple of inches shorter than I am, I should say – but he has a way about him. It must be something in the royal blood, don't you think? His father was the same. I met him, too, you know.'

'Look, *my lady*, I couldn't care less if you danced the hornpipe with His Majesty dressed as a Japanese princess—'

'Actually, since you mention it—'

'—you are not coming through and that is my final word on the subject.' He handed back the letters. 'Good day to you.'

There was movement behind him and one of the detectives spoke over the hubbub of the crowd.

'Everything all right there, Sergeant?' It was Inspector Sunderland.

'All under control, sir,' said the sergeant. 'I was just asking these two ladies to leave.'

'Which two . . . ? Good heavens. Lady Hardcastle and Miss Armstrong. Well, there's a surprise. How splendid to see you.'

'You too, Inspector dear.'

'Come for a look at our crime scene, eh?'

'In a manner of speaking.'

'I might have known,' he said with a friendly chuckle. 'Nothing to interest you here, though, I'm afraid. Simple street shooting. Foreign chap. Came from one of the boats in the harbour, we assume.'

Lady Hardcastle and I stepped to either side of the sergeant and approached the wooden barrier behind him. He puffed irritably again and began to take out his frustration on a courting couple who were craning their necks for a better view. I started to compile a mental list of at least a dozen more appropriate activities for a romantic rendezvous than trying to get a glimpse of a dead body, but it could just be that I was out of touch with the tastes and interests of the young.

Lady Hardcastle offered Inspector Sunderland the leather wallet.

'You know of our day jobs, Inspector,' she said, indicating that he should open the wallet and take a look inside. 'I'm afraid we're under orders from Whitehall to take over your investigation.'

Inspector Sunderland glanced quickly at the two letters before replacing them in the wallet and handing it back to Lady Hardcastle. I had worried he might be resentful of our usurpation of his authority, but he actually seemed rather amused.

'You'd better come through then, my lady,' he said. 'Sergeant. Move the barrier aside and let the ladies past, please.'

Making no secret of his annoyance, the sergeant complied, and we were admitted to the heart of the investigation.

◆ ◆ ◆

Clear of the obstructing barrier and the obstructive sergeant, we were finally able to get a proper look at the body. Or we would have been, had the body been there. It was not – the area still fully occupying the attention of two other detectives was entirely corpse-free. A small bloodstain on the footpath was the only evidence that a man's life had recently met a violent end there.

'The SSB wants this one?' said Inspector Sunderland as we approached the others.

'Apparently so,' said Lady Hardcastle. 'Though I'm not able to say why at this point.'

'It's all hush-hush, then?'

'Oh, I'm sure it would be – you know what we're like down at the Secret Service Bureau – but that's not why, I'm afraid. The plain truth is that I'm not able to explain our interest because I have no idea what it is. We received a call from my brother a little over an hour ago telling us to get down here and take over. He said no more. If you're certain the victim isn't British, you already know more than we do.'

'According to the first men on the scene, the labels in his clothes and the money in his pockets would have marked him as having at least visited another country, even if our witnesses hadn't heard him "speaking in foreign" as he lay dying.'

'Any idea what sort of foreign?' I asked.

'Nothing they recognized, but that's quite telling on its own. Bristol's a busy port. We've people here from all over Europe, the Indies, the Far East, Africa – anyone who lives in the city will have heard dozens of languages and accents over the years. But no one could place him.'

'What about the labels and currency?'

'I didn't see them myself – the mortuary boys had already taken him off to Gosling's lair by the time I arrived.'

'That was swift,' said Lady Hardcastle.

'Can't leave a murdered man in the middle of the city in the middle of a summer's day,' said the inspector. 'Robs the victim of his dignity and disrupts the lives of the living.'

'Though you've managed to do that pretty well with your saw-horses and gruff sergeants.'

'I made the very same point myself when I got here,' he said. 'Marsh?'

One of the other detectives turned round. I'd seen him before at the Bridewell but we'd never spoken.

'Sir?' he said.

'This is Lady Hardcastle, and this is Miss Armstrong. They're from the War Office and they're taking over the case. We're to give them every assistance.'

Marsh snorted. 'The War Office, sir? These two?'

'These two, Marsh,' said Inspector Sunderland.

'But why are we—'

'We're to give them every assistance, Marsh, and we are to treat them with the utmost respect. Do I make myself clear?'

'Quite clear, sir,' said Marsh with an insolent smirk.

'You were the first on the scene?' asked Lady Hardcastle.

'No, my lady, that would be Constable Hawkins over there.' Marsh indicated the second uniformed officer manning the barrier.

'Were you the first *detective* on the scene, then?' I asked, barely managing to suppress a weary sigh.

'That's right, Miss.'

'What did you see?'

'A dead body, Miss. He'd been shot.'

'So we're given to understand,' I said, as patiently as I could. 'You searched his clothing for some indication of his identity?'

'Of course I did. We know what we're doing down here, even if we're not fancy *ladies* from the War Office.'

'Marsh,' said Inspector Sunderland. 'Did I or did I not just tell you to treat them with the utmost respect?'

'Yes, but—'

'Just answer their questions.'

Marsh sighed. 'I searched his pockets. He had two shillings and sixpence, three farthings in English money, a door key, a notebook and pencil, and three banknotes. At least I presume they were banknotes. They looked like money but I couldn't make head nor tail of them.'

'Did you not recognize the language at all?' asked Lady Hardcastle.

'I couldn't even read the letters,' he said.

Lady Hardcastle took out her own notebook and mechanical pencil, both of which had been gifts from Inspector Sunderland not long after we first worked with him. He noticed them now and smiled as Lady Hardcastle wrote a few lines.

'Did it look like any of these?' she said, showing the book to Marsh.

'Middle one,' said Marsh, confidently. 'Definitely the middle one. Is it some sort of code?'

'It's Cyrillic,' she said.

Marsh frowned. 'From . . . Cyril? Where's that to?'

Lady Hardcastle smiled. 'In a manner of speaking, I suppose it is. It's an alphabet created by the followers of St Cyril and his missionary pal – whose name eludes me for the moment – to render the Slavic languages of Eastern Europe and parts of Asia. It's used in Russia and its neighbours, as well as in the Balkans and quite a few other places besides. Methodius, that was his name. I knew I'd remember if I just stopped trying. Where was our victim from?'

'No idea, my lady,' said Marsh. 'Somewhere in Europe, perhaps?'

'Not from Mongolia or anywhere like that, then? The labels in his clothes?'

'Same sort of writing.'

'Intriguing,' said Lady Hardcastle. 'Thank you, Marsh. You have witness statements, you say?'

'Yes – Channing and I took them down between us.' He indicated the other detective. 'It was broad daylight in the middle of the city. We're not short of people who saw the murder.'

'I'd like you to collate them and cross-check them, please. We'll need a decent description of the killer and as full an account of the events leading up to and immediately following the shooting as we can get—'

'I think we know how to compile witness statements—'

'And we'll need your men to make a thorough search of the ground,' continued Lady Hardcastle, without so much as pausing to acknowledge his interruption. 'Pay special attention to anywhere the killer was before and after he fired the fatal shot. Do we know what sort of gun he used?'

Marsh wearily consulted his own notebook. 'A pistol of some kind, apparently. No one seems sure what sort, but one man who was close by when the victim was shot said he thought it "wasn't a revolver".'

'In that case, be on particular lookout for a spent cartridge casing – it might help us to identify the weapon.'

Marsh was shaking his head as he put away his notebook. 'Will there be anything else, my lady?'

'See if you can find anyone who saw where the killer went after he shot our man, and let Inspector Sunderland have your full report no later than tomorrow lunchtime.'

'But that's hours of work.'

'Best not to spend any more time arguing with me, then, eh?'

Marsh sloped off, shaking his head once more.

'I doubt there's anything we can learn from the bloodstain,' said Lady Hardcastle once he was gone, 'so if your men want to arrange for that to be cleaned up, I'd have no objection.'

'Right you are,' said the inspector. 'What about clearing this cordon?'

'That's up to you, Inspector dear. Marsh will have an easier time of searching the ground if he's unimpeded by gawpers and gongoozlers, but I imagine they'll disperse anyway once they realize there's nothing for them to gawp at.'

'I'll let them know,' said Sunderland. 'What would you like me to do?'

'You said the body is at the mortuary?'

'Yes. And Gosling's there so he should have had a chance to look at it already.'

'In that case, might you be able to meet us there? We can have a chat about all this away from disapproving ears.'

'Of course. I'm more than a little curious to find out what this is all about.'

'You and me both. First, though, could you be an absolute love and pop back to the Bridewell? It's asking a lot, but could you make it plain to the top-hatters back at headquarters that we're taking over? It'll soften the blow if it comes first from you.'

The inspector laughed. 'Yes, I can do that.'

'You're sure?' said Lady Hardcastle. 'I don't want to cause trouble for you.'

'It will be fun.'

'That's the spirit – thank you. We'll drop in and confirm things later. Harry is supposedly sending telegrams to the chief constable and assorted other worthies so I'm hoping we'll face only harrumphing and resentment by the time we get there. If we turn up any earlier we'll have a great many more arguments.'

With a round of thanks and handshakes, we left the inspector and returned to the Rolls.

Chapter Two

The public mortuary was housed in a handsome new building in the Old Market area of the city. The facade was clean and sombre in the modern style, with a simple porticoed entrance. To the left was a tall archway leading to the rear of the building, large enough for the discreet coming and going of mortuary vans and hearses.

The forecourt provided ample room for the arrival of carriages, as well as parking spaces for several motor cars. I tucked the Rolls into a space beneath the shade of a large tree and we made our way to the main door.

We were met at the reception desk by a uniformed man with a neatly waxed moustache.

'Good afternoon,' he said softly. 'Are you here for a viewing?'

'No,' said Lady Hardcastle. 'We're here to see Dr Gosling. Lady Hardcastle and Miss Armstrong.'

'Dr Gosling is busy with an autopsy at the moment, my lady – he shan't be available for some time.'

'Yes, we know. The post-mortem is the reason for our visit.'

'Are you relatives of the deceased, my lady?'

'No, we're here on official business. Would you please be kind enough to tell Dr Gosling that we're here?'

'It's really most irregular. Dr Gosling does not like to be interrupted while he is at work.'

'None of us does. But please let him know we've arrived and that Inspector Sunderland of the Bristol CID will be here shortly, too.'

The man looked at us both for a few moments, then at the clock on the wall behind his desk. Then back to us. Then at the ledger open in front of him. Then at the clock.

'Very well,' he said at length. 'There are chairs over there if you would care to make yourselves comfortable while you wait. I may be some time.'

He disappeared through a door at the rear of his cubbyhole and we perched ourselves on the indicated chairs.

'Why didn't he just pick up the telephone?' I said.

'No idea, dear,' said Lady Hardcastle. 'Perhaps there's some sort of prohibition against holding a telephone while one is conducting an autopsy. Hygiene and all that sort of malarkey.'

'Perhaps. Or perhaps Dr Gosling is something of a tartar and our man there is terrified of him.'

Lady Hardcastle laughed. 'Wouldn't that be too precious? Dear, sweet Sim – a charming, affable duffer at home, an absolute martinet at work.'

We didn't have to wait long before the man reappeared through an entirely different door and coughed politely.

'Dr Gosling will see you now,' he said. 'Please follow me.'

He led us along green-painted corridors, his heels clicking softly on the newly laid linoleum. Eventually we arrived at a pair of heavy double doors with porthole windows. A sign above indicated that this was Autopsy Room 1.

The man pushed open one of the doors and stepped inside, holding it open for us to follow him.

'Lady Hardcastle and Miss . . . ?' he began.

'Armstrong,' said Dr Gosling. 'Thank you, Hathaway. Come on in, you two. What an unexpected treat. Come to see me in my lair?'

Hathaway had already retreated to the safety of his reception desk as we made our way further into the spacious room. It was white-tiled and gleaming. A cross between an operating theatre and a laboratory. It smelled of disinfectant and blood.

'Hello, Sim dear,' said Lady Hardcastle. 'We've come to see your body.'

Dr Gosling laughed. 'I say, that's rather forward of you, Em. I had no idea you felt that way.'

I tutted and indicated the murder victim on the examination table.

'You're worse than she is,' I said.

He grinned. 'And how do you know about John Doe here?'

'We know he was shot in the Tramway Centre—'

'What a terrible place to be—'

'Don't, dear. Flo's already in trouble for that one.'

'Sorry.'

'We know he was shot in the Tramway Centre,' continued Lady Hardcastle, 'that he came from Eastern Europe – Russia or the Balkans are most likely – and that the Secret Service Bureau wants Flo and me to take charge of the case.'

'The SSB?' said Dr Gosling, his cheerful smile disappearing. 'Who on earth *is* he?'

'Harry refused to say over the telephone. We know only that "we're" interested in him and that Harry doesn't want anyone else asking too many questions about who he is or where he's from.'

'Goodness me. So I have to sign the Official Secrets Act? Am I in danger?'

'Goodness you, indeed; not yet; and of course not. In that order.'

'Well, that's something, I suppose.'

'Do you have his clothes?' I asked.

Dr Gosling pointed to a paper sack in the corner of the room.

'Over there,' he said. 'I haven't had a chance to go through them yet.'

'Do you mind if I do?'

'Be my guest. It's your case, after all.'

I tipped the clothes and boots out on to the laboratory bench and started to examine them. The boots were well worn, but cared for. They had been recently resoled and the laces were almost new. The insole was loose at the heel of the right one and I thought for a moment that I might have discovered a hidden compartment . . . but sometimes a loose insole is just a loose insole.

The contents of the pockets of the man's jacket and trousers were almost exactly as Marsh had described, though he had missed a farthing in the left trouser pocket, making the total two shillings and sevenpence. The notebook was brand new and, as yet, unused.

I handed one of the banknotes to Lady Hardcastle.

'Serbia,' I said.

'It is indeed,' she agreed.

'Don't tell me you read Serbian,' said Dr Gosling, looking over our shoulders.

'Enough to spot the word "Serbia",' I said, pointing to the two instances of the word on the note. 'More than that and you'll have to speak to my translator here.'

'So he had Serbian currency and clothes,' said Lady Hardcastle, distractedly. 'He spoke a language that no one recognized, and he was shot in broad daylight in a busy part of town. Cause of death was the gunshot, I take it?'

'It was. It was a terrible shot, mind you. The bullet came from his left-hand side, grazed the left first rib and nicked the subclavian artery on the way, then lodged in the spine between the first and second thoracic vertebrae. Spinal cord damage means he would probably have lost the use of his arms immediately, but he would have bled to death very quickly anyway.'

'That *is* a terrible shot,' said Lady Hardcastle.

'Well, quite. It was more by chance than good shooting that the killer is a killer and not just a man with a gun. Miles from the heart, miles from the head – goodness only knows what he was aiming at.' Dr Gosling reached over to the bench and retrieved a polished kidney dish. 'This is the bullet.'

'Any idea of the calibre?' asked Lady Hardcastle.

'It's a peculiar one,' he said. 'Allowing for a little distortion it would have experienced on its deadly journey, my trusty micrometer puts it at a little over 0.35 inches. Not a calibre I recognize.'

Lady Hardcastle looked around and then plucked a ready reckoner from the bookshelf. She leafed through it for a moment.

'Roughly nine millimetres,' she said.

'If you say so, old thing,' said Dr Gosling. 'But that's a new one on me. Most often we see the Webley .455 in here – chaps brought them back from their time in the army. I've seen 7.63 millimetre bullets from the broomhandle Mauser – there's a local gang that loves that one.'

'There's the German Luger,' said Lady Hardcastle. ''That uses a 9 millimetre round. And there's a new one from Belgium, the FN 1910 – there's a variant of that which takes the same ammunition.'

'Well, I'll be blowed.'

'I'm going to ask you to do something, Sim dear,' said Lady Hardcastle, returning the book to its place on the shelf. 'I would never ask you to lie, nor would I ask you to submit substandard work—'

'But you want me to leave all that stuff out,' he said.

'Are you prepared to do that? I can't justify it. I can't say, "You must do this because the safety of the nation depends upon it," because at this moment Flo and I know only as much as you do. But I trust Harry. He's an infuriating bufflehead – I mean, really, you have no idea – but he knows his onions. He was insistent that we make every effort to dissuade the local rozzers from trying to find out too much about our victim.'

'I understand, Em, really I do.'

'Thank you. Can you list his possessions as blandly as possible, please? Make no mention of the fact that you now know the notes are from the National Bank of Serbia. If it's customary to record the calibre of the bullet, then obviously you must do so, but report it in inches and don't disclose that you know of European 9 millimetre weapons. Would that compromise you?'

'Not at all, old sport, not at all. I'm here to ascertain cause of death and I can describe that in the most excruciatingly tedious detail without giving the game away. The city pays detectives to detect, and ordinarily they would do just that based on my findings. But if you're in charge of detection then it's your job to detect that he was a Serbian killed with a German or Belgian gun, not theirs. And certainly not mine. It's not my place to speculate at all – I deal in primary facts, old thing. The abduction of hypotheses therefrom is entirely up to chaps like you.'

'Thank you, dear. If I knew more, I would tell you at once. Actually, I probably wouldn't. But you know what I mean. Thank you for trusting me.'

The door swung open and we all turned to see Hathaway ushering in a new visitor.

'Inspector Sunderland to see you, sir,' he said, before turning smartly on his heel and gliding back to his post.

'Sunderland,' said Dr Gosling, warmly.

'Gosling,' replied Inspector Sunderland.

'We were just discussing how little I know about your murder victim.'

'Lady Hardcastle's murder victim,' said the inspector.

'We discussed that side of it, too. Confusing, isn't it? I must say I prefer a good old-fashioned barney between good old-fashioned gangsters. A bit of a territorial dispute, razors at dead of night – you know the drill. Everyone knows who's running the investigation and everyone knows who can say what to whom. This hugger-mugger stuff makes my head spin.'

'Mine too, if I'm honest,' said the inspector. 'Do you have all the information you need, my lady?'

'For now, yes, I think so. Simeon has been most helpful.'

'In that case, may I take you away? The chief superintendent wishes to have words.'

'Does he, indeed? That sounds ominous. Was he frightfully cross?'

'Frightfully.'

'I'm so terribly sorry, Inspector dear. We shall come at once – I'll soon sort him out.' Lady Hardcastle kissed Dr Gosling's cheek. 'Thank you, Sim dear. We must have dinner with you and Dinah soon.'

'I'd like that,' said Dr Gosling. 'Enjoy your trip to the Bridewell.'

We left the mortuary and set off in the Rolls to the central police station, with Inspector Sunderland close behind in his own, police-issue motor car.

◆　◆　◆

Lady Hardcastle had met the chief superintendent at a charity function a couple of years previously, but neither of us had ever been to his office before. It was much smarter than Inspector Sunderland's, as befitted his rank, and the man himself looked extremely spiffy in his neatly pressed uniform with his rank insignia shining on his epaulettes and the blue and white ribbon of the King's Police Medal on his chest.

'Inspector Sunderland has spoken to me,' he said once the formal round of introductions, invitations to sit, and offers of tea had been dealt with. 'You told him, I gather, that you intend to take over the investigation of this afternoon's murder of an unidentified foreign man at the Floating Harbour.'

'That's correct, Chief Superintendent,' said Lady Hardcastle.

'I have to inform you that your request is denied.'

'It's not a request, Chief Superintendent. We are instructed by our own superiors in Whitehall that the murder is a matter of national security and that we are to take it over on their behalf.'

'And I'm supposed simply to take your word for it?'

'To be honest, I rather hoped you would have heard from them by now, but yes, in the meantime I expect you to take our word for it.'

'Based upon whose authority?'

Lady Hardcastle held out her hand to me and I passed her the document wallet.

'The Secretary of State for War,' she said, handing him the two letters.

'I don't care if it's on the say-so of the—'

'Of the King himself, Chief Superintendent? Honestly, if I had a shilling for every time someone has said that to me today I'd have . . . well, I'd have two and six.'

This last comment made the policeman pause and frown.

'I said it myself in the car on the way into town as I imagined out loud how much resistance we would meet when we arrived,' she said. 'That counts as half, hence the sixpence.'

He glanced at the letters and handed them back.

'This changes nothing,' he said. 'The War Office has no jurisdiction here. My officers are tasked by the Crown with the policing of the City of Bristol and that is what we shall do. Inspector Sunderland is the senior officer on the investigation and he will be reporting directly to me as always. You and your lady's maid will cease your attempts to interfere in this case and you will both go home to your village in the back of beyond where I sincerely hope you will live long, happy lives, far away from the important work of the Bristol Constabulary. Do I make myself clear?'

'Your wishes are as clear as the water of a fresh mountain spring,' said Lady Hardcastle. 'But as my dear mother always used to say: "If wishes were horseradish, dear, beggars would eat roast beef more often." That you wish a thing to be so does not make it so. And . . . so . . . unfortunately, I must insist that Miss Armstrong and I really are taking over this case on behalf of the War Office, no matter how much you fuss and bluster. Your officers will report to that government department through us. You will be kept informed, of course, and any information we uncover which is relevant to your work but not to ours will be handed over at once. Do *I* make *myself* clear?'

'Now look here, *my lady*—'

'Really, *Chief Superintendent*? If I had a shilling for every time someone has tried to diminish me by using my title sarcastically, I should be a millionaire, never mind the blasted two and sixpence. It's not an affectation – my late husband was knighted for his service to the Crown. Service, I might add, which saw him murdered by our nation's enemies.'

'It's merely a courtesy title,' harrumphed the chief superintendent.

'It is indeed, which makes it even worse that you should choose to use it so discourteously.'

'Well, really.'

The telephone on his desk rang and he picked up the earpiece irritably.

'What?' he barked. He listened for a moment and then sighed. 'Put him through . . . Good afternoon, sir . . . Yes, they're with me now. I was just . . . Yes, sir . . . Yes, sir . . . Of course, sir . . . Thank you, sir.' He replaced the earpiece in its cradle and sighed again.

'The case is yours,' he said after a long pause. 'The resources of the Bristol Constabulary are at your disposal.'

'Thank you, Chief Superintendent,' said Lady Hardcastle, standing up.

She offered him her hand but he declined to shake it, instead remaining seated and picking up his pen.

'Good day to you,' he said, and returned to his work.

We left him to fume.

◆　◆　◆

We made our way through the labyrinthine corridors of police headquarters and only had to double-back once, when we found ourselves suddenly and unexpectedly in the canteen. A few minutes later we were on familiar ground and making our way to Inspector Sunderland's office.

I knocked.

'Come,' said the inspector from within.

We entered.

'Ah, the cats,' he said with a welcoming smile. 'Come in. Make yourselves at home.'

'Cats?' I said. 'I'm usually a dog in these things for some reason.'

'She is,' said Lady Hardcastle. 'She's my little Welsh terrier.'

'You see?' I said. 'Wait a moment – aren't they the ones with the fat legs?'

'Don't take offence, dear, I think it's mostly fur.'

'So they're the ones with hairy legs? How is that better?'

'When you put it like that, I don't think it's any better at all. But no matter – the inspector thinks we're cats.'

'So he said.' I turned to the inspector. 'But why?'

'Among the pigeons,' he said. 'I've just had Gosling on the telephone wittering on about my having set the cat among the

32

pigeons. I suggested that it was actually two cats and . . . well, you get the gist. And now here you both are, looking as though you got the cream.'

'A needless battle, hard won,' said Lady Hardcastle. 'Your chief superintendent grumbled and harrumphed at us for a while until a call from . . . actually, I don't know who it was from, but probably the chief constable to judge from the way he tugged his forelock throughout the brief call. Anyway, the snarling and chest-beating ceased as soon as he had hung up, and he gracelessly invited us to get on with it. You are ours to command.'

'As always, my lady. What do you need from me?'

'To tell the dismaying truth, I'm not yet sure. Thanks to his vagueness on the telephone, it's not at all clear to me what Harry and the SSB want. He was insistent that we make every effort to keep the victim's identity under wraps. But he also mumbled something about making use of the local police to find out whatever we can about the shooting. We could shut your chaps out very easily by doing nothing at all now that we've grudgingly been given control of the case. But then how would we carry out his investigation for him? "Do these two entirely contradictory things, please, sis. You don't mind if I don't explain why, do you? Got to dash. Toodle-oo." Infuriating. Absolutely infuriating.'

'I can definitely make sure that our investigation concentrates on the killer rather than the victim.'

'It would be marvellous if you could. I should very much like to know more about who killed him, how they did it, and how they got away with it.'

'Exactly where we excel.'

'Indeed. It would be most satisfying to be able to supply the Basement with a decent account of the events surrounding the shooting. Exactly as infuriatingly instructed.'

'The Basement?'

'I'm sorry. It just popped into my head as a potential new way of referring to the SSB. I don't like to keep calling them "the SSB" – far too direct and potentially indiscreet for casual conversation. And something like "Harry's mob" is simply ghastly. I've been using "Whitehall" and "the War Office" a lot today but they both cover far too much ground – I could be talking about anything from weapons procurement to the ruminations of the Board of Agriculture and Fisheries. I thought "the Basement" might be at once specific and oblique. I've always joked that my dear brother and his cloak-and-daggerous pals are housed in a shabby basement in Whitehall. The truth is a little more salubrious, but the idea of them skulking in a basement still amuses me.'

'The Basement it is, then,' said the inspector. 'I've already spoken to Marsh. He still isn't in the least bit thrilled to be taking instructions from a . . . civilian—'

'It's all right, Inspector dear, you can say that he doesn't like being ordered about by women – we're quite used to it.'

'Whether you're used to it or not, it still gets my goat. I've known you for four years now and I'd trust you to run an investigation – to run a whole police division if it came to that – far more readily than I'd trust many of the men I've met on the Force.'

'Oh, I say.'

'I mean it. But Marsh is a good man and he'll have a report on the witness statements ready before lunchtime tomorrow, as requested.'

'Splendid. I presume that the usual procedure is to interview only the bystanders who were still there when the detectives arrived?'

'It's not the preferred procedure, but that's what happened at lunchtime, yes.'

'What exactly happened?' I asked. 'What was the sequence of events?'

'A beat constable responded to the gunshot a few minutes before midday,' said the inspector. 'He blew his whistle and attracted the attention of one of his colleagues, who ran back here with the news. Marsh and Channing hurried down to the Tramway Centre to take over, and I followed a few minutes later. I think I was there by about twenty past the hour.'

'And then Harry called us at one o'clock,' said Lady Hardcastle. 'I wonder how he knew so quickly.'

'If the victim was of interest to the Basement,' I said, 'he was probably being followed. His shadow would have been on the telephone within minutes.'

'That makes sense,' said Lady Hardcastle. 'So, we presume that Marsh and Channing, as professional and well meaning as they might be, took statements only from the most convenient witnesses. Might I ask, then, that you assign some men to return to the Tramway Centre a little before noon tomorrow to cast the net a little wider? Shopkeepers and street traders might have seen something, for instance. And by going down there at the same time of day, they might be able to find witnesses who pass through the area around noon every day.'

'Of course,' said the inspector, making a note in his notebook. 'I'll make sure there are officers there by about a quarter past eleven.'

'Thank you. Will Simeon send his report straight here?'

'Straight to me as the investigating officer, yes.'

'Can you check it for us, please? I asked him to be as professionally thorough as usual, but to skim over anything that might speak to the victim's nationality or speculate too accurately on the weapon used. We can rely on him not to let the cat out of the bag, but I'd like you to make sure he hasn't been too ham-fisted about it – he's a fine physician but he's not one of Nature's dissemblers. Ordinarily one would say that was a good thing, but in this case . . .'

'I'll take a look,' said the inspector with a smile.

'Splendidly splendid,' said Lady Hardcastle. 'In that case, we shall leave you to it. My apologies for landing you in the middle of all this territorial squabbling, but I'm glad to have you as our liaison. It's reassuring to have a friend one can rely on.'

'Think nothing of it, my lady. Politics and "territorial squabbling", as you put it, are increasingly part of the job. For my part I'm happy that the outside interference is coming from a friend and not some Whitehall mandarin.'

'In that case, good day to you, Inspector dear. You know how to reach us if you need us. Do give our love to Mrs Sunderland, won't you.'

'I will,' he said. 'Cheerio for now.'

Miss Jones, Lady Hardcastle's cook, had made a delicious pork pie before she left for the day, and I decided to serve it with a salad that would include tomatoes from our own garden.

Rather than actually helping, Lady Hardcastle fussed about the kitchen, offering advice on the best way to wash lettuce, and then umm-ing and ahh-ing about a suitable wine to accompany the pie.

Eventually she sighed and said, 'Dash it all, I suppose a glass of Mattick's Cider will do,' and proceeded to harrumph about in the pantry trying to find some.

'Remind me why we call this the wine cellar,' she called from inside. 'We've a perfectly good actual cellar we could use.'

'You said you didn't fancy trudging up and down the stairs,' I said. 'Even though it would mostly be me doing the trudging. And you said you didn't want to be forever brushing cobwebs out of your hair. Even though I'd be the one doing the brushing. So we put a wine rack in there and called it the cellar.'

'That sounds like me,' she said as she emerged with a large bottle of cider. 'But we ought to reconsider. I see myself as the sort of person who would keep a fine cellar. "There goes Emily," people would say. "I'd wager she keeps a fine cellar."'

'It would certainly leave more room for food,' I said.

'Well, quite. Poor Miss Jones is having to double-stack her mysterious bottles and jars so she can fit everything in. Is that nearly ready? I'm starving.'

It was a pleasant evening, so we ate beneath the apple tree at what we still thought of as the 'new' table, even though it was now almost a year old. As we munched, we discussed practical matters, preferring to leave work until we had retired to the drawing room for the evening. We talked about the payment of the telephone bill, the probable need to adjust the carburettor on the Silver Ghost, and the whereabouts of Lady Hardcastle's favourite summer shoes (in her wardrobe under a pile of silk scarves, for some reason).

Once properly settled in the drawing room, though, with the dishes cleaned, the brandy decanter close at hand, and Lady Hardcastle's notebook open on her lap, it was time to discuss business.

'A Serbian man—' she began.

'Or a man recently returned from a trip to Serbia,' I said. 'Or perhaps preparing for a trip.'

'I would have agreed with you based on the banknotes alone, but he was wearing Serbian clothes. More likely, I think, that Serbia was his home.'

'Fair point.'

'So, a Serbian man of interest to the Basement finds himself in Bristol, where, on a bright summer's day in the middle of one of the busiest parts of town, he is shot to death by an unknown assailant. I don't know about you, but I got the impression from our conversation with Harry that . . . I'm going to call the poor fellow Jovan for now – he deserves more than being "the corpse" or "the victim".'

'I take it that's the Serbian version of John?'

'It is. If memory serves, Srna would be Serbian for Doe. At least I think so. Anyway, he shall be Jovan Srna until we know better. But I rather think that Harry knows exactly who Jovan was. Unknown, uninteresting foreign visitors aren't trailed around the country by Special Branch.'

'Assuming we're right about that. About how Harry knew so quickly, I mean.'

'It's one of only two explanations that make proper sense. And certainly the most likely of the two.'

'I've been wondering about that second possibility,' I said. 'It would explain Harry's almost instant knowledge of Jovan's death, as well as the importance of hushing things up and his reluctance to say anything over the telephone.'

'It is a possibility, of course it is. But if the Basement had wanted Jovan dead, I like to imagine they would have done it a good deal more discreetly than that. Shooting him in broad daylight in the middle of a busy city is hardly our style. At least I hope not. One has professional standards, after all.'

'But what's going on in Serbia?' I asked. 'Why would the Basement be interested in a Serbian national? Was he a member of the Black Hand, do you think?'

'Perhaps,' she said. 'But what would they be doing here? They're nationalists, keen on unifying some of their Baltic neighbours under a Serbian banner. They're not gentle about it when they take action, but they haven't done much to cause headlines for nearly ten years, even at home. I certainly can't imagine what they might be up to in England.'

'Young Bosnia?' I suggested.

'Again, possible – we've intelligence that they might be working with the Black Hand. But the same objections apply – they want to split the Balkan countries from Austria-Hungary and unify as something they're calling "Yugoslavia". Swanning around in the West Country would do little to advance their cause.'

'Then perhaps we should stop worrying about who he is and concentrate on how someone managed to kill him right under the nose of his Special Branch minder.'

'A boy scout could kill someone under the nose of some of the oafs Harry manages to get from Special Branch. I'm sure there are some fine officers there, but they certainly assign some duffers to the Basement. Do you remember those two flatheads we met at Weston?'

'Perch and Tench,' I said. 'Real names Brownlow and Perlman.'

'Our hypothetical boy scout could have murdered Jovan Srna and the entire Hungarian Olympic team on stage at the Duke's Theatre without those idiots even noticing, let alone being able to do anything about it.'

'Then let's hope the inspector's men turn something up in their interviews tomorrow.'

'Let's hope. But there's not much we can do other than specu-late for now without some hard facts – what say we while away the evening with a few hands of cards?'

'A much more agreeable plan,' I said.

I set up the card table while Lady Hardcastle fetched her purse. She was going to need it.

Chapter Three

When viewed from the blissfully oblivious summit of Sunday evening, it had seemed that Monday would be a pleasantly calm day of pottering about and relaxed lunching with friends. At that point, the diary for Tuesday was entirely empty save for a vague, unconfirmed intention to visit the pub in the evening, when Joe the landlord would be holding one of his outdoor skittles competitions.

How quickly things change.

First, Jovan's murder had cast its tragic shadow across Monday afternoon. Now it was looming ominously over Tuesday, and possibly beyond.

I had taken advantage of the warm weather to complete my morning exercises under the apple tree rather than in the drawing room, and then joined housekeeper Edna and cook Miss Jones in the kitchen as they prepared for their own morning's work.

'Mornin', Miss Armstrong,' said Edna. 'I always likes watchin' you do they exercises in the mornin's. You looks so graceful.'

'Thank you, Edna,' I said. 'I keep telling you you're welcome to join me any time. It'll keep you strong and flexible. It's good for balance, too.'

She laughed. 'I think my flexible days are behind me, my lover. I has to put my foot on a stool to do up my boot buttons.'

'Then join me for a few sessions. We'll have you touching your toes in no time.'

'Poor Dan wouldn't know which way to look.'

It was my turn to laugh. 'Well, the offer's there,' I said. 'Give your husband a treat. You too, Blodwen, if you ever fancy it.'

Miss Jones looked up from her bread-slicing. 'I'm not sure I fancies givin' her Dan a treat.'

I tutted and shook my head. 'You've been spending too long in Herself's company. You know what I meant.'

'Well, I must say I's intrigued. Are you sure you wouldn't mind?'

'Not at all. I've offered before.'

'You ever tried to get Lady Hardcastle interested?' asked Edna.

'I learned long ago that it's not worth it,' I said. 'She used to sit with her back against a tree watching as Chen Ping Bo taught me when we were escaping across China. He and I both tried to get her to join us, but she just carried on writing her journal. Eighteen years I've been her lady's maid, and I don't think I've ever once seen her do any exercise, not for its own sake, anyway. She sometimes plays a little tennis or golf, but whenever I suggest some t'ai chi she just laughs that laugh of hers and changes the subject.'

'Do I need to wear pyjamas?' asked Miss Jones, indicating my Chinese garb.

'Not unless you really want to,' I said. 'We have spares if you do, but a dress is fine.'

'I'll think about it.'

'You do that.'

She had 'thought about it' many times over the past four years, but had yet to join me.

'I'll have Lady Hardcastle's starter breakfast ready by the time you's changed,' she said.

'Marvellous. Thank you.'

◆ ◆ ◆

I had been delivering Lady Hardcastle's starter breakfast – two rounds of toast and a cup of coffee – for quite a few years. It was originally tea, but lately she had expressed a preference for coffee. The routine remained the same, though. No earlier than seven o'clock each morning – though the time was flexible, depending on her schedule – I would arrive at her bedside with a tray. I would then open the curtains and field her complaints about being woken. After that we might chatter for a while about the day ahead, or I would leave her to come to while I got on with something about the house.

This morning she was already sitting up and reading some papers she had taken to bed with her the night before. She peered schoolmarmishly over her spectacles as I entered.

'Good morning, tiny servant,' she said, putting down the document she had been reading.

'And good morning to you, ancient one,' I said.

'Oh, don't. I'm feeling every one of my forty-four years this morning. It's no age at all, but I ache like an old woman.'

'I was just singing the praises of my morning exercises,' I said. 'Miss Jones inches ever closer to joining me. You could, too, you know – we'd fix those aches and pains in no time. And if you were to join us, we might persuade Edna to partake and then we'd have the whole household enjoying the benefits.'

She laughed her enchanting laugh. 'I've been reading Harry's briefing about the situation in the Balkans again. I still can't see anything in there that might prompt an operational visit to our sceptred isle.'

'Perhaps he was sightseeing,' I suggested. 'England is an earth of majesty, after all. A precious stone set in a silver sea, if you will. Who wouldn't want to visit such a demi-paradise?'

'Well, there is that, I suppose. But I remain unconvinced. Something else is afoot and we shan't know what until stupid Harry deigns to tell us.'

'Is that his full given name? I've often wondered.'

'Stupid Henry Infuriating Alfred Nitwit Percival Dunderhead Featherstonhaugh, dear – yes. He had to bribe the vicar not to use it at his wedding for fear Lavinia would flee back up the aisle in horror were she to discover the awful truth.'

'I can see why he prefers Harry, certainly. Though the story needs refinement – they were married in the blacksmith's shop at Gretna Green.'

'With us as their witnesses. It really was the most delightfully romantic day – quite the loveliest wedding I've ever attended. But he's still a nincompoop.'

'As you wish,' I said. 'But since your latest research has still revealed no clues to Jovan's background, why don't we just forget Harry's apparent failings and stick to our original plan? We can get ourselves down to the Tramway Centre for about half past eleven and monitor Inspector Sunderland's search for information.'

'You're right, as always.'

'I have my moments. Breakfast is at nine.'

'I shall be there.'

❖ ❖ ❖

The Tramway Centre had returned almost to normal by the time we arrived at half past eleven. The barricades had gone, and with them the crowds of gawpers. Everyday life had resumed. The trams were swishing about on the spiderweb of tracks in their elegant, clanking tramular ballet. The smaller boats that still came all the way up the Avon to the old docks were loading and unloading at the quays beside the transit sheds. The engines of motor cars and vans rumbled and clattered. Hawkers hawked. Shoppers shopped. Cartwheels scraped and horses clopped.

The only sign that there was anything unusual going on was the half a dozen uniformed policemen talking to shopkeepers and stopping passers-by to ask them if they'd been there the day before.

We found Inspector Sunderland standing with Marsh and Channing at the spot where Jovan's body had lain less than twenty-four hours earlier.

'Good morning, Lady Hardcastle,' said the inspector. 'The door-to-door and street interviews have begun, as you can see. There's a way to go yet, but so far the men have nothing to report.'

'They won't find anything,' said Marsh. 'The Somerset cricket team could perform *HMS Pinafore* right here dressed as Belgian nuns and no one would notice a thing.'

'Steady on, Marsh,' said Inspector Sunderland. 'No need for that tone.'

'Sadly, Inspector,' said Lady Hardcastle, 'I fear Mr Marsh is correct. Modern life carries us at such a tremendous pace, and I fear we are all so wrapped up in our own concerns that we scarcely perceive anything else. Still, one way to guarantee we find nothing is not to take the trouble to look, so I'm grateful for the efforts of you and your men.'

'Did anything come of the ground search?' I asked.

The inspector shook his head. 'I decided to let the uniforms get on with the interviews rather than delay them with a search. To be honest, I think it needs detectives' eyes anyway, so we were about to begin a sweep just as you arrived.'

'Marvellous,' said Lady Hardcastle. 'May we join you?'

'Do we have a choice?' asked Channing. This was the first time I had heard him speak and it was good to know he had an opinion, even if it wasn't an especially positive one.

'Not really, dear,' said Lady Hardcastle in her most infuriatingly cheerful tone. 'But one likes to ask. "Good manners cost nothing" and all that.'

Marsh and Channing both tutted, but were saved from another rebuke from Inspector Sunderland by the arrival of one of the uniformed constables. He was accompanied by a woman wearing a black dress with the sleeves rolled up to just below the elbows. There was a pad and pencil in the pocket of her slightly grubby white apron.

'Beggin' your pardon, sir,' said the constable. 'But I thought you'd want to 'ear this yourself.'

'Hear what, Constable . . . ?'

'Franklin, sir. This lady is from the greengrocer's over the way there.' He pointed in the vague direction of Denmark Street. 'She saw . . . well, missus, you tell 'em.'

She gave us all a look of confident appraisal.

'You all coppers?' she said.

'Yes, madam,' said Inspector Sunderland.

'They i'n't,' she said, pointing at Lady Hardcastle and me.

'They work for the government.'

She laughed. 'What as? Tottles?'

'I'm afraid my street-walking days are long behind me, dear,' said Lady Hardcastle. 'I simply don't have the flexibility required for the work any more. The curse of middle age, you see? But you saw something yesterday morning?'

'I like you,' said the woman.

'And I'm warming to you, too, Mrs . . . ?'

'Webb,' said the woman. 'Dilly Webb. With two Bs,' she added, peering over at the inspector's notebook to check that he was spelling it correctly. 'My husband – Mr Webb – he runs the greengrocer's down Denmark Street. I works with him.'

'And you were working there yesterday?' asked Lady Hardcastle.

'We always works there. We doesn't 'ave no time to be swannin' about on the Centre in our finery chattin' to passers-by like some people.'

'We'll not detain you for a moment longer than necessary, I promise. What happened yesterday?'

'I was comin' to that, but you keeps interruptin'.'

'I'm so sorry, dear. Do go on.'

'I was outside the shop, puttin' some bananas on the table – come in fresh on the refrigerator ship from the West Indies on Sunday, they did – an' I was out there stackin' 'em up all neat like, when I hears this bang from the Centre. 'Tweren't like when the motor cars does it. Higher-pitched, it was. Why does cars do that, that's what I've always wondered? They can't be designed like that, surely.'

'Either there's unburnt fuel exploding in the hot exhaust, or the ignition is happening too late so that it's going bang while the exhaust valve is open, dear,' said Lady Hardcastle. 'It's usually that the fuel mixture is too rich or that the timing is off.'

'Oo-er, don't you know a lot?'

'One has to have something to talk about afterwards, dear – that's how one makes the big money in the tottie business.'

Mrs Webb laughed again. 'So this bang goes off, and there's a few screams, and I thinks, "Hello, what's all that about?" But I couldn't see nothin', so I just carried on with me bananas. You 'as to treat 'em gentle like – they bruises so easy. I'm just steppin' back inside the shop when this fella dressed all in black comes harin' up the road.'

'He'd come from the Tramway Centre?' I asked.

'Wouldn't be no point in tellin' you if he'd come from the other way, would there?'

'You make a compelling point, dear,' said Lady Hardcastle. 'Did you see him properly before he ran past? What did he look like?'

'Black trousers, black boots, one o' they fisherman's smock things, funny-lookin' black cap.'

'His face?'

'Foreign.'

'He had a foreign face?' I said with slightly more incredulity than I'd have preferred to show a cooperative witness.

'You can tell. Dark hair. Unshaven. Too good-lookin' to be English.'

I gave a little chuckle. 'Fair point.'

'Did you notice anything else about him?' asked Lady Hardcastle.

'No. And I couldn't really tell what sort of gun he was carryin', neither.'

Lady Hardcastle and I looked at each other and rolled our eyes in unison.

'He was carrying a gun?' I said.

'I just said so, didn't I?'

'You did, dear,' said Lady Hardcastle. 'It's quite an important piece of information – you might have led with it.'

Mrs Webb nodded towards me. 'She asked me what he looked like, not what he was carryin' in his hand.'

'Another fair point,' I conceded. 'I did ask that. But he was definitely carrying a pistol?'

'One o' they modern square ones, not a proper revolver.'

'What happened then?' asked Lady Hardcastle.

'He goes peltin' off up towards the Hatchet and I lost sight of him.'

'I see. Well, I must say this is all extremely helpful, Mrs Webb. Thank you very much for sparing us so much of your valuable time. We ought to let you get back to your shop.'

'I a'n't finished yet,' said Mrs Webb with a shake of the head. 'You i'n't 'alf impatient for someone who's got nothin' else to do all day.'

'I'm so sorry, dear,' said Lady Hardcastle. 'Do go on.'

'So I'm tuttin' about what the world's comin' to, and gettin' ready to tell Mr Webb all about what I just seen, when another fella comes runnin' up after the first one.'

'Was *he* carrying a gun?' I asked.

'As a matter of fact, he was,' said Mrs Webb with an emphatic nod. 'He 'ad a Webley Mark IV in 'is left hand.'

'You recognized the make and model?' asked Lady Hardcastle.

'Mr Webb brought one back from the Boer War – I'd know it anywhere. I hates the thing. I don't know why he insists on keepin' it. Dangerous, they are.'

'And what did this other man look like?' I said.

'Very expensive suit. Grey, it was. Fancy little medallion thing hangin' from his watch chain. Homburg hat. Waxed moustache.'

'And he was definitely pursuing the first man?' asked Lady Hardcastle.

'Well, now. "Definitely"? I couldn't say "definitely". But when you sees two men runnin' in the same direction, one after the other a few yards apart, both of 'em carryin' guns, I reckon you'd be a fool not to think the second one was chasin' the first.'

Lady Hardcastle smiled. 'You would indeed.'

There was a lengthy pause.

'Well?' said Mrs Webb.

'Well what, dear?'

'Is that it? Can I go? Some of us has got work to do, you know.'

'Of course, Mrs Webb. We are most grateful for your help.'

With a nod of farewell, Mrs Webb set off back towards the greengrocer's.

Inspector Sunderland finished making his notes.

'Helpful, my lady?' he asked when he was done.

'Most helpful, yes.'

'How's that?' said Marsh. 'We started the day trying to establish the identity of one man – the killer of our John Doe – and now we have two men to worry about. We've doubled our problems.'

'And that's exactly why you should be grateful to have us here,' I said.

'Because of your great skill and experience as detectives?' he said with a sneer.

'Because we can reassure you that you don't need to worry about the second man.'

'And how can you do that? Who was he?'

'I'm afraid we can't tell you that,' said Lady Hardcastle. 'We government totties have to have our secrets, after all. But I can say with absolute certainty that he's no threat to the people of Bristol and of no concern to you.'

'I think we'll decide what concerns us,' said Channing.

'I think *I'll* decide what concerns us, Detective Constable,' said Inspector Sunderland. 'And *you* will respect our War Office colleagues.'

'If I could say more,' said Lady Hardcastle, 'I would. But for now, shall we all make ourselves useful and carry out one final search of the ground in case anything has been missed?'

There was a sullen 'Yes, ma'am' from each of the two junior officers.

'So . . .' began Lady Hardcastle. 'We now know that the killer ran off towards Denmark Street.' She pointed. 'From Dr Gosling's post-mortem we know that the victim was shot by someone standing to his left-hand side. The body was lying . . . here.' She indicated the spot on the pavement. 'With his head facing that way.' She pointed towards Denmark Street again. 'Has Dr Gosling submitted his report, by the way, Inspector?'

'He has, my lady. Nothing unexpected. It's all very much as we discussed yesterday.'

'Thank you. Since the killer was dressed in the manner of a sailor, and the flow of movement seems to be from left to right as we face the floating harbour, I suggest they came up from the eastern quayside.' She pointed. 'Our black-clad killer caught up with the victim here. And then legged it across St Augustine's Parade and up Denmark Street past the greengrocer's.'

'Hotly pursued by a man in an expensive grey suit,' said Channing.

'Whom we are ignoring,' said the inspector, 'because he is no concern of ours.'

'As you say, sir.'

'I propose we start on the quayside and follow the supposed route at least as far as the Webbs' shop.'

Without waiting for agreement, she strode off.

We followed.

◆ ◆ ◆

Lady Hardcastle led us along Broad Quay. I kept thinking she would stop so that we could begin our search, but she kept going. And going.

To be fair, she only took us four hundred yards or so to the end of the quay, but I'd been expecting to start much closer to the Tramway Centre so it felt a good deal further.

'Any reason for coming all this way?' said Marsh, sulkily.

'Why yes, since you ask,' said Lady Hardcastle, 'there is. I'm working on the assumption that either the victim, the killer, or possibly both, had some connection with a boat moored at this quay. Whether they came from it – or were going to it – might be important later, but for now what interests me is that there is almost certainly a boat involved. We have no idea which boat, but it seems short-sighted to rule out half the possible boats on this quay for a saving of only a couple of hundred yards.'

The two junior detectives sighed theatrically and the inspector shook his head. I was able to predict the carpeting they were going to get when they were back in the office, and I wondered why two apparently intelligent and perceptive young detectives weren't able to foresee it for themselves.

We spread out in a line and began our slow walk along the quayside. The cobbles were uneven and we had to step over the lines from the boats, all of which slowed our progress even further. But the quay had been kept reasonably tidy, and such mess as we could see was predictable enough: splinters of broken crates, torn sacking, and frayed ropes, for the most part. This, I thought, should make it easier to spot anything out of place, though I had no idea what form that thing might take.

We had progressed about fifty yards when a wiry man with a trim grey beard clambered up a ladder from a steam launch moored below and addressed Inspector Sunderland.

'You the coppers?' he said.

'We are, sir, yes,' said the inspector, showing his warrant card.

'You here about the fella that was shot over there yesterday?'

'Yes, sir, we are. Did you see anything?'

'No, I was round the corner in the pub. But I got his dunnage.' He hefted a canvas kit bag on to the cobbles. 'Don't reckon he's comin' back for it.'

Inspector Sunderland gestured for Channing to retrieve the bag.

'You're certain it was his?' asked the inspector.

'He left it here and said he needed to get himself some baccy from the shops over yonder afore we left. I told him not to hang about or we'd miss the tide. And then . . . well, he missed that tide and every one that followed, rest his soul.'

Channing tipped out the contents of the bag and began to rummage through them. I went to help.

'Where were you taking him?' asked Lady Hardcastle.

'Avonmouth Docks,' said the boatman.

'He was to meet another boat there?'

'I didn't ask and he didn't say. Just paid for his passage and left to get himself some tobacco.'

'Did you see a man dressed all in black following him?'

'Wasn't looking. I was stoking up, getting ready to leave. Tide had already turned on t'other side of Cumberland Basin. If we didn't get a shift on we'd have run aground before we got halfway to Pill.'

Jovan's possessions were unremarkable – just some clothes suitable for a sea journey. There was a woollen hat and a heavy coat, a couple of clean shirts, some underwear, a pair of thick socks, a shaving kit. Slightly more interesting was a notebook with a pencil tucked in the elastic band holding it shut. From its battered appearance, this one was a good deal older than the one found in Jovan's jacket.

Leaving Channing to continue his search, I stood and opened up the notebook. Disappointingly, despite my assumption that it must have been well used, it was empty. The first few pages had been torn out, so it might once have contained something interesting or important, but now there was nothing to see but clean, white paper. I flicked through it to make sure, and something caught my eye. One of the pages hadn't been torn cleanly and a larger fragment remained. On the back of this partially torn sheet was a word written not in Serbian Cyrillic as I had expected, but in Latin letters. It said, *Wharf*.

'Anything interesting?' asked Lady Hardcastle.

'No,' I said. 'Empty.' I held it open as proof.

Inspector Sunderland concluded his conversation with the boatman and instructed Channing to repack the kit bag so that it could be taken back to the station.

'Can't we give it to one of the uniforms?' said Channing.

'If we see one before you get back to the Bridewell, you have my permission to ask him if he'll carry it for you,' said the inspector. 'Though I rather think I can predict what his answer will be.'

Mumbling and grumbling, Channing repacked the bag – badly – and hefted it on to his shoulder.

We walked on.

We found nothing along the wharf, and began our slow, methodical march along the supposed route followed by Jovan and his killer across the Tramway Centre. There was a moment of excitement when Lady Hardcastle suddenly crouched down, but she was merely re-buttoning her boot.

The Tramway Centre and Denmark Street had been swept by the city street-sweepers that morning, so most of what we saw – and it's astonishing how much litter people manage to drop in just a few hours – was fresh.

Eventually, the search was done, and Marsh and Channing were released to return to other duties, with Channing still carrying the heavy kit bag.

'Thank you for that, Inspector,' said Lady Hardcastle once they were gone. 'It's been most helpful.'

'You're welcome as always, my lady,' he said. 'Are we free to pursue the black-clad man?'

'By all means make whatever enquiries you normally would, but be warned that you won't find him. He'll be long gone by now.'

'I see. Do you know who he is?'

'I'm afraid not, no. But I imagine he followed Jovan here, probably from London. He'll have returned as quickly as he could.'

'And the chap in the grey suit? I take it he's one of yours.'

'He is,' said Lady Hardcastle. 'Though it might be more accurate to say that he's one of yours. Or one of the Met's, at any rate. I rather think he's from Special Branch, seconded to the Basement – Harry does like his Special Branch chaps. And this particular chap will also have been London-bound on the first train he could catch.'

'Probably the same train,' I said. 'Special Branch bloke in first class and the killer in third.'

'Wouldn't that be precious?' said Lady Hardcastle. 'All that running about and all he needed to do was take a cab to the station.'

The inspector smiled. 'And how do you wish us to proceed?'

'As I say, Inspector dear, proceed entirely as normal. Make your enquiries, write your reports. Regrettably, you won't find anything or catch anyone, and for that I'm sorry. But in carrying out a normal investigation you'll have done us and the Basement a great service. With everything seen to be done by the book, with all t's dotted and i's crossed—' She crossed her own eyes and then giggled at her joke. 'With everything done exactly as normal, the attention of the press and public will drift away. Before long your chief superintendent will be quietly instructed to close the case and you can get on with "real" work. I hope you'll accept that the work you've done, and will do, is just as important, though, for all that it will yield no results.'

'I understand, my lady. If nothing else it's been a pleasure to see you again.'

'You, too, Inspector dear. We really must have dinner again soon. All of us. You and Dolly, Simeon and Dinah.'

'I should like that very much,' said the inspector with a smile. 'What are you doing next? Will you come to the Bridewell with us? I have Marsh's report.'

'I wasn't planning to. Does it contain anything we don't already know?'

'Not really. Confirmation of a man in black fleeing the scene, but no one saw the shooting itself. The sequence of events is much as we've already established.'

'In that case, no thank you. We ought to get ourselves back to the house where we can collect our thoughts and then report to Harry.'

'Very well. I'll have a copy sent out to you by messenger.' He stopped and thought for a moment. 'One day,' he said, 'even if I have to wait until I'm old and grey, will you tell me what on earth has been going on here?'

'I promise,' said Lady Hardcastle, touching his arm. 'Goodbye for now, though. We'll be in touch to arrange dinner.'

We left him to gather his men, and returned to the Rolls.

◆ ◆ ◆

We had missed lunch. I had my fingers crossed all the way home that Miss Jones hadn't had to dash off to some important appointment and might still be pottering in the kitchen and be prepared to help me make something nice. I had no idea what, but I definitely fancied 'something nice'.

We arrived home at half past one and I left Lady Hardcastle to her urgent visit to the WC while I went in search of the cook.

Miss Blodwen Jones — who, despite her very Welsh name, wasn't even a tiny bit Welsh – was, indeed, pottering in the kitchen.

'Hello, Miss Armstrong,' she said. 'I wasn't expectin' you two back. I hope you don't mind me still bein' here. I was experimentin' with puff pastry and the time sort of ran away from me.' She indicated the delicate vol-au-vents cooling on a rack. 'There's ham and boiled egg in a white sauce in them ones, and a sort of cheese and herb concoction in those others.'

'Are we allowed to eat them?' I asked, eyeing them hungrily.

'Of course,' she said with a laugh. 'It's Lady Hardcastle's ingredients I'm usin', after all.'

'You're an angel sent from heaven, Miss Jones. Is there any salad in the pantry?'

'Loads, Miss Armstrong. Weakley's lad came round with a delivery from the greengrocer's this mornin'.'

Along with Daisy Spratt (the butcher's daughter) and Cissy Slocomb (the dairyman's daughter), Blodwen Jones was one of my gang of pals in the village. Despite this off-duty friendship, we still usually addressed each other as 'Miss' at work.

I got on with washing and preparing some lettuce, cucumber and tomatoes, and arranged everything nicely on two plates with a selection of the pastries. I had always loved salad season.

'These look marvellous, thank you,' I said. 'Do take some with you, though. I'm sure your mother would love them.'

'I shall, ta. Oh, and I've cleaned a couple of trout for your dinner, and scrubbed some taters. I still reckon they doesn't need peelin' this time of year. There's peas, an' all.'

'Do we have any lemons? I might grill it with lemon and dill.'

'I was gonna suggest exactly that. You's almost as good as I am.'

'Would that I were, Blodders, would that I were. But for now I must take this through to Herself so I can get eating. I'm starving.'

I left her to her pastry and went through to the dining room, where I found Lady Hardcastle already at the table with a glass of white wine, reviewing her notes.

She looked up as I entered. 'Oh, I say. I thought something smelled delicious when we came in. Miss Jones is worth her weight in . . . in . . . I don't want to say gold – too boring.'

'Saffron?' I suggested. 'White truffles? Caviar?'

'Much more suitable, yes. But don't just stand there wafting it about – let's eat.'

I joined her and tucked in. Blodwen's experimental puff pastry was even more delicious than I had hoped, and we munched for a few moments in contented silence.

When the sharpest edges of our hunger had been dulled by the vol-au-vents, we found ourselves ready and eager to talk about the case.

'What was in the notebook?' asked Lady Hardcastle. 'I could tell from your face that it wasn't blank.'

'The word "Wharf" in Latin letters,' I said. 'It was the last word on the top line of a page that had been untidily ripped out. There were quote marks above it, as though it was part of a name.'

'That's suggestive. One would have thought he'd be writing in Serbian.'

'Exactly my thinking. So it's probably referring to the name of an actual wharf somewhere, then.'

'That seems likely, yes. And have a look at what I found.'

She fished in her jacket pocket and produced a spent cartridge casing, which she placed on the table between us.

'When you were "fastening your boot"?' I asked.

'At that precise moment, yes.'

I picked it up and examined it. There were letters stamped around the base of the rim, but no indication of its calibre.

'Is it 9 millimetre?' I asked.

'It is.'

'How can you tell?'

'I measured it,' she said, as though I had asked the stupidest question she had ever heard.

'So definitely a modern European gun, then.'

'Definitely . . . well, probably definitely. Definitely not a clunky old Webley, that's for sure.'

'And we now know for certain Jovan was being trailed by one of Harry's SBOs.'

'SBO?'

'Special Branch Oaf.'

Lady Hardcastle laughed. 'Yes. Yes we do. I'm not sure we know much more, though. We ought to—'

She was interrupted by the ringing of the telephone.

'Don't get up,' I said. 'I'll get it.'

I hurried through to the hall and picked up the earpiece.

'Good afternoon,' I said.

'And good afternoon to you, too, Strongarm. Is that how you answer the telephone these days?' It was Harry.

'I experiment,' I said. 'Someone barked "What?" into his telephone when we were in his office yesterday, but I feel that's a little brusque for the Hardcastle household. I considered "Wotcher", but while that's definitely friendlier, it might be a little too familiar for some of our more distinguished callers.'

'Have you thought of "What ho"?'

'Only buffleheads say "What ho", Mr Feather-Stone-Huff. Your sister told me that. And she used to say it all the time, so she should know.'

'*I* say it all the time, Strongarm.'

I remained silent.

'Ha!' he barked. 'One-nil to you, old thing. How goes the latest job? Locals behaving themselves?'

'We have them under control,' I said. 'Would you like me to brief you over the telephone?'

'Actually, Flo, that's rather why I called. I want you both in London by tomorrow afternoon at the latest – you can tell me all about it then.'

'Can I give Herself any details? Anything at all? You know she'll ask.'

'The details will have to wait, I'm afraid, old thing. Walls have ears and all that. Pack for a couple of weeks, bring work clothes as well as the usual paraphernalia. You'll stay with us tomorrow night.'

'And then . . . ?'

'And then time will have passed and events will have begun to unfold. Send me a cable as soon as you know which train you'll be on and I'll meet you at Paddington.'

'She's right about you,' I said.

'What does she say?'

'She says you're infuriating.'

'Ha! She's a fine one to talk.'

'I couldn't possibly comment,' I said. 'Oh, but what about the business here?'

'I'll take care of that. I'll make sure the local management quietly scale things down.'

'Right you are. Anything else?'

'No, that's it. See you tomorrow.'

'See you tomorrow. Give our love to Lady Lavinia and give Addie a big kiss.'

'Will do, Strongarm. Toodle-oo.'

He hung up.

I returned to the dining room.

'We're seeing Harry tomorrow, I take it,' she said. 'Here?'

'No, there,' I said. 'He wants us in London by tomorrow afternoon. He wants us to pack for a couple of weeks, including "work clothes". He'll pick us up at Paddington and we'll stay at his gaff tomorrow night.'

'That's rather presumptuous of him. We might have wanted to drive.'

'It would certainly be handy to have the Rolls. But if he wants us to pack "work clothes" I imagine there'll be trailing and nose-pokery to be done – the Rolls is a tad conspicuous for that sort of thing. It's a much faster journey by train, too.'

'True, true. We'll have to let Inspector Sunderland know we'll be away for a while and make sure he's happy with what's expected of him.'

'Harry's going to speak to the chief constable again. I think the inspector will be quietly stood down.'

'I'd still like to talk to him myself. He's been very cooperative.'

'He has. Do you need my cheerful voice with you on the telephone, or should I leave you to it while I go and make a start on the packing?'

'Pack away, dear thing. I'll look up the train times, too.'

As we finished the last of the vol-au-vents, we discussed whether we might need anything out of the ordinary for a 'couple of weeks' of non-specific SSB work in London. And then, with plans made, I cleared the table and helped Miss Jones with the washing-up before setting off upstairs for the very familiar task of packing for 'work'.

Chapter Four

Packing for the trip to London required some careful thought. Not only did we have only the vaguest idea how long we would be there, we didn't know where we'd be staying beyond the first night and had no clue what the actual job might entail.

We attempted to be prepared for any eventuality and included evening wear for us both as well as a variety of day dresses and outdoor togs. Shoes and boots took up a lot of room, as did weapons and tools. By the time we were done we ended up with a trunk, three suitcases, a hatbox, two Gladstone bags, and an artist's canvas satchel 'just in case'. Ideally we would have travelled a good deal lighter, but we couldn't see a way round it.

Necessity notwithstanding, it was a lot of baggage and I was dubious about our ability to get it all to the station. With Lady Hardcastle's unexpectedly enthusiastic assistance, though, everything was heaved on to the Silver Ghost's luggage rack before bedtime and secured with the stout leather straps provided by Rolls-Royce for exactly that purpose.

The 9.45 from Bristol Temple Meads would get us to London Paddington at two o'clock, and Harry had been advised of our planned arrival time as requested. But that meant that we had to be at Temple Meads no later than half past nine, preferably a little earlier, in order to change trains – getting all that baggage across the station wasn't going to be a straightforward task for whatever poor porter we managed to grab. Trains from Chipping Bevington to Temple Meads were frequent but lumbering, and that fifteen-mile hop would take us an hour on its own. Then there was the three-quarters of an hour we had to allow for the journey to Chipping, buying tickets . . .

I worked out that we would have to leave home at no later than half past seven.

I had gone to bed, dreading a morning fraught with hiccups and delays. And possibly more than one argument.

And yet, with Miss Jones's help preparing a very early breakfast, we were out the door at twenty past. Lady Hardcastle was more than capable of overcoming her innate reluctance to rise before eight when there was work to be done, and we were washed, dressed, and fed in plenty of time.

At Chipping Bevington station, Old Roberts – the porter – came out to greet us.

He touched the peak of his railway-issue cap. 'Mornin', Lady Hardcastle. Mornin', Miss Armstrong.'

'Good morning, Roberts,' said Lady Hardcastle. 'I trust you're well?'

'Quite well, thank you, m'lady.'

'And Mrs Roberts? How is she after her fall?'

'She's gettin' along fine, thank you, m'lady. She said to thank you for the flowers you sent if I saw you.'

'I'm jolly pleased to hear it. Tell her to keep active, though, won't you? She'll heal better if she keeps moving.'

'No one could stop her even if they wanted,' said the porter with an affectionate smile. 'Take more than a twisted ankle to stop our Winnie.' He indicated the teetering pile of luggage on the back of the Rolls. 'You goin' away?'

'For a couple of weeks, yes. We're visiting my brother in London. Can we prevail upon you to keep an eye on the motor car for us if we leave it here?'

'Of course, m'lady. Your usual spot in the corner of the yard is free – just leave it with us. You want Young Roberts to give it a wash for you?'

'Oh, no, don't go to any trouble.'

'Won't be no trouble, m'lady. He enjoys it.'

Lady Hardcastle laughed and gave him a handsome tip before heading off to get our tickets from Old Roberts's son, Young Roberts.

Meanwhile, Old Roberts started heaving our luggage down from the rack. 'You just leave this with me, Miss Armstrong. I'll get it tagged up and ready to load on the Temple Meads train. No need for you to worry about it.'

'Thank you, Mr Roberts. I'd better go and make sure Lady Hardcastle isn't distracting your son too much.'

The Bristol train was on time and we made it to Temple Meads with more than twenty minutes to spare. There was a moment of tension when we were unable to locate a porter to help us unload, but the guard – keen to get his train away on time managed to summon one up.

By 9.45 we and our baggage were loaded on to the London train and settled in our first-class compartment.

'It's at times like these,' said Lady Hardcastle as she sprawled on the seat in a most unladylike fashion, 'that I think we ought to keep a flat in London where we can store suitable dresses and hats and boots and pistols and knives and coshes and jemmies and picklocks. Even with charmingly helpful railway staff to heave the stuff from one train to the other, it's still an awful palaver to have to travel with so much impedimenta.'

'I've suggested a London flat more than once,' I said. 'Your response always begins "Ah . . . well . . . yes, Flo . . . you see . . . the thing is . . ." and that's usually the end of that. Once in a while I might chance my arm and counter with "Yes . . . but . . . bear in mind that . . ." but it never gets me anywhere.'

'It just seems like such an enormous expense simply to make life easier for occasional visits.'

'Property's always a shrewd investment. You told me that.'

'I did, and it is. But if I were to invest in property, I'd much rather buy our rented house from dear Jasper. It seems increasingly unlikely that he and his family are ever going to return to England and I'd value our home in Littleton Cotterell much more highly than a pied-à-terre in the metropolis.'

'Well, yes, but just bear in mind that I'd enthusiastically back any decision to buy a gaff in the Smoke.'

She laughed. 'Duly noted, dear. In the meantime, I wonder what's for lunch.'

◆ ◆ ◆

Lunch, it turned out, began with cucumber soup. I'd never been entirely certain about cucumbers. They always smelled so fresh and delicious, promising a mouthful of perfumed summertime . . . and yet they tasted mostly of water. Somehow, though, in soup form, they kept their promise. Perhaps it was that the word 'soup' had lowered my expectations. Soups can be thick or thin, savoury or bland, but their overwhelming characteristic is their wetness. Whatever else you might expect when you take a mouthful of soup, you know it will be distinctly soggy. And, somehow, that made the fragrant essence of the cucumber shine through.

Or so it seemed to me.

'This cucumber soup is disappointing,' said Lady Hardcastle. 'I mean, one has to admire the ambition of serving something so perilous as soup on a moving train, but I had hoped for more.'

'More than what?'

'More . . . actually, now I'm forced to define it, I have no idea. More than cucumber soup, I suppose.'

'You should have had the pâté.'

'Or the smoked salmon – I always enjoy smoked salmon. But then I couldn't have had the Dover sole.'

'Why not?'

'Two fish courses? Have you run mad, dear? People would talk.'

'You would be shunned.'

'Quite. And how could one pass up the opportunity to sample Great Western Railway's Dover sole as we pass through the Wiltshire countryside at dizzying speed?'

'How indeed? What are we doing again?'

'We are travelling to London at dizzying speed while we await the delivery of our Dover sole. I, for one, am enjoying this delicious bottle of Chevalier-Montrachet. Soon there will be angel parfait, followed by petits fours and a pot of coffee.'

I sighed. 'And why are we going to London, at dizzying speed or otherwise?'

'Ah, well, there you have me, dear thing.' She looked around, discreetly checking that we were clear of earwiggers. 'A Serbian has been murdered in Bristol on his way to a ship bound for who knows where. We were ordered to interfere in a police investigation – and don't ask me whether that's legal, I have no idea – but were then peremptorily summoned to London before we could find out more. No explanations have been offered by our . . . I was going to say "superiors" again but it will be glacial in Gehenna before I recognize Harry as my superior.'

'So you say. Often.'

'My tiresome repetition notwithstanding, we are still explanation-free and I should welcome any insights you were able to offer.'

'I've no more idea than you, I'm afraid. The Balkan element is troubling.'

'Anything involving the Continent is troubling at the moment. But I can't see any profit in speculating until my darling brother deigns to bring us properly up to date.'

She was right, of course, and as we worked our way through the rest of the meal we discussed the intriguing music of Gustav Mahler and the disappointing awfulness of Bram Stoker's *The Lair of the White Worm*.

Back in our carriage, we read our books, made up stories about our fellow passengers (always one of our favourite travel games), and snoozed a little in the warm sunshine streaming through the windows.

But I still wanted to know what on earth was going on.

By the time the train puffed majestically into Paddington station – dead on time – Harry, as promised, was on the platform to meet us.

'What ho, you two,' he said. 'Thank you so very much for coming.'

'Hello, Harry dear,' said Lady Hardcastle. 'Did we have a choice?'

'None whatsoever, but it's still good of you to come.'

'You're most welcome.'

Harry looked at the two porters puffing beside us, with their trucks groaning under the weight of our luggage.

'Good lord,' he said. 'Is all of that yours?'

'You said to pack for a couple of weeks,' I said. 'You didn't offer any further details and so' – I gestured towards the trunk, three suit-cases, one hat box, two Gladstone bags and one canvas satchel – 'that's what you get.'

'Ha! Well, that's me told. It'll never fit in my little Ministry motor, though – we'll have to have it delivered.'

One of the porters produced a pad on to which Harry wrote the delivery instructions. He paid the fee, Lady Hardcastle gave the two men her customary generous tip, and we were at last free to follow Harry out on to Praed Street, where he had parked the aforementioned little Ministry motor.

It took him three tries to crank the engine to life, and he was red-faced and puffing as he joined us in the car.

'All set?' he said.

'Raring to go,' said Lady Hardcastle.

'You can't claim that back, you know,' he said as he pulled out into the surprisingly heavy traffic.

'Can't claim what back?' said Lady Hardcastle.

'That enormous tip you gave those two chaps.'

'The thought had never occurred to me, dear.'

'I'll be claiming the delivery fee,' he said, holding up the receipt in one hand as he steered with the other.

'You jolly well will not. I'll reimburse you myself if you're going to be parsimonious about it, but the British taxpayer absolutely does not need to be paying for us to move frocks and hats across the capital.'

'But—'

'Butts are for bees, brother dear. There are people starving in our cities despite our government's best intentions and I shall not have the transport of my shoes and stockings given precedence over the needs of a hungry child.'

With a sigh, Harry put the receipt back in his jacket pocket.

'Did you have a pleasant journey?' he asked.

'Very nice indeed,' I said. 'Good food, good company, and even time for a nap. And it's quite the best way to see cows – from a distance, at speed, and protected inside a sturdy railway carriage.'

'You'll be safe from them for a while,' said Harry with a chuckle. 'Still plenty of horses in town, mind you. But the only cattle are at Smithfield market, and they're no longer a threat to anyone.'

Harry took the most direct route to Whitehall, down Edgware Road, past Marble Arch, down Park Lane, and round Buckingham Palace on Constitution Hill. Then to Birdcage Walk alongside St James's Park, on to Great George Street, and finally left on to Whitehall. He made an alarmingly reckless right turn beside the War Office on to Horse Guards Avenue and then left on to Whitehall Court.

Outside number 2, he parked as haphazardly as his sister always did and we struggled out on to the busy pavement, being tutted at all the while by dark-suited men scurrying about on very, very important government business.

Harry ushered us through the familiar anonymous door and we signed ourselves in before heading not for his office as I had expected, but for the office of his boss, Colonel Clifford Valentine.

Harry knocked and entered without waiting for a reply.

◆ ◆ ◆

Colonel Valentine's office was not luxuriously appointed. The furniture, scavenged from other departments, had seen better days. The carpet, barely large enough to accommodate his battered desk and visitor chairs, was threadbare in places. The King's portrait, in a chipped wooden frame, hung slightly askew.

The colonel himself, by contrast, was immaculate. His greying hair was smartly cut, crisply parted, and slick with Macassar

Oil. His luxuriant salt-and-pepper walrus moustache was neatly trimmed and freshly waxed. His khaki dress tunic and white shirt were clean and pressed. The scarlet staff tabs on his collar, and the medal ribbons on his chest, were so pristine that they seemed to gleam.

He was writing on a sheet at the front of a fat file with an expensive-looking fountain pen as we entered, but he put it down at once and stood to greet us.

He smiled warmly. 'Lady Hardcastle. Miss Armstrong. How wonderful to have our two best field officers back in the fold. Did you have a comfortable journey?'

'Very pleasant, thank you, Colonel,' said Lady Hardcastle as she settled into one of the visitor chairs.

'It always helps to have an agreeable travelling companion, too,' I said as I too sat down.

'Splendid, splendid. Ah, and here's the tea.'

A junior assistant entered with a tray and poured four cups before withdrawing, closing the door behind him. Harry stepped forward and took his, then returned to his spot against the wall where he leaned against a tall, wooden filing cabinet.

'Featherstonhaugh tells me you've kept the provincial peelers under control,' said Colonel Valentine as he reached for his own cup and one of the broken Rich Tea biscuits that sat forlornly on a chipped plate.

'We have a good friend on the Bristol police force,' said Lady Hardcastle. 'He understands that the Bureau might have valid reasons for interfering in the investigation of a murder, but clings to the hope that justice will be done, even if it's not his own force which brings that about.'

'Good man.'

'He is, Colonel. A very good man. And for my part, I cling to the hope that he's not being naive.'

'We shall do what the circumstances allow.'

'And what does that mean?'

'We operate in a grey area, Lady Hardcastle – you, of all people, should know that.'

'I'm well aware. Does that mean *we* killed Jovan Srna and that Inspector Sunderland won't see justice done?'

'Who? Oh, I see. Jovan Srna – John Doe. I say, that's terribly clever. Well done, you.' He smiled to himself for a few moments. 'How did you know he was Serbian?'

'Clothes and banknotes,' I said.

'Ah, of course. Not much gets past you two.'

'Did we, though?' persisted Lady Hardcastle.

'Did we kill him?' The colonel shook his head. 'Good lord, no. We'd have made a much more discreet job of it if we had, don't you think? Can you imagine any of our lot shooting someone in broad daylight on a crowded street?'

'Well . . .' I said. 'There are one or two.'

He laughed – a familiar upper-class bark. 'Ha! Quite right. There are one or two. But no, it wasn't us. I shouldn't have wasted your time with all that palaver in Bristol if it were us. Even if we had been clumsy enough to make such a hash of things, we'd have closed everything down quick-stick. Hushed it up, swept it under the rug. Move along now, nothing to see here. No need to drag you two away from luncheon with the local squire and his memsahib.'

'I see.'

'In fact, the dead man – Dragomir Kovač – was one of ours.'

'One of ours?' said Lady Hardcastle. 'From the Basement?'

'The Basement?' He looked around at his shabby office. 'Oh, I say, you're in fine form today. Perhaps that's what we should call ourselves, Featherstonhaugh, eh? The Basement. Ha! But no, he was an agent. Recruited in Serbia.'

'And the man who shot him?'

'One of theirs, we assume. He didn't have any personal enemies as far as we know, so we presume it to be the Turks, the Austrians, or the Serbians.'

'What was he doing for us?' I asked.

'Providing intelligence on the coming war between the Balkan League and the Ottomans. Frightfully unstable part of the world – has us all in a flap here. Everyone else has their eye on Kaiser Wilhelm and his imperialist ambitions – building up his navy, snarling at Russia – but I've a nasty feeling it'll be the situation in the Balkans that sets us all on the path to destruction and damnation.'

'The Russians aren't helping,' said Lady Hardcastle. 'Helping to form the Balkan League to take Macedonia from the Ottomans wasn't a move designed to promote peace.'

'Well, quite. They'll be at war down there soon. By the autumn, we assume.'

'That doesn't bode well,' I said. 'It's bound to upset Austria-Hungary, for a start. They've a lot of influence in the area at the moment – if local independence and nationalism mean they lose that, they'll not be best pleased. And if they're unhappy, Germany is honour-bound to be unhappy on their behalf. And if the two of them start blaming Russia . . .'

'You have a decent grasp of it, Miss Armstrong. You see why I think of you two as my best officers? Instability in the Balkans could set the whole of Europe at each other's throats.'

'And where did Mr Kovač fit in to all this?' asked Lady Hardcastle. 'He was providing intelligence, you say?'

'Just so. He was a former military man with contacts in the Balkan League as well as the Black Hand. We brought him to London to help with a project we've been working on here, but things are escalating in his homeland and we needed him back in the old country to keep an eye on developments there. Obviously we didn't want our Teutonic chums and their allies to get their paws on him, which meant that land routes were out – no way to get home without passing through Germany, Austria or Italy. So he was going to travel by sea out of Bristol. Hell of a journey, but it would be difficult for hostile forces to keep an eye on a little steamer chugging its way through the Med and the Adriatic. What we hadn't bargained for was someone getting wind of his movements and doing the poor chap in before he boarded his boat.'

'The killer was a dark-haired man in nautical garb,' I said. 'The witness who saw him fleeing the scene described him as foreign.'

'How the devil did she come to that conclusion?'

'Too good-looking to be English, she said.'

'Ha! Well, we know what he looked like – one of Featherstonhaugh's chaps gave chase.'

'Brownlow,' I said.

The colonel's mouth hung open for a moment. 'How . . . I mean to say . . .'

'A faintly inept, left-handed Special Branch officer with expensive taste in clothes and a medallion on an Albert chain? It's a Balliol medallion, by the way. Homburg hat, waxed moustache? That'll be Brownlow. We met him at Weston-super-Mare.'

'Ah, yes, so you did. I'd quite forgotten that little bit of business. Missing scientist?'

'That was it.'

'Wasn't Brownlow the chap you . . . ?'

'Knocked on his backside?' I said. 'Yes, that's the one.'

'He's not one of your admirers, I must say.'

'He's an oaf and a bully. The feeling is entirely mutual.'

'Ha! But yes, it was Brownlow who was tasked with keeping watch on Kovač, and Brownlow who chased—'

'And lost, presumably.'

'Chased and lost Kovač's killer, yes. A killer the Bristol police shan't be getting anywhere near, thanks to you.' He tapped a closed file lying on his desk. 'I have a copy of the post-mortem report, for instance. It's admirably anodyne – well done. Did you edit it?'

Lady Hardcastle shook her head. 'The police surgeon responsible is also a friend. He, too, was persuaded to be honest but bland.'

'Splendid, splendid. What did he leave out?'

'We asked him to neglect to mention that the bullet that killed Kovač was a 9 millimetre.'

'Modern round,' said the colonel, thoughtfully. 'Luger, or . . . ?'

'FN 1910?' said Harry. 'The Italian Glisenti? Although the Americans have been using 9 millimetre rounds for a few years as well, don't forget – that little Colt pocket pistol shoots something similar. Was it short or long?'

'Our witness said only that it was square and modern,' said Lady Hardcastle.

'Not the gun, sis, the bullet.'

'Compared with what, dear?'

'Well, the Luger and the Glisenti, for instance, take a round two millimetres longer than something like the FN.'

She fished in her bag and handed Harry the spent cartridge case. 'So a round I haven't seen is a shade over a sixteenth of an inch longer than another round I've never seen. I'm not sure how—'

'Doesn't look like a Luger round to me,' said Harry. 'My money's on the FN 1910. Nice little pistol.'

'I'll take your word for it, dear.'

'Anything else that's not in the official reports?' asked Colonel Valentine.

'I found a notebook,' I said. 'There were a few pages ripped out and the only word that remained was "Wharf" written in English.'

The colonel sat for a few moments in contemplation. After a while, he said, 'And the local chaps know nothing of any of this?'

'Dr Gosling is aware of the size of the bullet, obviously,' said Lady Hardcastle. 'He dug it out of Kovač's spine, after all. But no one has seen the cartridge case, and no one knows of the writing in the notebook.'

'Good show. In that case we can close down the Bristol investigation entirely. See to that, would you, Featherstonhaugh? And then bring your men back here.'

'They're already back,' said Harry.

'Even better. Nothing more to be done there. We can return our focus to London.'

Lady Hardcastle frowned slightly. 'And what's our role to be in all this? Surely you have men who can track down an enemy operative in London – you hardly need us. And if he's already gone home . . .'

'Kovač was working on another matter. Fan— Harry will brief you on the full situation in due course, but that's why we need you here. It very much requires your special talents.'

'I see,' said Lady Hardcastle. 'In that case, we are at your service.'

'Marvellous. Knew I could count on you. Make the necessary arrangements, Featherstonhaugh. Set the ladies up with accommodation and transport as necessary.'

'Already in hand,' said Harry.

'Good man. Get them some identification as well, would you? Might come in handy to keep the local rozzers in their place. "My War Office identification trumps your warrant card" – that sort of thing.'

'I'll see to it.'

'Thank you. I'll leave you to brief them on everything that's been going on. Splendid to have you on board, ladies.'

We said our goodbyes and followed Harry to his own office.

Harry's office was just as shabbily furnished as the colonel's but he had somehow managed to make it more welcoming. The King's portrait hung straight. There was a photograph of Lady Lavinia and little Addie in a silver frame on his desk. He had a fireplace, and there were nick-nacks and mementoes on the mantelpiece. It wasn't exactly homely, but it definitely avoided the spartan, utilitarian feel so effortlessly achieved by Colonel Valentine.

'Sit yourselves down, ladies,' said Harry as he closed the door. 'Make yourselves at home. More tea? I could get more tea.'

Even his visitor chairs were padded, and a good deal more comfortable than those in the colonel's office.

'I'm fine, thank you,' I said.

'Me too,' said Lady Hardcastle. She looked at her brother for a moment. 'What's going on, Harry? If we're not here to track down Kovač's killer, then why *are* we here?'

Harry sat in his own chair and swung his feet up on to the desk. 'Longish story, sis.'

'Precis, then. You can do it — you're a bright boy.'

'Because.'

'I shall instruct Flo to murder you in your sleep. She won't want to – for reasons of her own, the poor deluded woman seems to like you – but she's loyal to me and she'll do as I ask.'

'She's right,' I said, 'I will.'

'Very well, then.' He sighed. 'Kovač was recruited a couple of years ago. He was over here from Belgrade on some sort of business mission – railways or ships or something—'

'Serbia is landlocked, dear,' said Lady Hardcastle.

'Probably railways, then, eh? Or maybe telephones. Not chemicals – they'd have gone to Germany for that. I honestly don't know. The important part of the story is that some enterprising chap from the Foreign Office sidled up to him at a drinks reception and started talking to him about the political situation at home. It transpired that young Dragomir Kovač not only had some extremely useful contacts in the Serbian army, and even the Black Hand, he was also becoming increasingly alarmed at the state of Balkan politics. Enquiries were made into his credentials – checking his life story, that sort of thing – and he was duly recruited as an agent. When our merry band was formed in '09, we inherited Kovač and continued to make use of his intelligence-gathering skills. Time, as it has a dispiriting tendency to do, passed. Earlier this year we started to hear rumours that something was afoot, so we sent a coded telegram to Kovač in Belgrade asking him what he knew. He replied saying that he'd heard something, but he needed to come to London to confirm it. We made the arrangements at once.'

'Overland?' I said. 'I thought that was too risky.'

'Train to Dubrovnik, from there by sea to Marseille, and then up through France. Hopped the channel to Dover, *et Robert est ton oncle*. The French are our pals, remember?'

'Why not use that route to get him home?'

'Because. Look, we can go into the intricacies of our operational decisions if you like, but I thought you might be more interested to know why we were so amenable to the idea of Kovač coming over here in the first place.'

'I'm so sorry,' I said. 'Do carry on.'

'Thank you. Kovač was still a minor functionary in the Serbian trade ministry and had kept up with his contacts in the army, the Black Hand, and now the Balkan League. We hoped his inside knowledge would help us confirm or refute our worst fears.'

'Which were?' said Lady Hardcastle.

'On Monday, the twenty-second of July – a shade under two weeks from now – our government will be playing host to a trade delegation from Austria. Trains again, I think. Honestly, I don't care. What I do care about are the rumours we've been hearing that politically motivated Serbian agitators are planning to disrupt the visit.'

'Violently?' I asked.

'I'm not sure they know any other way. So, yes, almost certainly violently. Kovač arrived in London in one piece, despite the lengthy journey. The story he'd heard matched the one we'd heard, but he wanted to make some enquiries in London before he would commit. He would disappear for days, but would then surface saying he nearly had it. Until one day he just vanished. Went to ground. He left word that he had to get out sharpish but didn't say anything else. Now, despite our callous reputation, we actually do care about our agents' safety, so we made the necessary arrangements to get him out of town and put him on a Balkan-bound boat.'

'Having told you nothing,' said Lady Hardcastle.

'Not a dickie bird.'

'Why not just ask him before you packed him off to Bristol?' I asked.

'We had no opportunity to talk to him. He'd gone to ground, as I said. By this point we were communicating by messages hidden in a hole in a tree in Hyde Park, and they were short, functional things – mostly in a prearranged code. We sorted out two boats for him – one from the city docks, then one from Avonmouth – and sent the details by coded message. Finally we knew where he would be: he'd have to be at the Floating Harbour in time for that first boat from Bristol. So we sent Brownlow down to have a quick word before he sailed. We could have arranged a meeting in London, of course, but we decided that would be too dangerous – the chaps who were after him were here. But surely Bristol would be a safe place for a quiet meeting.' He shrugged. 'The rest you know.'

'Whatever he was looking into in London was down at the Thames,' I said. 'He'd have made his notes in his own language, but he wrote the English word "Wharf" – it must have been the actual name, not just a description.'

Harry nodded. 'Can't say I disagree with you, Strongarm, and it would fit with the little we know of his movements – he was *very* good at evading our surveillance, by the way. The problem is—'

'Who was trailing him?' asked Lady Hardcastle.

'Perlman and Brownlow. Perch and Tench as you knew them.'

'I'll always think of them as Oryx and Kudu. They didn't impress me in any other way, but some of their *noms de guerre* were inspired.'

'Well, their talent for impenetrable code names notwithstanding, when they inevitably lost him – every blessed day, I have to tell you – he was going south towards the river. So the idea that he was heading for a wharf is entirely plausible. The trouble is, there are hundreds of wharves. Literally. One might hyperbolically say there are "hundreds" of a thing, but in this case it's dismayingly true. There are more than five hundred named wharves between Isleworth and Southend. And almost four hundred of them lie between Westminster and Canning Town.'

Lady Hardcastle frowned at him curiously. 'How on earth do you know that, dear?'

'A boy has to have a hobby. Actually, I counted them one day. One of our jobs is to keep an eye on the comings and goings along the river and it struck me how many times the word "Wharf" came up in daily reports. So I got a chap at the Port of London to send me a list. Charming fellow. Long list.'

'Then it's a good thing we're here,' I said. 'We'll find your wharf and your Serbian ne'er-do-wells in no time.'

Harry gave one of his famous smiles. He and his sister could both light up a room with their smiles – it was most disconcerting at times.

'I'm not questioning your abilities,' he said, 'but how?'

Lady Hardcastle tapped the side of her nose. 'We know people. And those people know other people. We've worked these streets—'

Harry's smile turned to a broad grin.

'Oh, don't be so childish, dear,' said Lady Hardcastle, shaking her head. 'We were investigating unsavoury goings-on in the Pool of London while you were still meekly plodding about in the Foreign Office making tea for people much stupider than you but, unaccountably, a good deal more senior. If our network can't track down a gang of Balkan terrorists, I'll eat my . . . I was going to say "hat", but it's such a lovely hat – it seems a shame to risk sacrificing it to hubris. I'll certainly eat my lunch, though. We'll start first thing in the morning.'

'That's the spirit,' said Harry. 'Before you go skulking off into your beloved underworld, though, I've arranged for you to meet some of the British delegation who'll be taking part in the trade talks – the London Trade Confederation. It won't take long, but I thought it might help. They should be able to give you up-to-date information on the plans for the talks.'

'A splendid idea, dear, thank you.'

'You're most welcome, sis. Now, what say we adjourn for the day and pop home to Bedford Square to see Jake and Addie?'

Harry's wife, Lady Lavinia, had been known as Jake since her schooldays. The etymology of the nickname (Lavinia – Lav – Lavatory – Jakes – Jake) meant that Lady Hardcastle was never comfortable using it, and always called her Lavinia. Harry, of course, had no such qualms and, in truth, Lady Lavinia didn't seem to mind. I avoided the whole complicated issue by trying not to use her name at all. Sometimes being a lady's maid had its advantages, even when the words 'notional' and even 'former' started to be added to my job title.

'I thought you'd never ask, dear,' said Lady Hardcastle. 'As enchanting as it's been to visit the offices again, I'm itching to give little Addie a big, squidgy, materteral hug and teach her some swear words.'

'Jake will be so pleased. We'll just go and see Halliday on your way out – he'll give you your new credentials.'

◆ ◆ ◆

The Featherstonhaughs rented a rather pleasant Georgian townhouse on Bedford Square, just round the corner from the British Museum. Harry parked the SSB car right outside the door with the same carelessness as he had shown on Whitehall Court. Dazzling smiles and shambolic parking – two key Featherstonhaugh family characteristics.

Lady Lavinia was pleased to see us, as always, while Addie – now almost eighteen months old – nearly burst with excitement at seeing Aunt Emmy and Fo. I rather liked being Fo.

We all made ourselves comfortable in the drawing room and had yet more reviving tea.

As she had promised she would, Lady Hardcastle gave Addie the warmest hug and then lifted her up to sit on her knee while she tried to get her to repeat a Russian word. It took a few tries, but eventually Addie had it.

'That's pretty,' said Lady Lavinia, who was sitting beside them on the sofa. 'What does it mean?'

Lady Hardcastle leaned over and whispered in her ear.

Lady Lavinia exploded with laughter. 'Oh, Emily, you utter beast. She can't say that.'

'Nonsense, dear – it might come in very handy one day.'

Addie looked earnestly at her father and repeated the word once more.

'You might have a point,' said Lady Lavinia, still laughing. 'And it can be very helpful for young ladies to have good language skills.'

'You're welcome.'

With family news and village gossip exchanged, Lady Hardcastle and I went upstairs to settle ourselves in our usual rooms. I, for one, had another nap before getting changed for the evening.

Refreshed and rejuvenated, we joined Harry and Lavinia in the drawing room for drinks.

'Have we missed Addie?' said Lady Hardcastle as she accepted her gin and tonic.

'Hours ago,' said Lady Lavinia. 'She was most put out you weren't there.'

'You should have woken me – I would love to have said good-night to the little poppet. Oh, and I would have fetched Flo. She could have read her a story.'

'Oh, she would have loved that. She's very fond of stories, even when she doesn't fully understand them.'

'Of course. Everyone loves a story.'

'Would you not want to read to her, though?'

'Oh, no, dear – I'm absolutely hopeless. I'm far too self-conscious to do the voices – I sound like I'm reading a trade report to a parliamentary committee. Flo, on the other hand . . . Flo has some sort of magical gift. She does the voices, the actions, the animal noises. She's like a one-woman theatre show.'

'How did you find that out?' asked Harry with a laugh. 'Does she read to you?'

I smiled. 'I sometimes read for the younger children at the village school,' I said. 'I did it one day to help out when the teacher wasn't well and I sort of got stuck with it.'

'Then you shall most definitely have to read to Addie,' said Lady Lavinia. 'But only if it's not too much of a bother.'

I smiled again. 'I look forward to it.'

'It's lovely of you to put us up at such short notice,' said Lady Hardcastle. 'We had no idea we'd be coming until last night.'

'Really?' said Lady Lavinia. 'We've known since last week, haven't we, Harry?'

Lady Hardcastle and I turned to look at Harry.

'Well, now,' he said. '"Known"? "Known" is a strong word. "Known" connotes certainty. I'd be more comfortable with "thought very strongly there might be a possibility that". But "known"? I wouldn't say that.'

'Ah, I seem to have put my foot in it,' said Lady Lavinia. 'Sorry, darling.'

'I had a choice,' said Harry. 'I could either say, "We might need you in London by next Wednesday, better start packing," and then have you annoyed with me when it didn't happen. Or I could keep quiet and then have you annoyed with me when I called you down at short notice. Either way it seemed to me that I'd be on the wrong end of some annoyance so I tossed a coin. Short notice won.'

Lady Hardcastle and I shook our heads in unison.

'On the other hand,' he said, 'knowing since last week . . . *strongly suspecting* since last week has given me the chance to organize a flat, a car and some staff for you. You'd be welcome to stay here, of course. Always. But given your duties it might be more discreet for you to have a gaff of your own.'

'It would, dear, thank you. Though we might turn down the offer of staff. Someone to pop in now and again to titivate the place a bit and make sure there's tea and coffee in the larder would be splendid. But you're right about the need for discretion, and I really don't want to be having to keep my voice down so the maid doesn't hear something she oughtn't.'

'You make a compelling case. I'll get on to the agency in the morning and change the arrangements.'

'Thank you. Oh, and for future reference: if something like this ever comes up again, do take the "giving plenty of notice" option, won't you.'

'Right you are, sis. Sorry.'

A gong sounded in the hall.

'Dinner at last,' said Harry, standing up. 'I'm starving.'

Chapter Five

A housemaid brought me coffee and toast at seven o'clock the next morning. I was sitting up in bed, reading a book.

'Mornin', miss,' she said as she put the tray on the bedside table. 'Mr Featherstonhaugh says as how you like a bit o' toast before you get up.'

'That's kind,' I said. 'Thank you. We've not met, have we? I'm Flo.'

'Yes, miss. I'm Sarah, miss. Sarah Turley.'

'It's a pleasure to meet you, Sarah. Have you been in to Lady Hardcastle yet?'

'Not yet, miss, no.'

'She'll be pleased to see you once she's awake, but don't worry if she grumbles at you at first – she's not very good at mornings.'

Sarah laughed. 'Right you are, miss. I'll remember.'

'When's breakfast?'

'Eight sharp, miss. Mr Featherstonhaugh likes to leave the 'ouse by 'alf past so 'e can walk to work. Though he might leave later this mornin' – 'e's got a motor car outside.'

'Thank you. I'll be ready.'

'Can I get you anyfing else?'

'No, I'll be just fine.'

Sarah left me to my toast and coffee.

Toast eaten and coffee drunk, I readied myself for the day before putting away the few things I'd taken from my case. Even before he announced the renting of the flat, I had gathered from Harry's original telephone message that we might not be staying at Bedford Square for long, so I hadn't unpacked properly.

At a quarter to eight, I went to Lady Hardcastle's room to make sure she was vertical and presentable.

'Good morning, Flo dear,' she said as I entered.

She was up, at least, and sitting at the dressing table, but still looked as though her hair had been styled by an overenthusiastic small child.

She gestured to the offending tangle. 'I say, you couldn't do something with my barnet, could you? I just can't seem to get it right.'

I fixed her hair and repacked for her. Like me, she had only unpacked a few things, but her magical gift for chaos made it appear as though the room had been ransacked by an angry burglar. With Herself and her possessions finally neat and tidy, we went down to breakfast together.

Harry and Lady Lavinia were already there, chatting about something Harry had just read in his copy of *The Times*.

'Good morning, you two,' said Lady Lavinia. 'Do help yourselves. I recommend the kedgeree, though – Cook has a marvellous way with kedgeree.'

We loaded our plates and joined them at the table.

'Where are we off to, then?' asked Lady Hardcastle as she tucked in.

Harry folded his newspaper. 'Off to? The London Trade Confederation? It's in the City, but that's not until lunchtime. No rush.'

'This morning, dear. You said we were to move in to our new digs.'

'Oh, yes, of course. The flat. It's not far.'

'You'll love it,' said Lady Lavinia. 'The building belongs to one of Fishy's friends. It's frightfully nice.'

Lady Lavinia's brother was Lord Riddlethorpe, the owner of Riddlethorpe Racing, known to his friends as Fishy. It was easy to imagine that he had friends who between them owned most of London.

'We can stroll up there after breakfast,' said Harry. 'Are you packed? We can leave your traps here and get them sent up this morning.'

'All squared away, dear. Flo gave me a hand.'

'I imagine Flo did the lot, sis. You were never the tidiest girl. I always used to wonder how you ever found anything in your nightmare of a room.'

'I always know exactly where everything is.'

'On the floor,' I said. 'It's actually a rather clever system when you think about it. You never have to wonder "Where's my hat?", "Where's my favourite pen?", "Where's that cup of coffee Flo just made me?" The answer is always the same: on the floor.'

Harry barked, 'Ha!'

Did they teach them that at school, I wondered? Were there special lessons where the boys were all taught how to laugh like gentlemen? It seemed warm and charming when Harry did it, but it was the same sound made by upper-class Englishmen throughout the Empire.

'Never mind my uniquely enchanting way of organizing myself,' said Lady Hardcastle. 'The important thing is that we are packed, and ready to flit at a moment's notice.'

'Are you packed, Flo?' asked Lady Lavinia.

'She's always packed, dear. Even when she's unpacked, she's packed. She's like one of those paradoxes in children's riddles.'

'I am, thank you,' I said, ignoring her.

'Good show,' said Harry. 'What do you think of the kedgeree?'

◆　◆　◆

By the time hats had been pinned on, and Harry had made telephone calls to rearrange the staffing of the flat and to book someone to move our luggage, it was raining. The plan to walk to the flat – a distance of less than a mile, we were assured – was abandoned and we clambered instead into Harry's Ministry car with our Gladstone bags.

It would have taken us only twenty minutes to walk to the rented flat on Southampton Street, just off Fitzroy Square. Thanks to a coal wagon parked in the middle of one street, a skittish horse on another, and workmen digging up the road on Harry's third-choice route, it took twenty-five minutes to drive. Still, at least we would keep dry.

By the time we arrived, it had stopped raining.

The comparative narrowness of the street ought to have prompted Harry to park more neatly, but he stopped with the car at the same devil-may-care angle as always. Other motorists would end up wishing they had walked, too.

The building was another terraced block of townhouses, strikingly similar to Harry's and probably, I thought, built by the same eighteenth-century builder. If not, then someone had been copying someone else's homework.

Harry let us in to a shared entrance hall and then strode confidently up two flights of stairs to a door on the second floor. He unlocked it and we followed him inside.

The flat was tastefully decorated and comfortably furnished in a surprisingly modern style, and the brief tour confirmed that we had enough room to be comfortable for a lengthy stay. Since the Austrian delegation would be arriving in less than two weeks, we would definitely not have time to grow frustrated by any perceived lack of space.

'I asked our chaps to make sure there were some basic groceries in the larder,' said Harry, 'so you should be all right there. The agency will send a charlady on Mondays, Wednesdays and Fridays at ten in the morning if that suits, but if not feel free to vary the arrangement as you will. The telephone was connected last week and the Bureau will take care of the bill.' He took his watch from his waistcoat pocket and flipped open the lid. 'There's a motor car due any time—' A noise outside made him look out of the window. 'Oh, now, as it happens. I say, he's making a complete pig's breakfast of parking it. Anyway. As you can see, there's a blue Austin 10 hp at your disposal. Keep receipts for petrol and whatnot and the Bureau will reimburse you.'

I looked out of the window at the pleasingly anonymous little blue car.

Lady Hardcastle sighed. 'That's kind, dear, but I do so hate forms.'

'Don't worry, sis, I'll take care of the paperwork. Consider it my way of saying thank you. Monstrously grateful to have you two on the case, to tell you the truth. Can you imagine the hash Pilchard and Sardine would make of it?'

'I shudder at the thought.'

'We'll try not to let you down,' I said. 'And this flat will do marvellously.'

'It will, Harry,' said Lady Hardcastle. 'Thank you very much indeed. It will be fun to be back in London for a while.'

Harry beamed. 'Good show. Got any paper?'

Lady Hardcastle rummaged in her handbag and produced her notepad and mechanical pencil. Harry scrawled an address on a blank page and handed it back.

'I have to get back to the office, I'm afraid. Would you mind awfully meeting me at the Trade Doo-dah offices at midday?'

'Map?'

'On the bookshelf, old girl. Street maps, *Bradshaw's*, and a schedule of planned shipping movements at the Port of London for the next two weeks. Anything else, just ask.'

'Give our regards to the Basement,' said Lady Hardcastle. 'We'll see you at the Trade Doo-dah at lunchtime.'

Harry handed over the keys and was gone.

◆　◆　◆

The London Trade Confederation occupied one floor of an impressive Palladian building in the heart of the City of London, not far from the Bank of England.

We parked in a side street at five minutes to twelve, and made our way to the imposing entrance door with its gleaming paint and brass furnishings. A uniformed commissionaire opened the door for us and ushered us into the building, where we consulted the board and found that the LTC were on the first floor.

We were already walking towards the broad marble staircase when we heard a voice behind us.

'What ho, sis. Wait for me.'

Harry caught us, and we set off up the stairs together.

'You found it all right, then?' he said.

Lady Hardcastle turned to look at him, but said nothing.

'Ah, yes. Obviously you did. Sorry. The chap we're meeting is Sir Montague Winfield, chairman of the LTC. Managing director of a tram company. Rich as Croesus, doesn't suffer fools – gladly or otherwise.'

'Self-made or inherited?' I asked.

'Inherited. His family owned cotton mills in Lancashire for a few generations. No longer, though. When the textiles market began to flag, he sold up to fund his new business ambitions.

His poor widowed mother was horrified, but his gamble paid off.'

'Do you like him?' said Lady Hardcastle.

'Not my place to like or dislike, sis. I am but a humble civil servant, assigned to ensure the safety of his confederation's trade talks with the Austrians.'

We arrived outside a polished oak door bearing a brass plate declaring it to be the offices of the London Trade Confederation. Harry opened it and entered.

We found ourselves in a small reception room, decorated with a portrait of a dour, bewhiskered man in early-nineteenth-century clothes. There was a forlorn, slightly wilted aspidistra on an inlaid, mahogany stand, flanked by two uncomfortable-looking chairs. A corridor stretched off into the distance, lined with more oak doors.

A smartly dressed man in his twenties appeared as though from nowhere. A second glance confirmed that at least one of the door-sized oak panels around the room was actually a concealed door.

'Good afternoon, Mr Featherstonhaugh,' said the man with a slight bow.

'What ho, Rackley,' said Harry. 'Splendid to see you again. How's the arm?'

'Improving, sir, thank you.'

'Rackley's a rather talented cricketer, sis – a fast bowler of unusual cunning. Injured his arm against your lot in Gloucestershire the other week. Soon have you back on the field, though, eh?'

'One hopes so, sir. Sir Montague is expecting you. Would your . . . family care to wait here? I can have tea sent up.'

'No need, Rackley, dear boy – they're with me.'

'As you say, sir. This way.'

Rackley led us the entire length of the corridor to a pair of oversized doors. He knocked, and then ostentatiously threw them both open without waiting for a reply.

Where the SSB offices had been tatty and barely functional, the LTC chairman's office was entirely devoted to the expression of power and wealth through luxury and opulence.

The carpet was deeply piled, the silk wallpaper hand-painted. The portraits of past chairmen hung in frames whose gilt was richly burnished. The furniture – every item of which perfectly complemented every other – was plushly padded and lustrously polished. The chairman's desk, as is the way with men who wish to convey an impression of their importance, was at least the size of a tennis court.

I estimated that the man himself was in his early fifties. He was well on the way to being portly, but so immaculately tailored that only his jowly face gave him away. Even then, the effect was artfully camouflaged by a fastidiously trimmed George V beard.

'Mr Featherstonhaugh and . . . guests to see you, sir,' said Rackley.

Sir Montague stood, smiling broadly. 'Featherstonhaugh! Marvellous to see you, my dear chap. Come in, come in. Sit, sit.'

Rackley backed out of the room and closed the doors almost silently.

Sir Montague seemed to notice Lady Hardcastle and me for the first time. 'What's this, Featherstonhaugh? Brought your family?' He chuckled.

'Actually, yes, Sir Montague. May I have the pleasure of introducing my sister, Lady Hardcastle, and my dear friend Miss Armstrong? Ladies, this is Sir Montague Winfield, chairman of the London Trade Confederation.'

After the customary round of handshakes and how-do-you-do's, we settled into delightfully comfortable visitor chairs on the other side of the colossal desk from our still-smiling host.

'Charmed to meet the ladies, Featherstonhaugh, of course. Utterly charmed. But I was under the impression you were bringing chaps from your Bureau. The chaps who are going to oversee the security arrangements for our trade talks.'

Harry gestured towards Lady Hardcastle and me with a smile. 'These *are* the chaps from the Bureau.'

Sir Montague looked at us quizzically, and then laughed. 'I know when a fellow's having me on, Featherstonhaugh. Most amusing. Very funny indeed. Seriously, though, when are your men getting here? Things are moving apace and I want them to meet the organizing committee this afternoon.'

'Honestly, these are our officers. Lady Hardcastle and Miss Armstrong will be coordinating the security for the Austrian visit and investigating a potential threat already identified by an agent of the SSB.'

Sir Montague had stopped smiling. 'I've heard a lot about you, Featherstonhaugh. "He's a good egg," they say, "but he doesn't take things seriously enough." I like a joke as much as the next fellow, but I really don't have time for your shenanigans. I can see you're fully committed to your little joke and I'll have to graciously accept being played for a fool, but can I at least count on your men being here in time for the committee meeting this afternoon?'

'My "men" are here, Sir Montague, as I said.'

'Now look here Featherstonhaugh, I—'

Lady Hardcastle held up her hand. 'Forgive me for interrupting, Sir Montague, but perhaps I might be able to help. What were you doing in 1898?'

'What was I doing in ninety-eight? What an odd thing to ask. I was . . . let me see . . . I was managing two of my family's mills in Lancashire. Why?'

'I just wondered. Miss Armstrong and I were in Shanghai in ninety-eight, spying on the Germans on behalf of Her Majesty's Government.'

He regarded us coolly for a moment. 'You two?'

'Us two. How about 1904?'

'Still just about at the mill, but about to sell up and invest the proceeds in a new tram business. I launched it in 1905 and built it into one of the most successful in the country.'

'Well done, you. We were escaping from the Bulgarian secret police disguised as . . . ?' She looked to me for confirmation.

'Policemen,' I said.

'I say, it *was* policemen, wasn't it. And we were getting away from a gang of smugglers, not the secret police – I always get that part muddled. But the secret police were most definitely involved – we'd stolen some important documents from them, hadn't we? I get it mixed up with the time in Berlin with the military plans and the embassy ball.'

I nodded. 'That time we escaped the secret police disguised as an American heiress and her governess.'

'Oh, we did. I seem to recall you were wearing a dirndl at one point for some unfathomable reason.' Lady Hardcastle smiled fondly.

I turned to Sir Montague.

'That was at the ball,' I explained. 'Fancy dress. The general was Bavarian and fiercely proud of it, so we decided to ingratiate ourselves by turning up in traditional costume. Well, I did, anyway. Lady Hardcastle went as a European brown bear. She has a particular fondness for bears.'

'We were a great hit,' said Lady Hardcastle. 'If you wish to curry favour with Bavarian generals, dirndls and bear costumes are the key.' She paused to enjoy the memory. 'The thing is, Sir Montague,' she continued after a moment, 'one doesn't usually like to boast about one's past achievements – most of them remain top secret, for one thing – but I thought it might save some time. Going back and forth as though we were at a pantomime – "oh yes, they are – oh no, they're not" – is amusing in a theatre full of excited children at Christmas time, but it's less fun when the safe conduct of an important trade meeting is at stake, don't you think?'

Sir Montague didn't respond. Instead he turned to Harry.

'This is most irregular, Featherstonhaugh,' he said with a frown. 'Most irregular. I can't say I'm happy with it. Not happy at all. I shall be having words with Colonel Valentine. Strong words. We can't have a joker like you fobbing us off with his sister and her pal, no matter how many times they've escaped from foreign cities disguised as washerwomen.'

'That was Vienna,' said Lady Hardcastle. '1906.'

'I shall put a stop to this nonsense,' said Sir Montague. 'Get some proper men on the job.'

'By all means,' said Harry. 'You have Colonel Valentine's telephone number. Before you call, though, it might be helpful to know that it was his idea to give Lady Hardcastle and Miss Armstrong the job in the first place. You know, before you start explaining what a damn fool plan it is. Forewarned is forearmed and all that.'

Sir Montague harrumphed. 'Don't know what the blessed War Office is coming to,' he muttered.

Lady Hardcastle and I both smiled sweetly.

'There's a meeting of the organizing committee this afternoon, you say?' said Lady Hardcastle. 'Where and when?'

'I don't see what business that is of yours. This is not resolved. Not by a long chalk. I'll not have two . . . women attending confidential committee meetings and pretending they're in charge of security. You'll have to come, Featherstonhaugh. Until I've settled this with your superiors, you'll be looking after things.'

'So where's the meeting?' asked Harry.

Sir Montague smiled triumphantly. 'Committee room down the other corridor. Three o'clock. You'll be there?'

Harry slapped his thighs and stood. 'No can do, I'm afraid, old bean – I'm on other duties.'

'More important than a trade deal with Austria-Hungary at this tense time?'

'I'm really not at liberty to say, I'm afraid. National security and all that – you know how it is. Lady Hardcastle and Miss Armstrong will attend the committee meeting and coordinate the security arrangements for the Austrian visit.'

Lady Hardcastle and I stood to leave, too.

'We'll see you at three,' said Lady Hardcastle.

Sir Montague glared.

'Don't worry, old chap,' said Harry. 'We'll see ourselves out.'

◆ ◆ ◆

Harry scooted off to do whatever jolly important thing it was that he had to do, while Lady Hardcastle and I went to a nearby restaurant for lunch.

We presented ourselves to the maître d'hôtel and Lady Hardcastle asked for a table for two.

The man looked us up and down – he clearly didn't want two women occupying a table in this favourite dining spot of bankers and stockbrokers. 'We're rather full, madam. Have you booked?'

'I fully intended to, but do you know, I'm such a scatterbrain I can't remember whether I actually did. Lady Hardcastle is the name.'

His resolve seemed to falter at the sound of her title and he consulted the diary. 'No, my lady, it appears you did not. But I think . . . yes, I think we can squeeze you in.' He clicked his fingers and a waiter appeared. 'Table twelve for Lady Hardcastle and her . . . companion. *Bon appétit*, ladies.'

Table twelve, it turned out, was in the furthest, darkest corner of the dining room, next to the door to the kitchen and partially concealed behind a large indoor palm.

'I'm not sure they want us here,' said Lady Hardcastle.

I nodded. 'That's how I read it. Afraid we'll discomfit the native wildlife at their favourite watering hole.'

'It might work in our favour.'

'How so?'

'They might be so eager to get us out that they give us the best service we've ever had.'

And so it proved. Once ordered, our meals arrived in double-quick time.

'We should eat in places we're not welcome more often,' she said, as she tucked in to her pork chop.

'We should. And I'm not surprised we're not welcome here. Look at those chaps over there.'

I indicated a group of men in black jackets and starched white shirts with unfashionable collars.

Lady Hardcastle glanced at them as they guffawed at something one of them had said. 'Stockbrokers, do you think?'

I shook my head. 'A secret cabal of undertakers. They meet here on the second Thursday of the month to discuss . . .'

'To discuss their plans for transatlantic air travel. They intend to build gigantic aeroplanes that will transport passengers and their luggage from London to New York in hours instead of days.'

'Why would that be of interest to undertakers?'

'Everything is more interesting than undertaking. They long for lives where fashioning coffins and embalming the earthly remains of the recently deceased are but dim memories. They hate the life of the undertaker. They wish to fly free.'

'Then why not simply find alternative employment?' I said. 'They have cabinet-making skills and a reassuring manner. They could fashion furniture for the nervous and easily upset.'

'And yet they choose to put their energy into fanciful dreams of intercontinental travel.'

'And the telling of jokes.'

'And, as you say, the telling of jokes. I say, that was quick.'

She nodded towards the waiter bringing the pot of coffee we had ordered only moments earlier.

'Perhaps there have been complaints from the undertakers,' I said.

'The undertakers, madam?' said the waiter as he set down the coffee pot and cups. 'Have you received complaints?'

'They were complaining about the— Never mind. Thank you for the coffee.'

'I shall bring your bill.'

And before we had taken more than two sips, he did just that.

We finished our coffee, Lady Hardcastle settled the bill, and we were back out on to the street in less time than it would usually take to hang up our coats and peruse the menu.

'It's a quarter to two,' said Lady Hardcastle as we stood on the pavement outside the restaurant. 'What shall we do to pass a pleasant hour before the meeting?'

'We could go for a walk down to St Paul's,' I said. 'I know how you love to see the cathedral. Or sit a while in Finsbury Circus Gardens and bask in the sunshine.'

'Both splendid ideas.'

'But,' I continued, 'I suggest we head back to the LTC offices.'

'Because . . . ?'

'If someone I didn't much like had told me they were coming to my meeting at three, I know what I'd do.'

'Oh, Flo, you tiny Welsh marvel. Of course they'll move the blessed meeting. An hour earlier, would you think?'

'Assuming everyone has otherwise busy lives, I'd say that would be the most they could manage.'

'Then we should get ourselves back there at once and make sure we don't miss anything.'

There was no sign of Rackley when we let ourselves in to the LTC's suite of offices, but that was a good sign – there was every chance he was at the rescheduled meeting.

The 'other corridor' of which Sir Montague had spoken was a good deal shorter than the one that led to his office, but the double doors at the end were just as needlessly huge. We approached and took one each, opening them in unison and stepping briskly inside.

Sir Montague was talking to the six other men around the enormous conference table. '. . . which means we need to be done before three.'

All seven men laughed.

The laughter died first on the lips of those facing the doors, and their surprised expressions caused the others to turn in their seats to see who had come in.

'Is it not three now?' said Lady Hardcastle as she pulled out two chairs for us. 'I really must get this watch fixed.' She tapped the offending instrument on her wrist and then held it to her ear. 'Stupid thing. But I'm glad we haven't missed anything, timepiece malfunctions notwithstanding.' She smiled. 'How do you do, everyone? I'm Lady Hardcastle, and this is Miss Armstrong. We're your government security liaisons for the Austrian trade visit.'

We made ourselves comfortable at the table while the men – none of whom had stood up – muttered their how-do-you-do's.

'Do you have a spare copy of the agenda, Sir Montague?' said Lady Hardcastle. 'Just the one will do – we can share.'

Sir Montague shook his head and gave Rackley a weary flick of the fingers to indicate that he should furnish us with the requisite document. Two copies were passed along the table to us.

No introductions were made, and in one sense the meeting proceeded as though we were not there. Nothing was explained to us and we were not invited to comment or question. We were not acknowledged in any way. In another sense, though, it seemed that our presence was very much being taken into consideration.

The planned visit was discussed only in the most general terms, with nod-and-wink references to matters 'as previously discussed' and to the actions of 'the parties we spoke about at the previous meeting'. It wasn't too difficult to read between the clumsily drawn lines, though, and we began to get an impression of the nature of the visit.

The principal business would involve a series of meetings with a group of unnamed Austrian businessmen and government officials. They were to arrive in London on Monday the twenty-second – which we already knew – and would stay for a week. As well as the meetings there were to be informal receptions and lunches with interested parties, and a formal dinner hosted by the Board of Trade. There was still some doubt as to whether David Lloyd George himself would be present, but the committee was still hopeful.

During Any Other Business, the committee member sitting directly opposite me indicated that he would like to speak.

'Mr Chairman,' he began, 'I wonder how the arrangements are progressing for the visit of—'

Sir Montague cleared his throat loudly. 'I don't think this is the correct forum for the discussion of those particular arrangements.'

'Yes, Mr Chairman, I quite understand. But—'

'We should discuss this in private, I think,' said Sir Montague, none too subtly nodding towards where Lady Hardcastle and I sat.

The man backed down. There were one or two other piffling matters to attend to before the meeting was wrapped up, dead on time, at two minutes to three.

'Thank you, gentlemen,' said Lady Hardcastle as we rose to leave, 'that was most edifying. Does our department already have the itinerary for the visit?'

'It's . . . ah . . . it's still being finalized,' mumbled Rackley.

'That's fine, dear, but please do make sure we get a copy, won't you? We can't protect you all if we don't know where you'll be.'

There were tuts and harrumphs from the departing committee members. Sir Montague just glared at us.

We took that as our cue and left the meeting without saying goodbye.

◆　◆　◆

We set off to return to Southampton Street. The traffic was terrible, with carts, wagons, buses, vans and motor cars everywhere. Grimly determined pedestrians weaving between the vehicles and manure on the road added an extra dimension to the journey, and Lady Hardcastle amused herself by trying to strike up conversations with them as I inched along the crowded roads.

When we finally arrived at our temporary home, I parked extremely neatly outside the front door and we clambered easily up the stairs. We let ourselves in to the flat, where we found our luggage and a note from Lady Lavinia inviting us to dinner.

The unexpected rescheduling of the meeting left us with plenty of time to unpack, take baths, and dress for dinner. Lady Hardcastle even found a quarter of an hour to moan about the absence of a piano.

It was a pleasant evening so we decided to stroll the three-quarters of a mile to Bedford Square.

Birds were singing, and butterflies flitting. A prowling cat eyed us suspiciously before approaching to mewingly demand we scratch her ears. Finely dressed people were heading out for dinner or the theatre, and vehicles were clattering, rumbling and buzzing according to their nature. I was reminded once again how much I loved being in London.

As we walked down Tottenham Court Road, a passing bus splashed through a still-wet pile of horse manure, splattering my skirt and boots, and I was reminded once again how much I hated being in London.

Eventually we arrived, and Harry's butler, Weatherby, welcomed us in, taking our hats and light summer coats. He showed us through to the drawing room, where Lady Lavinia was playing the piano and Harry was intently studying his Scotch and soda.

'What ho, sis,' said Harry, waving the cut-glass tumbler in our direction, but not standing up. 'What ho, Strongarm. I say, you chaps know a lot about things – why do bubbles form in a chap's drink?'

'Because, dear,' said Lady Hardcastle.

'Good enough for me. Something scientific, eh?'

'Do you really want to know?'

'Not really, no.'

'I thought not. Hello, Lavinia dear.'

Lady Lavinia turned her head towards us but carried on playing. 'Evening, Emily. Evening, Flo. You'll have to help yourself to drinks, I'm afraid – Harry has become unaccountably obsessed with the bubbles in his glass.'

Harry waved his glass again. 'What can I say? I'm a curious chap.'

'I've always found you decidedly curious, dear,' said Lady Hardcastle. 'Imperfections in the glass give the dissolved carbon dioxide something to cling on to. When the bubble gets big enough, it breaks free and floats to the surface.'

'Nucleation,' I said.

'Nucle – as Flo so rightly says – ation.'

Harry frowned, and cocked his head like a puzzled dog. 'I say. Really? But questions remain, old thing. We'll get to how the nuclifated carbolic flimfloxinide gets into the water in just a moment—'

'We won't, dear – it will bore you.'

'As you say, sis. But glass is as smooth as . . . well . . . as glass. It doesn't have any imperfections.'

'And yet . . .' said Lady Hardcastle.

Harry nodded. 'I see. Science, eh?'

'Science. Be a pet and make me a gin and tonic – I'm gasping.'

'And for me, please,' I said, flopping into my favourite Featherstonhaugh armchair.

'I'm not entirely certain why you can't get it yourself,' said Harry.

Lady Hardcastle made herself comfortable on the sofa and gestured as she spoke. 'Host. Guests. I'm happy to accept that you can't quite grasp the mechanism by which dissolved gas makes its way out of your soda water, but you do at least understand how all the hospitality nonsense works by now, surely? Even if that charming social convention eludes you as well, consider how hard we've been working on your behalf all day – the very least you can do is splash some gin in a glass and top it up with a little Indian tonic water. Some ice and a slice of cucumber wouldn't go amiss, either.'

'Salad? In your gin?'

'Indulge me, brother dear.'

Harry rang for the maid and asked her to fetch some cucumber slices from the kitchen. She left looking only slightly puzzled – odd requests from her employer were clearly nothing new.

'How did the committee meeting go?' he asked as he fussed about at the sideboard with the drinks.

'They moved it to two o'clock.'

'The cheeky blighters. So you missed it?'

'No, we were there at two. Flo predicted the move.'

'I say, well done you.'

I tugged my forelock. 'Thank you, Mr Feather-stone-huff.'

Harry gave his familiar bark of laughter.

'They weren't pleased to see us,' said Lady Hardcastle. 'But they ungraciously allowed us to stay. They did their best to talk in riddles and generalities so as not to include us in their important business, but we got the gist. The only thing we couldn't quite grasp was an oblique reference to a special visit of some sort. Sir Montague shut that one down rather briskly.'

'I can't understand why. He knows who you work for, and it was the SSB who told them about it in the first place.'

'It was just petty point-scoring, then. So who's visiting? What's going on?'

'We can't confirm anything at this point, but it's almost certainly a member of the Austrian royal family. Our people in Vienna have noticed diaries being cleared, bodyguards being reassigned, travel arrangements being discreetly made – all things that would generally precede an official visit. The problem is that the main things that would precede an official visit – an official invitation and an official acceptance – are oddly absent.'

'Surely the Foreign Office would know,' I said. 'Even about an unofficial visit.'

'Oh, they know all right. But for reasons of their own they're not letting us in on their little secret. More petty point-scoring, I'm afraid. We in the SSB are the poor relations, even though we're responsible for providing the intelligence required to ensure the safety of such things.'

'Have they told Special Branch, at least?' asked Lady Hardcastle.

Harry shrugged. 'They may well have, but we're not their favourites, either. Why do you think we get all their duffers when we need bodies on the streets?'

'Who are the most likely candidates for this putative visit?' I said.

'From the now empty diaries and the reassigned bruisers, we're thinking the heir presumptive himself. Emperor Franz Joseph wouldn't so much as go to the shops without a full ceremonial whatnot—'

'Do emperors go to the shops?'

'A chap has to get an ounce of baccy and a newspaper once in a while. Even emperors. And we know old Frankie-Joe is partial to humbugs, too – they can't keep him out of the corner shop. It's an absolute nightmare for his protocol secretary – all those announce-ments in the press, the imperial trumpeters for the fanfare, invita-tions to the local mayor. And don't even talk about how much work it is for his security detail. Fuss and folderol follow Franz Joseph wherever he goes. But his nephew and heir, the Archduke Franz Ferdinand, accompanied always by the love of his life – his dear wife, the Duchess Sophie – are known to flit about hither, thither and yon without a care. They've been all the way round the world, you know. They're quite the imperial gadabouts.'

'And you think they're coming here?' said Lady Hardcastle.

'We do. There's an official visit pencilled in for next year, but we believe they're tagging along with the trade delegation this year as well.'

There was a brief pause while the maid delivered the cucumber slices and Harry finished preparing the drinks. With a tut and a shake of the head, he handed Lady Hardcastle and me a garnished gin and tonic each and sat on the sofa next to his sister.

Lady Hardcastle sighed wearily. 'We'd better make sure we shut down the Black Hand or the Young Bosnians or whoever else might want to cause trouble, then, eh?'

'You better had, sis. You better had.'

'And what will you be doing while we save Europe from conflagration?'

'I shall be saving Europe from conflagration. You had dealings with Autumn Wind in Calcutta, did you not?'

Lady Hardcastle stopped mid-sip. 'How on earth do you know that?'

'I'm in the intelligence game, sis – surely you noticed.'

'Yes, but that whole business was extremely hush-hush, entirely on the QT, and not to be discussed with anyone anywhere ever.'

He grinned mischievously. 'And yet . . .'

'I can neither confirm nor deny it, dear. How much do you know?'

Lady Lavinia stopped playing for a moment. 'Don't mind me, darlings – I've heard more state secrets than I've had glasses of warm champagne at embassy receptions. I know how to keep mum.' She resumed her skilled interpretation of Schubert.

'My darling wife makes a good point,' said Harry. 'Perhaps we shouldn't talk about them too much. Suffice it to say that we're reasonably certain they're mounting a new operation. Something big. Potentially catastrophic.'

'You and your mysterious newspaper advertisements again?' asked Lady Hardcastle.

Harry nodded. 'I still can't get to the bottom of the advertisement business. No, this is more conventional intelligence.'

'What are they up to this time?' I asked.

Harry sipped his Scotch. 'I think Jake is right – we probably shouldn't be talking about it.'

The dinner gong sounded and Lady Lavinia stopped playing mid-phrase.

'What say we dine instead, and talk about lighter things,' she said. 'Come along, ladies – you can tell me all about your Littleton Cotterell art exhibition and Basil Westbury's Shakespeare.' She stood and led us out of the drawing room. 'Was Westbury's book really as exquisite as the newspapers made out? Or was it a tasteless monument to arriviste gaucherie?'

Lady Hardcastle laughed. 'A little of both, dear.'

We went through to the dining room to eat.

Chapter Six

We rose early on Friday morning and breakfasted together in the tiny kitchen. The elegant dining room with its high ceiling and understated, modern decor would have been an altogether classier and more appropriate place to eat, but it was rather too gloomy in the morning. It was at the rear of the flat, where it faced just far enough north of east to miss the rays of the morning sun, and the view, though not exactly unpleasant, was only of the backs of the neighbouring houses and Richardson's Mews below. The kitchen was on the same side and just as sun-free, but kitchens have a homely cosiness about them that overcomes any inadequacies of light and vista.

Harry's minions had stocked the larder with bread, eggs and a pound of sausages, as well as the promised tea, coffee and milk, so I was able to cobble together a hearty meal to start the day. Whoever had placed the grocery order had also thought to provide us with a bottle of tomato ketchup. We had the sauce at home, much to Miss Jones's disgust, but I would never have classed it as a staple. Perhaps it was more popular than I thought.

Its provenance notwithstanding, Lady Hardcastle was very keen on the silky, scarlet sauce and splatted a hearty dollop of it on to her plate.

'I don't know how we managed to survive so long without this magical elixir,' she said. 'If Mr Heinz were an Englishman we would knight him for services to the culinary arts. Or find a way to elevate him to the peerage. Lord Heinz of the Breakfast Table.'

'I'm more interested to know how it got here,' I said.

'By ship from America.'

'Most amusing. I meant *here*. To this flat.'

'Harry knows we have it at home and I think he's rather keen on it himself – he'll have instructed whichever of the Basement goblins was tasked with filling our larder to add it to the order. He's probably hoping there'll be some left by the time we return to Littleton Cotterell so he can sneak it home without enraging his cook. Cooks can be funny about shop-bought sauces.'

'I doubt there'll be much left at the rate you're going,' I said, helping myself to a much daintier dab of the stuff. 'What are our plans for the day?'

'Down to Wapping for some tree-shaking, I think. We'll do a tour of our usual haunts and see who knows anything about anything.'

'It's been a while.'

'They'll remember us. And we should have more luck than usual. Last time we were there we were looking for an Englishman who was working for the Austrians, don't forget – someone who fitted in. This time we're after actual Serbians. Or Bosnians. Either way, they're up to no good and they'll be keeping themselves to themselves. Everyone knows everyone down there, so strangers will be easy to spot. Someone will know something about something.'

'You're probably right,' I said. 'Are we taking the Austin?'

'I think so. Taxis are easy to come by round here, but we've waited ages in the East End in the past when we wanted to get back. We had to get the bus that time, remember?'

'I don't mind taking the bus. We fit in better on a bus.'

'We do indeed. And they're fast and convenient, too. But if we drive down to the Tower of London and park somewhere near there, we can have the convenience of motorized transport across town exactly when we need it, and the anonymity of Shanks's pony as we make our way around the East End. We'll have the best of both worlds and we shan't have to cross our fingers and hope a cab comes by.'

I tidied away the breakfast wreckage while Lady Hardcastle packed a few essentials into her bag, including spare ammunition for her favourite Colt Vest Pocket pistol. The gun itself was carried in a specially reinforced – and very discreet – pocket I'd made for her skirt.

'Are you knived, dear?' she said as she checked her mechanical pencil.

I patted my right forearm, where my own favourite weapon was strapped. I was a fair shot, but as the daughter of a circus knife-thrower I took extra pride in my skills with a blade.

Lady Hardcastle nodded. 'Then one more quick visit to the you-know-what and we're ready to go.'

◆ ◆ ◆

We parked on Tower Hill, and walked the fifteen minutes down towards St Katharine Docks. It looked set to be a hot day, and the bright morning sunshine was doing its best to make London look glorious. The soot-stained buildings seemed to glow with some mysterious inner light as the morning rays hit the blackened stone and brick, while pigeons and starlings iridesced in the river of sunlight that washed the paving stones.

We were dressed unassumingly for our trip. There was no need to go overboard and try to disguise ourselves as dock workers' wives, but Lady Hardcastle's beautiful summer morning dress would have drawn too much attention, and not a little suspicion. We needed people's help, not their resentment, and so we were both dressed plainly and inexpensively.

Lady Hardcastle was an accomplished linguist and had a musician's ear for the subtleties and nuances of accents. So while she was an embarrassingly poor mimic – her attempts to impersonate her friends were always hilarious in their awfulness – she was nevertheless adept at adopting different accents should the need arise.

On our previous missions in the East End we had been the wives of shipping clerks, out on our own for a few drinks and a lark. At first we had drawn some suspicious stares, but there was no actual hostility, and after a while we were accepted. Lady Hardcastle's generosity at the bar had been a big help in this regard, and we soon made some very useful friends among the stevedores, porters and lumpers of the docks, as well as a few thieves and chancers. The women we met were barmaids, wives and sweethearts for the most part, but our most helpful contacts there, as in any busy port, were the street girls who made their living from the thousands of sailors, their pockets stuffed with backpay, who came ashore looking for a good time.

We had been more honest about our real work with the friends we made, and established a useful network of eyes and ears around the city. But it had been several years since we were last in the area and we couldn't be certain we'd be remembered.

We came up blank at our first stop, where the landlord had changed since our last visit and we were told, in no uncertain terms, that 'your sort' were not welcome. We didn't stop to ask what exactly our sort was – with so many other pubs and drinking dens to visit, it wasn't worth the bother.

We received a warmer welcome at the next pub where the landlord remembered us, even after a few years away. He regretfully told us that one of the regulars we sought had died two years earlier, and that his friend – who was also a good source of Dockland gossip – hadn't been seen for a few months and was rumoured to be doing time in Pentonville. We thanked him, and Lady Hardcastle left a few shillings for the dead man's widow.

Three more pubs followed, each with a landlord surprised, but not displeased, to see us, and a mixed clientele of locals and visitors. But there was still no sign of our old contacts. We chatted for a while nevertheless, trying to sound people out – a stranger is just an informant you haven't met, after all.

Queenie, the madam at our favourite bawdy house in Shadwell, was positively thrilled to see us. She greeted us warmly when we knocked on her door before making her customary offer of work.

Lady Hardcastle gave her customary reply: 'I'm getting too old for all that, love. Can you imagine anyone paying for an old biddy like me?'

The customary laughter ensued, and we were invited to come in for a cup of tea.

The half-dressed girls in the front room looked up as we passed the door on our way to the parlour, but on seeing that we weren't prospective customers they returned to their conversations.

The parlour – Queenie's lair – was a good deal cosier than the rest of the house, and we were invited to sit in a couple of over-stuffed armchairs while Queenie herself bustled with the teapot.

'I ain't seen you two for years,' she said. 'You been away?'

Now that we were in private, Lady Hardcastle reverted to her normal accent. 'We live in the West Country now. It was getting far too dangerous for us round here.'

'And yet here you are, back again.'

'And yet here we are, yes.'

'Sommat important?' Without waiting for a response, she turned to me. 'You want a biscuit, Flo love? You always look like you need feedin' up.'

I patted my stomach. 'I'm fine, thank you, Queenie. Saving myself for lunch.'

'There's a lovely pie and mash shop up the road. Just tell Frankie that Queenie sent you – he'll see you right.'

'Thank you,' I said. 'We might well do that. But yes, it is important. We're trying to find a killer.'

'Plenty of them round here, darlin'. Most days you can't chuck a stone up Cable Street without hittin' a killer.'

'This is a very particular killer,' said Lady Hardcastle. 'Possibly part of a gang. Almost certainly Serbian or Bosnian. If there is a gang of them, they'll most likely be young men. Earnest. Keeping themselves to themselves.'

'Who'd they kill?'

'Someone who had important information. Information that might prevent . . . You know there's a war coming, don't you?'

'Everyone knows there's a war comin', darlin'. Not one of us knows why, but you'd 'ave to be livin' in a cellar somewhere not to know it's comin'.'

'Well, quite. Europe, as they say, is a powder keg. Britain, France and Russia on one side, Italy, Germany, Austria-Hungary and the Ottomans on the other. All jockeying for position, all seeing who can shout the loudest, who has the biggest navy, who has the strongest army. It will explode eventually – there doesn't seem to be any getting away from it. But there are other things going on across the Continent, largely unconnected to the squabbles between the Great Powers. Things that are just as important to the people involved. Things that most definitely need to be resolved. And the gentlemen we seek are part of one of these struggles. It ought to be a local matter, but the outcome will affect the Great Powers nonetheless, and in their efforts to settle their own local affairs, groups like the one behind this murder might accidentally light the fuse that sets the whole mess off.'

Queenie regarded us in silence for a moment. 'So it is important, then.'

'Very,' I said.

'Well, we ain't 'ad no earnest young gentlemen in 'ere, Serbian or otherwise. All my clients are fun-lovin' lads. Some are locals, some come in off the boats. I don't doubt some of 'em would slit your throat soon as look at you, but your lot sound . . . different, somehow.'

Lady Hardcastle nodded. 'I think you'd know if you'd met them. If they're here at all, these will be idealistic young men with a mission. I doubt they'll make any effort to fit in.'

'I'll put the word out,' said Queenie. 'Frightenin' young men, keepin' to themselves, probably from . . . Serbia, was it?' She looked at the large map of the world pinned up on the parlour wall.

'Or Bosnia, yes,' I said. 'Across the Adriatic from Italy.'

She took a magnifying glass from the pocket of her black dress and inspected the map.

'I've got you,' she said. 'Don't see many from there.'

'Why do you have—' I began.

'The map, love? I like to know where my customers come from. When some burly deckhand says, "I come from Odesa," I like to know what he's talkin' about. Try to make conversation, like. "Oh, yes? I bet the Black Sea's lovely this time of year," I'll say. It's friendly, see? Makes 'em feel welcome. And if they feel welcome, they'll come back here next time they're in London, won't they?'

Lady Hardcastle smiled and handed back her empty teacup. 'You're a shrewd businesswoman, Queenie dear.'

'You do what you 'as to, don't you?'

'You do indeed. And I'm afraid we have to get moving again. We've been away a long time and we're still trying to establish contact with all our old friends. We've not had any promising information yet, and time is somewhat against us.'

'Right you are, love. You'd better get goin' in that case. It's been lovely to see you, no matter how short a visit. You can drop in any time, you know that.'

I stood and handed her my own teacup. 'We do, Queenie. Thank you.'

'And you're sure I can't tempt you to do a couple of shifts?'

'A woman in Bristol thought it might be our line of work,' I said. 'Maybe we're more suited to it than we like to think.'

Queenie laughed – a delightfully uninhibited, throaty chuckle. 'I don't have to tell you to look after yourselves – I know you can. You remember that Polish fella who tried to take advantage of Flo that time? I bet he walked funny for a week.' She laughed again at the memory. 'But you get your job done, my darlin's. If there's a war, it'll be the young lads round here they'll send off to die, and the longer we can give 'em before they 'ave to go, the better.'

'We shall do our utmost,' said Lady Hardcastle.

'I know you will. And I'll put the word out. If I hear any-thing . . . what then? How do I get in touch with you?'

Lady Hardcastle scribbled an address on a page of her note-book, tore it out, and handed it to Queenie.

'For the next hour we'll be at Frankie's – is that what it's called?' she said. 'After that, send a telegram to me care of this address and they'll pass the message on to us no matter where we are.'

Queenie put the scrap of paper in her pocket. 'Cable Street Pie and Mash, love. And thank you – I'll let you know as soon as I hear anythin'.'

'We'll make sure you're reimbursed, of course.'

'Don't you worry about that – old Queenie can afford the price of a telegram on a matter of national importance.'

She kissed us both goodbye and saw us out along the passage, past the front room and a completely different set of girls, then out on to the street.

The tiny restaurant was as splendid as advertised – neat, clean and welcoming. And once we'd dropped Queenie's name, the owner – 'Call me Frankie, darlin'; everyone does' – treated us like visiting royalty.

We both had the house speciality – pie, mash and liquor – while Lady Hardcastle indulged one of her gastronomic passions by adding jellied eels to her meal. All this was washed down with 'a nice cup of Rosie and satin'.

Full and contented, we settled up with the voluble Frankie, who assured us that he would always have a table waiting for any friend of Queenie's. We were about to leave when a young boy burst in and looked around. Seeing Lady Hardcastle and me together, he strode confidently towards us.

'You two Mrs Brown and Mrs Jones?' he asked.

Those were the names we used when we were out and about so I said, 'We are.'

'Friends of Queenie Pearce?'

'Good friends, yes,' said Lady Hardcastle. 'What can we do for you?'

'I got a message for you, ain't I.'

'From Queenie?'

'No, from Marie Lloyd. Who d'ya fink?'

'Less o' your cheek, Billy Burgess,' said Frankie. 'Just give 'em the bleedin' message or I'll tell your mother.'

The boy stuck out his tongue and handed Lady Hardcastle an envelope. She dug in her purse for a few coppers, which she gave him with her thanks.

As he scampered off he called, 'Kiss my aris, Frankie Pie Man,' over his shoulder, and the door slammed on his laughter.

'I'll clout that little snot one of these days,' said Frankie. 'I do beg your pardon, ladies.'

'Think nothing of it,' said Lady Hardcastle. 'If he brings word from Queenie, we can put up with all the cheek in the world.' She opened up the envelope and quickly read the note within. She checked her watch. 'We'd better get our skates on, Mrs Jones – we have an appointment at the Prospect of Whitby. Thank you for your hospitality, Frankie. We'll visit again soon, I hope.'

'Ta-ta, ladies.'

It was only about ten minutes' stroll to the pub on the river in Wapping, but Lady Hardcastle was bustling along as though every minute taken was a minute wasted.

'What was the message?' I asked.

'It seems word of our arrival has spread, and dear Benny Butcher has been looking for us. He remembered our friendship with Queenie so he sent a lad to her place on the off chance we might have been there. She sent a note on to the pie and mash shop.'

'And we're practically running because . . . ?'

'Because he's only going to wait there for us until half past one.'

'It's barely a few minutes past one now and the Prospect is only just up the road.'

'I know, dear, but Benny is the key to this part of town. The veritable linchpin. If we have Benny back on our side, we have the whole of London's underworld in our delicate, ladylike hands.'

Benny Butcher was, indeed, an important figure in the East End, as well as a good and trusted friend. He was a villain, to be sure, and we were under no illusions about him – virtually every-thing he did beyond the basic essentials of life was against one or more laws – but he had a strong sense of what was proper. He was prepared to burgle and rob his way through life, with as much violence as the job required, but he still believed there were lines you just didn't cross. There were people you didn't steal from, and people you didn't hurt, and that meant he was well respected by everyone in the area. When youngsters and incomers behaved in ways Benny thought inappropriate and suffered the consequences of his irritation, they would get no sympathy, even from competing criminals and gangs who would nod sternly and say, 'Well, you shouldn't 'ave done it, should you?'

Unlike his fellow criminals, he wasn't above working with the rozzers if that meant keeping the wrong sort of crook off the streets, and his strong sense of patriotic pride meant he was always ready and willing to help us when the need arose. Lady Hardcastle was right: if we could get Benny Butcher to help us, the job was more than half done.

We arrived at the old pub just before a quarter past one, and found Benny in the corner surrounded by three friends. He caught sight of us as we approached.

'That'll do for now, lads,' he said. 'I've got some business to attend to.'

Without a murmur of complaint, the three men rose and walked away, leaving Benny on his own. He stood.

'As I live and breathe,' he said with a smile. 'If it ain't *Mrs Brown* and *Mrs Jones*. Must be, what, five years? I thought you'd finally crossed one too many foreigners and been left in a ditch somewhere.'

'It was always a possibility,' said Lady Hardcastle.

'It still is,' I said. 'How are you, Benny *bach*?'

'Mustn't grumble. I mean, I could – my knees are playin' up somefin' rotten – but it don't do no good, do it? Who's gonna listen? Can I get you a little somefin' wet to celebrate your continuin' good health?'

'I'll get them, Benny,' said Lady Hardcastle. 'We come in search of your assistance – it's only fair we should buy the drinks.'

'That's very decent of you. I'll have another light ale.'

Lady Hardcastle handed me some coins. 'And I'll have a brandy, dear. A large one.'

I frowned. 'You said you were going to get them.'

'Pay for them, dear, pay for them. I can't possibly go all the way to the bar – Benny's not the only one with gammy knees.'

With a tut and a shake of the head, I went to the bar.

By the time I returned with the drinks, Lady Hardcastle was mid-anecdote. '. . . flipped him on his back and told the police he'd slipped on the polished floor in the ballroom.'

Benny laughed and accepted his beer with a nod of thanks. 'She's just tellin' me about your quiet life in the country.'

'It had its moments,' I said. 'Cheers.'

Glasses clinked.

Benny took a hearty swig of his beer and smacked his lips. 'So what brings you back to the nation's proud capital?'

Lady Hardcastle quickly ran through the story again, including a few of the details we'd left out when we'd spoken to Queenie. She made a special effort to play up the potential danger to Britain's security should war break out too soon, and Benny listened intently. He asked a few clarifying questions as she went, and when she finished he took another swig of beer while he digested the information.

'No one like that this side of the river,' he said emphatically.

'No one at all?'

'I'd know, darlin'. I might not be the man I was twenty years ago—'

'Who is, dear? I look in the glass in the morning and wonder why my mother is looking back at me.'

'Ha, yeah, I know that feelin'. We're lucky our mothers was such 'andsome women, ain't we? But me fadin' good looks and dodgy knees don't mean I ain't still got me finger on the pulse, and there ain't no gang of Serbians nor Bosnians gone to earth between Wappin' and Beckton.'

'But "Wharf" is all we've got to go on,' I said, dejectedly.

'Hundreds of wharves on the other side of the river too, though, don't forget.'

The way he said 'other side of the river' made it sound as though he was talking about another country.

'Do you have contacts over there?' asked Lady Hardcastle.

'I know a couple of geezers in Bermondsey, bloke in Rotherhithe. I'll 'ave a word.'

'We'd be most grateful, dear. There's a fiver in it for you.'

Benny raised his eyebrows. 'Proper serious, then. But you know I ain't interested in your money.'

'Oh, it's not my money, dear – His Majesty's War Office will cough up the rhino.'

'In that case, I shan't say no. But not until you get 'em – I ain't no payment-on-account sort. When I deliver, King George can pay up.'

'We can't say fairer than that.'

'Give us a day. I'll be 'ere same time tomorrow with whatever news I got.'

We stayed with him for a little longer and brought him up to date with some of our more interesting cases. He laughed at the ineptitude of amateur crooks and assured us that if he'd been responsible for any of the crimes we'd solved since we last met, we'd never have caught him.

Eventually we left him to return to his shady business with his shady friends and made our way back to Tower Hill and our waiting motor car.

Back at the flat, we sat down in the drawing room to enjoy the cakes we'd bought on the way home, washed down with the inevitable cup of tea.

'I miss the crime board,' said Lady Hardcastle as she added her recollections of the day's conversations to her little notebook.

'We're in London,' I said. 'The shopping capital of England. I'm sure we could have a blackboard and easel delivered by tomorrow afternoon if you're missing it that much.'

'It wouldn't be very secure to have details of a sensitive operation on display, would it? We've got a char coming in on Monday. I'm sure Harry hasn't vetted her – he said he just got her from an agency.'

'Then your notebook will have to suffice. What do we have so far?'

'Precious little, I'm afraid. We believe Dragomir Kovač was murdered in Bristol by a fellow Serb, probably a member of the Black Hand or the Balkan League. Unless he was a Young Bosnian.'

'Are young Bosnians predisposed to murder people in Bristol?'

'Stealing my jokes now, dear? You know very well who the Young Bosnians are. But anyway . . . I concede that our dark-haired young man might well be acting alone, but his ability to track Kovač to Bristol, despite the efforts Kovač made to keep himself hidden, suggests the involvement of an organization with significant resources. I'm prepared to hypothesize that there is a group of Balkan revolutionaries active in London.'

'I think we have to consider it, at least,' I said. 'A lone man with political ideals *might* be able to cause a fair amount of trouble, but an organized and determined group definitely could.'

'Quite. If we take Benny at his word, no such group exists in the East End, so we're awaiting his reports from his contacts on the other side of the river. And even if we establish the presence of

Balkan revolutionaries in south London, we're not any nearer to knowing what they plan to do.'

'They don't have many things to choose from, though, do they? Men who murder their opponents in the street aren't the sort of people simply to hold up placards and shout slogans. They won't be trying to engineer a scandal by setting up elaborate schemes to bring about someone's social or financial ruin. They're the sort of men who take violent action. They're going to want to sow terror, to cause death and destruction. They're going to kill one or more of the people involved in the trade discussions, and if they've heard the rumour that a member of the Austrian royal family might be in the party, they'll definitely be after him. They might try a bomb, a sniper, or a frontal military-style assault with guns blazing.'

Lady Hardcastle pursed her lips. 'Indeed. We really need that itinerary if we're to work out what their best options are for an attack. I might have to ask Harry to apply some pressure – I wouldn't put it past Sir Monty to withhold it just to prove some puerile point.'

An unfamiliar ringing came from the corner of the room.

'Good heavens,' said Lady Hardcastle. 'Is that the telephone? Who would ever have dreamed of putting a telephone in the draw-ing room?'

I stood. 'Should one of us answer it, do you think?'

'You do it, dear. You have a special knack for telephones.'

I picked up the earpiece and spoke for a few moments, scrib-bling a few notes on the pad left conveniently beside the telephone.

We concluded our conversation and I returned the earpiece to its cradle.

I returned to my seat. 'That was Harry. We are invited to dine at a restaurant in Mayfair at eight o'clock. I have the address.'

'With Harry and Lavinia?'

'And a special guest.'

'Who?'

'He didn't say.'

'You didn't ask?'

'You were sitting right there. Did you hear me ask?'

'Why didn't you ask?'

'He said it was to be a surprise. Asking would have spoiled it.'

Lady Hardcastle harrumphed. 'We have a couple of hours. How shall we amuse ourselves?'

'I don't know about you, but I could do with a nap – I've been on the go all day. If I have to be sparkling company for a surprise special guest, I need at least forty winks. Possibly fifty.'

'I shall catch up with some correspondence, then. Would you like me to wake you?'

'I'll be fine.'

I hauled myself to my feet and shuffled off to bed.

We arrived at the restaurant on the dot of eight, and were led to our table by a waiter who had that magical waitery gift of being both obsequious and supercilious at the same time. Parisian waiters were the masters, of course, and I wondered with a smile if one of them had set up a training school somewhere to teach Englishmen the mystic art of being simultaneously fawning and condescending.

We found Harry and Lady Lavinia already seated. Their surprise guest had her back to us, but I knew her at once – it was Helen Titmus, Lady Lavinia's old schoolfriend. We had met her at Lady Lavinia's family home in 1909, during a murder-filled motor-racing weekend at Riddlethorpe Hall in Rutland.

As Harry stood – clearly keen to impress either his guest or the waiters with his good manners – Miss Titmus turned round.

Her face lit up with pleasure and surprise as she saw us. Clearly our presence had come as a surprise, too.

'Emily,' she said excitedly. 'Flo. How wonderful to see you both. Jake said we were to have special guests for dinner but I never imagined for a moment it would be two of my favourite people in the whole wide world.'

We had bumped into Miss Titmus a few times since that weekend at Riddlethorpe Hall and it was always a pleasure to see her. She had been timid and slightly lost when we first met her, but since opening her own photographic studio and shop in Brighton, she had become a different person. The bright, confident woman who took studio portraits, and sold photographic equipment and paraphernalia from her shop, would be unrecognizable to the girls who had once called her Titmouse.

'Hello, Helen dear,' said Lady Hardcastle as we sat down. 'It's wonderful to see you, too – a proper treat. I confess I was braced for Harry's "special guest" to be someone dreary from the office. I was somewhat apprehensive, I must say. Lord knows I've met enough boring civil servants over the last few years to last me a lifetime.'

Helen grinned. 'Instead it's a boring photographer from Brighton. What about you, Flo? Who were you expecting?'

'The same,' I said. 'Or a member of the London Trade Confederation.'

'The who?' asked Helen with a laugh.

Lady Hardcastle pulled a face. 'A shower of odious men who imagine themselves to be much more important than they really are.'

'But why—?'

'We're trying to help them with something,' I said, 'but they're being tiresome about it. I think it might have something to do with the way we dress.'

Lady Hardcastle nodded. 'I fear she's right. A certain type of gentleman finds ladies' fashion quite unacceptable.'

'How so?' said Helen.

'It's mostly because of the sort of person who wears it, I think,' I said.

Helen looked at us quizzically for a few moments.

'Ohh,' she said as realization finally dawned. 'I see what you mean. Not keen on the idea of women in the workplace?'

I shrugged. 'I'm sure they don't mind as long as the workplace is somewhere far, far away from their own.'

Lady Hardcastle picked up her menu. 'But let's not be boring about our work. What have you been up to since last we met, Helen dear? How's your shop? We really ought to come down to Brighton and see it for ourselves – I confess to being rather envious.'

'Of my shop? Surely not.'

'A photographic studio? All the latest equipment? People in and out all day in awe of your skill and expertise? How could one not envy you, dear?'

Helen beamed. 'I suppose when you put it like that I'm the luckiest woman in Brighton. And the business is thriving, thank you. I've even employed a young photographer to set up on the seafront between the Palace Pier and the West Pier. Charlie Boxell is his name. He's a charming young fellow – terribly popular with the ladies – and somehow he manages to persuade dozens of people every day to pay for a photograph. Oh, and he has a little hand puppet – an adorable little bear called Algernon – that he uses to keep the children's attention while he snaps them.'

'How enchanting,' said Lady Hardcastle. 'A bear called Algernon would certainly keep my attention.'

'I sometimes wonder if Algernon is more of a draw than the prospect of yet another seaside photograph.'

'Perhaps you should sell Algernons in the shop,' I suggested.

'I certainly thought about it, but his mother made him. From the look of him I think he's a homemade body with a Steiff head. I'm not sure she could keep up with demand even if we could source sufficient toy bear heads.'

'I'm delighted for you, dear,' said Lady Hardcastle. 'Are you in town long?'

'A couple of weeks. I have some business matters to attend to, and one or two little photographic projects I never get time for at home.'

'She's staying with us,' said Lavinia.

Lady Hardcastle smiled. 'How very wonderful. We're here for at least a couple of weeks ourselves – we shall have to dine again.'

'Is Betty with you?' I asked. Betty Buffrey and I had become friends when Lady Hardcastle and I stayed at Riddlethorpe. Betty had been working for another of Lady Lavinia's friends when I first met her, but once the dust had settled on the business at the house, she found herself employed instead as Helen Titmus's lady's maid.

'No, sadly not – I'm having to struggle on without her for a couple of weeks. She's had to go and see to a family matter. She'll be sorry she missed you.'

'I'm sorry, too. Please give her my love, won't you?'

A waiter approached to take our orders but Harry waved him away with a smile and a shake of the head. The Parisian training was in evidence as the waiter bowed respectfully while tutting impatiently, before sliding away.

We got down to the serious business of choosing food and catching up with Helen's news from the seaside.

Chapter Seven

I was awake early on Saturday as usual, but now we were settled in the flat and the proper work of trying to track down the killer had begun, Lady Hardcastle had reverted to her customary sleep patterns and was still abed.

And so, having nothing better to do, I took myself down to Fitzroy Square to exercise beneath one of the plane trees. The London plane, with its big leaves and its eccentric habit of shedding its bark, was one of the few trees I could recognize by sight, and for a short while I was distracted from my meditative Chinese exercises by the smugness that came from being able to name it without having to ask Lady Hardcastle for help.

By the time I returned to the flat there was still no sign of the great woman, so I made her some coffee and two rounds of buttered toast.

I took it in to her and put the cup and plate on the bedside cabinet. I was amused to see that her head was completely under the covers as usual, though her dark hair was just visible above the sheet, having been fanned out on the pillow rather than plaited neatly like a sensible person's.

I opened the shutters and a grumpy groan emanated from the lump in the bed.

'Good morning,' I said, as infuriatingly cheerfully as I could. 'It's a lovely summer's day. Birds are singing, milkmen are whistling, parlour maids are . . . actually I didn't see any parlour maids, but I know from bitter personal experience they'll be busy.'

The sheet flipped down, revealing a familiar sleep-rumpled face. 'You've been out among the birds and the milkmen?'

'And the coalmen and dustmen. But not the parlour maids. And it's beautiful in the square, the absence of junior servants notwithstanding.'

'I'm sure it is. Is that coffee and toast I smell?'

'It's the safest way I know to wake you.'

She struggled upright, getting slightly tangled in her nightdress on the way to verticality, and I handed her the plate of toast before heaving myself up to sit on the edge of the bed beside her.

'You're a living marvel, Flossie Armstrong,' she said. 'Thank you. But what time is it?'

'Eight.'

She groaned again. 'But we don't have to meet Benny at the Prospect until after one. Could I not have been allowed a nice lie-in?'

'I thought we might go down to Bond Street and do a little shopping – you always enjoy our time there. And how about the Burlington Arcade? Go on – you know you want to, really.'

She laughed. 'Oh, all right then.'

'And we've never been to Selfridges.'

'I am curious, I must confess.'

'There you are, then. A morning browsing London's finest shops will be much more exciting than an extra hour of fitful dozing and occasional snoring.'

She took a bite of toast and smiled appreciatively. 'I have come around to your over-energetic plan.'

'I knew you'd see sense.'

'In the end, dear, I always do. Do you need any help making breakfast?'

'I hadn't given it any thought. What do you feel qualified to do?'

'Ah . . . well now . . . you have me there, I'm afraid. I confess I was merely offering to be polite. Sorry.'

I slid down off the bed and stood once more on the rug beside it. 'Then leave it to me. Will half an hour give you enough time to come to?'

'More than enough. I shall see you in the kitchen in half an hour.'

I left her munching her toast.

◆　◆　◆

The shopping trip was a roaring success. Dresses, skirts, jackets and blouses were ordered from Lady Hardcastle's favourite dressmaker. Hats, boots and shoes were bought, and delivery to Littleton Cotterell was arranged. And just when exhaustion threatened to overcome us, a nice sit-down and a reviving pot of tea were supplied by the café in the Selfridges department store.

And even after all that excitement, we were still home in plenty of time to change into our East End clothes before setting off for our meeting with Benny Butcher.

It took four tries before the engine caught. I had become accustomed to the electric starter motor – designed by Lady Lavinia's brother and fitted to the Rolls – and had come to believe that this tiresome ritual of trying to crank the engine to life using nothing but Florence Power was a thing of the past. After the third failed attempt I was swearing colourfully and creatively in Welsh. This alarmed a passing nanny with a perambulator, who quickened her pace to hasten her precious charge away from the mad lady with the motor car. Meanwhile, my performance greatly amused

Lady Hardcastle, who had no firm idea of what I was saying but always found the sight and sound of a frustrated Flo unaccountably hilarious.

Finally, the engine spluttered to life and I hopped grumpily into the passenger seat.

Lady Hardcastle was still laughing.

'You might want to think twice about mocking me while I have a starter handle in my hand,' I said.

'Oh, but you look so adorable when you're cross. How could one not feel joy?'

'Just drive the stupid car.'

I sulked as we made our way through the West End traffic towards the City of London, but my mood had lifted by the time we arrived at Tower Hill and I had my own chance to chuckle as Lady Hardcastle parked on the street with her customary ebullient carelessness.

We set off to walk down to Wapping Wall.

It was Saturday lunchtime, and even though the Port of London didn't stop for such frivolities as the weekend, there were still plenty of workers in the area for whom the week's work was done. The Prospect of Whitby was busier than it had been the day before, with groups of cheerful men having a quick 'pig's ear' before heading home to the 'trouble and strife'.

Benny Butcher was on his own at the bar, chatting to the land-lord. He picked up his pint as he saw us approaching and nodded towards a door marked *Private*. We followed him into a back room, where he invited us to sit at the landlord's dining table.

'Sorry, ladies,' he said as we made ourselves comfortable. 'I should 'ave got you a drink 'fore we come back 'ere. You want somefin'?'

Lady Hardcastle smiled. 'You're very kind, Benny dear, but I'm fine, thank you.'

'Me too,' I said. 'But is there anything to eat?'

'Danny does a nice roast beef sandwich if you're peckish.'

I paused for a moment, weighing up this generous offer.

'With piccalilli,' added Benny, to sweeten the deal.

'Sold.'

'I'll have one of those if you're offering,' said Lady Hardcastle. 'I'm famished.'

Benny disappeared for a good few minutes before returning with two doorstop sandwiches to rival Old Joe's at the Dog and Duck, as well as two small glasses of porter. He set everything down on the table.

'Thank you, Benny dear, this is most generous of you. But you must let me pay – you're doing us a favour, after all.'

'Don't be daft.'

'For the beer, at least? I insist.'

'No, it's my treat. Anyway, you can't 'ave a sandwich without somefin' to wash it down. Good 'ealth.'

He took a heroic swig of his own beer and we raised our glasses in salute.

Lady Hardcastle bit hungrily into her sandwich and was lost for a moment in the simple pleasure of fresh bread, butter, roast beef, and a generous dollop of piccalilli.

Eventually she swallowed her mouthful and was free to speak. 'So tell us, Mr Butcher – what have you found? Are there wrong 'uns from south-east Europe skulking about on the other side of the Thames?'

'I reckon there might be,' said Benny with a satisfied nod. 'I 'ad a word with one of the fellas I know down in Bermondsey' – again he spoke as though he were talking about a foreign country, not somewhere less than four hundred yards away, across the river – 'and 'e says some of his lads 'ave been talkin' about seein' the sort of blokes you might be lookin' for. He says there's an abandoned ware'ouse round the back streets down by Farrand's Wharf. The wharf is busy, of course, but the ware'ouse 'as been empty for a couple of years now. Shouldn't be no one there 'cept maybe the occasional dosser, but they reckon they've seen "swarthy, foreign-lookin' blokes" goin' in and out for a few weeks.'

'This is one of the busiest ports in the world,' I said. 'Isn't it teeming with foreign-looking blokes?'

Benny laughed. 'That's what I said. But he insisted they ain't sailors. Not dressed right, he said. Wrong sort of 'ats.'

'They wear the wrong hats?' said Lady Hardcastle.

Benny laughed. 'So 'e says. I didn't like to argue – didn't want to fall out over a description of a titfer. All 'e said was they wasn't sailors' 'ats. And 'e's convinced there's somefin' goin' on.'

'What sort of something?' I asked.

'The sort of thing they didn't ought to be doin' on someone else's manor, he says.'

'Something dodgy, then.'

'Yep. He don't know what they're up to, but 'e'd bet his granny it ain't legal.'

'I'm assuming his own business dealings aren't strictly above board either, though,' said Lady Hardcastle before taking another bite of her sandwich.

'I don't reckon he's made an honest penny in his life, but I can't hold it against him – I ain't, neither. But that ain't what bothers us. You don't do nothin' dodgy on someone else's beat without askin' permission. Ain't polite.'

I'd already finished my own mouthful so I took over. 'How would they know who to ask?'

'You always knows. But it ain't difficult to find out even if you don't.'

'And your pal is the man they should have asked?'

'Runs the whole place from Tower Bridge down to Surrey Water. Ask anyone in Bermondsey or Rotherhithe – they'll point you at Big Spencer Harris.'

'This is most helpful,' said Lady Hardcastle. 'Thank you. How do we find this abandoned warehouse?'

'You're goin' down there?' Once more the incredulous tone suggested we'd be mad to undertake a journey all the way to Bermondsey without engaging a bearer party and armed guards.

'We have to see for ourselves, dear. If these *are* the gentlemen who intend to scupper the trade mission, we have to stop them. But first we have to be certain. And the only way to be certain is to take a good look at the place and observe the comings and goings of the "swarthy, foreign-looking blokes". There's no other way.'

'But . . . I mean . . .'

'Benny dear, how long have you known us?'

'Gawd knows. A few years, definitely.'

'Then you should know enough to trust us to look after ourselves, even south of the river. If everything goes according to plan, he'll never know we're there, but could you clear it with Mr Harris for us just in case, please?'

Benny nodded and scrawled an address on a scrap of paper he dug out of his pocket. 'I'll make sure he knows you're all right. When you goin'?'

'Tonight, I think. We don't have the luxury of time.'

'Then I'd better get over there sharpish. He should be all right, though. He's a patriotic man.'

'Don't tell him too much about us, please, dear.'

Benny looked offended. 'What do you take me for? I know what's what. I'll tell him just enough to make sure he knows you're not . . . encroaching. He'll make sure his lads leave you alone if I vouch for you.'

'Thank you, that would be most appreciated.'

'What names shall I give 'im?'

'Names, dear?'

'Well, you ain't goin' as yourselves, are you?'

'Oh, yes, of course. But—'

I didn't think we should trouble Benny with the details of our usual means of sneaking about city docks at night, so I said, 'I'm Nelly Maybee. With two e's.'

Benny chuckled. 'He won't ask how to spell it, darlin'. What about you?'

Lady Hardcastle sighed. 'I no longer have a *nom de guerre* suitable for this kind of work, I'm afraid. We had to retire Millie Mason in '07 after blackmailing an industrialist from Düsseldorf – we didn't want him coming after her. I . . . umm . . . Flo? You're good at this – what do you think?'

'Evie Stilwell,' I said without hesitating. 'A laundress, originally from Kent. You're the one who took Nelly under her wing and saved her from a life of petty crime and prostitution by getting her a job as a trainee seamstress.'

'There you are, dear Evie Stilwell. We'll be armed, so make sure Big Spencer's men know not to push their luck. We wouldn't want any unfortunate accidents.'

Benny frowned and cocked his head, but thought better of doubting our abilities again. Instead, he said, 'I'll tell 'im you're workin' for me – tell 'im these geezers are interferin' with my work. There ain't no obvious profit in your bein' there so 'e won't object. There might come a day when 'e wants to sort someone out up the East End, so doin' me this small courtesy'll be to his advantage.'

Lady Hardcastle polished off the last mouthful of her porter and stood to leave. 'Your efforts are greatly appreciated – this won't be forgotten.' She rummaged in the sleeve of her dress and produced a neatly folded, white five-pound note, which she handed to him between the first two fingers of her right hand. 'Don't spend it all in the same place, dear.'

Benny took the money and inclined his head in thanks. 'Be careful.'

'Always, dear, always.'

We said our goodbyes and slipped quietly back through the lunchtime pub crowd and back out on to Wapping Wall.

◆ ◆ ◆

Despite their modest cost and unassuming appearance, the clothes worn by Mrs Brown and Mrs Jones were still unsuitable for our planned mission of observing the comings and goings at abandoned warehouses at night. If we were to move about the docks of south London without drawing even the smallest amount of attention, we would need to dress more appropriately.

It was in anticipation of this need that Lady Hardcastle's trunk had been packed with a variety of suitable outfits for us both to wear in any circumstance, from a night on the Dockland streets to an elegant evening at an embassy ball. The three suitcases contained her own clothes, of course, and if challenged on the necessity of bringing so much, she would point out that many ladies of her station would travel with a dozen or more.

We took care over it, but by eight that evening, after a light dinner at a delightful little restaurant not far from the flat, we were dressed and ready.

As far as Big Spencer's men would be aware, there would be two women called Evie and Nelly on their territory, but if all went well they would never see them. The strangers watching the abandoned warehouse near Farrand's Wharf wouldn't be women at all.

Lady Hardcastle's impressive mane of hair had been pinned up and concealed beneath a battered bowler hat, while my own was tucked into a loose cap. I had made good use of the few tailoring skills I'd picked up over the years to make adjustments to the cut of our suits, the better to conceal our true shapes, though I'd been careful not to make too many repairs, leaving ample evidence of wear and tear. Both our jackets were slightly frayed at the cuffs, and the elbows of mine had been patched with leather.

The most expensive items were our boots, which had been handmade for us by a discreet shoemaker in St James's. He had disguised their origins by expertly ageing and distressing them, but they fitted perfectly and were as comfortable and practical as any shoe I had ever owned. We had learned the hard way that ill-fitting men's boots might complete the ensemble, but were absolutely useless if we needed to run or fight. Far better to have bespoke footwear that *looked* like a man's well-worn work boot but which would still allow us to do what needed to be done if things cut up rough.

Lady Hardcastle inspected herself in the glass by the front door. 'Will I do?'

I looked her up and down. 'You'll be fine. The sun's setting soon, so it'll be gloomy by the time we get there, but no one will pay us the slightest attention anyway.' I patted the small of her back. 'Is that gun all right there?'

'Is it too obvious?'

'I saw it, certainly, but I know to look for it. I'm sure it will be fine. I was thinking more about comfort and convenience.'

'Well, it's not the most comfortable spot for it, that's for sure, but it's less obvious than having it on my hip, and it's easy enough to get to. I tried it in my jacket pocket but it's so dashed heavy – it quite ruined the line of my suit.'

'What about the little Colt? Wouldn't that be better?'

'Already strapped to my ankle, dear. One can never be too careful. These aren't the sort of chaps who deal with disputes by a cordial airing of conflicting views over a pint in the pub – they settle their differences with a poorly aimed shot to the chest.'

I tapped my favourite knife in the sheath strapped to my right forearm. 'I feel underdressed now.'

'I pity the man who tries to get the better of you, dear, spare blade or not.'

'We should have got the shoemaker to make room for a sgian dubh. One of those beautiful ornamental ones we saw in Edinburgh would look very fetching tucked into my boot.'

'Something to bear in mind for next time. Are we ready, though, do you think?'

'As we'll ever be.'

'Come then, tiny servant, we shall hie with all speed to Bermondsey.'

◆　◆　◆

We parked in what had become our usual spot at Tower Hill, but this time, instead of heading east towards Wapping, we made our way past the Tower of London to Tower Bridge, gateway to Southwark.

Tooley Street took us to St Saviour's Dock and across the invisible boundary to Bermondsey, where we strolled casually towards our destination like two workmates out for an evening drink.

Farrand's Wharf was about a mile and a half from where we'd left the Austin, and the journey took a little over half an hour. By the time we arrived at the corner of Bermondsey Wall and Marigold Street it was well on the way to being dark – or as dark as England gets in the middle of summer.

'It's down this way,' said Lady Hardcastle, pointing towards the brick buildings that loomed over us on either side of the road.

Even though it was already a little after nine o'clock in the evening, the wharves, warehouses and granaries were still very much alive with busy workers. The pub on the corner was full to bursting with noisy Saturday night revellers, too. An out-of-tune piano was belting out the accompaniment to a music hall song, and the singing could probably be heard in Rotherhithe.

Things were not a great deal quieter even as we got down to the smaller building on the corner of Pottery Street that seemed to be our goal.

'Papered-up windows,' I said. 'Notices pasted to the doors – I'm going to go out on a limb and say this is our abandoned warehouse.'

Lady Hardcastle nodded. 'It's certainly the address Benny gave us. Not very well situated for discreet surveillance, though, is it?'

I looked around. 'There's a doorway over there we could loiter in. It doesn't look like it's used much. It's not well lit, either – it's as if that street lamp had been positioned specifically to create a shadowy space for lurking.'

'That might be our only option. I'd prefer to be properly concealed, but needs must and all that. We'll need a story if the local bobby comes round.'

'We just start a row about football. I imagine a decent bit of argy-bargy about the relative merits of Millwall and West Ham will convince him we're just a couple of local drunks. Then we mumble polite apologies when he tells us to move along and scoot round the block. By the time we get back he'll be long gone.'

'Sounds good to me. I'll follow your lead.'

We settled into the doorway, well back in the shadows, and waited.

As we had made our plans for this evening's outing, I had mentally braced myself for a long night of standing about watching nothing very much and trying not to wish I was sitting in a comfy armchair with a cup of cocoa and a good book. Observation duties were seldom a source of boundless excitement, or even mild interest, and I had been prepared for the worst. I had wondered if we might find somewhere safe to hide so that we could at least pass the time in quiet conversation, but had considered it more likely that we would be hiding silently in the shadows. For hours.

I was half right.

We had been hiding in the shadows for only about a quarter of an hour when a young man dressed all in black came walking quickly down the street from the river. He glanced about to check that no one was looking before knocking on the door of the abandoned warehouse. It took a few moments for anyone to answer his knock, and he kept to the shadowed side of the doorway as much as he could while maintaining a nervous lookout for observers. The door opened just wide enough for him to enter and he slipped inside. The door closed.

'Serbian,' said Lady Hardcastle quietly.

'Absolutely,' I agreed. 'The hat.'

As he passed beneath one of the street lamps we had both noticed that he was wearing a *šajkača* – a military cap with a V-shaped top that we had seen everywhere the last time we were in Serbia. Big Spencer had been right – you could tell who they were by their titfers.

'It's not exactly proof of anything,' said Lady Hardcastle, 'but it's very suggestive, wouldn't you say?'

'Very. Good thing we didn't break in.'

'It certainly crossed my mind to try. But there's definitely more than one of them and we'd have been in serious tr— Hold on.'

The door had opened again, and the man re-emerged, this time with three companions, all dressed in black and sporting *šajkačas*. The last one out locked the door and they strode purposefully up the street towards the river and its many wharves.

'What do you think?' I said. 'Do we hang around to wait for them come back or have we seen enough?'

'Or,' she replied, 'do we break in? We know there's no one there now.'

'We strongly suspect there's no one there,' I corrected her. 'We don't know the others didn't just tell them to lock the door on their way out so they didn't have to get up from their game of cards.'

'True, true. Still, some progress has been made. We should definitely report this to Harry.'

'Excellent,' I said. 'We can go down to the Basement first thing on Monday.'

'Monday be beggared. We're going to tell him now.'

'It must be half past nine already. We won't be home until half past ten at the earliest. Then, by the time we've changed—'

Lady Hardcastle pushed against the brickwork she'd been leaning on and stood properly upright. 'We're not getting changed, silly. Where would be the fun in that? Come on, let's get back to the motor car.'

◆ ◆ ◆

It was more like a quarter to eleven by the time we pulled up outside Harry's house on Bedford Square. The Austin's brakes squealed and the engine clattered to stillness. A couple got out of a taxi a few doors down, dressed for dinner and a little the worse for drink. The man eyed us suspiciously as we got out of our own car and approached Harry's door.

'I say,' called the man. 'You there. What's your business here?'

'Just callin' on an old pal,' said Lady Hardcastle in a terribly unconvincing husky voice.

'Not at this time of night you're not,' said the man. 'Clear orf.'

The door opened to reveal Harry's astonished face. 'What the—?'

'Hello, Harry dear. May we come in? We seem to be upsetting your neighbours.'

Harry poked his head out of the door. 'What ho, Jimmy,' he called. 'Nothing to worry about. Just some colleagues.' He waved to his friend and ushered us inside.

Lady Hardcastle handed him her hat. 'Thank you, dear. I didn't want to have to shoot him.'

'It would have caused quite a stink,' agreed Harry. 'What the blue blazes were you thinking of, coming round dressed like that?'

'More to the point, dear: since when did you answer your own front door?'

'Since the staff all went to bed. We don't usually have callers at' – he checked the hall clock – 'a quarter to eleven. I take it you've been working.'

'Surveillance, brother dear. Sarf of the river.'

'Good heavens. Bandit country, eh? And it was imperative that you visit me at dead of night because . . . ?'

'Because we thought you might enjoy hearing about our evening.'

Harry sighed. 'Couldn't it have waited?' He turned to me. 'Why didn't you try to talk her out of it, Strongarm?'

'I have no control over her, Mr Feather-stone-huff, you know that. I just do as I'm told. Whither she goest and all that.'

He led us up the stairs and reached for the handle of one of the doors leading off the hall. 'We're in the drawing room.'

Lady Hardcastle put out a hand out to stop him. 'Is Helen here?'

'She is.'

'Then can we have a quiet word in private? It's not that I think she's a security risk or anything, but . . . you know . . . protocol and all that.'

'Quite right, sis, quite right. Come through to my study.'

He led the way to a room at the front of the house almost completely filled by an absurdly large desk, and invited us to sit on the sofa that took up the remaining space.

'Could you not find a bigger desk, dear?' said Lady Hardcastle.

'Don't you recognize it? It's Pa's. From the Treasury.'

'Good gracious, so it is.' She got on her hands and knees and crawled into the knee hole. 'I signed my name on the underside of the drawer. It's still there.'

'That's nothing,' said Harry, reaching down and pointing to something else underneath. 'Carved my initials with my new pen-knife when I was seven.'

Lady Hardcastle crawled free and returned to the Chesterfield. 'It's charming. But it needs a bigger room.'

'Never mind the desk, sis, what's been going on? You didn't say a word at dinner last night.'

'Helen was there, dear. I thought we'd covered that.'

'Fair enough. So . . . ?'

'So what?'

Harry sighed. 'Florence: what have you been up to?'

'Oh, you know, this and that. We had a lovely morning's shopping. I bought a new hat. And some charming new underwear. It has—'

'I imagine you're both armed,' he said, 'but I will try to kill you nonetheless. The ice is melting in my Scotch downstairs while you mess me about.'

'Well now,' said Lady Hardcastle, sitting up straight and putting her hands on her lap. 'In that case I suppose we ought to tell you. Yesterday we visited a fair few of our old haunts in the East End. Queenie Pearce—'

'Who's Queenie Pearce?'

'A brothel keeper in Wapping, but that's not terribly relevant. Anyway, she was most cooperative and promised to get in touch with you if she hears anything.'

'With me? You told a brothel keeper to contact me?'

'Of course. It was no good giving her the telephone number at the flat – we're hardly ever there. The Basement, on the other hand, is manned twenty-four hours a day.'

Harry tutted and shook his head. 'Very well.'

'Meanwhile, our good friend Benny Butcher—'

'Now Butcher I *have* heard of. Underworld aristocracy. I didn't think he was very keen on our lot, though. He promised Brownlow and Perlman he'd have their throats slit if he ever saw them again.'

'To be honest,' I said, 'I feel the same about those two. But even if they'd had a magical transformation of character, he still wouldn't like them – they're Old Bill. We, on the other hand, are perfectly delightful and he loves us like sisters.'

'And we helped him with a spot of bother he was having in '07,' said Lady Hardcastle.

Harry frowned. 'Do I want to know?'

'Best you don't, dear. But he had already heard something, and he put us on to an abandoned warehouse in Bermondsey, near Farrand's Wharf.'

'Kovač's notes mentioned a wharf.'

'Well remembered. So we crossed the river to Bermondsey this evening—'

'Hence the manly clobber.'

'Hence our present appearance, yes, and we took a look at this warehouse. Lo and behold, what should we see but four Serbian gentlemen using it for . . . actually we don't know what they're using it for. But we think it worthy of another look.'

'How do you know they're Serbian?'

'Their hats,' said Lady Hardcastle and I together.

Harry frowned again. 'Very well. What do you propose doing next?'

'Now we know where they are,' I said, 'we can ask more specific questions of our pals in the area. Benny has contacts south of the river and he's already making enquiries for us. And Queenie might have something new.'

'You'll do this when?'

'Tomorrow,' said Lady Hardcastle. 'Then we'll report to the Basement on Monday. It might be that we'll be in a position to tell Colonel Valentine to arrange a raid.'

Harry laughed. 'You'll *tell* Valentine?'

'Of course, dear. There's no point in asking for things – one never gets them. If a raid is justified, we'll tell him so.'

'As you wish, sis, as you wish. Is there anything else?'

'No, I think that covers the pertinent points. Oh, Queenie offered us a job but we had to turn her down – busy on other matters, you see.'

'Shame. Well, in that case, would you care to join us for a nightcap?'

Lady Hardcastle indicated our tattered suits. 'I think not. Helen is the sweetest thing, and she knows about our work, but we can't really explain our togs without also explaining exactly what we've been up to. And I really don't want to be doing that yet, if it can be avoided.'

'Understood. Well, good luck tomorrow and I'll see you at the office on Monday.'

'Bright and early,' said Lady Hardcastle. 'Good night, dear.'

We returned to the Austin – which started first time – and drove the short distance back to the flat.

Chapter Eight

On Sunday morning, I exercised beneath my plane tree in Fitzroy Square again. There were fewer tradesmen about, but there was a young man on the other side of the square completing his own exercises with Indian clubs. He was either shy or politely discreet, and kept himself mostly out of sight behind a tree of his own, and I didn't see very much of him.

Feeling invigorated, as much by the early morning sunshine and birdsong as by the Chinese exercises, I stretched a little and padded back towards the flat on Southampton Street, my black plimsoles making no sound. I looked to see if Indian Clubs Man was still there – I'd often wondered about exercising with clubs and I was keen to see how it was done. He caught sight of me and turned away at once with a look of disgust, presumably horrified by my Chinese jacket and trousers. I smiled and carried on.

To my surprise, Lady Hardcastle was already in the kitchen by the time I entered the flat at half past seven.

'Good morning, Flossie,' she said as I went in to see what she was up to. She had taken to using my family's pet name for me since my sister had come to stay with us the previous autumn. Gwen always called me Flossie, just as our mother had, and it seemed to amuse Lady Hardcastle. I was never quite sure if she meant it teasingly, but I rather liked it so I never complained.

'Good morning to you, too. Are you all right?'

'Am I all right? Oh, because I'm up and about, you mean? Yes, thank you, dear, quite all right. I thought I might make us some breakfast.'

'Good heavens.'

'There's no need to sound so surprised. I can make breakfast.'

'You *can*,' I said. 'We both know you're an accomplished cook – though you'd never dream of letting anyone find out – but I don't remember the last time you actually demonstrated your skills by making breakfast.'

'Then put a note in your diary so that you remember I made it today.'

'It's much appreciated. If you'll excuse me, I'll get changed into something a little less exercisey while you finish off.'

'You might as well put Mrs Jones's dress straight on, dear,' she called as I left. 'I want to go over to Wapping as soon as we can.'

I returned to the kitchen in my Mrs Jones dress as suggested and sat at the table.

Lady Hardcastle put fried eggs on to two plates and brought them over.

'What do you do out there in the mornings in your Chinese garb?' she asked.

'The same thing I do at home in my Chinese garb. You've seen me doing my t'ai chi exercises.'

'And you need to do that outside? It never looks terribly energetic – it seems like the sort of thing one might happily do indoors.'

'Energy flows, sunlight, trees, nature – it would take too long to explain and you'd mock me anyway.'

'I hope I wouldn't. But it seems to do you good.'

'I enjoy it. It both relaxes and energizes me. And it's good for circulation and flexibility. You really ought to try it. I can teach you.'

'You offer regularly, and regularly I decline. I get all that from my piano.'

I smiled. 'The offer will always be open. I'm hoping to get Edna and Blodwen interested.'

'I wish you the best of luck. Though if you get Edna Gibson exercising under the apple tree in pyjamas, I might join you just so I can say I saw it with my own eyes.'

'If I can convert her, I might get the rest of the village.'

'I would actually *pay* to see that. Can you imagine Dr Fitzsimmons and Mr and Mrs Newton on the village green, moving elegantly in unison under your instruction?'

I had to admit that the thought of the village doctor and his servants spreading their wings like the white crane was an amusing one.

'Old Joe and Mrs Arnold would definitely retire.'

'Or,' I said, spearing a sausage with my fork, 'they might be so rejuvenated that they cast aside all thoughts of retirement.'

'Daisy wouldn't thank you for that.'

'Perhaps I ought to rethink the entire plan, then. I wouldn't want to stand in the way of Daisy Spratt's tavern-running ambitions.'

'Does she have ambitions, do you think?'

'You never know with Daisy. Time was when we thought her a self-centred flibbertigibbet with far too much interest in handsome cricketers. And now look at her.'

'Indeed. From village floozy to organizing the drinks for Gertie's party. Oh, I say.'

'Oh, you say what?'

'Gertie's party,' she said. 'We recklessly promised to sort out the entertainment.'

'*You* recklessly promised. I merely observed like a startled bystander at a railway disaster.'

'Why didn't you stop me?'

'Have you ever tried to stop you? Do you know how difficult you are to stop?'

'What shall we do?'

'*You* will think of something marvellous,' I said. 'You always do.'

'Hmm. Perhaps Queenie will inspire something.'

'The Cocottes Chorus? Now that would be worth seeing.'

'Or perhaps she knows some musicians.'

'Or that. Shall we go soon?'

'As soon as I've finished this toast.'

◆ ◆ ◆

The City was quiet as we walked from the motor car, but the docks, of course, were as alive as ever.

'Do you think they ever get any peace?' I asked as we made our way past the busy warehouses of the Western Dock.

Lady Hardcastle shook her head. 'It's the same the world over. Do you remember Shanghai?'

'I do. And Hamburg. Port Said. Marseille. This seems even busier, though, somehow – more excitingly alive.'

'It really does. One wonders how long it can survive, though.'

'What do you mean?'

'The population grows, trade increases. The tonnage of goods coming in and going out goes up every year. But the docks have to stay the same size. They're hemmed in on all sides by the city they serve – there's no room for them to expand. Ships are getting bigger, too. There must surely come a time when it's no longer practical to sail all the way up the Thames – some of the bigger ships already favour Tilbury.'

I gestured at the homes all around us. 'I wonder what will happen to all this.'

'I have no idea. If the docks close, it will end a whole way of life.'

'It's rather sad when you put it like that.'

'There's always an element of sadness to any change, don't you think?'

We walked on in silent contemplation.

A short while later we arrived at Queenie's, where Lady Hardcastle rat-a-tatted on the lion's-head door knocker.

There was a lengthy delay while bolts were thrown and a key turned in the lock, before the door opened a crack and Queenie's face appeared.

'Sorry, darlin', we're not open yet. Got to give the girls a bit of a rest . . . Oh, I'm sorry, I thought you was a customer.' She opened the door wider. 'Come in, come in. I've just made a pot of tea.'

We made our own way through to the parlour, while Queenie relocked the door. After the hustle, bustle, hurly and burly of the docks, the house was almost eerie in its silence.

'We were just wondering if there was ever any peace round here,' I said.

A black and white cat emerged from the front room as we passed and mewed as it rubbed itself against my legs.

I crouched down to tickle its chin. '*Bore da, cath.*'

'That's Lord Kitchener,' said Queenie from behind me. 'Very fond of the ladies, is Lord Kitchener. We 'as to keep 'im out of there when we're open, though – 'e can't stand men. But no, it ain't never quiet. I could stay open all day and all night if I didn't need me sleep.'

I stood up and the cat cheerfully trotted alongside me as we entered the parlour.

Lady Hardcastle was already pouring three cups of tea, and I wondered once again if she was quite all right.

Queenie took her cup gratefully and settled into her armchair. 'Sit yourselves down, make yourselves at 'ome. You come about your Balkan boys? I ain't 'eard nothin', I'm afraid.'

'We have,' said Lady Hardcastle. 'They're south of the river. Bermondsey.'

If Queenie had crossed herself at the mention of *the other side* I wouldn't have been in the least bit surprised, but the look of disgust on her face said quite enough about her opinion of 'south of the river'.

'To be expected, I s'pose. If there's anythin' sly goin' on, it'll be down there.'

'We think they're holed up in an abandoned warehouse on the corner of Pottery Street and Marigold Street,' I said.

'Funny enough, I know exactly where you mean. There's a pub up on the corner by Bermondsey Wall. Gawd, that takes me back. I used to go over there sometimes when I was younger. I still got some pals over that way – you want me to ask around?'

'That would be most helpful, dear,' said Lady Hardcastle. 'Thank you. We're interested in finding out when they arrived, how many of them there are, what else might have been going in and out of the building. You know the sort of thing.'

I was about to take a sip of my tea, but lowered my cup. 'Make sure you tell your pals not to go poking around, though,' I said. 'If these men are who we think they are, they're very dangerous. They've killed one man already – shot him in broad daylight on a busy street in Bristol. They won't hesitate to kill again.'

Queenie nodded. 'They're sensible girls. Well, I say "girls" – we ain't none of us gettin' any younger, are we?'

'We're not, dear,' said Lady Hardcastle. 'Though I'm not entirely sure I'd like to. I'd quite like my knees returned to their former creak-free flexibility, but I can't even begin to contemplate the horror of being sixteen again.'

Conversation turned towards the perils of ageing as we finished our tea. Queenie catalogued her various ailments – she was a martyr to her sinuses – while Lady Hardcastle and I nodded sympathetically.

We left Queenie talking affectionately to Lord Kitchener and let ourselves out into the bright Wapping sunshine.

◆　◆　◆

Our next port of call was to be the Prospect of Whitby, where we hoped to meet Benny Butcher. Ideally we would have made direct contact, but that wasn't how our relationship worked – it was important to Benny that he was seen to be in control, so we usually waited to hear from him. But with the Austrian delegation due to arrive in eight days' time, and only a suspicion of the whereabouts of the Serbian nationalists who had killed Kovač, we had to try to hurry things along.

It was shaping up to be another glorious summer's day, and the walk down to the river was a pleasant one. Sunshine and warmth made the dilapidated houses and oppressive warehouses glimmer and sparkle in the same way it enlivened the blackened Georgian buildings of the City.

Children were playing in the streets, neighbours were gossiping on doorsteps, and the smells of cooking filled the air. Even the distinctive aroma of boiled cabbage – or, more likely, over-boiled cabbage – brought back happy childhood memories.

More familiar smells, this time of tobacco smoke and beer, greeted us with ferocious cordiality as we opened the Prospect's door and walked in. The pub was busy, as usual, but a quick tour of both rooms revealed an absence of Benny.

The landlord caught my eye as we made a second pass of the bar.

'Nice to see you again, ladies,' he said. 'You lookin' for Benny?'

I smiled and nodded. 'We are.'

'I ain't seen 'im today, but 'e told me to look after you if you dropped in, like.'

'That's very kind of him,' said Lady Hardcastle. 'And of you, too. But we need to speak to him. Are you expecting him?'

'Expectin'? I wouldn't say you ever expect Benny Butcher – he comes and goes as 'e pleases. He's usually in 'ere by now if 'e's coming, though, so we probably won't see 'im today, darlin'.'

'Do you have his address?' I asked.

'He won't take too kindly to you droppin' in unannounced. He's a bit funny like that.'

Lady Hardcastle shrugged. 'It's a chance we'll have to take. It really is very urgent, I'm afraid.'

The landlord looked at us appraisingly for a few moments, then started hunting around behind the bar. 'Hold up, let me get a bit of paper. He told me never to say it out loud, y'see. "Walls 'ave ears, Danny, mate," 'e always says. And I says, "I always wondered what was in them sausages." And that makes him laugh every time. He likes a laugh does old Benny.'

He finally found Saturday's edition of *Boxing* tucked beside a gin bottle on the shelf beneath the mirror. The back page was entirely taken over by an advertisement and seemed a likely spot to write a note. He checked there was nothing of interest on the inside back page, took a pencil from behind his ear, and wrote an address in the margin of the advert. He ripped off the whole back page and handed it to me.

'There you go, darlin'. But be careful. Benny don't much like visitors and 'e don't like surprises. Surprise visitors are in twice as much danger.'

I took the paper. 'Thank you . . . Danny, did you say?'

'That's it, love. Be lucky.'

We waved our goodbyes and went back out into the fresh air.

I looked at the advertisement.

Luis Hardt – who claimed to earn 'the salary of a cabinet minister' by performing feats of strength and showing off his muscular physique in music halls – was exhorting us to buy a pair of Sandow's Spring Grip Dumb-Bells. We could get a pair suitable for ladies over the age of fifteen for just ten shillings and sixpence (gentlemen's dumb-bells were twelve and six). Mr Hardt had cured himself of a weak chest following Sandow's system of Physical Culture and was most particularly impressed by the spring grip dumb-bells.

I was not tempted, even by the offer of a seven-day free trial and the gift of a photograph of the man himself.

On the other side was provincial boxing news of no interest to East End fight aficionados.

I showed Lady Hardcastle the address and she nodded.

'I know it,' she said. 'It should only take us twenty minutes.'

A quarter of an hour later we arrived at Betts Street. We walked up past the public baths and the Ratcliff Highway Refuge towards a terrace of houses at the end of the street. A number of people had gathered near one of the houses and I could just about see a policeman's helmet outside the front door. I presumed there was a policeman underneath it, but this was the East End so you could never be certain.

'This doesn't look good,' said Lady Hardcastle. 'I do hope it's not Benny's house.' She counted off the house numbers. 'Blast it – it is. I suddenly wish we were more impressively dressed.'

The crowd was growing and I wasn't confident we'd make it to the door to see what had happened, but Lady Hardcastle once again employed the trick she had used at the dockside in Bristol – some sort of witchcraft.

'We're coming through because we need to get to the door,' she said loudly in her normal voice, and the crowd parted before us as though by magic. Even though I had seen it work before, I still expected resistance, perhaps even a little pushing and shoving, or a 'What the bleedin' 'ell d'ya fink you're doin'?' But they just got out of her way and I followed in her wake.

Within moments we were face to face with the young constable manning the door.

'I'm goin' to have to ask you to step back, please, madam,' he said. 'There ain't nothin' to see here.'

Lady Hardcastle rummaged in her pocket and produced the smart leather holder into which the young man at the SSB had put her new identification card. She presented it to the policeman.

'I am Lady Hardcastle and this is Miss Armstrong. What's going on?'

'I don't care if you're the Queen of Sh—'

'If I were the Queen of Sheba, Constable, I should be resting on my throne in my palace on the Red Sea just up the road from Aden, where I would be impressing passing notables with my fine collection of camels, spices, gold and precious stones. Since I am here before you, and since I bear not exotic spices but War Office identification, it's much more likely that I am, in fact, Lady Hardcastle, just as it says' – she tapped the card – 'right there. Please tell us what's going on.'

'I'm under strict instructions—'

'From whom?'

'I beg your pardon?'

'Who gave you the instructions?'

'My sergeant.'

'Is he here?'

'He's gone back to the station to get the chief inspector.'

Lady Hardcastle sighed. 'I'm not asking for access to the property. Not yet, at least. I just want to know what's going on.'

'And I'm tellin' you that—'

'Constable,' I said, calmly. 'Here's my identification. It's exactly the same as Lady Hardcastle's apart from the name. Do you see? F. Armstrong. That's me. Florence. My friends call me Flo. Can you see what it says on the other page? Under that very impressive-look-ing government crest?'

He looked closer and muttered as he read. 'Let me see . . . acting under the authority of the Secretary of State for War . . . requests and requires . . . all persons . . . help and assistance . . .' He mumbled his way through the rest of the flowery paragraph which, in essence, said, 'The bearer of this card is a great deal more important than you think.'

'Splendid,' I said. 'Now, I think you would be rendering us help and assistance if you were to tell us what's going on, don't you?'

'Well . . . I . . . er . . . when you put it like that. A man's been found dead inside the 'ouse.'

'Who?' said Lady Hardcastle.

'I don't know, m'lady. Sorry. No one said.'

'How did he die?'

'I'm not at liberty to s—'

'Don't let's start that again, dear. Just let us in and we'll see for ourselves.'

'I can't do that, m'lady. I'm under strict—'

I tapped my card. 'Help and assistance, Constable. We'll square it with your chief inspector.'

The poor lad wrestled with it all for a good few seconds before reluctantly pushing open the front door for us and letting us in.

◆ ◆ ◆

I checked the door frame as we entered and confirmed that the reason the constable had been able simply to push the door open was that it had been forced – the frame had splintered around the lock when someone had kicked it in.

The door opened straight into the front parlour, where a man's body was sprawled on the rug in front of the fireplace. A short length of lead pipe lay by his outstretched hand. He had been shot three times – once in the shoulder, once in the leg and once through the heart.

It was not Benny.

'Looks like the same killer,' I said.

Lady Hardcastle was still looking round the room. 'How so?'

'Terrible shot. Compared with you I'm hopeless with a gun, but even I could get three shots closer together than that from a couple of yards away.'

'At least four. Look at the window frame.' She pointed at a splintered hole in the wood at about what would have been the dead man's head height. 'Do you have your knife, dear?'

'I'll do it,' I said and drew my knife from its sheath on my forearm. It took a little digging but I eventually freed the stray bullet.

I handed it to Lady Hardcastle. 'What do you think?'

She fished her reading glasses from her pocket and looked closely. 'It *could* be another 9 millimetre. It certainly looks like the one Simeon dug out of Kovač to me.'

'To me, too. But the police will assume Benny killed him.'

'They will. We shall have to persuade them to look elsewhere.'

'We shall. So who's this chap, I wonder?'

'A trusted lieutenant, one presumes, left to look after the house while Benny was away.'

'And killed for his trouble. So, what do we think? The killer kicks in the door, chummy here gets up with his lead pipe and starts for the door, but the killer's too quick. He starts firing and gets off four shots—'

'Five,' said Lady Hardcastle, pointing to the wall above the mantelpiece. 'No, six.' There was another bullet hole in the floorboard beside the armchair.

'Six shots, then. Three of them hit Benny's man, with one of them – by the most amazing stroke of luck, it seems – hitting him in the heart and killing him. The killer flees.'

'That doesn't sound unreasonable. One presumes the killer came to shoot Benny but had no idea what he looked like – he just shot whoever was in the house. There must be a dozen or more people on either side of the river who would want Benny dead, but one wonders how many of them would favour a 9 millimetre hand-gun. From past experience, razors and lead pipes are the weapons of choice in these parts.'

'The only pistol I remember seeing round here was another of those wretched Webleys,' I said. 'Does the army not keep track of them? Are soldiers just free to stuff them in their kit bags and take them home?'

'It would appear so. But this was definitely a smaller weapon than that, so let us presume that the Serbians killed Benny. This means—'

'And who the bloody hell are you?'

The speaker was a tall, neatly presented man in a bowler hat.

I took out my SSB card and held it up for him. 'I'm Miss Armstrong and this is Lady Hardcastle.'

'So the constable told me. Perhaps I should rephrase my question: what the bloody hell do you think you're doing interfering at the scene of a murder on my manor?'

'We're not "interfering", Chief Inspector . . . ?' began Lady Hardcastle.

'Cromwell. How did you know I was a chief inspector?'

'The constable told us he was waiting for a chief inspector. Moments later you arrive and complain that we're interfering with your murder. But we're not, as I said, interfering. We believe this murder is connected with a matter we're working on and it was important that we find out as much as we can, as quickly as possible.'

'I don't care if—'

'We've encountered quite enough not caring about what we do already this afternoon, thank you. You've seen our credentials, so you know who we are. Whether you care about that or not is a matter for you, but you must also know – or at least suspect – that what we do is not trivial. We are not employed by His Majesty's Government to *interfere* in police cases to satisfy the petty whims and idle curiosity of Whitehall mandarins.'

'Until I hear different from someone a great deal more senior to you, *my lady*, this is my district and this is my murder. Unless your case involves Mr Benedict Butcher, who clearly murdered this man, it has nothing whatsoever to do with you. I shall thank you to step outside so that I may examine the scene of the crime.'

'Another shilling in the pot, Armstrong,' said Lady Hardcastle.

It took me a few seconds to remember the conversation with the chief superintendent in Bristol.

I laughed. 'You'll be a millionaire in no time. Might I suggest something to help smooth things over, Chief Inspector?'

'You can do what you like once you're back outside on the street where you belong.'

'Is it far to your police station? Or to the nearest telephone?'

'There's a telephone in the public baths down the road.'

'Then please send your constable to the baths and ask him to call this number.' I wrote Harry's telephone number on a corner of the dumb-bell advertisement and held it out to him. 'Tell him to ask for Mr Featherstonhaugh and he'll explain everything to you. We can all wait here until we hear back from him. I'm happy to make us all a nice cup of tea in the meantime – I don't know about you, but I'm gasping.'

'You can get out and leave my men to get on with their job, that's what you can do.'

I sighed. 'We both know that's not going to happen. Now, we could stand here and argue about it, or you could clear it all up by having your constable make a simple telephone call.' I waved the scrap of paper.

The chief inspector glared at me for a moment, then took the number. '*I'll* make the bloody call. Sergeant?'

A uniformed sergeant appeared at the door. 'Sir?'

'I'm going down the road to make a telephone call. Watch these two jokers and don't let them touch anything.'

'Right you are, sir.'

'May I touch the teapot?' I said.

The sergeant nodded enthusiastically. 'I'd love a cup of rosie, sir.'

Chief Inspector Cromwell stalked out. 'She may touch the bloody teapot.'

◆ ◆ ◆

Freed from the immediate influence of his superiors, Sergeant Bryer turned out to be very good company. He sat in the kitchen with Lady Hardcastle and me as we drank our tea and chatted to him about the area. He had grown up not far from Betts Street and had joined the police as soon as he was able.

'My dad wanted me to work on the docks – it's a good livin', but it ain't 'alf tough work. I reckon I'd 'ave done all right, but there'd been an old sergeant when we was kids – Sergeant Steel, 'e was called. His beat brought 'im past our 'ouse and 'e always told us it was his job to keep us all safe, to look after everyone. He made sure the villains kept to themselves. "You want to steal from the docks, you can take your chances, but you leave these people alone – these are your people. You come round 'ere makin' trouble and I'll 'ave you in the clink so fast your feet won't touch." Tough as old boots 'e was, but he always had a kind word for us. I wanted to be like him.'

'You're a credit to the uniform, Sergeant,' said Lady Hardcastle.

'I try to be.'

'Do you know Benny Butcher?' I asked.

He laughed. 'Everyone knows Benny Butcher, miss. They all love him round here. He's a wrong 'un, but he's what you might call a noble villain. He grew up under old Sergeant Steel's watchful eye an' all, see? He cheats and robs his way through life and I daresay the detectives'll catch up with him one of these days – I don't reckon he's earned so much as an honest farthin' since he was old enough to walk. Gawd knows he belongs in gaol, but he looks after the people round here. Him and his lads don't nick nothin' from honest people, and woe betide any chancer from outside who tries.'

'We've known him for a while, and we've seen that for ourselves. Have you any idea where he is?'

'None at all, miss. When they told me Benny's door had been kicked in and someone killed, I thought it would be him. His luck was bound to run out sooner or later. If our lads didn't arrest him, one of his rivals would do for him.'

'Do you know who the actual victim is?'

'That's Tommy Adams – one of Benny's bravos.'

'Do you agree with Chief Inspector Cromwell? Do you think Benny killed him?'

Bryer laughed. 'Not a chance. Best mates, them two. And it ain't Benny's style – Benny likes the razor. He wouldn't shoot no one, and certainly not in his own gaff. Tommy must have been lookin' after the place while Benny was away.'

'Why might that be necessary?' asked Lady Hardcastle.

'Can only mean trouble with another gang, I reckon. Benny must've thought him or his drum were gonna be a target.'

'Another gang? Any likely suspects?'

'Too many to name.'

'It looks like Tommy was shot with a small pistol,' I said. 'Is that the weapon of choice for any of the local gangs?'

'Nah. They all prefer blades and cudgels. If they use a shooter it's more likely to be a sawn-off shotgun. Or one of them army pistols. Bane of my bloody life, them things.'

A church clock chimed and I realized it had been at least half an hour since Chief Inspector Cromwell had left to make his telephone call. I was about to comment, but we were interrupted by a sudden commotion. To judge from the high pitch of the engine and the loud squeal of the brakes, a motor car had arrived outside the house at inappropriate speed. If she hadn't been sitting next to me there in Benny's kitchen I might have assumed Lady Hardcastle was at the wheel.

We were made aware of the opening of the front door by the sudden increase in the sound of the babble from the street. It ceased just as abruptly as the door closed.

The brief silence was broken by Chief Inspector Cromwell. 'Sergeant!'

We stood as one, and walked through to the front room with Sergeant Bryer in the lead.

The chief inspector had company.

'Perch and Tench,' said Lady Hardcastle. 'As I live and breathe. How are you, gentlemen? It's been a long time.'

'Not long enough, if you ask me,' said the junior of the two, who had originally been introduced to us as Tench. The last time we met there had been a slight disagreement over his manners – I didn't think he had any – and he had ended up being thrown painfully on to his back in Lady Hardcastle's hotel bedroom in Weston-super-Mare. We were not friends.

'Who?' said Cromwell. 'I thought you said your names were Perlman and Brownlow.'

'Just Lady Hardcastle's little joke, Chief Inspector,' said the other man. 'I am Perlman, and my colleague is Brownlow, just as we said.'

'Has Harry sent you to take over?' asked Lady Hardcastle.

'He has indeed, my lady.'

'Splendid.'

'Now, look here—' spluttered Cromwell, who despite his lengthy phone call was clearly still unwilling to relinquish the case.

Lady Hardcastle ignored him. 'The house belongs to Benny Butcher, but the victim is one of his associates, Tommy Adams. It looks very much as though he was shot with the same weapon used in your other recent case in Bristol, and from the poor marksmanship it could well be the same man, too.'

'The chap you lost, Brownlow,' said Perlman. 'Tut-tut.'

Brownlow glared but said nothing.

'We'll look for Butcher,' continued Lady Hardcastle, 'but the nature and timing of this killing does rather indicate that our other enquiries were on the right lines. Can we leave it with you?'

'Of course, my lady, of course. It will be our pleasure, won't it, Brownlow?'

Brownlow continued to glare and continued to say nothing.

Perlman turned to Cromwell with a smile. 'Thank you for your help, Chief Inspector. Your men have done exemplary work, but they can stand down – we'll take it from here.'

Cromwell was still fuming. 'Now look here—'

'This is a Special Branch matter now, my dear chap. If you would be good enough to get your men to disperse the gawkers, that would be most helpful, but your work is done.'

Against all the evidence, Cromwell had clearly believed he could retain at least some control, but he could see he would get nowhere with Perlman. There was cold menace beneath the Balliol charm and Cromwell was forced, however reluctantly, to admit that he had met his match.

'Get that shower out there to go home, Sergeant,' he said. 'I'm going back to the station.'

He left. He attempted to slam the door behind him, but with the lock broken it just hit the jamb and bounced open again.

Sergeant Bryer shrugged apologetically. 'Is there anythin' else I can do for you, sir?'

Perlman shook his head. 'No, thank you, Sergeant. If you and the constable could just deal with the crowd, we'll be grand.'

'Should we collect witness statements?'

'Were there any witnesses?'

'I shouldn't think so, sir. No one even reported hearin' the gunshots. We only found out somethin' was up when we passed by on our beat this mornin' and saw the door had been kicked in.'

'I think we can spare you the trouble. No point in you wasting your time only to find out no one saw anything.'

'Right you are, sir.'

The sergeant left, too.

Now we were alone, Perlman turned to Lady Hardcastle. 'Featherstonhaugh suggested you might have found our Balkan friends.'

'We think we might have,' said Lady Hardcastle.

'South of the river?'

'Indeed.'

'We were so busy trying to keep up with Kovač we never had a chance to look over there. If the fool hadn't been so intent on losing his tail we might have had some men to spare to go looking for the threat.'

'We don't know if we're right, mind you, but we'll collect our thoughts and report to Valentine tomorrow.'

Perlman tapped the brim of his homburg with his black-gloved index finger. 'Right you are. I do very much hope you have found them – I look forward to seeing them get their comeuppance. Good day to you, Lady Hardcastle, Miss Armstrong.'

We left the two Special Branch men to look after things.

Chapter Nine

At half past nine on Monday morning, Lady Hardcastle, Harry and I were in Colonel Valentine's office to give our report. Tea and biscuits had been served.

'Featherstonhaugh tells me you think you've found our chaps' lair,' said the colonel, carefully dunking a Rich Tea into his cup. He nodded to himself as he counted slowly to four and then withdrew the biscuit. It held, so he took a bite.

'We believe so,' I said. 'We got a tip from our man Benny Butcher—'

'The fellow who disappeared? We sent Perlman and Brownlow to the East End to his home yesterday to take over the investigation of the murder of one of his associates.'

'The very same. Perch and Te— I mean Perlman and Brownlow persuaded the local nick not to try to arrest Benny, I hope? He's definitely not guilty of the murder and it's important he remains at liberty – he's one of our principal contacts in the area.'

'They did. The chief superintendent interrupted my bridge game to advise me of his displeasure at having his officers' authority usurped by "bloody Special Branch" but I set him straight.'

'Thank you.'

'All part of the service. But I interrupted, Miss Armstrong, do go on.'

'Benny spoke to someone he knows south of the river and they said there'd been unusual activity at a disused warehouse. Lady Hardcastle and I took a look on Saturday night and we saw at least four Serbians coming out.'

'How d'you know they were Serbians?'

'Their hats,' said Lady Hardcastle, Harry and I in unison.

'Ah, yes. *Šajkačas*?'

'Exactly,' said Lady Hardcastle. 'They're either too dull-witted to realize their caps give them away or they're too proud of their homeland to give them up. Either way, at least four of them seem to be holed up in a warehouse in Bermondsey. You need to authorize a raid as soon as possible.'

Colonel Valentine held up his hands. 'Hold your horses, there. Yours isn't the only operation we're running and we don't have unlimited resources. I can't commit manpower to raiding an abandoned warehouse just because you've seen some Serbians. They could be sailors saving their pay by dossing down in an empty building. They could be . . . well, they could be anything. Being from Serbia isn't a crime.'

'Shooting a man in the street and another in his friend's home most certainly is, though.'

'Granted, but unless and until you can show me that these distinctively behatted individuals in Bermondsey have anything to do with those murders in Bristol and Wapping, I'm going to have to politely decline your . . . *request* for a raid. I'm sorry, but there it is.'

'But they were clearly trying to kill Benny when they burst into his house. Surely that proves he was on to something,' I said.

'On to *something*, yes. I'm happy with that assumption. But on to what, exactly? Until you can speak to him you have no idea whether it was his tip about the warehouse that got him into trouble or whether he blundered into some other hornets' nest. No, I'm sorry, but you'll have to keep digging.'

'But—' said Lady Hardcastle.

'*Šajkače*, dear lady. All you have is *šajkače*. Bring me maps, plans and incriminating documents. Bring me guns and explosives. If I want hats I can go to Jermyn Street.'

Lady Hardcastle sighed. 'Very well.'

'That's the ticket. Do you have anything else for me?'

'No.'

'Off you pop, then. Keep digging. Bring me gold and I shall summon every man in the Bureau to your aid.'

We all stood to leave.

'Not you, Featherstonhaugh. I want a word about your other operation.'

We left them to obviously more important things.

The cheerful sunshine illuminating Whitehall Court was at odds with our dejected mood as we left the office. As we trudged towards the little blue Austin, Lady Hardcastle turned to me with unexpected suddenness and grabbed my arm.

'Flo!' she said.

'Good grief. What?'

'We need to go shopping.'

'We really don't – we went shopping on Saturday.'

'Then we must do something else. Something fun.'

'Like what?'

'Elevenses at the Ritz.'

'It's only just gone ten,' I said.

'A walk in St James's Park, then. We could feed the ducks, marvel at the pelicans.'

'I do like a pelican.'

'It's one of your more endearing traits. They were a gift from the Russian ambassador in 1664, you know.'

'You tell me that every time. And then I wonder if they're special pelicans or if all great white pelicans can live for more than two hundred and forty years.'

'What fun we have,' she said. 'Shall we go and see them?'

'Will it find Kovač's killer or stop the potential disruption of the Austrian visit?'

'No, but it will stop us moping and give us a chance to get things straight in our heads.'

'All right, then. Shall we take the car?'

'No, let's leave it here – it's not far to walk. We can cut through Downing Street and wave to Mr Asquith as we pass Number Ten.'

And so we did exactly that.

The policeman standing guard at the door to the prime minister's residence tapped the brim of his helmet in salute and called out, 'He's not at home, ladies, but I'll pass on your regards.'

We emerged from the other end of the street, crossed Horse Guards Road, then strolled between the ubiquitous plane trees and across the grass to the path that ran around the perimeter of the park. We were at the very end of the lake by the Swiss-styled Bird Keeper's Cottage, so a turn in either direction would take us past Duck Island. We opted to go left.

With the prospect of a pleasant pelican-filled walk before us, I had thought Lady Hardcastle might be calming down a little, but then she sighed. 'I sometimes wonder why they bother to employ us if they're not going to listen.'

'It does seem a little short-sighted,' I agreed. 'You were spying for Britain when chummy there was still at Sandhurst.'

'Not quite, dear. Valentine's entry in *Who's Who* says he's sixty-one, so that would have made him around thirty-seven when Roddy and I first started our little double act. He was a major, then, training the Egyptian army.'

'He still ought to show a little more respect.'

'He ought. But if he's going to stand in our way, we'll just have to find a way to work round him.'

'Or work harder to persuade him?' I said.

'Or that, yes. But we need to do something, and that right soon. It could be that our Serbian friends are merely smugglers, or perhaps they're engaged in some other economic mischief. Kovač could have been barking up entirely the wrong tree – they may present no threat to the meeting at all.'

'But then why kill him?'

'We're still not absolutely certain that they did. It could have been anyone.'

'Anyone who uses an unusual 9 millimetre pistol,' I reminded her.

'True, but it's not as though he was stabbed to death with a unicorn's horn. Our presumed weapon might not be commonplace, but such a thing isn't unobtainable to people with the right connections.'

'Very well, but let's stick with the idea that it's the Serbians and their hats. We're assuming they also killed Benny's man, so if they're not planning something as serious as assassination, why murder two people?'

Lady Hardcastle stopped and gazed out at the lake as she spoke. 'I think it's the second killing that's muddying the waters for me. Harry has his rumours of an attempt to disrupt the meeting, and says Kovač had heard the same. Kovač came to England to help investigate, but was killed before he could confirm anything. At first glance that appears to be confirmation enough on its own – he got too close to the truth and had to be silenced.' She was distracted briefly by the sight of a swan leading her four fluffy, brownish cygnets across the water. 'But then they tried to kill Benny – a powerful and influential man in the London criminal fraternity. It doesn't entirely scotch the political hypothesis, but it definitely elevates the possibility of it being more mundane criminality. If they're trying to move in and set up shop as smugglers, let's say, then they would want to silence anyone who stood in their way – Kovač, Benny . . . and anyone else who posed a threat.'

'True,' I said. 'We've seen people killed over a few bob, never mind a profitable smuggling business.'

'Indeed. But if the intelligence is accurate and they're here to disrupt the trade talks, then . . . well, what are they up to? It could be anything from stink bombs to actual bombs. And if an angry young Serbian manages to kill the heir presumptive to the Austro-Hungarian Empire, we shall be at war before you can say, "Ooh, look, a pelican."'

'Ooh, look, a pelican.'

'Exactly like that.'

I pointed. 'No, look. Over there. A pelican.'

A great white pelican was standing on the island, stretching its wings.

Two little girls – sisters to judge from their matching coats – stopped when they heard my exclamation and looked towards the island.

'Lily? Evie?' said their guardian. 'What have you seen now?'

'A pelican, Aunt Kristie,' said one of the girls.

'So it is,' said the woman. 'Aren't they lovely. But we can't dawdle, we have things to do.'

The family moved on.

'How enchanting,' said Lady Hardcastle when they had gone. 'Did you know—'

'—that the pelicans were a gift from the Russian ambassador to Charles II in 1664? I did, as a matter of fact. They look well for two-hundred-and-forty-eight-year-old birds, don't they?'

'We could make a fortune as a music hall act, you know.'

'We'd need better material than that.'

'Nonsense. Every comedian knows that endless repetition makes something funny. How do you think catchphrases work?

And it wouldn't be our whole act. You could throw knives at me while I play the piano.'

'The act might last more than one performance if I throw knives at a target, narrowly missing you while you play the piano,' I said.

'There, you see? It's all coming together nicely. We shall contact the management at the Empire in Bristol as soon as we get home.'

'Until then, though? What next?'

'First, an afternoon of rest and recuperation. Perhaps we should find a matinee performance in the West End.'

'Not on a Monday. Matinees tend to be Wednesdays and Saturdays.'

'A trip to the British Museum, then?' said Lady Hardcastle. 'It's on our way back to the flat.'

'More or less. If we go the long way round. But after that?'

'We need to drop in on Harry at home – try to persuade him to back us up.'

'I'm sure he'll be willing to help.'

'Willing, yes – for all his many terrible faults, he's a loyal brother. But I wonder if he'll be able. Valentine is a stubborn chap, and there's a whole world of internal politics at the Basement to which we are not privy.'

'So if we can't get his support?'

'Then we get evidence, tiny one. We mount our own surveillance operation and gather proof that the Serbs are up to no good – then Valentine has to act, internal politics or not.'

'Museum, Harry, surveillance,' I said. 'That's a plan.'

Our walk around the park was punctuated at intervals with pauses where we would sit on a park bench and bask in the July sunshine while watching the wildlife and the passing humans with equal fascination. By the time we had completed a circuit of the lake, it was almost lunchtime.

'What now?' I said as we crossed Horse Guards Road on our way back to Whitehall. 'Home for lunch before the British Museum?'

Lady Hardcastle shook her head. 'Do you really want to prepare lunch on a day like today?'

'Not in the least. I thought with your newfound fondness for life in the kitchen that you might want to make us something.'

'You do make me laugh, dear. How about the Metropole?'

'Oh, I do enjoy it there. Yes, please.'

And so we strolled to the elegantly decadent hotel on the corner of Whitehall Place and asked ever so politely for a table for two.

A waiter led us to a corner table with an excellent view of the dining room and settled us in our seats without even a hint of sneering condescension. Evidently the Metropole eschewed Parisian training in favour of treating diners with courtesy and kindness. I hoped it would catch on. He left us with menus and glided away.

'This will do very nicely,' said Lady Hardcastle. 'Backs to the wall and a good view of the two exits – I couldn't have chosen better myself.' She nodded towards a nearby table. 'And it provides ample opportunities for discreetly observing senior government officials and civil servants in the wild.'

Sure enough, there were two cabinet ministers, two members of the shadow cabinet, and at least three Permanent Secretaries of State, deep in discussion.

'I wonder what they're up to,' I said.

'Planning the golf club summer ball, I should imagine. Open deals are done in the House of Commons dining room, secret deals in locked rooms in private members' clubs. Social events are planned at the local restaurant over a bottle or two of claret and a good cigar.'

'Pity. We could have sold their secrets to a foreign power. Or the newspapers.'

'Sadly, we shall have to seek our fortunes elsewhere for now.'

Luncheon was delicious, and from the snippets of conversation that drifted over from the politicians' table, they were, indeed, planning a social event. So much for intrigue.

Full, and in a much more optimistic frame of mind, we retrieved the Austin from Whitehall Court and drove straight to Harry's house on Bedford Square. We judged that he would still be at work, so we left the car there and walked round the corner to Great Russell Street.

The British Museum was as intriguing as ever, though I was struck halfway round, as I so often was, by an attack of museum melancholy. Obviously there was the nagging feeling I always got that many of the artefacts had been looted from their homelands, and properly belonged to other people, but that wasn't the sort of thing you could say out loud without being accused of treason.

But that wasn't what made me properly sad.

The melancholy came from seeing useful things locked away. Things created for a purpose – a cup to be drunk from, a knife to prepare food, a vase to hold flowers, an instrument to make music – sealed for all time in glass-topped tombs, denied the touch of a human hand, condemned to live out the rest of their existence as nothing but reminders of how they were once essential parts of their owners' lives.

It was still too early to see Harry by the time we had exhausted all the entertainment possibilities the museum had to offer, so we retired to a nearby tea room for a reviving pot of tea. And buttered buns. It seemed rude not to at least try them.

With our energies replenished, we set off round the corner to Harry and Lavinia's house, and arrived at Bedford Square just as Harry strode in from the other side.

'What ho, sis,' he said. 'I saw the car and thought you must already be here.'

'We've been to the museum,' said Lady Hardcastle.

'You should have invited Jake.'

'We needed to talk, dear. To contemplate the mysteries of departmental bureaucracy. Poor Lavinia would have been bored senseless.'

'And now you wish to see me?'

'If it's convenient. We need an ally at the Basement.'

'Of course, but wouldn't you rather come to dinner? Helen is out visiting friends so we'd be delighted to have company.'

'If you're sure Lavinia won't mind, that would be delightful.'

'She secretly loves work talk. Eight?'

'Eight it is.'

'See you then. Toodle-oo.'

Harry let himself in, and we took the Austin back to Southampton Street.

At eight on the dot, and properly dressed for dinner, we presented ourselves at Maison Featherstonhaugh. Weatherby took our hats once more and led us through to the drawing room.

'Hello, you two,' said Lady Lavinia from her customary seat at the piano. 'I'm afraid you've missed Addie.'

'Hours ago, I should imagine,' said Lady Hardcastle. 'Hello, dear.'

Harry waved his Scotch and soda. 'What ho, sis. Evening, Strongarm.'

Lady Hardcastle sat down while I went to the drinks cabinet. It amused Herself to bully her brother into making us drinks, but we needed his help so I thought it might be more profitable to keep him on our side. I set about mixing two gin and tonics.

Lady Lavinia stopped playing. 'I'm so sorry, Emily darling. I always forget what a dab hand you are at the old Joanna – would you like a turn?'

'Later perhaps, dear. For now, I should like a word with the master of the house.'

The Mozart resumed. 'Only in his private daydreams.'

'One has to pander to their egos – they're fragile creatures.'

'I say. Fragile and powerless, I may be,' said Harry, 'but my hearing is perfect.'

'My apologies, dear,' said Lady Hardcastle. 'Oh, thank you.'

This last was in response to my handing her a drink. I sat down beside her.

Harry raised his glass. 'Your good health.'

Lady Hardcastle raised hers. 'Long life and happiness, may the sun be always at your back, may the road rise to meet you, and Thomas's Soap – the Bristol soap for Bristol folk.'

'Hurrying the clock to Jelloid time,' I said. They looked blankly at me. 'What? I thought we were doing advertising slogans.'

'Ha!' said Harry. 'So what can I do for you both?'

'How much influence do you have over Valentine?' asked Lady Hardcastle.

'None whatsoever, sis. To give him his due, he does at least listen to me when it's obvious I know more than he does about a given subject – he's happy to take advantage of experience gained by my years in the Foreign Office. But once he has all the information he thinks he needs, he'll make a decision and no power on Earth will make him change his mind.'

'But he doesn't have all the information,' I said. 'The purpose of raiding the warehouse would be to gather more information.'

'For the moment, though, Strongarm old thing, he has all the information he *thinks* he needs. I'm completely convinced by your assessment and if I were sitting behind his desk I'd summon my forces – or my Special Branch cast-offs, at least – and storm the citadel. We would swoop in like avenging whatnots, arresting Serbians and gathering evidence as we flushed the evil-doers from their riverside lair.'

Lady Hardcastle took a sip of her drink. 'That's most comforting, and I'm grateful for your familial loyalty—'

'It's not mere loyalty, sis. I said I was convinced, and I meant it.'

'Thank you, dear. But where does that leave us?'

'Up Deptford Creek without a paddle, I'm afraid. *You* know there's something going on in Bermondsey, *I* know there's something going on in Bermondsey, and we *both* know something needs to be done about it. But our knowing isn't the same as our being able to prove it to Valentine. And until you can bring him fresh information, preferably in the form of irrefutable proof, he won't budge. His mind is made up.'

Lady Lavinia carried on playing, but turned to look over her shoulder at Harry. 'Can't you do something to help them get their irrefutable proof, darling?'

'Would that I could, lambkin—'

The playing stopped. 'Lambkin?'

'I'm trying it out.'

'Well don't.'

'But Shakespeare used it.'

'I'm not married to Shakespeare.'

'Right you are. But lambkins notwithstanding, I'm up to my collar stud in my own investigation. You remember I mentioned Autumn Wind the other day?'

'I do,' said Lady Lavinia, returning to her Mozart. 'I persuaded you that such talk was not for my delicate lugholes.'

'Sometimes I think life would be much simpler if we simply had you sign the Official Secrets Act – then I wouldn't have to make such heroic efforts to be discreet.'

'I think we can trust her, dear,' said Lady Hardcastle. 'Lady Lavinia, do you solemnly swear, affirm, cross your heart, et cetera, blah, blah, secrets, blah, blah, even unto death?'

Lady Lavinia laughed. 'Absolutely.'

'There you are, dear, she's one of us now. What are Autumn Wind up to now?'

Harry looked at his drink for a few moments. 'We believe they're trying to hasten the arrival of all-out war. I mean, war's on the cards anyway, but they see profit in it and they'd like it to happen sooner rather than later.'

Lady Lavinia stopped playing again. 'I'm sorry, darling, but you can't say something like that and then not tell me more. What on earth . . . ?'

The dinner gong sounded in the hall.

'You'll have to explain everything,' she continued. 'Over dinner.'

◆　◆　◆

Lady Lavinia waited patiently for dinner to be served and for the servants to withdraw before turning to Harry, fork menacingly in hand, and saying, 'Come on then, Secret Service Man – tell me about this Autumn Wind and their plans for war.'

'I think Em and Flo know more about them than I do,' said Harry. 'I've been going from their heavily censored reports.'

'Censored?' said Lady Hardcastle. 'What on earth is the value of that?'

'Couldn't say, old thing. When I finally managed to get the files from Section W at the Foreign Office, everything was there – or seemed to be, at least – but great chunks of it had been blotted out with fulsome dabs of India ink. I know . . . I *think* I know what they're up to now, but I know little of their history or what they were up to in Bengal at the turn of the century.'

'How very odd. Not to say slightly suspicious. Very well, we shall assume that you have the requisite authority to know. As for you, Lavinia dear . . . you're infinitely more trustworthy than my brother, but do please say you understand the need for discretion.'

'Of course, darling,' said Lady Lavinia. 'Though if you'd prefer not to say . . .'

'No, no, I'm happy to tell you.' Lady Hardcastle paused for a moment to marshal her thoughts. 'It was 1903 and we had begun making plans to return home. We'd been away for more than seven years by this point—'

'We spent two of those years thinking they were dead,' interrupted Harry.

'Well, quite. So it was high time we returned home. But as we were making the arrangements, we were contacted by one Colonel Richard "Dickie" Mussellwhite – a lovely chap. He started out in military intelligence but by the time we met him he was running Section W for the Foreign Office. Is he still there?'

'Died in '08, I'm afraid.'

'Oh, that's a shame. He wasn't terribly old.'

'Seventy-five.'

'Good heavens. So he was seventy when we met him? He certainly didn't look it. Well I never. Anyway, he knew of our work and wanted us to take charge of an important matter before we sailed home. There had been a series of apparently unconnected events, you see. Scandals, sabotage – eventually a kidnapping and murder.'

'All in north-east India?' asked Lady Lavinia.

'Yes, dear. It had begun when the prominent owner of a tea plantation was publicly accused of having improper relations with his houseboy. His reputation was destroyed and his business backers abandoned him, leaving him no option but to sell his plantation at a loss and return to England in disgrace.'

'Heavens.'

I nodded. 'Next came a violent attack on a party of bearers bringing a large shipment of tea down from a hill station to the port at Calcutta. Ten men were killed and the entire shipment stolen, with just one badly wounded survivor left behind to tell the tale.'

'I do remember that one,' said Harry. 'Caused quite a stink.'

'Indeed,' said Lady Hardcastle. 'In the following weeks, another tea trader was accused of embezzlement, and yet another of cheating at cards. Meanwhile there were two further robberies, and a clipper was badly damaged by fire while at anchor in the harbour.'

I took over. 'Suspicions were growing that these events were linked somehow, but the local police were at something of a loss. It was when the wife of another plantation owner was kidnapped and murdered that someone finally thought to ask Section W if they knew anything about it. And they did – it all appeared to be the work of a secret organization known as Autumn Wind.'

'All of this is missing from the file,' said Harry. 'I only know about the tea shipment ambush and the damage to the clipper because both were in the papers.'

'Most peculiar,' said Lady Hardcastle. 'I can understand the need to play the scandals down, of course. They were all fabricated – not a grain of truth in any of them – so no one wanted false gossip spread too widely. But to remove it from our internal reports, too? Fishy. Decidedly fishy. But anyway, it fell to us to investigate.'

'Why you, though, darling?' asked Lady Lavinia. 'I mean, I know you're the very best – Harry never stops telling me – but surely there were other suitable officers in the region. You were trying to get home.'

'Ah, well, to explain that, one has to know a little about the history of Autumn Wind. It began life innocently enough in 1666, shortly after the Great Fire of London. A group of London merchants would meet regularly in a coffee house to exchange news and gossip as they rebuilt their businesses after the conflagration. Eventually, they formed themselves into a society to protect their interests and named themselves after the wind that had fanned the flames of the Great Fire. In a way, the catastrophe had served them well, giving them all the opportunity for a fresh start, so they commemorated the event by calling themselves Autumn Wind. They enjoyed a brief period of popularity among the trading classes, but slowly their public profile diminished – it seemed everyone simply lost interest. By the mid-eighteenth century it was believed that the society must surely have been disbanded.'

'I've certainly never heard of them,' said Lady Lavinia, 'and I was fascinated by the seventeenth century when I was at school. One would have thought the name would have come up.'

'That was deliberate, I think – making them disappear from the public mind, I mean. Though they didn't manage it entirely, of course. One can never completely eradicate something like that. The idea of the society lingered in some quarters, and Autumn Wind became a bogeyman, someone people could blame for whatever ills had befallen them. When something rum was afoot it was because "they" were up to something. Unexplained shady business dealings, political shenanigans, and public scandals were often blamed on "the Wind". One story even noted how much they had profited from the fire in 1666 and hinted that they had been responsible for it, but most thought it all a myth. Most people, apparently, except those in a tiny room hidden away in Whitehall who had been keeping a close eye on the activities of suspected Autumn Wind members. Section W didn't think they were a myth at all. They'd been tracking the society for years after they went underground and were reasonably sure they were behind all the tea-related unpleasantness.'

'But I still don't see—'

'We were the safe bet,' I said. 'Like most societies, secret or otherwise, which dealt in power and influence, Autumn Wind was a strictly all-male affair. Section W's problem had always been that it didn't know who to trust – anyone with wealth or connections could be a member. But we couldn't be. We didn't have the right . . . credentials.'

'And so you investigated the scandals and brought the whole sinister cabal down?' said Lady Lavinia.

'Hardly,' said Lady Hardcastle. 'We conclusively established their involvement, certainly, and one or two prominent men became a great deal less prominent. But there was . . . pressure. We never really got to the heart of it all, and as soon as a few sacrificial lambs had publicly paid penance we were loaded on to a ship bound for home.'

'So it's still active, then, this Autumn Wind?'

'That's where I come in,' said Harry. 'It's all whispers and suspicions, but the SSB believes they're at it again. This time, instead of trying to get rich by taking control of the tea trade, they seem to be positioning themselves to make a fortune from war.'

'How does one make money from war, darling? Surely it's all expense and national debt, and inventing income tax to pay for it all?'

'That's true if you're a government, but if you own the mines and the steel mills, or if you manufacture the arms and equipment, you can make a metaphorical killing in business while men and boys are doing the literal killing and dying at the front. There'll be a war, and it will be the first war to be fought as much in the factories as on the battlefields. There is, I'm appalled to say, profit in war, and we strongly believe Autumn Wind is working to bring it about sooner rather than later.'

'But how?'

'That, my darling, is what I'm trying to find out.'

Chapter Ten

We had asked Harry for one favour before we set off to find a taxi to take us home. We planned to spend as much of Tuesday as possible observing the comings and goings at the disused warehouse in Bermondsey, and we needed him to find us a safe place from which to do that.

'Preferably elevated,' Lady Hardcastle had said. 'People never look up.' She pointed to a sketch plan she had drawn on a piece of Lady Lavinia's writing paper. 'We need sight of that main door, there, and if we had a decent view down both Pottery Street and Marigold Street, that would be super. An upstairs window in this building here would suit us perfectly.'

Harry had promised to see what he could do as soon as he got to the office the next morning, and said he would telephone the moment he had any news.

And so we waited.

I exercised in Fitzroy Square as usual, to the evident irritation of Indian Clubs Man, who packed up and left as soon as I arrived. From there I went to a nearby bakery and then to a newsagent's. Armed with a fresh loaf and a couple of morning newspapers, I returned to the flat.

Lady Hardcastle was sitting in the kitchen when I arrived, having made her own starter breakfast of coffee and toast.

'Good morning,' I said as I put my purchases on the kitchen table. 'Are you all right?'

She put down her toast. 'Nightmares.'

'I'm so sorry. Is there anything I can do?'

'No, dear – one has to forbear.'

'You never talk about it.'

'I know I should . . . but . . . well, I feel so foolish. It's not as though I'm the only person ever to get shot in the line of duty. I'm sure things will get back to normal soon.'

'I hope so. But if you change your mind . . .'

'Thank you, dear.'

'Do I have time to get washed and dressed before breakfast?'

She laughed. 'I've made a rod for my own back there, haven't I? I knew I should never have offered to cook on Sunday morning.'

'There's no need if you don't want to. I just thought you were enjoying it.'

'To be honest, I have rather enjoyed helping. You know what I'm like when things go quiet while we're working – all that pent-up nervous energy has to go somewhere. Doing something useful with it has been rather satisfying.'

'I'll certainly never stop you, but I'm willing to take over if you prefer. Whatever happens, though, I do need to get changed.'

'You go and beautify yourself, dear. I'll make a start on the drudgery.'

Breakfast was pleasantly companionable, interrupted only briefly by a commotion in Richardson's Mews below. For reasons unknown, someone had driven a motor car down the little alley that led to the mews from Warren Street, and had found himself stuck. As he noisily and ineptly tried to manoeuvre himself back out again, his car backfired, alarming the milkman's horse. While the milkman tried to calm the startled beast and save his cart, a resident came out of his front door and remonstrated with the motorist. A lady's maid in a house on Fitzroy Square leaned out of an upstairs window to tell everyone to quieten down because her mistress was under the weather. The motorist told her what her mistress could do with herself and the mews resident punched him in the chops, having first given stern advice on how properly to speak to a lady.

Order was restored when the local beat bobby arrived. He kept his voice admirably calm so we were unable to make out what he said, but the effect was almost magical. The resident retreated to his home to resume his breakfast, while the motorist managed to find reverse gear and gingerly backed out on to Warren Street. The maid closed the window. Even the horse seemed to bow to the policeman's quiet authority and resumed its patient examination of the cobbles.

We couldn't leave the flat – we were awaiting Harry's call. There was no point in starting anything we couldn't drop at once – his call could come at any time. And so we sat in the drawing room with a newspaper each, dressed as Mrs Brown and Mrs Jones.

I had the *Daily Mirror*. 'I see *Fanny's First Play* is on at the Kingsway.'

Lady Hardcastle laughed. 'Is it? Is it, indeed?'

'It is. I wonder—'

The telephone rang and I was out of my chair without finishing my thought.

'Ahoy?' I said.

'Strongarm?'

'None other.'

'Why did you—? Never mind. I have good news. The manager of the offices in whose doorway you loitered on Saturday night has agreed to let you have the use of an empty room at the corner of the building. It's on the second floor and has windows on Pottery Street and Marigold Street as requested.'

'You, sir, are an absolute marvel, no matter what they say.'

Harry laughed. 'Do I wish to know what they say?'

'It would be best to remain blissfully ignorant, I think. Instead, I shall tell Herself the good news and we'll set off for the other side of Tower Bridge at once.'

'Ask for Bill Hughes. Mention my name.'

'Thank you, Mr Feather-stone-huff – your place in Heaven is assured.'

'If only that were all there was to it. But I await your report with interest. Good luck, Strongarm.'

I replaced the earpiece.

'Do we have an eyrie?' asked Lady Hardcastle, putting down her copy of *The Times*.

'A vantage spot so perfect it could have been built especially for us.'

'Then we must away. I made sandwiches while you were getting dressed, but we shall have to prevail upon the building's manager—'

'Bill Hughes.'

'Strong name. Welsh?'

'Alas, Harry neglected to include that level of biographical detail. I was vouchsafed his name and position in the company hierarchy, but nothing else.'

'No matter. We shall charm Mr Hughes into bringing us tea, but we'll have our own rations, at least.'

'Lavatories weren't mentioned, either.'

'We'll manage. Are you ready?'

'As I'll ever be.'

Everything was falling into place. Even the Austin cooperated, starting first time.

Mr Hughes was an absolute poppet, and set us up with chairs and a table in the storeroom on the corner of the second floor of the office building he managed on behalf of Messrs Prevost, Mildred and Radden, Shipping Agents and Hauliers. Tea was supplied, as were instructions on how to find the lavatory.

We took an open window each and watched the streets below. The field glasses, should they be needed, were on the table along with the teapot, cups, a jug of milk, and the greaseproof paper packages holding our sandwiches.

'I think Mr Hughes fancies you,' I said.

Lady Hardcastle *pff*d. 'He fancies his chances of some sort of medal for helping the SSB, more like. Anyway, why me? Why not you?'

'I am professionally unnoticeable – it's part of a maid's training. And I'm not the one he was fawning over.'

'You are silly – he was just being polite. Though if he was sniffing around for honours, we ought to let him know there's a queue. You need to be knighted before even the most obliging shipping agent gets an Order of Merit.'

'Oh, wouldn't that be marvellous? I'd outrank you.'

She inclined her head. 'That would be hilarious, my lady. It's such a pity there are so few honours available to women.'

'Perhaps we should have the vote first. I mean—' I stopped talking and grabbed the field glasses. 'Look out. Movement.'

I had spotted one of the hats opening the warehouse door. He checked his surroundings thoroughly to make sure he was unobserved but, as predicted, he did not look up. He stepped out on to Marigold Street and walked north towards the wharves.

Lady Hardcastle made a note. 'That's one. What shall we call him?'

'Hat Number One?'

'How shall we distinguish him from the other hats?'

'He has a scar on his left cheek.'

'Then he is Scar Hat. It's' – she checked her watch – 'five minutes to eleven.' She noted the time.

'I wonder where he's off to.'

'He will pay a visit to his tailor to replace those ghastly trousers, then meet a young girl in a tea room where they will discuss their plans for a romantic dinner, and perhaps a trip to see *Fanny's First Play.*'

'Does she like George Bernard Shaw?'

'Everyone likes George Bernard Shaw. But she is particularly fond of satirical plays so it doesn't matter who wrote it. But just like Mr Shaw, she is weary of drawing room comedies, and despairing of theatre critics. It is likely to become her favourite play.'

I lifted the glasses again. 'There's another.'

A second hat left the warehouse, following the same, almost professional security routine as his comrade. When he was sure he wasn't being watched, he set off westward along Pottery Street towards Southwark.

'Less than a minute apart,' said Lady Hardcastle, making another note. 'Methinks they are decamping for a day of conspiracy and wickedness, and not trysts with rebellious young ladies at all. Name?'

'Limping Hat – he favours his left leg.'

Within five minutes, three more hats left the warehouse one by one, with the last carefully locking the door behind him.

'Key-Holder Hat,' I said as he walked off up Marigold Street. 'Do you think that's it? Five of them?'

'I'd not like to say for certain. We thought there were only four the other night, and yet there goes a fifth.'

'But do we think they've all gone?'

'I wondered that last time – you were the one who suggested that the last man out was just being friendly by locking the door behind him to save the others getting up. I think we should give it a few minutes before we do anything rash.'

We waited another half an hour.

I was just about to suggest we break in and have a look round, when the door opened and yet another man came out. He relocked the door and took the road to the wharves. It was likely that all the men were all heading for the same location, and I couldn't help but admire their efforts to take different routes to get there, even if it was only two different routes among six men.

'How about now?' I said.

'Unless they have an actual army in there, I think we're probably safe in assuming the warehouse is finally empty. Shall we break in?'

'I thought you'd never ask.'

With our windows open, the office storeroom had been well ventilated and comparatively cool. Out on the street it was a different story, and the heat came as something of a surprise. It was still a long way from the tropical temperatures we had enjoyed early in our careers (I had enjoyed them, at least – Lady Hardcastle had complained quite a lot) but it was a definite contrast to the office.

The streets were as busy as ever, with carts, wagons and motor vehicles coming and going, and pedestrians everywhere. Dockers, sailors, messengers, managers, clerks, loafers and children moved about the streets with varying levels of speed and urgency according to their purpose.

Here in the heart of the warehouses and wharves there were few women about, but our emergence from the shipping agents' offices lent us some much needed invisibility – just a couple of bookkeepers out for a lunchtime stroll, perhaps.

We crossed the road to the locked warehouse door and Lady Hardcastle shielded me from view while I picked the lock.

We were inside in less than thirty seconds. I must have been getting slow.

I locked us in and we took our first look round. It was, as expected, a huge, empty warehouse. The main ground-floor room seemed to stretch forever – a vast space, its high ceiling supported at intervals by iron pillars. It was dirty and dusty, with old, broken packing cases and barrels stacked haphazardly against the walls. A pile of hessian sacking seemed, from the abundance of droppings, to be home to a colony of rats. As always, I wondered what they could possibly find to eat in an abandoned building, but 'Resourceful chap, Johnny Rat' as Sir Hector Farley-Stroud would probably have said.

There was an old table in one corner, surrounded by an assortment of obviously scavenged chairs. They appeared to have an oil stove and a kettle, but I couldn't see a source of fresh water, though there must have been one somewhere. The original occupants had to have some way of keeping the place clean.

At the same end of the room were six thin mattresses, with blankets and pillows.

Newspaper had been pasted on the lower windows, presumably for privacy, so the light, such as it was, had to struggle in through the upper ones.

It was damp, gloomy and, I suddenly realized, smelly. Not an unpleasant smell – if you discounted the rats – but a familiar smell somewhere between burnt caramel and bananas. A dangerous smell.

'There's dynamite here,' I said.

'I was thinking the same thing. But where?'

I looked around. A section of the space was hidden from view behind stacks of packing crates forming a small room. There was a blanket draped over a broom handle to form a door. We approached cautiously.

I lifted the blanket and Lady Hardcastle peered inside.

She swore colourfully and inventively. 'That'll be why we can smell explosives, then.'

I followed her into the improvised room and looked around. There were ammunition cases and small wooden boxes on the floor. A tall workbench stood against the back wall of the room, partially obstructing a door. Lined up on the bench were half a dozen sets of dynamite, each comprising seven sticks carefully taped together in neat hexagonal bundles. Beside them were two clocks and two batteries, already wired together, along with several coils of wire and a box of detonators, all awaiting the completion of what would eventually form at least two bombs with timers, and possibly more with conventional fuses. On another table were six automatic pistols and several boxes of ammunition. Some of it was 9 mm and presumably for the pistols, while some looked more like rifle rounds to my untrained eye. I pointed it out to Lady Hardcastle.

'Yes, I saw,' she said. 'The pistols are the FN 1910, exactly as Harry and I thought. Those other rounds, though . . . I'm not so sure.' She picked up one of the boxes. '7.62 by 54 millimetre. Russian, too.' She indicated the Cyrillic writing on the box. 'A Mosin-Nagant, perhaps? I think that takes this sort of round.'

'I've heard of the rifle,' I said, 'but you know me and guns – I don't remember all the technical details. I'll have to take your word for it.'

'Well, whatever it is, there's no sign of it, so they're not keeping it here.'

'I can't imagine what they'd need it for, to be honest. They've enough explosives here to kill scores of people. And with those timing whatnots they needn't be anywhere near the place when it happens – they just have to place the bombs and get as far away as possible.'

'Indeed. And they'll have no more than an hour. Look at the way those two timers are set up.'

The faces of the two clocks had been drilled at the twelve o'clock position and a pin inserted in the hole. There was a wire attached to the pin and another on the minute hand. When the hand touched the pin, the firing circuit would close. *Boom*. As Lady Hardcastle had noted, it could give someone anywhere between a minute and almost an hour to get away.

Lady Hardcastle picked up a discarded scrap of waxed paper from the floor and presented the torn edge to a large piece of wrapping on the bench. The letters 'DY' on the scrap perfectly fitted the letters 'NAMITE' on the remnants of the explosives packaging.

She put the smaller scrap in her pocket. 'I'd say we've enough evidence to get Valentine to seek a warrant and raid this place now.'

'Preferably with the Hats still in it,' I agreed.

I was about to say more, but Lady Hardcastle held up her hand for silence. She cocked her head to listen.

'They're back,' she murmured. 'This door?' She pointed to the door behind the workbench.

'Tight squeeze,' I murmured back, indicating the small gap between the bench and the door frame.

She shrugged. 'It's that or get caught.'

I tried the handle and, of course, found the door locked.

There was someone in the main room now, but from the footsteps and absence of conversation, it seemed he was alone. I could hear him pottering about as my picklocks struggled with the recalcitrant lock. It was obvious that the door hadn't been unlocked for a while, but this, I thought, might be good news. If the door had been locked and unused for the entirety of the Hats' tenancy, they wouldn't trouble to check whatever room lay beyond. We might be stuck in there for a while, but no one would bother us.

The lock resisted valiantly, but eventually succumbed. There was an alarmingly loud click as the bolt withdrew and we both froze, but the Hat seemed oblivious. Perhaps he couldn't hear us over his tuneless whistling and the clumping of his boots as he went about his business, or perhaps the crates and blankets rendered the bomb-making area soundproof. Whatever it was, he didn't seem to be coming our way, so I slowly twisted the doorknob.

Or I tried to, at least.

It wouldn't budge.

Lady Hardcastle made helpful hurry-up gestures, and I gave her a what-do-you-think-I'm-doing look.

After a few more moments of trying, the latch struggled free with another dismayingly loud grind and clonk.

We froze again, but still there was no reaction from our friend in the main room.

I pushed the door but it held fast. I pushed harder, and with the grating of wood on wood and the low protests of rusted hinges, it began to open.

The whistling stopped and we held our breath.

I turned towards the blanket door and slipped my left hand inside my right sleeve to rest on the handle of my trusty knife, but there were no clumping footsteps. After an agonizingly long moment, the whistling resumed.

The door slowly yielded to our cautious pushing and we eventually opened it enough to allow us to enter whatever room lay beyond. As long as we could squeeze through the tiny gap.

I went first, being the smaller, and found myself in a room which, to judge from the dilapidated desk and rickety chair, had once been used as an office. More important than its decrepit furniture, though, was the window, which gave an unappealing view of the wall of the building next door. It admitted only a dim light and added little cheer to the dreary room, but it would open – at least I hoped it would open – to allow us to leave the warehouse and slip out along the litter-strewn alleyway between the two buildings.

I turned to find out what had happened to Lady Hardcastle. She was stuck.

I grinned.

She glared, and gestured for help.

I smiled and shrugged.

She gestured again, this time more urgently.

I crossed silently to her and leaned close to her ear. 'Sit on the edge of the bench and swivel in – that way only your calves have to clear the gap.'

She snorted impatiently, and gestured towards her hips, which were jammed in the space between the workbench and the door frame. 'Obviously. But how do you propose I get myself free to do that?'

I grinned again. 'Well, I suppose I might be able to push you out.'

'Can't you pull me in?'

'I'm strong, but not that strong.'

Her glare was positively menacing. 'Then you'd better push me, hadn't you.'

'Brace yourself. We don't want you falling over and giving the game away. One . . . two . . . three . . .'

I gave her a hefty shove and she popped out of the narrow gap. With her hips no longer wedged, she was free to hoist herself up and swing her legs into the office.

As quickly but quietly as I could, I shut the door behind her.

'Does that window open?' she murmured.

'I haven't had a chance to check yet,' I said. 'I've been helping you get into the room.'

'I should be more effusive in my thanks if you hadn't been so insufferably smug about it.'

'Sooner or later all those little jibes about my size were bound to come back to bite you. It would appear there are some advantages to being a "tiny servant" after all.'

She harrumphed and tried the window. The latches were stiff but to my surprise it opened easily once they were undone.

I placed my hands on either side of her hips and compared the measurement with the open window.

'You should make it,' I said, 'but I think you should go first, in case you need a little push.'

'I'm going to start putting your favourite things on high shelves and hiding the stool.'

By standing on the rickety chair, she was able to get herself on to the windowsill and through the opening. She dropped gracefully to the ground and dusted off her skirt. I followed and waited for her to close the window behind us.

The alleyway was blocked to the south by a teetering pile of rubbish, but the way north, towards the river, was clear.

We emerged unnoticed on to the busy Bermondsey Wall, and set off westwards, back to Tower Bridge and our little Austin on the other side of the river.

◆ ◆ ◆

It was nearly two o'clock by the time we arrived at the Basement, seeking an audience with Colonel Valentine. Sadly, we found only Harry. He gave us the frustrating news that Valentine was at the Ministry of War all afternoon and couldn't be contacted, but he was kind enough to listen to our account of our morning's work. He agreed that Valentine would be foolish to deny our request for a raid now, and promised to speak up on our behalf.

'That's very kind of you, dear,' said Lady Hardcastle. 'Thank you.'

'I live to serve, sis, you know that. Is there anything else I can help you with?'

'No, that will be sufficient, thank you. Unless you have any ideas for how we might amuse ourselves until tomorrow morning, of course.'

'I'd invite you for dinner, but I'm afraid my presence is required at one of Jake's charity functions. I don't suppose you'd enjoy an evening at the London home of Lady Henrietta Galston?'

'Lady Henrietta . . . that name rings a bell. Tall woman with an inexplicable fondness for yappy dogs?'

'The very same.'

'In that case, I think we shall pass. I'm not sure she likes me very much – there was an incident with a Pomeranian at a garden party a few years ago.'

'Probably best you don't come, then. Long memories, Pomeranians.'

'Quite. Is Helen going with you?'

'Titmouse? No, she's at a loose end as far as I know.'

'Then we shall invite her out to dinner. May I use your telephone?'

◆ ◆ ◆

We picked Helen up in a motor taxi at eight o'clock that evening and made our way together to a hotel in Mayfair that Harry had recommended.

The hotel was unassuming from the outside, but rather grand within. The *maître d'hôtel* took our coats and we were seated in the spacious and airy dining room by an actual French waiter who was more attentive and polite than any of his English counterparts had been. He probably wasn't from Paris.

Our table was near the stage, which, though set with chairs and music stands, was empty of musicians.

'Strange not to have a small ensemble belting out the overture to *The Merry Widow*,' I said.

Lady Hardcastle made a face. 'A blessed relief if you ask me. You know how I feel about Lehár.'

'What's wrong with Lehár?' asked Helen with a laugh.

'He writes dreadful, sentimental nonsense,' said Lady Hardcastle.

'He speaks very highly of you,' I said.

Helen pointed to the drum set at the other end of the stage. 'Does *The Merry Widow* feature much in the way of percussion?'

I looked over and saw that not only was there a bass drum, side drum, cymbals, and a bewildering assortment of other things to be struck with sticks, but a double bass with a familiar scratch on its shoulder.

'Isn't that—?' I began, but events overtook me.

A door next to us opened and a group of men and women in evening dress filed in, some of them carrying instruments. At the back of the line were the familiar figures of our old friends Ivor 'Skins' Maloney and Bartholomew 'Barty' Dunn. Neither of them noticed us, and they took up their positions with the band.

When everyone was settled and apparently ready to play, the side door opened again, and out stepped a woman in a beautiful white gown. There was a ripple of applause from the other side of the room as she made her way to the stage and took up her position in front of the band.

'Good evening,' she said, in a Glaswegian accent. Her voice was unforced, but carried easily to the back of the room. 'We are the Rip-Roaring Revellers, and this is "Melody in Motion".'

With a syncopated flourish from Skins on the side drum, they were off. The music was lively ragtime, and the singer's voice somehow managed to be both powerful and delicate. They were going to be a wonderful accompaniment to our meal.

Helen was clearly impressed. 'I say, they're rather jolly, aren't they? Have you heard them before?'

'Not this specific band,' I said, 'but we know the rhythm section.'

'The what?'

'Bass and drums,' said Lady Hardcastle. 'We've been friends since we first moved to Littleton Cotterell in 1908. They were involved in our very first case as detectives.'

'I say. How glamorous. Murder and musicians. It rather puts my humble efforts in the shade.'

'Nonsense, dear. I can think of few things more glamorous than setting up one's own photographic business from scratch. You shouldn't be so modest.'

'Oh, it's mostly just sales and bookkeeping. Half the time I might just as well be running a milliner's or a greengrocer's.'

'Surely you still take photographs,' I said.

Helen nodded. 'Portraiture, mainly. Though I do have one or two personal projects on the go. I'm off to somewhere in Kent tomorrow to get some snaps.'

'What's in Kent?'

'Orchards and hop fields, as far as I can make out, but I'm interested in a disused quarry. I had this idea of trying to capture the juxtaposition of the solidity and permanence of rock with man's capacity for destruction. Formations formed millions of years ago that withstood everything Nature could throw at them, until men came along with their pickaxes and their explosives, and smashed it all to pieces in search of building materials.'

Lady Hardcastle was intrigued. 'This is part of a project, you say?'

'I'm hoping to mount an exhibition in Brighton, yes. The working title is "Man the Destroyer of Worlds", but I'll come up with something better before we open.'

'You must tell us when,' I said. 'I'd love to see your work.'

'Me, too,' said Lady Hardcastle. 'Ah, *bonsoir, monsieur.*'

She said this last to the waiter who had materialized beside her. She charmed him with a brief conversation in French and he took our orders with friendly enthusiasm, steering us away from a few dishes he thought weren't up to standard and making suggestions for accompaniments.

◆ ◆ ◆

During the lull between our main courses and puddings, when Lady Hardcastle had ordered yet another bottle of champagne, the singer announced that the band was going to take a break, but assured us that they'd be back to keep us entertained in just a short while.

Most of the musicians filed off stage and out through the door, but Skins, Dunn and the singer stayed behind, chatting, while Skins made unfathomable adjustments to one of his drums. It had been a few months since we had seen the boys and I'd had no idea they were in a new band, so I couldn't let them get away without saying hello.

I excused myself and went over to them. 'Hello, you two.'

Skins beamed. 'Florence Armstrong, as I live and breathe. What the bleedin' 'ell are you doin' 'ere?'

'I might ask the same of you. When did you join the Rip-Roaring Revellers? Hello, Barty.'

Dunn nodded and smiled. 'Flo.'

'We've been with you, what, three months now?' said Skins to the singer.

'Aye, about that. They're very good. I'm Jessie, by the way. Jessie McKenzie. I could tell these two numpties werenae gonnae introduce me.'

'Flo Armstrong,' I said and held out my hand. We shook.

'Pleased tae meet you,' she said. 'How do you know these two reprobates?'

'Oh, we've been friends for years, haven't we, boys?'

'Since we was nippers,' agreed Skins. He turned to Jessie. 'Did you ever meet Roland Richman?'

'Aye. Nasty wee fella. I auditioned for him once, years ago. Didnae get the job. Isn't he in gaol now?'

'He is. But just before he got sent down, we was in his band – Roland Richman's Ragtime Revue. We played an engagement party at Flo's mate's gaff. When was that? '08?'

'It was. Though they were more Lady Hardcastle's mates at the time.'

'You boys pal about wi' toffs, then?' said Jessie. 'You're full o' surprises, you are.'

Skins nodded. 'We're well connected, ain't we, Barty. Is she 'ere?'

'She is,' I said. 'Do you have a few minutes to come over?'

'For Lady H? All the time in the world.'

Our table was a large one, and there was plenty of room for the three additional chairs our new waiter friend managed to magic up from somewhere. I sensed a mixture of envy, resentment and disapproval from our fellow diners, but it was fun to spend time with our old friends so I didn't much care.

After a round of introductions, Lady Hardcastle turned to Skins. 'Why didn't you tell us you were in a new band?' she said.

Skins grinned his cheeky grin. 'Why didn't you tell us you was doin' . . . whatever it is you're up to.'

'Touché.'

'What *are* you up to?' asked Dunn.

'Oh, this and that,' said Lady Hardcastle. 'We can't really say, dear, you should know that by now. Your inamorata's aunt is in our line of work, after all.'

'Make a note of that one, Barty. "Inamorata". I like it.'

'And how is Ellie?' I said. 'She's not written to me for ages.'

'She's all right,' said Skins. 'Frustrated with life in Annapolis, but she's keepin' 'er chin up.'

'Do you have any plans to see her?'

Skins laughed. 'What, me? How am I gonna get the readies together to go to America? But somethin' will turn up. Always does, don't it, Barty?'

'You always land on your feet, son,' said Dunn. 'Nothing to worry about there.'

'Is it your band, Miss McKenzie?' asked Helen.

'It's Mrs, but please call me Jessie. And, yes. I sort of inherited it, you might say. My late father was band leader, and when he passed it fell to me to keep it goin'. I couldnae let it fold – you've seen how many of us rely on the income.'

'Was your father a ragtime aficionado?'

Jessie laughed. 'No, not at all. Under my father we used to be a bit more . . . staid, you might say. Selections from light opera – *The Merry Widow* and the like. But I've tried to bring it a bit more up to date – that's why I hired these two cocky chancers.'

'You're such wonderful fun,' said Helen. 'What does your husband think of it all?'

'He's very happy. He's the clarinet player.'

'A family affair, then. And do you have children?'

'Aye, four. Ma sister takes care of them while we're on the road.'

Lady Hardcastle's attention had been uncharacteristically wandering during this part of the conversation, and I was about to ask her if everything was all right.

Suddenly, though, she was back with us. 'Do you get a lot of bookings?'

'We keep ourselves busy,' said Jessie. 'We could always do with more, but the bailiffs are nae knockin' on the door just yet.'

'That's wonderful. I—'

She was interrupted by the opening of the stage door. A man's head peeped round. He gestured to Jessie.

'That's ma husband,' she said. 'We should be gettin' back there – I want to make some changes to the second half. It was lovely tae meet you.'

She stood.

'It was lovely to meet you, too, dear,' said Lady Hardcastle. 'Do you have a card?'

'Not with me, but these two can always find me.'

Skins and Dunn nodded.

'We'd probably better be goin' an' all,' said Skins. 'I need to see a man about a dog.'

Dunn shook his head. 'Classy, mate. Very classy. Are you ladies in town much longer?'

'At least until the beginning of next week,' I said. 'Why?'

'Though we might get together and have a proper chat.' He scribbled a number on a bus ticket he dug out of his jacket pocket. 'Give us a call if you're free.'

'You have a telephone now?'

'What? No, not me. I've got digs above a sweet shop. That's the owner's number. Lovely old girl. Doris.'

Lady Hardcastle smiled. 'Then if we're free at all before we head home, we shall telephone Doris and leave a message.'

'You do that.'

'You'd better go, dear. Poor Skins is starting to fidget.'

They left us to our meal.

Chapter Eleven

We were at the Basement at eight o'clock on Wednesday morning, and sitting in Colonel Valentine's office by ten past. Harry joined us, and took up his customary position, leaning against a filing cabinet by the door.

'A deputation, I see,' said Valentine with an irritatingly patronizing air. 'And to what do I owe the pleasure? You have news on the mysterious warehouse?' His smirk didn't help.

Lady Hardcastle, as always, was unfazed. 'We do, Colonel dear. Armstrong and I spent yesterday morning observing the comings and goings at the abandoned warehouse on Marigold Street, and we can confirm that it is occupied by at least six men – there were bedrolls and blankets for six – and they appear at first glance to be Serbian and are definitely engaged in terrorist activities.'

'And how do you know that? Did they have terrorist badges on their *šajkačas*?' He seemed very pleased with his little joke.

'We broke in to the warehouse and found a cache of small arms, ammunition for a rifle – Russian – and at least forty-two sticks of dynamite. These last were bound into six bundles, with two clockwork timers for delayed detonation. I should probably have mentioned all this earlier.' She produced the fragment of dynamite wrapper from her notebook and put it on his desk, smiling her most infuriating smile.

The colonel looked shocked. 'What do you make of this, Featherstonhaugh?'

Harry waved his hand airily. 'It's Emily and Flo, sir. I'd trust their assessment of any situation – they've been at this longer than the two of us put together.'

Valentine puffed out his cheeks and stared up at the smoke-stained ceiling for a moment.

'Is there any chance they know you were there?' he asked eventually.

'There is, unfortunately,' said Lady Hardcastle. 'We took all the usual precautions, but no plan of operations survives with any certainty beyond the first encounter with a man in a suspicious hat. One of their number returned to the warehouse while we were examining the munitions. We were concealed, and made our exit as stealthily as we were able. He gave no indication that he was suspicious, but he might have been aware of our presence, or might have discovered some sign of our snooping once we were gone. I can offer no guarantees.'

'Then we must raid the place at once. If they have any suspicions, we can't give them time to clear out.'

I didn't say that if he'd ordered the raid on Monday when we first alerted him to our own suspicions, then we wouldn't be worrying about them doing a moonlight flit. Instead, I said, 'They have enough explosives to destroy a small building – we need to round them up and relieve them of it at the earliest opportunity. If we fail, none of us can guarantee the security of the Austrian visit.'

'Quite. Make the arrangements, Featherstonhaugh. Get as many Special Branch men as you can find. If you can't find enough, get on to Scotland Yard and get more. Make sure you're armed.'

'Right you are, sir.'

'Now, Featherstonhaugh.'

Harry gave an ironic salute and pushed himself upright. He opened the door and left the room.

'Thank you, ladies,' said Valentine. 'We'll let you know how we get on.'

'We'll be going with them,' said Lady Hardcastle.

'You jolly well will not.'

'Let's not fall out over this, Colonel. We'll be going on the raid. You heard what Harry said – I've been doing this sort of thing since you were in North Africa, training the Egyptian army. Armstrong is almost as experienced. This won't be our first raid, nor the most dangerous thing we've ever done. It won't even be the most dangerous thing we've done this week.'

Valentine harrumphed. 'Very well. You'd better get cracking.'

We left him and joined Harry as he made the plans in his own office.

Harry quickly cobbled together a party of ten men – six from the SSB's own Special Branch strength and a further four from their main team at Scotland Yard.

'And how will you get the SBOs there?' I asked.

'SBOs? Special Branch Officers?'

'Special Branch Oafs.'

Harry laughed long and loud. 'I say, that's splendid. I shall use it henceforth. They'll be "Officers" in public and "Oafs" to those in the know. I have arranged for the loan of a light truck to carry the SBOs . . . SBOs – I love it . . . Anyway, a light truck will carry the men with their cudgels and blunderbusses to Bermondsey. I thought we three might make the journey by motor car.'

'You're coming with us?' said Lady Hardcastle. 'Are you feeling quite well?'

'Don't sound so surprised – I shall be leading the raid. I do plenty of fieldwork when you're not around, you know.'

'I was teasing, dear. How's your shooting?'

'Not as good as yours, but I can look after myself.'

'We shall be sure to stand behind you.'

'You do that. Do you need to draw a sidearm from the armoury?'

Lady Hardcastle patted her bag. 'I come prepared.'

'What about you, Strongarm? Can I tempt you? We have some natty little pistols that would suit. Small but powerful.'

'A kind offer,' I said, 'but if I can't run away, I prefer the open hand or the blade.'

'Not fists?'

'Never strike anyone with a closed fist, Mr Feather-stone-huff. You should know that by now.'

'I stand corrected. Shall we go, then?'

'Ready when you are, dear,' said Lady Hardcastle.

◆ ◆ ◆

It felt strange to be travelling into Dockland in a motor car instead of on foot. Stranger still to be in our own clothes rather than in our disguises as Mrs Brown and Mrs Jones. I also noticed for the first time how impossibly busy Tower Bridge was. On foot, I had been aware of the cars, lorries, buses and carts, but I hadn't properly registered quite how many there were nor how infuriatingly slowly they were moving.

'Is it always like this?' I asked.

'What, the traffic?' said Harry.

'Yes. How do you all get about?'

'I seldom venture south of the river, so I don't know if the bridges are all like this. But London is definitely busier since you last lived here.'

Lady Hardcastle turned to look behind us. 'We've lost the SBOs, dear. There's a coal cart between us and them.'

'I saw,' said Harry. 'They'll catch us up once we turn off on to Fair Street.'

'How on earth can you know that?'

'That cart says "Elephant and Castle Coal Merchants" – it'll be carrying on down Tower Bridge Road. You're not the only one trained in observation, sis.'

'I've underestimated you all these years, dear.'

Sure enough, when we turned left towards Bermondsey, the coal wagon carried on and the SBOs' borrowed truck fell into line behind us. We progressed to the warehouse without any further complications.

With an efficiency and precision I would never have expected, the ten SBOs jumped down from the back of the truck and lined up on the pavement on either side of the door. The two at the front were armed with sledgehammers, and at Harry's casual signal, they proceeded to smash their way in.

The door gave up its valiant resistance on the fourth blow and swung open. The men with the sledgehammers stepped smartly aside and put down their tools while the others streamed inside, guns drawn. Harry followed them in, with Lady Hardcastle and me bringing up the rear.

The main room looked strangely different. Obviously it was full of armed policemen, which would change the appearance of any space, but there was something else.

It took me a while to fathom what the difference was, but eventually I realized that it was the table and chairs in the corner. Everything had been tipped over and pushed against the wall, including the stove, which was leaking oil on to the flagstone floor. The mattresses and blankets had gone, as had the kettle. The Hats had moved out.

Two of the SBOs approached the makeshift room, revolvers raised.

'Go easy in there, gentlemen,' said Lady Hardcastle. 'That's where we saw the explosives.'

Cautiously, one of the men raised the blanket while the other kept his weapon trained on the opening. The others turned towards them, alert for danger. The man with the raised gun edged into the explosives room.

'Nothing here, sir,' he said. 'Some scraps of waxed paper, a few little bits of wire, but no bombs or weapons.'

'Dynamite and guns,' said one of the SBOs, shaking his head. 'Women.'

'That'll do,' said Harry as he pushed his way through to the small room.

We followed him, running the gauntlet of smirks and sniggers from the now superfluous armed officers.

Harry picked up one of the scraps of waxed paper and sniffed it. 'Definitely dynamite.' He bent to sniff the workbench. 'And gun oil. Looks like we're just too late.'

There was a *pfft* from one of the men outside. 'Hours too bloomin' late. They cleared the place out.'

'If they were ever here at all,' said another voice. 'Those two useless aprons probably put the wrappers and gun oil there to make themselves look important.'

We stepped back into the main room, and another of the SBOs, one of only two who hadn't so far made any disparaging comments, approached Harry.

'Do you need us any more, sir?' he asked. 'Only my men have work we need to be getting on with back at the Yard.'

'Thank you, Chief Inspector,' said Harry. 'You may stand down. If you could take the SSB lot back with you, they can get back to their other duties, too.'

'Right you are, sir. Come on lads, back to the truck.'

The SBOs filed out, guns holstered, smirks firmly fixed in place.

'I'm so sorry, Harry,' said Lady Hardcastle. 'They were most definitely here.'

'I never doubted you for a second, sis. If Valentine had given the go-ahead when you first told him what you'd seen, we'd be rounding them up and taking them to the Tower now.'

I smiled – it's always pleasing when someone agrees with you unbidden.

'We're convinced they've gone?' I asked.

Harry gestured around the empty space. 'This most definitely has the air of a former residence. We'll not be seeing them again. Why?'

'We didn't get a chance to search the place properly yesterday – I was going to suggest that we have a really good look round. Our experience is that even the most painstaking evacuation will overlook something. They might have left traces – something to give us a clue what they're up to.'

'I shall be guided by you,' said Harry.

And so we split the room into thirds and each walked carefully up and down our assigned segment, scanning the floor for anything that might have been left behind. Notes or a scrap of map would be too much to hope for, but nothing was to be discounted. The crates and barrels against the walls were to be searched and lifted.

The pile of sacking was in Harry's part of the room, and we told him about the possibility of rats, but he was made of stern stuff and pooh-poohed our rodent warnings.

It took a good while, and we found nothing apart from a scrap of apple peel, some pencil shavings, and a good amount of tobacco ash. Of the supposed rats there was no sign – perhaps even they were in the pay of the Hats and had accompanied them to their new digs.

We were about to give up when I glimpsed something shiny under the remains of a smashed packing case. It was probably just an old nail, but I was the one who had insisted that nothing should be discounted, so I lifted the piece of wood.

It was a piece of pressed steel, maybe two and a half inches long and folded into a long, square U-shape. At either end of the channel, the steel had been cut and bent so that it formed spring-like clips. It was unmarked, but it was slightly greasy. I sniffed it. Gun oil.

'Do you two know what this is?'

Lady Hardcastle and Harry came over to me.

'Stripper clip,' they said in unison.

'From a Mosin-Nagant,' said Lady Hardcastle. 'I was right – one of them has a rifle.'

'What's a stripper clip?' I asked.

'It makes it easier to load the weapon. It holds five rounds by the base so you can load all five in one go rather than laboriously slotting them into the magazine one by one. You just push down on the top round and all five pop into place, then you discard the clip and you're ready to shoot.'

'Ingenious.'

'We always are when it comes to finding ways of killing each other, dear – you know that.'

'It was worth making the search, then,' I said.

'It certainly was,' said Harry, giving the place one last look. 'We need to marshal our thoughts before we report to Valentine. What say we retire to my palatial abode, get Cook to supply us with sandwiches and cake, and get our stories straight?'

'Get our stories straight, dear?' said Lady Hardcastle. 'We simply tell him what happened.'

'Figure of speech, sis. But we need a plan or he'll just huff and bluster and tell us what nincompoops we all are.'

'I've been called a nincompoop by far more impressive men than he. But you're right. We need to go to him with a new plan.'

We left the warehouse and returned to Bloomsbury.

◆ ◆ ◆

I was very fond of Lady Lavinia, but it felt odd discussing SSB business in her presence and I was pleased when Lady Hardcastle suggested that, rather than going straight to Bedford Square, we have our discussion at the flat instead.

'Why?' said Harry.

'Security,' said Lady Hardcastle.

'Security? We can rely on Jake's discretion, surely you know that.'

'I do, dear.'

'And, as it happens, she's out for the afternoon – one of her charity committees – so it doesn't really matter anyway.'

'I trust Lavinia implicitly. And Helen. And we can rely on your servants, too, I'm sure. But I can't help but feel that the fewer people who hear our conversations, the better. No matter how trustworthy they may be, the more people who are privy to confidential information, the less time it can manage to remain a secret.'

Harry seemed about to say more, but wisely thought better of it. 'Your place it is, then.'

'That sounds like a splendid plan. Thank you, dear.'

And so we drove to Southampton Street, where Harry parked his car a short bus ride from the kerb and we all went inside.

I made a pot of tea, and when I brought the tray through to the small drawing room I found Lady Hardcastle slumped on the sofa with her feet up on the coffee table.

'Must you?' I said, pointing at her dusty boots.

She sat up with a sigh and put her feet back on the rug. 'Fusspot.'

'Slattern.'

'She was like that as a child,' said Harry.

We both looked at him sharply.

'Yes . . . Well . . .' he said. 'What are our thoughts on the empty warehouse?'

I poured the tea.

'I wonder,' I said, 'if we were less discreet than we imagined yesterday.'

'How so?'

'We thought we escaped unobserved, but what if Returning Hat knew we were there all along?'

Lady Hardcastle shook her head. 'He would have confronted us, surely.'

'Perhaps. But what else might have prompted them to move out in such a rush?'

'I think it more likely that it wasn't a hurried withdrawal at all, but part of the plan.'

'How does a move fit with any sort of plan?' asked Harry. 'Doesn't that just make things more complicated?'

'Complicated, perhaps,' said Lady Hardcastle, 'but not unnecessarily so. One needs peace and quiet to assemble a couple of bombs – somewhere spacious and anonymous where one can come and go unobserved. An abandoned warehouse in Dockland is ideal. At least, it appears so to the uninitiated – they were clearly unaware of the vigilance of the Dockland criminal fraternity. So the warehouse is a good place to prepare their munitions, but it's miles from anywhere the delegation will visit, so it's highly unlikely the Hats plan to strike from there.'

'Why not?'

'It's getting harder and harder to move about the city – we commented on the traffic on Tower Bridge ourselves today – so they won't want their attack to fail because they find themselves stuck behind a slow-moving brewer's dray, or because their motor car takes a wrong turn and then stalls when they try to reverse their way out of trouble. They'll want to be near wherever they plan to strike so they can reach it easily – at some point they will need to move up to a forward position in preparation. When we broke in yesterday all the dynamite was neatly bundled and the two timing devices assembled. With that done, they had no further need to be there.'

'You make a vague sort of sense,' conceded Harry. 'But why move now? Why not wait a little longer?'

'Or, to put it another way, why wait at all? The Austrians arrive on Monday. Moving now gives them time to settle, check their equipment, dry-run their routes. No rushing about, no drawing attention to themselves, just calmly going about their business with plenty of time to spare if there are any unforeseen problems.'

Harry mulled all this over for a while.

'Either of these things could be true,' he said at length, 'but how do they help us? On the one hand, perhaps your presence was noted by the chap who came back and they decided to do a moon-light flit. On the other, their move was a scheduled part of their plan to disrupt the talks. Whatever the truth of it, we still have no idea where they've gone.'

'True,' I said. 'Although we do know what they're up to. In the broadest sense, at least. They're going to blow something up.'

'I'm still at a loss to see what help that is.'

I smiled. 'At the moment, very little. But if we could see the itinerary we could identify the most likely points of attack. They must have finalized it by now.'

'They might well have, but they're not sharing it. I've asked for a copy every day since you first mentioned it, but they're ignoring me.'

'Then you must huff and puff, dear,' said Lady Hardcastle. 'Tell them that the Big Bad Hats are threatening to blow their house down.'

'If I had the time, I would, but I have work of my own, you know. We're still no closer to Autumn Wind.'

'That's our plan for our forthcoming meeting, then. When Valentine starts smirking and well-well-well-ing about what nincompoops we are, we'll tell him we can solve the whole thing if he can put some pressure on the London Trade Confederation to release the full details of the visit.'

Chapter Twelve

Once more we found ourselves in Colonel Valentine's office, though this time less full of ourselves. Our surveillance of the warehouse the previous day had gone well, but we had received precious little praise for our success. Our morning raid on the warehouse had been a good deal less impressive, and I could only imagine the level of grumpiness that would greet our failure.

Lady Hardcastle gave our report in her usual precise, concise way. She tried to keep things positive, and mentioned finding the additional scraps of dynamite wrapper as well as noticing the smell of gun oil – Harry backed her up on that – to confirm our earlier assertion that the Hats were the terrorists we were after. But everything else was a report of things that were missing: the Hats themselves, the explosives, the guns, the beds and bedding. By the time she was finished, even I was ready to give us a severe wigging for messing things up so badly.

Colonel Valentine beamed. 'Well done, all. Well done indeed.'

'I beg your pardon,' said Lady Hardcastle. 'You did understand the part where I explained that our suspects and all their munitions were missing?'

'Of course, of course.'

I frowned. 'It means that there are six armed men on the loose in London, in possession of enough explosives to severely damage the headquarters of the London Trade Confederation and kill scores of people. Actually, that's a point: how did they manage to get all that dynamite? And all the ammunition we saw? You can't just go down to the hardware shop on the corner and buy forty-two sticks of dynamite and several cases of ammunition.'

'They'll have help,' said Valentine. 'The Black Hand is a powerful organization. But that's of only academic interest. The point is that we know what they're up to. You've seen their explosives, so we can plan to protect ourselves from a bomb attack. We know they all have sidearms, so we can prepare for that, too. And you've spooked them. Perhaps you haven't foiled their plot, but they know we're on to them and they've had to hop it.'

'I don't want to boringly repeat myself,' I said, 'but they've hopped it with all their guns, ammunition and explosives. They're on the run, whereabouts unknown, and armed to the teeth.'

'But confounded. Off balance. Their best-laid plans have gang agley. They need a new base of operations, their transport arrangements will need to change . . . everything about the scheme – whatever it was – has been disrupted. By the time they've regrouped, the Austrians will have returned home. That's if they hang around at all. There's a decent chance they've done a bunk and are already on a boat back across the Channel.'

'You're willing to take that chance?' asked Lady Hardcastle.

'We'll not be taking any chances. We'll advise the police to be on the lookout for six men in *šajkačas* carrying bombs' – he chuckled to himself at the image – 'but we know exactly what they're up to and I'm happy to tell the LTC that we have everything in hand.'

'Even though we have no idea about the specifics of their plan?' I said.

Valentine nodded as he fussed with his pipe. 'Even though. I have a meeting with the LTC tomorrow morning at which I shall be passing on the good news. You're most welcome to come.' He put down his tobacco pouch and looked up sharply. 'As long as you don't start with all this "but we don't know where they've gone" nonsense. We stick to "the Serbians plan to use bombs, but their operation has been disrupted and they're on the back foot so we can beat them easily". No need to start introducing doubts. Don't want to frighten the horses.'

'We'll be in a much better position to thwart them when we know exactly what's happening on Monday,' said Lady Hardcastle. 'Do you have a copy of the trade delegation's itinerary yet?'

'Not yet, no. It's damned frustrating, honestly. I shall definitely be pressing them for it.'

'In that case we'd very much like to join you. When and where?'

'Tomorrow morning, eleven o'clock, LTC's offices in the City.'

'We'll meet you there.'

We ate a leisurely breakfast on Thursday morning, making sure to keep the kitchen window open – the better to enjoy any repeat performance from our neighbours in the mews. Sadly, everyone was on their best behaviour and we were obliged to entertain ourselves as we ate our sausages and eggs.

'What do you make of Valentine's reaction to the raid?' I asked during the lull, while Lady Hardcastle painstakingly constructed a sausage sandwich.

'I think he's been behind a desk for a good long while and has become far too accustomed to playing the political game. He'd rather tell those oafs at the LTC what he thinks they'd prefer to hear than actually take steps to make sure they're all safe. I very much get the feeling that he's interpreted his brief as being not to "frighten the horses", as he puts it. I suspect his masters in Whitehall have applied pressure in that regard, too. Obviously no one wants any harm to befall the Austrian delegation, but neither do they want it to appear that London isn't a safe place to do business.'

'It's up to us to quietly see to it that no harm *does* befall them, then.'

'As it always was, tiny one – our brief hasn't changed. And if we have to do it without the overt support of the Bureau . . . then . . . well, that will hardly be a new experience, will it?'

And with that firmly agreed between us, we set off just after ten o'clock to drive once more into the City.

We were unable to park outside the building that housed the LTC's offices – there was a wagon in the way – but there was plenty of room round the corner and we arrived in good time. Colonel Valentine, his dress uniform as immaculate as always, was enjoying a cup of tea in the waiting area as he chatted amiably to Rackley about cricket.

'Ah, here they are,' said Valentine as he stood. 'Punctual as always. Good morning, ladies.'

We greeted them both.

Valentine gestured along the corridor towards the meeting room. 'I believe the committee is already in session – is that the correct term? Monty said we should just go in as soon as you arrived. Shall we?'

We followed him to the huge double doors, which he opened without knocking.

'Clifford,' said Sir Montague, warmly. 'Bang on time. We were just about to move on to the trade delegation visit. Ah, I see you've brought your little terriers with you.'

'What ho, Sir Monty,' said Lady Hardcastle, making herself comfortable without being invited.

'Yes . . . well . . . quite. Please . . . er . . . please sit down, won't you. What news from the Secret Service Bureau, Spencer? Are we safe and secure?'

'I believe we are,' said Valentine. 'Lady Hardcastle and Miss Armstrong have identified and, we believe, neutralized a serious potential threat.' He went on to describe our surveillance and raid of the abandoned warehouse, carefully shaping the narrative to show, as he had said he would, that it meant the gang knew the jig was up.

Sir Montague looked pleased. 'You've definitely gone above and beyond. Thank you, ladies. I must say we didn't know what to expect of you, but you've done a magnificent job. We thought you'd be raking through dusty files and reading police reports – we certainly didn't imagine you'd be whirling round the hovel ends like that.'

The board members all smiled knowingly and nodded.

Valentine smiled, too. 'Our assessment is that the gang is either long gone or, at worst, trying to regroup for a revised, less effective attack.'

'And is this also your assessment, Lady Hardcastle?' asked Sir Montague. 'Should we stand you down?'

Lady Hardcastle smiled. 'We're available until the end of next week come what may, so why not make use of us? It's not as though you're paying. I suggest we plan for the worst possible case and make suitable security arrangements to eliminate – or at least mitigate – any realistic threat.'

'And what do you suggest that threat might be?'

'The gang has a substantial amount of dynamite, along with a couple of clockwork timers, so we should start with a thorough assessment of the itinerary to determine the most likely opportunities for a bomb attack. The police can search likely targets at the appropriate time.'

Sir Montague nodded. 'That doesn't seem unreasonable.'

'To do that, though, we really do need to see the final itinerary. We asked you for it a week ago – is it ready yet?'

'We're just adding one or two more details. We should be able to let you have it tomorrow.'

'That would be splendid, thank you.'

Colonel Valentine stood. 'Do you need us for anything else?'

'No, no,' said Sir Montague. 'That will be all. Thank you for coming.'

We trooped out towards the waiting area.

'Thank you, ladies,' said Valentine. 'I think that went rather well. You've made us look very good. Very good indeed.'

'If you can keep on at him about the itinerary and make sure we really do have it by tomorrow at the latest, we can make the Bureau look even better,' said Lady Hardcastle.

'I shall, I shall. I take it you have transport? We gave you a motor car, didn't we?'

'You did indeed.'

'Splendid. I shall see you tomorrow. Cheerio, ladies.'

We left him to do whatever it was senior members of secret services did, and made our way back to the Austin.

◆ ◆ ◆

It was more than a little frustrating to find ourselves kicking our heels once more, but we managed to pass a pleasant enough afternoon on Bond Street and its environs, wondering whether yet more new clothes would be a ridiculous indulgence or an essential professional purchase. We sometimes had to look spiffingly *au courant* in order to blend in with the smart set, after all.

We decided our money would be better spent with the dressmakers of Bristol – their prices were more reasonable and it felt somehow virtuous to support our local economy – but we did entertain ourselves by making up stories about the women we saw parading along the street and going in to the shops.

We had afternoon tea at an absurdly fashionable tea room somewhere in St James's, where I was certain I saw two famous actresses, an officer of the French intelligence service, and the wife of a cabinet minister. Disappointingly, though the service was enjoyably fawning and the clientele glamorous and exotic, the sandwiches and cakes were mediocre at best. We left amused but dissatisfied, and decided to drive back to the flat. Harry had invited us for dinner again, so we made sure to be home in plenty of time for baths and a change of clothes.

'Sometimes I miss my uniform,' I said later, as Lady Hardcastle buttoned me into an evening dress. 'As long as it was starched in the right places and looked reasonably clean, no one expected me to change it four times a day. I mean, obviously I look utterly splendid, but life is simpler when you can just chuck on a frock before breakfast and shrug out of it at bedtime.'

'It's an essential part of upper-class living, though, dear. How else would people know one had more money than good sense?'

'If that's what's important, why not simply wear your most recent bank statement on an elegant chain around your neck, and forget about the tyranny of morning dresses and afternoon dresses and dinner dresses and everything in between.'

'You speak a good deal of sense as always, but for now, you do look utterly splendid, and unless we manage to hail a cab in the next five minutes we shall be late.'

'We're not walking?'

'I've been trudging about all day. We shall take a cab and hang the expense.'

'I just need to find my shoes and I'm ready.'

Despite Lady Hardcastle's fears of tardiness, we tumbled inelegantly out of a taxi on Bedford Square at exactly eight o'clock and rang the doorbell. Weatherby led us through to the drawing room, where Harry was already busy at the drinks cabinet. Helen and Lady Lavinia raised their glasses in salute.

'What ho, sis,' said Harry, waving a gin bottle. 'Your usual?'

'I'm not wholly convinced I have a usual, dear, but a gin and tonic would go down a treat.'

'Ice and cucumber?'

'No, that didn't work at all – it would need a different type of gin, I think. Lemon or lime will be fine, thank you.'

'Right you are. Strongarm?'

I settled on the sofa. 'I'll have the same, unless you have anything that isn't gin.'

'We have *everything* that isn't gin,' said Harry, sweeping his arm to display his collection.

'What's in the green bottle? Absinthe?'

'A Bohemian girl, eh?'

'I'm a good deal more worldly than people give me credit for.'

'Absinthe it is, then. And you know what they say?'

Lady Hardcastle shook her head wearily. 'Harry dear, don't say it.'

'Say what?'

'You know perfectly well. You say it every time someone asks for a glass of absinthe.'

'I'm sure I don't know what you mean, sis. But I do know that absinthe makes the heart grow fonder.'

'You're an idiot.'

'She's right, darling,' said Lady Lavinia, 'you *are* an idiot.'

Helen laughed. 'I think it's utterly delightful, Harry. Makes the heart grow fonder. You're such a card.'

Harry bowed as he handed us our drinks.

'So what have you two been up to since I last saw you?' said Helen. 'Anything you can talk about?'

'This and that, as always, dear,' said Lady Hardcastle.

'Have you averted the war yet?' asked Lady Lavinia.

Helen almost choked on her sherry. 'War?'

Lady Hardcastle smiled, kindly. 'Most of our work revolves around averting war, I'm afraid. I wouldn't read too much into it.'

'You're teasing me, I know it.'

'No,' said Harry, 'that's very much what our little bureau does. We hear the whispers on the wind and advise our nation's leaders accordingly.'

'Whispers on the wind?' said Lady Hardcastle. 'For goodness' sake, Harry, where do you get this rubbish? We poke our noses in, Helen dear. We read people's letters, we steal their files, we trick them into revealing things they oughtn't. We break in to their offices and workshops and snoop about. It's grubby, underhand, and often surprisingly tedious. Once we have this surreptitiously gathered intelligence, we piece it together and try to produce an up-to-date picture of our country's enemies. If we can glean their plans and intentions as well, so much the better. Whispers on the wind, indeed. I ask you.'

'The reality's a little mundane, sis, that's all. I thought I'd try to spice it up with a little poetry.'

'Hmm. But to answer your question: at the moment, we've ever-so-slightly lost track of the latest threat to European peace, but we're confident we can stop them before everything goes completely awry.'

'And what would be the consequences if things did go "awry"?' asked Helen.

'A number of very horrible deaths,' said Lady Hardcastle, 'followed by huffing and puffing by several nations' diplomats, and then . . . well, war really isn't out of the question.'

'Gracious.'

'Gracious, indeed. So you understand why we make light of it all.'

'I do. I'm sorry.'

'What about you, though,' I said, changing the subject. 'How did your trip to Kent go yesterday?'

'Oh, yes, I'd forgotten I told you about that. It was everything I hoped for. I got some marvellous shots of the rock formations, as well as some wonderful old abandoned machinery. Exactly what I'd planned.'

'"Man the Destroyer of Worlds",' said Lady Lavinia. 'I think it's frightfully clever.'

'Man the destroyer of everything, if Emily and Flo are right about this war business.'

'We'll do our best to keep it at bay for as long as we can,' I said.

'But if you have any spare capital lying about,' said Lady Hardcastle, 'invest in munitions.'

Harry tutted. 'That's rather cynical, sis.'

'Your pals the Autumn Wind seem to think they can make a few bob out of it, dear. Why not the rest of us?'

'Was there much clambering?' I asked, keen to get us back on to less terrifying ground.

'You wouldn't believe it. I wanted some shots from the bottom of the quarry looking upwards – you know, to give some sense of the scale of the place – and then some from the top looking downwards. So lots of clambering, and a dismaying amount of tidying. People can be so messy.'

'Messy?'

'It was terrible. I was happy with whatever remained of the old quarry works – you know, sheds, rusted picks, rotting carts. There was even a derelict steam engine – that's going to look marvellous if I managed to get the lighting right. But then there was just general rubbish. And not from the time the quarry was working – this was recent stuff. Beer bottles, cigarette ends, scrunched-up sandwich wrappers. I had to clean it all up so it didn't spoil the images.'

'It must be a popular spot for young people,' suggested Lady Lavinia. 'I remember when I was young I used to meet a boy I knew—' She stopped talking and looked around. 'Sorry. Probably best not to recount that one. Husband present and all that.'

Lady Hardcastle laughed. 'I could tell you stories about Harry's adolescent dalliances if that would help balance things out.'

'Don't you dare,' said Harry.

'Well, anyway,' persisted Helen, her face slightly flushed. 'I managed to get all that squared away, as well as what looked like a shattered wig block, and—'

Lady Hardcastle had stopped laughing. 'A what, dear?'

'A wig block. At least that's what I thought it was. It looked as though some ruffians had been driving spikes into it until it was completely destroyed. So I cleared all that away and took my photographs. I thought things would be better at the top, but there was rubbish up there, too.'

'What sort of rubbish?'

'More of the same – sandwich wrappers, beer bottles, cigarette ends. Oh, and two of these. I rather like them – I think they might come in handy for something at the studio, though I don't know what yet. I was hoping one of you might know what they are.'

She reached into her dainty evening purse and produced two pieces of pressed steel, about two and a half inches long. She held them out.

Lady Hardcastle took one. 'How high would you say the escarpment was, dear?'

'Oh, I don't know. Two hundred and fifty feet, perhaps? A little more? I'm no good at judging heights. I'd say it was a bit taller than Nelson's Column, but not as tall as Big Ben.'

'And how far away from the base of the cliff was the smashed wig block?'

'Lord, I don't know. A hundred and twenty yards, perhaps?'

'Helen, dear, I think you might have marched us one step further away from war.'

Chapter Thirteen

At nine o'clock on Friday morning, Lady Hardcastle and I stood behind Harry as he knocked on Colonel Valentine's office door.

'Come.'

Harry opened the door a tiny bit and popped his head in. 'Do you have a moment?'

'Of course, Featherstonhaugh, come in.'

Harry opened the door wider and stepped inside. Lady Hardcastle and I followed.

Valentine, it seemed, was not overjoyed to see us. 'Dash it all, Featherstonhaugh, I wasn't expecting a deputation.' He sighed. 'Good morning, ladies, what can I do for you? I thought we were meeting at the LTC offices at eleven.'

'We are,' said Lady Hardcastle, 'but we wanted to speak to you first.'

'Not more burbling about the Serbs, I hope. I told you we have it all in hand, thanks to you three.'

He gestured to his visitor chairs and we took up our customary positions.

'We have indeed come to burble about the Serbs,' said Lady Hardcastle. 'We have fresh intelligence from which an alarming new possibility arises.'

'But everything is under control. All we need from you now is a plan to thoroughly search every part of the archduke's route for bombs, as well as every building he and the duchess will be visiting.'

'So Archduke Franz Ferdinand really is coming?' I said.

Valentine nodded. 'Confirmation released by the Palace this morning. Announcement made as late as possible, for security reasons.'

'But they've known for some time?' said Lady Hardcastle.

'Apparently so. Takes a lot of organizing to host foreign royalty, they tell me. But they felt it prudent to keep it on the q.t. until the last possible moment – the fewer people who know a secret, the longer it stays secret.'

Lady Hardcastle nodded. 'I was saying the same thing myself only the other day. It doesn't seem the wisest course to keep such a thing secret from the people responsible for the visitors' safety, though. And one might suggest it was a misplaced fear in the first place, when those people make their living from keeping secrets.'

'We have voiced exactly that opinion to the Palace, but they have their ways of doing things.'

'Since we're now dealing with a royal visit,' I said, 'our new information is even more important. When we thought it was going to be some government officials and a handful of business-men, a simple bomb attack would have been sufficient to disrupt things and cause trouble for the Austrians. But if the heir presump-tive to the Austrian throne and his wife will be here, then a more precisely targeted assassination attempt would have more impact.'

Valentine began fussing with his pipe. 'A bomb would do that job just as effectively, I should say. More so, perhaps – difficult to miss with a well-placed bomb.'

'Nevertheless,' said Lady Hardcastle, 'we have evidence that our behatted terrorists have a sniper in their ranks.'

Valentine dropped his pipe. 'A sniper?'

'Armed, we believe, with a Russian-made Mosin-Nagant rifle – a reliable and very accurate weapon.'

'Evidence?'

'There was a decent amount of 7.62 millimetre ammunition in the warehouse, as well as a stray stripper clip from a Mosin-Nagant.'

'Why did you not mention this before?'

'You were irritated when we came to you with incomplete intelligence – I thought it best to wait until I was certain.'

'And what makes you so certain now?'

'Quite by chance, we learned that someone has been practising at a disused quarry in Kent. They were shooting a head-sized target from the lip of the quarry at a distance of about a hundred and twenty yards.'

'That could be anyone. Young lads mucking about with their father's old army rifle, for example. We see it all the time.'

'Not at that range. It would take a decent marksman to hit a wig block from that range.'

'And not unless their father had a Mosin-Nagant,' I added. 'There were more stripper clips at the supposed firing point.'

Valentine resumed his pipe-fussing.

'Careless,' he muttered. 'But it's still likely to be a coincidence.'

'I doubt there are very many Mosin-Nagants in the country,' said Lady Hardcastle. 'I don't think we should discount the possibility that, in addition to a bomb attack, our Serbian friends intend to take a shot at the archduke from an elevated position at some time during the visit.'

Valentine thought for a moment. 'No, I don't think so. We shall visit the LTC at eleven and press them for the final version of the itinerary. You will draw up your security plan based on the assumption that the threat is an explosive one, and we shall deploy our resources accordingly. You will not at any point startle the members of the LTC with your unfounded sniper theories. They're a conniving bunch and I don't want to give them any excuses to undermine this bureau with accusations that we were unable to track and contain a group of foreign miscreants. We have foiled their bomb plot, and that is all they need to know.'

'Why would they want to undermine—' I began.

'Power and money,' he said. 'They want as much of both as they can get their hands on, and they detest the idea of an intelligence organization that might be able to stand in their way.'

'Might we?' asked Lady Hardcastle.

'Might we what?'

'Stand in their way. And in the way of what?'

'I've no idea. But in my private conversations with Monty, he's let slip a few grumbles about government interference. We do nothing to give them an excuse to go telling tales to their chums in parliament.'

I was unconvinced. 'But if we ignore the threat and allow the Hats to kill the archduke, that will give them an even bigger stick to beat us with.'

'We'll cross that bridge if ever we come to it,' said Valentine. 'For now, perception is everything, and it is important that they believe we have everything under control.'

I shrugged.

'If that's all,' he said, picking up his pen, 'I have some paperwork to take care of before the meeting.'

He stopped short of giving us a military-style 'Dismissed', but we knew when we'd been told to leave.

◆ ◆ ◆

The meeting at the LTC was a swift one. Once again, our presence was greeted with contempt mingled with irritation and a dash of resentment, but we were given a dossier detailing the arrangements for the Austrian visit, for which we thanked them.

Lady Hardcastle wasn't keen to return to the Basement, so we made our way back to Southampton Street. I put the kettle on while she cleared a space at the dining table for us to make our plans.

By the time I arrived, she was already reading the itinerary and making notes on a sheet of foolscap.

'The Austrian party arrives at Dover early on Monday morning,' she said.

I put down the tea tray. 'And who's coming?'

'It might be quicker to list who isn't coming. If Austria were to conduct a census next week, they'd undercount their population by about half.'

'Surely you exaggerate.'

'But not by much. Anyway. So far I have the archduke, the duchess, three government ministers, six company chairmen, assorted secretaries and assistants, and a bewilderingly huge contingent of personal servants, royal household staff, and civil servants from various Austrian ministries. There'll be a general and a lieutenant colonel from the Austrian army, along with their own staff, and a hand-picked detachment from the Imperial-Royal Landwehr, and between them they'll form the royal bodyguard.'

'They're bringing their own security, then.'

'The royals are, certainly. Unless they happen to be close to the royal family when anything untoward happens, though, I suspect the businessmen, secretaries, valets, ladies-in-waiting, and assorted lackeys and hangers-on will have to fend for themselves.'

'How does the War Office feel about having foreign troops wandering about the place?'

'Their reaction is not recorded – this is an LTC document – but I imagine they'll be keeping a discreet eye on things. Travelling royals always have their own guards, though – it's not as though it's a covert invasion.'

'True. What happens next?'

'A special train has been laid on – though I'm beginning to wonder if one will be enough – to bring everyone from Dover to Victoria station, where they'll be met with all due pomp. Then the archduke and the duchess – together with their personal retinues – will go to Buckingham Palace to stay with the King and Queen, while the politicians and businessmen are taken off to Claridge's. The military contingent are to be the guests of the Foot Guards at Wellington Barracks.'

'These aren't arrangements that have been cobbled hastily together over the past few days.'

'Indeed not – this will have taken weeks of planning. One wonders why it has been kept from the Bureau for so long.'

'Power politics? Isn't that what Valentine said?'

'Little boys playing king of the castle? A dismaying but very real possibility, I'm afraid.'

'What happens next?'

'There's a gala reception in the Great Hall of the building that houses the offices of the LTC on the first night. The guest list is extensive but unremarkable – all the usual ministers, junior ministers, titans of industry, and assorted other moneyed ne'er-do-wells. And after that, a series of meetings at a mix of venues small and large. Some will be attended by the archduke, but most will not – he and the duchess have better things to do, one presumes. If all goes according to plan, there will be a final meeting on Friday next, at which documents will be signed, signalling a new era in international trade, etc, etc, blah, blah.'

'So where are the danger points?' I mused as I looked at the notes she'd been making. 'The boat should be safe enough crossing the Channel.'

'It will have a Royal Navy escort once it's in British waters, so it'll be fine.'

'The dock at Dover is easy enough to secure.'

'The Royal Marines will be providing all the stamping and shouting and royal-saluting a foreign royal could ever dream of. Even if he's heir presumptive to a country that might end up being our enemy, he will be properly looked after by heavily armed, highly trained men.'

'It's all but impossible to protect the train between Dover and London, and the sniper practised in Kent, so that's something we might worry about.'

'Ah,' said Lady Hardcastle, 'but the Hats made their base in London, so they're more likely to attack there.'

'You said they were moving up to a "forward position". Why would their forward position not be a barn by the railway in Kent? They could bomb the train as it made its way through the country-side and then take pot shots at the survivors.'

'Helen said the practice shots were from a couple of hundred feet up, at a range of about a hundred and twenty yards. We could scan the Ordnance Survey maps for suitable spots, I suppose, but I'm not hopeful we'd find any between here and Dover. Even then, there are too many unpredictable variables. The bomb or bombs would have to detonate at the precise moment the train passed by, or over, it or them. Having blown, there's no real way to know how much damage the explosives would do. And any survivors being shot at would be able to use the wreckage as cover. It's all far too messy.'

'Fair enough. We're going to assume they're safe until they arrive at Victoria, then?'

'I think so, don't you?' said Lady Hardcastle.

'Probably, yes. So the train pulls in to the station and everyone disembarks. Fanfares and flags? Speeches of welcome?'

'All due pomp, as I said, yes. Bunting, speeches of welcome – you know the sort of thing. They'll be at the station for quite a while, I imagine. A few members of the LTC board will be on hand to greet the delegation, with flunkies to direct everyone to the motor cars that will take them to their various destinations.'

'Cars for all of them?'

She flipped to the back of the document and consulted the appendix. 'Actually, no. There'll be two charabancs to carry the lower orders – one to take the servants to the palace, the other to take the Austrian civil servants and admin people to . . . oh, to a boarding house in Paddington. I'd assumed they were to be staying with their masters at Claridge's.'

'No point wasting money on luxury accommodation for the lower orders. We get ideas above our station when you start treating us well.'

'Just look at you, after all.'

'Well, quite,' I said. 'But this dispersal adds complications.'

'I'm not sure it does. Without wishing to appear to under-value the importance of servants – either personal or civil – I don't think either of the charabancs or their occupants are useful targets for someone wanting to make a splash. And once they reach their respective digs . . . well, the palace will be as secure for the royal household staff as it will be for the archduke and the duchess themselves, and a couple of bobbies making regular passes of the boarding house on their beat should keep the clerks safe.'

'You make a compelling case. So we just need to look after the royal car and the convoy heading to Claridge's. The hotel itself should be easy enough to secure, and we can make sure there's a thorough sweep for bombs before they get there. The same with any meeting venues.'

'That would seem to be it. I'm sure we can come up with a plan that everyone will agree to.'

'And express it in a way that won't alarm the LTC,' I added.

'That shower of oafs? Scaring the life out of them would do them the world of good.'

I poured more tea and we set about drawing up our plans.

◆ ◆ ◆

There were many things I would wish to be doing on a Saturday morning in July other than attending an extraordinary meeting of the management board of the London Trade Confederation. But, as Lady Hardcastle so often said, if wishes were *hors d'oeuvres*, beggars would host more parties. As it was, we found ourselves once more in the main boardroom at the LTC's headquarters, where we stood at a blackboard while we explained our security proposals.

Sir Montague seemed determined to be unimpressed. 'I had been under the impression that we were to be provided with a detailed document outlining your plans, and yet here you stand like a couple of village schoolmistresses about to teach us our ABCs.'

The other board members laughed.

Lady Hardcastle waited for the mirth to subside. 'I suppose we do, rather. Obviously we'd much prefer to present you each with a neatly typed dossier, complete with maps, diagrams and detailed staffing requirements, but there was some sort of hold-up with the itinerary and so this is the situation we find ourselves in.'

She smiled.

Sir Montague harrumphed. 'Yes. Well. What do you have for us?'

'As you know, we perceive the principal threat to be from a group of supposed Serbs—'

'"Supposed"?' said a florid-faced board member. 'Why only "supposed"? We know they're up to something.'

'We're sure they're up to something, Mr . . . ?'

'Watson.'

'We're sure they're up to something, Mr Watson, but we merely suppose them to be Serbs.'

'I thought that was all settled, too,' said a handsome board member whom I'd never heard speak before. 'The Serbs have been behind this whole thing from the beginning. They've got it in for the Austrians and they mean to disrupt the talks.'

'I'm reluctant to make such an assertion without definitive proof,' said Lady Hardcastle. 'A consequence of my scientific training, I'm afraid. Our working hypothesis – based on the existing antagonism between the Balkans and Austria-Hungary – was that the Serbs might be involved. The death of a Serbian informer and the presence at the warehouse in Bermondsey of men wearing distinctively Serbian hats—' She had to pause for more laughter.

A portly gentleman with a cigar found it particularly amusing. 'Hats, she says. Hah! Hats. Well I never.'

'Those two things added weight to the hypothesis,' continued Lady Hardcastle, 'but we have no actual proof of Serbian involvement, and so, for the time being at least, it has to be labelled a supposition.'

'What scientific training?' said Florid-Faced Watson.

'She studied Natural Sciences at Girton,' said Handsome Man.

'They let women do that sort of thing?'

'It's the twentieth century, Watson, old boy – they do all sorts of things. They'll be voting, soon.'

'Over my dead body.'

That, I thought, irritably, *would be very easy to arrange.*

Obviously, I said nothing.

Lady Hardcastle raised her voice and retook control of the room. 'As I was saying, the main threat comes from a group of at least six men, whom we know to be armed with automatic pistols. We also saw six bundles of dynamite, each comprising almost three pounds of the stuff. There were two clockwork timing devices. We have no way of knowing if both timers will be used, nor how many bundles will make up each bomb if they do use both. If they use all the dynamite in one bomb, the effect would be devastating, but even singly the individual bundles are destructive and very deadly.'

In an attempt to keep their attention, she began drawing on the blackboard. She started with a decent sketch of one of the bundles of dynamite with the timer attached, then moved on to draw a representation of the south of England, including the Kent coast and the railway line to London.

'The Austrians will be guarded by the Royal Navy while in British waters in the Channel, and by the Royal Marines once at the docks at Dover. We judge it impractical to attack the train en route to London, so the first danger point is here' – she stabbed the board with her chalk – 'at Victoria station.'

There were murmurs around the table, but no actual interruptions.

She went on to recount the plans we had drawn up the day before. The station would be searched; Claridge's would be searched. Armed men would accompany the vehicles, with look-outs along the proposed routes. Meeting venues would be searched in the same way.

By the time she finished, the board seemed, if not actually impressed, then at least unable to think of anything annoyingly negative to say. We left them with a promise to deliver a written version of the plan before the end of the day, and set off for the Basement.

Once there, we manage to enlist Harry's help in persuading one of the Bureau's clerical staff to help us turn our notes into a presentable document, and a messenger was able to deliver it to the LTC shortly before five o'clock.

With the plan properly drawn up, it was time to contact the relevant departments to advise them of the security work that would be expected of them on Monday. Fortunately, Harry and Valentine had already given most of them plenty of notice that *something* would be required, so the only complaints we received were that making the final arrangements would require their officers to work on a Sunday.

By the time the last cable had been sent it was getting on for dinner time, and so we packed up our notes and maps, bid farewell to the night staff, and drove off in the general direction of the flat in search of somewhere to eat.

Lady Hardcastle had a system for locating promising restaurants in unfamiliar locations. The trick, she insisted, was to look at people as they left. If they seemed content then it was a fair bet that their meal had been a good one. If they were also jolly it might be reasonable to assume that the atmosphere inside was a convivial one.

By this uncharacteristically unscientific method, we determined that an otherwise uninspiring-looking eatery somewhere near Tottenham Court Road would be a suitable place to dine. And we were right. The food was splendid, and the company good-humoured without being annoyingly exuberant.

Hunger satisfied, we set off to return to the flat. On the way, Lady Hardcastle spotted an off-licence and screeched to a halt outside.

'We need a little something,' she said as she hopped out of the Austin and strode purposefully inside.

'Good evenin', ladies,' said the elderly proprietor. 'And what can I tempt you with? I've a nice cream sherry? Some port, perhaps?'

'What do you have by way of cognac?' asked Lady Hardcastle.

'I 'ave two or three fine brandies that might interest a fine lady such as yourself.'

Lady Hardcastle inspected the indicated bottles but it was obvious she was somewhat underwhelmed.

'I can see you're a lady of distinction,' said the shopkeeper. 'Just wait a moment – I think I have exactly the thing.'

He disappeared into the stockroom in the back and was gone for a good few minutes, before he reappeared with dirty sleeves and what seemed to be a cobweb in his brilliantined hair.

'I've 'ad this a few years now,' he said, brandishing a dusty bottle. 'Sorry I bought it, tell you the truth. Got 'alf a case of the bleeders to cater to the West End crowd, but they don't seem to come up this far no more and I can't shift 'em. And there ain't much call for it round here from the locals. Too expensive, y'see?'

Lady Hardcastle took the bottle and inspected it.

'I say, this is splendid. Half a case, you say?'

'Still got 'em all. Like I said, can't shift 'em.'

'We'll take the lot. Name your price.'

After only a small amount of haggling – he seemed to expect it – they settled on a price that seemed to make him very happy indeed, and we left in possession of six bottles of the finest cognac. Which I carried out to the motor car. And then up to the flat. Obviously.

There were no brandy snifters in the flat, and Lady Hardcastle came close to telephoning Harry to complain. For reasons that were not adequately explained, it was deemed that neither wine glasses nor tumblers would do – though the idea seemed perfectly fine to me – and so we sipped our cognac from teacups. This seemed like the worst of all the possible solutions, but it had a pleasing eccentricity about it that added a much-needed modicum of light relief as we addressed the serious business of the Austrian visit.

'I'm not at all happy that we're making no formal plans to defend against a sniper,' I said. 'I mean, I agree with Valentine that we have no proof, and that it could have been anyone shooting in the quarry, but to discount it completely seems reckless and foolhardy.'

'I absolutely agree, dear,' said Lady Hardcastle. 'But it won't be the first time we've had to work round the objections of bureaucrats and their massive, yet oddly fragile, egos. Where do you think a sniper is most likely to strike?'

'You're the gun person – you tell me.'

She pulled out the draft versions of the sketch plans she had drawn for the security dossier. 'If Helen's estimates of elevation and distance are accurate and we agree that it's not practical to attack the train en route, then we start at Victoria station. A sniper could lurk in the roof at the far end of the platform and take a shot as the royals disembarked. That might give him his hundred and twenty yards, but from memory the roof is nowhere near two hundred and fifty feet high. It's also a terrible place to try to escape from – he'd be terribly exposed up there in the rafters.'

'Not there, then. The journey to the palace?'

'Possibly. The plan is that they go straight there, though – up Buckingham Palace Road and on to Buckingham Gate. The whole journey's barely half a mile and there are no tall buildings within a hundred and twenty yards of the route.'

'And if the target is a government minister or one of the businessmen?'

'Their route to Claridge's should take them round the back of the palace, up Park Lane and into Mayfair. As before, there's nowhere high enough.'

'What would be high enough?'

'Not much. A church tower, perhaps?'

'It has to be one of the meetings, then,' I said. 'Or on the journey to or from. There are plenty of churches in the City.'

Lady Hardcastle agreed, and we spent the next two hours poring over maps and sketches trying to fathom exactly where an attack was most likely to take place.

Chapter Fourteen

It was another mild but overcast morning as I completed my exercises beneath my favourite tree in Fitzroy Square on Monday. Indian Clubs Man failed to make an appearance, and I hoped I hadn't put him off with my outlandish garb and peculiar, almost balletic movements. Perhaps he'd come back when he knew he was safe from the likes of me.

Meanwhile, at the flat, breakfast was cooking. Bacon was sizzling, toast was browning, and their tempting aromas were mixing with the smell of a pot of coffee.

'Do I have time to change?' I called.

'You were only complaining the other day about having to change for dinner, dear,' Lady Hardcastle called back. 'I don't think you need to change for breakfast as well.'

'I'll just be a couple of minutes. I'm . . . sticky.'

'What an enchanting picture you paint. But hurry – it'll get cold.'

True to my word, I was at the table, knife and fork in hand, in less than five minutes.

Lady Hardcastle dropped the final plate of sausages on the table.

'Is that how you're going to do it?' I said.

'Do what?'

'You're just going to plonk it down there with a clatter? No grace? No finesse?'

She gestured towards the front door. 'I'm told the Russell Hotel serves a delightful breakfast if the service here isn't up to your exacting standards.'

'I'm grateful, really. Thank you.'

'You're more than welcome. We'll need a big breakfast.'

'I always need a big breakfast.'

'You do, don't you? I don't know where you put it all – there's so little of you. But today we both do – I'm not hopeful of getting a chance to break for lunch. No one's going to take kindly to our sloping off before the Austrians arrive, and they're not due at Victoria until 2.13. The fanfare and folderol will take up to an hour, then we have to get everyone safely aboard their cars and charabancs. By the time we receive notification that everyone is safely at their destinations, it will be long past teatime.'

'Boiled eggs.'

'I beg your pardon?'

'We'll take a few hard-boiled eggs. If we make sure we have pockets in our jackets so we can carry them, we can have a discreet snack if things drag on.'

'Good plan. I was going to suggest sandwiches, but eggs would be a much better idea.'

'Much less squishy. I'll see to it as soon as we finish here. Do you want that last sausage?'

'Help yourself – I've already had far too many.'

We arrived at Victoria station at eleven o'clock to find Harry already coordinating the security preparations. His own Special Branch officers and some on loan from Scotland Yard were leading teams of uniformed policemen as they searched the station.

'What ho, sis,' he said. 'Come to join in the fun?'

'We always enjoy an outing, Harry dear, especially to railway terminuses.'

'Termini.'

'You know my feelings about pretentious Latin plurals, dear. They're fine if one is an actual ancient Roman or a medieval monk, but for the rest of us an English plural will do.'

'Where do you stand on octopi?'

'I try not to – they're delightful, intelligent creatures who do not respond well to being stepped upon. As for the name . . . really? Ma and Pa spent a fortune on your classical education and you can't spot a word with Greek roots? If one wishes to be pretentious the plural would be "octopodes", as well you know. "Octopuses" will be fine, thank you very much. "Octopi" was invented by schoolboys as a joke, to make everyone look foolish.'

I gave Harry my most withering look. 'Must you?'

He grinned. 'Must I what?'

'Must you goad her like this? You should know this lecture by heart by now. I certainly do.'

'Oh, but Strongarm, it's such fun. She gets so worked up. It's a joy to behold.'

I shook my head and tutted. 'As for you, *my lady*, "octopi" has been used by scientists since at least the middle of the last century, as well *you* know. You can rail against it all you wish, but the octopus has bolted. The squid has sailed. The train – loaded with many, many ungrammatically pluralized cephalopods – has left the station.'

Lady Hardcastle smiled. 'Quite right, dear. Quite right.' She looked round for a moment. 'But talking of ships and trains, how went the transfer at Dover?'

'Entirely according to plan,' said Harry. 'The Austrians disembarked on schedule and were aboard their train with a tiny amount of fuss and only the smallest delay.'

'Caused by . . . ?' I said.

'A dispute over the seating arrangements. By all accounts it was like a society wedding, with everyone complaining about their tables.'

'Although you wouldn't know,' said Lady Hardcastle.

'Why do you think Jake and I eloped to Gretna Green? Her family is large and illustrious, and most of them can't stand each other. Sorting out the table plan had become such a monumental task that elopement was the only way to avoid full-scale internecine war.'

'I enjoyed it,' I said. 'Although I should have liked to go to Westminster Abbey, too.'

'Another area of contention. One faction insisted that the family of the Earl of Riddlethorpe should marry at Peterborough Cathedral, as had been tradition for . . . actually, for about twenty years, since Uncle Edgar married his housekeeper. Honestly, I couldn't be doing with any of it.'

'The delay at Dover, dear,' said Lady Hardcastle.

'Ah, yes, sorry – you were the one who got me on to the wedding. Apparently a manufacturer of doodahs had been promised private access to both a manufacturer of thingumajigs – an industry heavily reliant upon doo-dahs – and the minister for whatnots, in order that he might promote and expand his business. A clerical error saw him seated instead next to a landowner from Styria who is only on the trip because of a distant familial relationship to the Habsburgs. He has no interest in doodahs, thingumajigs or even whatnots, and is, in fact, making the journey in order to further his research into the architecture of English churches – a subject upon which he has already written several tedious but well-respected books. A row ensued.'

'But it's all sorted out now?' I asked.

'Harmony has been restored, and everyone is sitting with their preferred travel companions. My anticipated two-minute confirmatory telephone call with the senior port official lasted a quarter of an hour while he vented his frustration, but the train is underway and should be able to make up the time lost. We are still expecting its arrival at thirteen minutes past two.'

Lady Hardcastle shrugged. 'No plan of operations extends with certainty beyond first contact with a self-important businessman, but at least everyone is safe. What news of the searches?'

'The building has been scoured top to bottom – no nook or cranny overlooked. The bridge has been searched, too, as per your excellent plan. Every member of staff – from management to maintenance – has been accounted for.'

'What about members of the public?' I asked.

'As you can see, there are plenty about – it's a busy station – but we have complete control over the area around the main Continental arrivals platform. No one gets in or out without one of our chaps' say so.'

'What about the non-royal trains?'

'We've managed to divert everything else to other platforms until after the royal train has been cleared. Some will have to be held on the other side of the river for a short while until there's space for them, but the schedulers are enjoying the challenge. They've made it their mission to ensure that no one is delayed for more than fifteen minutes.'

'And the bridge?'

'The bridge is sealed off at either end by armed officers, with a regular patrol on the river to make sure no one sneaks up from underneath.'

'I take it there has been no sign of the bombs,' said Lady Hardcastle.

'None whatsoever, sis.'

I shook my head. 'Well, there wouldn't be, would there?'

'How so?' said Lady Hardcastle.

'It only has a one-hour timer – we saw it on the workbench, remember? It can't be placed until after a quarter past one. Any earlier and it'll certainly cause death, injury and destruction, but we'll be the ones who cop it – the visiting Austrians will still be clickety-clacking their way through Kent and the south-eastern suburbs of London.'

'One step ahead of you, Strongarm,' said Harry. 'There's another full sweep scheduled to begin at one-twenty. The station will be bomb-free by the time the train arrives.'

Lady Hardcastle patted Harry's arm affectionately. 'I'm not sure you needed us at all.'

'Nonsense. You were the ones who found the Serbs and their bomb factory. We'd have no clue what we were looking for if it weren't for you.'

'You're right, of course – we are as invaluable as ever. Would you mind if we took a look around for ourselves?'

'Not at all.' He fished a couple of green armbands from his jacket pocket. 'Put these on so everyone knows you're part of the security section. Don't want you being frog-marched off to chokey by overzealous rozzers on suspicion of nefarious ne'er-do-wellery.'

'It would only end badly for them if they tried,' I said, 'but thank you.'

'Uniformed policemen won't be wearing them, of course, but everyone else who has access to the platform will. They're colour-coded. We're in green, railway staff are blue. Other authorized visitors will wear yellow. Anyone beyond the ticket barrier not wearing an armband should be challenged, please – they're probably not supposed to be there.'

We put on the armbands and commenced our exploration of the platform.

'It seems they have everything in hand,' I said as we set off along the main Continental departures platform. It seemed eerily quiet with the newsagent's stand closed and no tea cart, thought it was obviously going to become more lively later, bedecked as it was with red and white bunting.

'I do hope so,' said Lady Hardcastle. 'I'm still decidedly uneasy about the official decision to ignore the sniper.'

'Me too. But we've been over all the planned routes – nowhere matches the profile of the practice site. Look at this place. It's exactly as you said: there's nowhere high enough to match the cliff at the quarry. Even if Helen's estimates were off, there's nowhere to hide up there.' I indicated the vaulted roof, with its exposed skeleton of girders, trusses and ties.

'True enough. It's just . . . well, someone was most definitely practising with a Mosin-Nagant at the quarry, and I really don't think there are enough of the blessed things in the country for that to be a mere coincidence.' She pointed out of the station. 'What about that chimney there, behind the building with the *Daily Mail* advertisement painted on it?'

'It's nowhere near two hundred and fifty feet high,' I said. 'And it would take a skilled steeplejack to get up there even if it were.'

We walked on.

At the end of the platform, we stopped and looked along the tracks as they curved gently out of sight towards the river.

'Everything seems all right,' I said. 'But I have to say that if I were trying to cause the maximum outrage, I'd try to kill the archduke here. Even though it's not an official visit, there's something about being blown up at a train station that will very much capture the world's attention.'

'I can't disagree – this would be the ideal spot. We'll just have to trust Harry's men to keep everything properly buttoned up.'

My fear that we might be too busy to eat proved unfounded, and we took ourselves – our hard-boiled eggs still in our pockets – to the Grosvenor Hotel for a delicious lunch.

Full and happy, we returned to the station concourse at a quarter past one, just in time to see Harry briefing his men for the bomb search. This was a more dangerous mission and I was pleased to see that a major from the Royal Artillery was on hand to defuse any live bombs they might find.

At Harry's command, the men dispersed and we approached him.

'Anything we can do to help?' asked Lady Hardcastle.

Harry smiled. 'Actually, yes, if you wouldn't mind. I could do with a couple of pairs of experienced eyes on the platform. You know the sort of thing we're looking for better than anyone.'

'Of course, dear. It would be a relief to be active. This waiting is doing my nerves no good at all.'

'Why so nervous?'

'We all know who'll be blamed if anything awful happens. I'm sure we've covered every eventuality, and I'm reasonably certain we're safe from the eventualities we've deliberately ignored, but I shan't be at peace until Archduke Whatshisface is safely at the palace, sipping schnapps with the King and Queen. As soon as he's through those wrought-iron gates, he's someone else's problem until Wednesday, when the poor chap sets off for his first dreary trade meeting.'

'Then you should most definitely go and anxiously prowl the platform. Keep those beady eyes peeled for wickedness.'

'Right you are, dear.'

'How about you, Strongarm?' asked Harry. 'Are you similarly fretful?'

'Honestly?' I said. 'No. Sorry. Happy to prowl, though. I do love a good prowl.'

'Off you trot, then, the pair of you. Let's make sure Victoria station is fit for an archduke.'

'And a duchess,' said Lady Hardcastle. 'Sophie always gets overlooked.'

'A rather splendid woman, by all accounts. Now go. I have things to do.'

We went.

Once more we strolled along the Continental arrivals platform. This time it was a good deal busier, with uniformed policemen diligently searching every inch. The newsagent's shutters had been raised and two men were going through the interior. Men on the tracks checked beneath the overhanging edge of the platform, and I caught sight of two brave souls edging out along one of the girders high above our heads, making sure nothing had been left in the roof.

I pointed them out. 'I'm not sure how they imagine anyone would have got up there in the past two hours without anyone seeing them.'

'Well, quite. But imagine how awful we'd all feel if someone had managed it.'

We walked on, nodding acknowledgement to the tipped hats and knuckled foreheads that came our way every time we saw another policeman.

At the end of the platform we looked out again at the leftward curve of the tracks.

'I'd very much like to see the bridge for myself,' said Lady Hardcastle.

'We can if you want to,' I said. 'It's only, what, about half a mile? A ten-minute walk at worst.'

'And we'll be safe if we stick to the tracks – the only train arriving on this line is the one we're waiting for.'

'Come on, then. Last one there buys dinner.'

I was about to descend the sloping end of the platform to the tracks when Lady Hardcastle stopped me.

'Railway staff are wearing blue armbands, yes?' she said.

I nodded. 'They are.'

'So that chap over there in the overalls who looks the absolute spitting image of one of the Bermondsey Hats ought to be wearing a blue armband if he really was a railway engineer.'

I looked in the indicated direction. 'And not the green one he's wearing.'

'He's coming this way. Don't alarm him or he'll bolt.'

The man was dressed in the familiar dark boiler suit issued to railway employees, and was carrying a wooden toolbox. He was whistling a jaunty tune as he strolled along the tracks towards us. He mounted the platform and greeted us with a smile and a nod.

'Afternoon, ladies,' he said in a distinctly English accent.

'Good afternoon,' said Lady Hardcastle. 'Is all well?'

'Very well indeed, thank you.'

We allowed him to pass between us and I waited until he was just slightly behind me before driving my right foot into the back of his knee. He stumbled and swore, but he was still encumbered by the heavy toolbox and his reactions were slow. By the time he had jettisoned his burden and was free to try to turn, I was already upon him.

He fought back somewhat more expertly than I was expecting, and I worried for a brief moment that I might have met my match.

Fortunately, though, he made the same mistake that my larger opponents almost always made and decided to use his bulk and strength against me. This was just what I'd been waiting for, and he was soon lying flat on his back, winded and bewildered. He snarled some choice abuse and began to struggle upright.

His attention was caught by the soft metallic snick of Lady Hardcastle's Colt Vest Pocket pistol as she racked the slide.

'You really shouldn't speak to ladies like that,' she said.

He sighed. 'You're not going to shoot me in cold blood. Put the gun down and let me go and we'll say no more about it.'

'I wouldn't put money on it,' I said. 'She does like to shoot men who are rude to me.'

'Who the bloody hell *are* you?'

'Oh, just a couple of ladies out for an afternoon stroll,' said Lady Hardcastle. 'More to the point, though, dear: who the blue blazes are you?'

'I'm your worst nightmare,' he snarled, and once more made a move to get up.

The little pistol let out more of a pop than a bang, but it caught his attention once more. A trickle of blood seeped out on to the sleeve of his overalls.

'You bloody shot me.'

I tutted. 'Oh, don't make such a fuss – she grazed your arm. I did say she'd shoot you.'

The commotion and the shot had attracted the attention of two policemen further down the platform, and they ran towards us.

They were panting heavily as they arrived.

'Are you all right, ma'am?' asked the taller of the two.

'Quite all right, thank you, dear,' said Lady Hardcastle. 'Arrest this man and take him to Mr Featherstonhaugh. Tell him we have gone to search the bridge.'

◆　◆　◆

Eight minutes later, and puffing slightly ourselves, we arrived at the Grosvenor Railway Bridge and looked around. All was calm. The search parties were a little way behind us, with the final search of the bridge still to come, and part of me wanted to leave them to it – ten men could make a quicker and more thorough search of the bridge than the two of us could manage. But then I saw the storage bin.

To our left, just before the bridge itself, was a very large wooden box – I presumed it was for storing important stuff like tools, or electrical cable, or even some other essential gubbins like paint or grease. Its mere presence, though, wasn't what caught my eye. What drew my attention was that the lid was open and a pair of legs clad in dark blue serge, with feet wearing police-issue boots, were on the ground beside it, their owner partially concealed.

I pointed. 'There. Beside that grey wooden box.'

Lady Hardcastle looked. 'Good lord.'

We hurried over and checked the policeman. He was alive but unconscious, with a bloody wound on the back of his head. I left Lady Hardcastle trying to bring him round while I inspected the box.

As predicted, it contained a jumble of tools and equipment – huge spanners, a shovel, coils of rope, a drum of electrical cable, some old rags – but nothing worth clobbering a policeman for. It was far from full, though, so perhaps it had once contained something more interesting.

The policeman was coming round.

'Steady, dear,' said Lady Hardcastle. 'You've taken quite a clout.'

'Man,' said the policeman. 'Overalls . . . wrong armband . . . broke into box . . .'

'We've got him,' I said. 'Did you see what he took out?'

'Duffel bag.'

'Heavy?'

'Hefty, certainly . . . made it look easy . . . but he was a big lad.'

'Did you see where he was going?'

He shook his head, and the movement made him wince. 'Tussled . . . he clumped me . . . don't remember nothin' after that.'

'Can I borrow your whistle, dear?' asked Lady Hardcastle as she unclipped a chain from his tunic button and tugged the whistle free of his pocket. 'Shield your ears.'

She gave three loud blasts on the brass police whistle, and uniformed men began to converge on us as fast as the treacherously uneven surface of the railway ballast would allow.

We left the stricken man in the care of one of his fellow officers who had been trained in first aid, while Lady Hardcastle quickly explained what she wanted the others to do.

'A man has just been arrested on the station platform, having come from this direction. We believe he took one or more explosive devices from their hiding place in that storage bin before attacking your colleague. He was carrying nothing when he was arrested, so we must assume that he placed the bombs somewhere between where you were searching and the other side of the bridge. I think the bridge is more likely, but two of you should make a careful search of the area beside this track between here and the bend there just in case.' She pointed. 'The rest of you split into twos and search the bridge. I want one pair on the tracks; the rest of us will try to find a way to search the arches and look for anything he might have used to get underneath. Pay particular attention to the centres of the arches and the tops of the piers – those will be the best places to place explosives to bring the whole thing down. Two whistle blasts if you find anything.' She held up the borrowed whistle by way of illustration.

'And who are you to be tellin' my men what to do?' asked a burly sergeant.

We produced our SSB identification cards.

'We can argue about who has the authority here, Sergeant,' said Lady Hardcastle, 'or we can find the bombs before they destroy the bridge and kill the visiting dignitaries. Which do you think the most prudent course of action?'

'Now look here—'

She sighed. 'Just get on with it, Sergeant. We really don't have the time.'

Lady Hardcastle and I stepped on to the bridge, leaving the policemen to settle it among themselves. I could hear a good deal of sulky muttering, but they soon followed and dispersed along the span of the bridge to carry out the search.

It wasn't long before I spotted the abandoned canvas duffel bag scrunched up against the wall at the side of the bridge. I pointed it out to Lady Hardcastle and we leaned over the parapet to see what we were up against.

'He won't have just dangled the bombs from ropes and hoped for the best,' I said. 'They'll have needed to be placed carefully.'

'Well, quite. But how?'

I looked around.

'There's a ladder there.'

An iron ladder with a curved top lay on its side a short distance away. It looked as though it would hook over the top of the parapet to allow engineers to climb safely down the outside of the bridge to inspect the structure beneath our feet.

We worked together to lift it and slide it over the edge, and managed it fairly easily. A man on his own might find it awkward but not impossible, and the Hat we'd just met was, as the groggy constable had observed, a big lad.

I tested the ladder's fastness before climbing up and turning awkwardly to begin my descent.

'These things weren't designed with dresses in mind,' I called up as I climbed down.

Lady Hardcastle was leaning over the edge. 'Almost nothing is, dear. I think it would be too expensive to redesign our entire world to accommodate long skirts, though.'

'Perhaps it might be easier to allow us to wear trousers.'

'Trousers? Good heavens, think of the scandal. Even men had difficulty getting society to accept trousers. Did you know that the Duke of Wellington was once refused entry to Almack's Assembly Rooms in London for wearing trousers instead of knee breeches?'

'I'm a little busy at the moment,' I shouted, my voice echoing beneath the bridge. 'Can we discuss the history of gentlemen's tailoring at a more convenient time? I think I can see something.'

The piers of the bridge were built from stone blocks in the form of two stacked oval shapes, with the ironwork supported by the larger bottom oval. The upper oval, which looked reminiscent of a column when seen from the river, served mainly as a decorative facing for the clever arrangements of iron beams and trusses that formed the arch of the bridge.

I had stopped partway down this top section, and there, barely visible in the lattice of iron girders, was something that looked familiarly like a hexagonal bundle of small tubes.

'Bomb,' I called.

'We need that artillery major chap,' Lady Hardcastle called back.

'We might not have time for that,' I said, but I was drowned out by two loud blasts from her purloined police whistle.

I stepped from the ladder on to the curved girder and hauled myself up into the iron lattice.

The suspicious shape was definitely the dynamite. It had a clockwork timer taped to it, with a wire leading off into the gloom, presumably to its siblings.

I edged closer.

The clock was ticking.

It was dark under the bridge, but I could just about make out the clock face and could see that it was set to detonate in twenty minutes' time, which I estimated to be more or less when the Austrians' train was due to arrive.

I shuffled back to the outside of the bridge and looked up to see Lady Hardcastle and four policemen looking down at me, but no Royal Artillery major.

'It's definitely the bomb,' I called. 'From the look of it there's at least one dynamite bundle – possibly more – further across the bridge, but the timer is at this end.'

'How long?' Lady Hardcastle called back.

'Twenty minutes.'

'Then you'd better get out and let the expert deal with it.'

There was a commotion above as all five heads withdrew.

I waited.

A few moments later, Lady Hardcastle reappeared. 'There's a slight problem.'

'What sort of problem?'

'They found another bomb in a flower tub on the platform. He's dealing with that.'

'So that means there's only one timer down here.'

'What?'

'We saw two timers at the warehouse,' I yelled. 'If one's in the flowerpot, then there's only one down here.'

'I suppose so. How does that help?'

'Makes it simpler for me to disarm the bomb,' I said and crawled back towards it.

I thought I heard 'Florence Armstrong, don't you dare!' but it could just as easily have been the sound of water against the bridge piers.

As the member of the partnership specializing in close combat and lock picking, I had only the most basic understanding of bombs, but they seemed uncomplicated. Dynamite went bang, but only if you used some sort of detonator to set it off. This bomb, we assumed, used electrical detonators. An electrical detonator needed electricity, and in this bomb that came from a battery. And so, I reasoned, if I disconnected the battery, the detonators wouldn't work. And if the detonators didn't work, the dynamite wouldn't go bang.

I examined the bomb more closely.

Reassuringly, I was able to trace the wires from the battery to the clock, and from the clock to the bundle of dynamite – I assumed the detonator had to be inserted into one of the sticks somehow.

I took one of the wires in my right hand and folded it into a loop. I carefully took my knife from its sheath.

I cut the wire.

Chapter Fifteen

It took only a few more cuts to disconnect all the wires – better safe than sorry – and then it was a simple matter of pulling out the first detonator and cutting the battery and clock free of the dynamite. With everything separated, it seemed safe to crawl back to the outside of the bridge.

'Well?' called an anxious Lady Hardcastle.

'Well what?'

'Did you do it?'

'I think so.'

'Then bally well get back up here this instant.'

I clambered back out on to the ladder and shinned up it, hopping nimbly over the parapet to land on the bridge beside her.

'You're an idiot,' she said.

I smiled. 'I'm the idiot who just disarmed a bomb that was going to bring the bridge down.'

'A task that should have been left to the expert.'

'An expert who was otherwise engaged.'

'Yes . . . well . . . just . . . just don't do it again.'

I touched her arm. 'There's no point in doing it again – it only needed defusing once.'

'I'm not above shooting you, you know. You've seen me do it.'

The brave men of B Division had found places to be that weren't near unexploded bombs, so we were left alone on the bridge while we waited for Major Whatever-his-name-was to finish work on the flowerpot bomb and join us.

He arrived a few minutes later, puffing slightly, with a bulging haversack slung over his shoulder.

'What ho,' he said jovially as he arrived. 'You're the SSB ladies, yes?'

'We are,' I said.

'They tell me you've found a bomb.'

'We have.'

'Down there, is it?' He pointed towards the ladder and the river beyond.

'It is.'

'Soon have it defused for you. Why don't you get back to the station while I make it safe?'

'It's already safe,' I said. 'Timer disconnected, detonator removed. It just needs tidying up.'

I expected more of the usual bluster but he just grinned. 'Hah! That's the spirit. Not much to a bomb, really, is there? But don't let on – you'll do me out of a job.'

He scampered off towards the ladder.

'Do you need us to wait for you?'

'No need,' he said just before his head disappeared from view. 'Soon have everything shipshape and Bristol fashion.' He was gone.

'Back to the platform, then,' said Lady Hardcastle. 'Idiot.'

'Fusspot.'

'Noodle head.'

'Nag.'

'Buffle.'

'Shrew.'

'I'm glad you didn't blow yourself up.'

'I am, too. Hard-boiled egg?'

We found Harry on the main concourse in conversation with Colonel Valentine and Sir Montague Winfield.

'Here they come,' said Harry.

Valentine beamed. 'Well done, you two. I hear you found another bomb.'

'Found it, defused it, made it safe,' I said. 'Boiled egg?'

'I beg your pardon?' He looked at the proffered snack. 'Oh, I see. Thank you, no. But well done. One man in custody, two bombs disarmed – you've more than earned your pay this afternoon.'

'There's pay, too?' said Lady Hardcastle. 'How delightful. Put away your boiled egg, Armstrong – tonight we shall dine like kings.'

'Yes, well,' said Valentine. 'Good work.'

'This won't be forgotten,' said Sir Montague. 'We've perhaps not seen eye to eye over the past week, but I'm not afraid to admit I was wrong about you both. You've saved the trade talks. Thank you.'

'All in a day's work,' I said.

'This visit will be of immense economic and political benefit to our nation, and it's thanks to you that it's going ahead. A terrible tragedy has been averted.'

'We still need to keep our wits about us,' said Lady Hardcastle. 'We believe there were six men in the gang and we only have one in custody. The bombs might be accounted for but there are still five armed men out there.'

Sir Montague shook his head. 'They'll be scrambling to get on the next boat back to the Continent by now. And since we're all safe, what do my security advisers think about a slight change to the plan? We were taking the archduke and duchess by the most direct route to Buckingham Palace, but now we know there's no more threat, I'd like to propose a small diversion.'

'A diversion?' said Valentine.

'The tiniest. Their Royal Highnesses are Roman Catholics, of course. I wonder if we might show them the neo-Byzantine wonders of the new Westminster Cathedral. It's only just round the corner, and I know it would mean a lot to them. It would be a chance for us to show off our architectural prowess, too.'

Lady Hardcastle took a breath to speak, but Valentine cut her off.

'I can't see a problem with that,' he said. 'Featherstonhaugh?'

'Well, sir, I do wonder if we—'

'Splendid. That's agreed, then. Come along, Monty, let's make the arrangements.'

Valentine led Sir Montague away, leaving Harry, Lady Hardcastle and me on our own.

Harry waited until they were out of earshot. 'I sometimes wonder why Valentine bothers to employ us, I really do. I've lost count of the number of times he's ignored my advice and just gone ahead and done the politically expedient thing instead.'

'That, brother dearest, is why we shall never be invited to run the Bureau. We might have years of experience of gathering and analysing intelligence, but we're inept novices when it comes to playing the politics game.'

Harry sighed. 'I suppose so.'

I was about to say something consoling, but I was forestalled by the arrival of a man in a railway uniform.

He held out a message slip to Harry. 'Mr Featherstonhaugh, is it?'

'The very same.'

'Message from the stationmaster at Beckenham Junction, sir. There's donkeys on the line and the royal train is delayed.'

'Donkeys? In Beckenham?'

''S what they said. You'd be surprised the sort of things we see. But the train was 'eld up for fifteen minutes and they reckoned it'd take another fifteen to make sure everythin's safe.'

'So, a half-hour delay, then?'

'Or thereabouts, sir, yes.'

'Thank you – I'll let my team know.'

The railwayman slipped away.

Harry took his watch from his waistcoat pocket and consulted it, despite the presence of the enormous clock above us. 'I'd better tell the chaps.'

'You'd better had,' I said.

He looked around gloomily. 'Care to join me? Everyone's going to be frightfully miffed by a half-hour delay. I could do with some moral support.'

Lady Hardcastle laughed. 'You're a big brave boy, dear. I think we'll leave you to it, if you don't mind. We might go back out to the Grosvenor for half an hour and have a cup of tea. Is that agreeable, Flo?'

'Sounds good to me,' I said.

'Would that I could join you,' said Harry. 'Back here for the grand arrival, though?'

Lady Hardcastle kissed his cheek. 'Wouldn't miss it, dear. Come, tiny intelligence officer, let us drink tea and yarn about the good old days.'

'Can I wash my hands and face first? I've been clambering in the filth trying to save the world.'

'You do look a little grubby. Ladies' waiting room, then tea.'

We left Harry trying to look important and set off for a well-earned break.

◆ ◆ ◆

Lady Hardcastle was in a pensive mood as we sipped our tea.

'You look troubled,' I said. 'Still worrying about the sniper?'

'It's partly that, certainly,' she said. 'But there's been something else niggling at me for days now. I just can't put my elegantly manicured finger on it.'

'What sort of thing?' I asked. 'And do you want a ginger biscuit?'

'Don't mind if I do. And I don't know. But not in that order. It was something someone said. Something that tickled an unreachable memory. I've been trying to scratch it but it keeps evading me.'

'When was it?'

'I think it was at the LTC meeting on Thursday – when we fibbed to them about how we'd smashed the assassination plot. Which we absolutely hadn't, by the way – two bombs at Victoria station and only one man in custody.'

'One apparently English man.'

'Yes, no one's mentioned that. We'd been telling everyone we supposed they were *šajkača*-wearing Serbs, and yet when one of them turns out to be as English as I am, no one bats an eyelid.'

'I would have made more fuss, but I was busy battling a trained fighter.'

'And that's another thing. These revolutionary types tend to be younger and greener. They're egged on by the old men, but the ones fizzing with fervour on the front lines tend to be inexperienced striplings barely old enough to shave. That chap was thirty if he was a day, and he carried himself like a soldier. The others we saw at the warehouse were no spring chickens, either.'

'Perhaps the Serbs have hired local mercenaries?'

'Perhaps.' She lapsed into contemplation once more.

I looked about the hotel dining room. Mostly travellers on their way to or from somewhere exotic, I imagined. If Brighton could be considered exotic. Perhaps it could. I quite fancied a trip to Brighton now I came to think of it. It was a couple of years since we'd spent any time at the seaside, and that had been at Weston-super-Mud where we'd seen little of the sea and some-one had tried to shoot us. *We should have a break somewhere*, I decided, and we could visit Helen Titmus. We needed ice cream and sticks of rock. Punch and Judy shows and deckchairs on the beach. Brighton's beach was pebbly, though, rather than sandy. I wondered if there was a seaside resort where—

'John Clare,' said Lady Hardcastle, slightly more loudly than I thought necessary.

'What?' I said, slightly irked to have my seaside reverie so harshly interrupted.

'John blasted Clare. That's what's been niggling me.'

'Is he the chap with the bombs?'

'No, he's a poet. Or he was. Early 1800s? I can't remember.'

'Did he have much to say on the subject of assassinating Austrian royalty?'

'Not as far as I'm aware, no. But he did write one pertinent poem, and it's just come back to me. One of the London Trade Confederation board members said something odd when we were describing our efforts in the East End and Bermondsey. He said, "we certainly didn't imagine you'd be whirling round the hovel ends". I thought at the time it was a peculiar thing to say, but they're peculiar men, so it just wandered sullenly off into the back of my mind, there to irritate me as I tried to go about my business. But I've just remembered that it's a quotation. Or a paraphrase, at least. "As round the hovel end it whirled." It had already fanned the feathers of the bird, you see, and ruffed the robin's ruddy breast. Only then did it feel it appropriate to whirl around the hovel end and set off to sob and gallop o'er the west.'

'And what was "it"?'

'It, my dear Flo, was "The Autumn Wind". I never cared for the poem but it was a favourite of one of my governesses, and so I was compelled to learn it. He rhymes "find" and "mind" with "wind", and that bothered me as a child, but she insisted that it used to be pronounced as "wined", so it was all right and I should stop being such a picky-knickers.'

'You *are* a picky-knickers – she wasn't wrong there.'

'She was a perspicacious woman, her dubious taste in poetry notwithstanding.'

'But how does this help us?'

'It doesn't, particularly, but it was everyone's reaction to it, as though they were in on some shared joke. I'd wager they all knew the poem.'

'I'm still not entirely with you. Are you saying that because they all knew an obscure poem, they're all members of Autumn Wind? It's a bit of a stretch.'

'Oh, it would never stand up in court, but it's suggestive, don't you think?'

I gave what I hoped was a helpfully encouraging smile, but I wasn't convinced.

Lady Hardcastle slammed down her teacup. 'Oh.'

This time her outburst caused the other diners and tea drinkers to turn and tut.

I tutted myself. 'What now?'

'Westminster blasted Cathedral.'

'I rather like it, actually. It's quite striking, don't you think? I mean, London has more than its fair share of older buildings, some of them also striking in their own way, but if you were a visiting Catholic, wouldn't you want to see the largest Catholic church in the country? I mean . . . Oh.'

'Oh, indeed. The bell tower must be at least two hundred and fifty feet high. Probably a little more. It has a good view along the road, wouldn't you say?'

'Ashley Place.'

'How do you remember these things?' she said.

'How do you not?'

'But it must be, what, a hundred and twenty yards to the turning?'

'About that, yes.'

'Do you still think it's a stretch to believe that the LTC is just Autumn Wind with a new name and a smart suite of offices in the City?'

'It's looking more and more likely that they are,' I said. 'And—'

'And Colonel-blasted-Valentine as well, I'd wager, yes. No wonder he was so desperate to pooh-pooh the sniper idea. We were never supposed to find out about that.'

'It was only by the most absurd coincidence that we did. What were the odds of our photographer friend going to exactly the same quarry the Hats had used for target practice?'

'Infinitesimal. But sometimes these things work in our favour.'

'Far too often if you ask me.'

'One should never look a gift whatsit in the thingummy, dear,' said Lady Hardcastle.

'Duly noted. What now, though? How do we stop them? Whom can we trust?'

'No one but Harry for the moment. The SBOs will obey Valentine unquestioningly – they don't know he's a wrong 'un. And even if they do, they might follow him anyway. We need to get a message to Harry and then get ourselves to the cathedral.'

She paid for our tea and we set off to find the concierge.

He was, we were relieved to discover, exactly where he was supposed to be – at his desk.

'What can I do for you, ladies? Tickets for a show? Dinner? There are a few lovely restaurants I can heartily recommend.'

'That would be enchanting,' said Lady Hardcastle, 'but not just now. We need something altogether more mundane, I'm afraid. Might I trouble you for a piece of paper and an envelope?'

'Certainly.'

He produced the stationery, along with a pencil, and Lady Hardcastle hurriedly wrote a note. She sealed it in the envelope.

'And do you have a messenger?'

'Of course, madam.' He rang a bell and a uniformed lad appeared at a run.

'Excellent. Good afternoon, young man. I need you to take this letter on to the station concourse. You must find Mr Harry Featherstonhaugh. He's a tall gentleman in a grey tweed suit and black Oxford shoes. He's wearing a dark grey homburg hat at what he imagines is a rakishly jaunty angle, and he has a green armband on his right arm. He looks, if you can imagine such a thing, a little like me – he's my brother.'

'Right you are, ma'am.'

'Do you think you can recognize him?'

'Easy as pie, ma'am.'

'By all means ask a uniformed policeman if you can't find Mr Featherstonhaugh, but please do not speak to anyone else. When you track him down, hand him this envelope. There's no need to wait for a reply.'

'No reply,' repeated the boy.

'This is the most important part, though: under no cir-cumstances give the envelope to anyone else. If someone says, "Don't worry, lad, I'll see it gets to him," politely refuse. If they insist, kick them in the shins and run like the clappers. Only Mr Featherstonhaugh can have this letter.'

The boy grinned, and I imagined him hoping he might meet some resistance. 'I understand, ma'am.'

'Good lad.' She handed him an absurdly large tip. 'Off you go. Quick as you can, please.'

The boy scurried off.

'Will that be all, madam?' asked the concierge. 'We like to make our guests' stays as enjoyable as possible.'

'Oh, we're not guests, dear. But thank you anyway.' She gave him a huge tip of his own and we hurried out of the hotel.

◆ ◆ ◆

We burst from the hotel's main doors on to Buckingham Palace Road like characters in a slapstick comedy film, and screeched to a halt in much the same style. Coming towards us were two men wearing green armbands.

'Do we know those two?' I asked.

'Never seen them before,' said Lady Hardcastle. 'But they've not seen us – let's cross the road.'

Dodging between the afternoon traffic and taking off our own armbands, we reached the safety of Grosvenor Gardens, where we strolled nonchalantly along the path, intermittently concealed by the trees.

'The cathedral's the other way,' I said.

'Well, yes, but those two aren't part of the Basement's SBO detachment, and they weren't with us on the warehouse raid. Unless and until I learn differently, I'm going to assume that everyone is against us. Where are they going?'

As casually as I could, I looked over my shoulder. 'Into the Grosvenor. They might just be trying to deliver a message.'

'Or they might have been sent to make sure we don't scupper Autumn Wind's plans. Are they in?'

'Safely in, with the doors closed behind them.'

'Then we'd better hurry.'

We were only going a few hundred yards round the corner – surely it couldn't be dangerous. Nevertheless, we crossed the road and ambled along, doing our best impersonation of two fashionable ladies out for a stroll. If anyone had troubled to look closely, they would have seen the grime on my clothes and the blossoming bruise on my cheek where Suspiciously English Hat had landed a lucky punch. Fortunately, we were in London, where everyone was far too wrapped up in their own concerns to pay any attention to two strangers.

I kept a weather eye on the opposite side of the road as we passed Victoria Underground station, but so far we were in the clear.

As we drew level with the Duke of York, though, I spotted two more green armbands heading up Wilton Road from the mainline station. I nudged Lady Hardcastle towards the door of the pub and we went inside.

Familiar smells, a familiar choking fug of tobacco smoke, and, as a quick look round told us, only one way out – back the way we came in.

'Not my finest choice of escape route,' I said. 'Sorry.'

'Heigh-ho,' said Lady Hardcastle. 'Not to worry. We only have to wait long enough for the Windies to stroll off in the wrong direction, then we can resume our journey.'

'Is that what we're calling them now?'

'The Windies? Yes, I think so. Do you like it?'

'Not a great deal.'

'I do like to give silly names to villainous gangs. It makes them much less scary, don't you think?'

'I suppose. How are we doing for time?'

She consulted her wristwatch. 'I'd say the train is due in another twenty minutes or so.'

'We still have a little while, then, if we add disembarking, formal welcome, speeches, boarding the cars.'

'But not long enough for us to tarry unduly. We must take our chances.'

We left the pub and resumed our walk, this time with a little more urgency.

We crossed the road to Carlisle Place, where we felt safe enough to hurry a little more. At the turning to Ashley Place, we stopped and looked up.

A hundred and twenty yards away, the red-brick campanile of Westminster Cathedral stood sentinel over the surrounding streets. It was a tall, square tower, banded with white stone. The top sections were circular, supported by radial buttresses, and the whole thing was topped with an ornate cupola.

I started scanning the openings, of which there were many. There were single-arched windows at regular intervals on each side of the square section, but I decided we could ignore those – we expected the sniper to be around two hundred and fifty feet above ground. The final openings on the square part of the tower were double the width, and I squinted in the bright sunshine to see if anyone lurked there, but there was no one.

The arches in the first circular tier looked more promising and seemed to offer a perfect vantage spot for a would-be assassin. He would have a choice of angles, and both the brick and stone pillars that supported the tier above would provide adequate concealment.

The sun was slightly behind us now, but still high in the sky, and I tipped the brim of my hat slightly to try to shield my eyes a little.

'Can you see anything?' I said.

'Not yet,' said Lady Hardcastle. 'If I were going to take a shot from up there, I'd choose those arches on the bottom tier beneath the cupola. But there's no one there as far as I can see. The observation platform is further up, I seem to recall – the level with the birds on the parapet. Are they eagles, do you think? Hold on. Movement.'

I looked again, and sure enough, there was a figure, just about visible between the stone birds. He squatted down, apparently busy with something.

He was out of sight for a minute or so, then slowly reappeared. He raised what looked alarmingly like a rifle and pointed it towards our end of the street.

As calmly and naturally as we could, hoping to betray no sign that we had been looking his way, we began to walk quickly towards the cathedral.

Chapter Sixteen

There was a small gaggle of clerics on the steps outside the main door of the cathedral, deep in conversation with a man wearing an expensive-looking suit whom I recognized from the LTC board meetings.

'What's the proper name for a group of priests?' I asked.

'No idea, dear,' said Lady Hardcastle. 'A mass?'

'Well, it looks like that mass of priests is being briefed by someone from Autumn Wind.'

'A Windy, you mean?'

'That's not going to catch on. You know that, don't you?'

'And yet I shall persist. But yes, I think his name's Furlong. Or Baldwin. Or is it Millington?'

'We may never know. Or care overmuch.'

'Well, quite,' said Lady Hardcastle. 'But I imagine he's giving them the good news that an important visitor would very much love to see their beautiful new cathedral.'

'And making the news sound sufficiently exciting and important that it needs everyone outside so that they don't notice that there's a killer in the campanile, about to defile their sacred building by using it as a vantage point from which to commit murder.'

'Somehow that makes their ghastliness even more ghastly, doesn't it. But the important question is: did he come alone?'

That question was swiftly answered as we passed the clergymen and saw two dark-haired men coming out of the main doorway, each wearing a green armband. Their suits weren't as well tailored as the LTC man's, and struggled to conceal the guns they were so obviously carrying. They stood 'at ease' with their hands clasped behind their backs. They seemed familiar, but perhaps it was simply their bearing – former soldiers all carried themselves the same way.

We strolled past.

'. . . and that's when Elsie decided she'd had quite enough of his nonsense,' said Lady Hardcastle.

'I'm not surprised,' I said. 'The way he's been carrying on I thought she would have snapped years ago.'

'Well, quite. I'm surprised she hasn't done something drastic. Especially after the incident with the parlour maid.'

I cast a sly glimpse at the burly men and saw that they were completely ignoring us. I was briefly put out that they weren't enjoying our impromptu performance. If I'd been in their position I would certainly want to hear more about Elsie's marital woes, and I'd be especially curious to find out more about the incident with the parlour maid.

We rounded the front of the cathedral and turned right on to Ambrosden Avenue, where almost at once we met another door.

It was locked.

'I could pick that in a moment,' I said. 'Although it might be bolted. Those two ex-soldiers at the front have probably secured it.'

'I was thinking the same,' said Lady Hardcastle. 'Let's see if there are more ways in.'

Sure enough, less than fifty yards further on, we found another door, and this one was open. With a carefully discreet look around to make sure we were unobserved, we slipped inside.

Closing the door quietly behind us, we found ourselves in a small enclosed porch with another door to the right. This led to a small lobby which in turn opened into the main body of the cathedral itself.

The interior was made gloomy by its dark ceiling and was only sparsely lit, but even by the dim light of the candles I could see that it was a magnificent space.

Lady Hardcastle looked around for a moment to get her bearings, then pointed along the aisle to the right.

'That way to the campanile, I believe,' she said softly.

We had no way of knowing if there were more Autumn Wind henchmen lurking about the place, but we didn't want to be spotted and challenged by anyone, friend or foe, so we moved as stealthily as we could across the parquet floor, keeping to the balls of our feet.

We passed three small chapels to the side and then came to a large, wooden double door.

'Is this it?' I asked.

Lady Hardcastle peered about. 'I think so. That looks like the end of the building there, so that locked door we found should be just around the corner. And that would make this the way to the campanile. Try it.'

The door opened and we did indeed find ourselves inside a square tower, with wooden stairs leading upwards. We began our tiptoed ascent.

Two hundred and fifty feet really isn't a very long way to travel along a city street or a country lane. A journey of two hundred and fifty vertical feet is an entirely different matter.

Having spent my early childhood living in a circus caravan, I had once found staircases to be an exciting curiosity. What an adventure it must be, I used to think, to have to go upstairs to bed. Imagine the fun you could have in a house that was so huge it actually had several floors stacked on top of each other.

These romantic notions were snuffed out when we moved back to my grandmother's tiny cottage in Cwmdare and I learned that the first floor was no more thrilling than the ground floor – it was just higher up. And when I entered service as a scullery maid in a grand house in Cardiff, I came to resent stairs as a source of thigh-aching trudgery.

Now here we were in an Italianate cathedral bell tower, and my previous experiences with stairs seemed like gentle strolls through sun-splashed meadows.

Hearts thudding and lungs protesting, we trudged upwards.

As the one with the pistol, Lady Hardcastle took the lead while I followed, keeping an ear and half an eye out for any danger that might be sneaking up on us from behind.

The stairs wound upwards in a squared spiral following the four walls of the tower. At each turn there was a small landing, and after a few minutes' weary climbing Lady Hardcastle stopped.

I tried to catch my breath to speak but she held up her hand for silence and cocked her head to listen.

I listened, too.

I couldn't hear anything. I shrugged and again opened my mouth to speak.

She glared at me and held her finger to her lips.

This time I heard it – the shuffle of shoe leather on wood and a weary sigh as some unseen watcher shifted his weight and contemplated the tedium of his assigned duty.

At Lady Hardcastle's signal, we resumed our climb, this time taking even more care to be as quiet as we possibly could.

Things went well for the next two flights, but then one of the boards creaked. Not the sort of gentle sound that might be mistaken for the wood settling itself after a bit of a stretch, but the sort of raucous screech that most definitely said, 'Look out, Mr Lookout, there's someone coming up the stairs.'

We froze.

The man above us – two flights closer now – shuffled his feet. 'Is that you, Winter?'

Lady Hardcastle and I looked at each other and shrugged. It crossed my mind to give a non-committal guttural grunt, but though the quality of my animal impressions was unsurpassed, I didn't think I could convincingly portray an armed thug of unknown age, weight and provenance.

'Who's there?' said the lookout. 'The tower is closed. You'll have to go back down.'

With another shrug, we resumed our careful ascent. Lady Hardcastle holstered her tiny pistol.

The arrangement of the stairs left an empty square space down the middle of the tower, which I thought would be an excellent place for a lift shaft to save visitors the effort of all this climbing. But the absence of this modern convenience did mean that we were able to see not only to the top of the flight we were on, but also to the top of the next one at right angles to us. I thought this offered us a tremendous advantage in being able to spot the guard, right up until the moment we spotted the guard. Obviously an arrangement that allowed us so easily to see him meant that as he stepped out of the room where he had been stationed, he could also see us.

'You're not supposed to be up here,' he said. 'The tours are cancelled for the afternoon. Essential maintenance.'

He looked familiar, and I realized – as I imagined his head topped by a *šajkača* – that he was one of the men from the warehouse. That must be why I'd thought I recognized the two men outside the main door, too. These were the Hats.

We carried on climbing.

'Oh dear,' said Lady Hardcastle with exaggerated breathlessness. 'Really? A charming young chap in a clerical robe said it would be all right. We just want a little look. It's such a marvellous place, don't you think? Who would have thought people would still be building magnificent cathedrals in this day and age?'

'It's a thing of beauty,' said the man. 'But this is as far as you can go – the observation platform is closed.' He pointed upwards. 'I'm afraid I'm going to have to ask you to return to the ground floor. It's really not safe up here today. You can come back tomorrow.'

Still we climbed.

'Tomorrow is no good, dear – we have to be elsewhere tomorrow. This is our only chance.'

'I'm sorry, madam, but I really must insist.'

By this time, Lady Hardcastle was almost level with the guard, just one step down from the landing where he stood.

She was still talking. 'Surely you can make an exception, dear. We've climbed all this way and there can't be much further to go. Just a few more flights, surely—'

She tripped on the top step and stumbled into him.

'I really am most terribly sorry, dear. I'm not usually this clumsy – it must be the climb.'

She put her hand behind her back and I saw at once the reason for her feigned clumsiness – she had picked his pocket and was holding his gun. She waggled it and I interpreted this as an invitation to take it from her.

I stepped out from behind her and levelled the familiar 9 mm pistol at the guard. His hand went at once to the empty holster beneath his jacket.

I smiled. 'Oops, that was careless of you. I believe the phrase is "hands up".'

He looked briefly bewildered, but after a moment's pause, he lunged for the pistol. Fortunately, he telegraphed the move so plainly that I was able to step aside in plenty of time, and his hands flailed at the empty air where I once had been. Lady Hardcastle must have been paying attention to my encounters with wrong 'uns over the years, because she correctly spotted the moment he was most off balance and gave his arm a hefty tug to send him tumbling down the stairs. His downward progress was arrested by the wall at the turn of the staircase, and he stopped at the next landing, out cold.

I held the pistol out for Lady Hardcastle with the look of distaste I usually reserved for dealing with dead rats.

She took it and, with a tut and a roll of her eyes, pointedly flicked the safety lever down with the tip of her gloved finger. She used the gun to gesture into the room recently vacated by the guard.

A quick look round revealed that we were on the level near the top of the square section of the tower – the one with the double-width windows. There was a door in the corner, beyond which we found another staircase, this time a spiral.

Once again, Lady Hardcastle took the lead and we tiptoed upwards. Despite all the racket we had already made, we still somehow imagined that silence might save us, and we made our way with exaggerated stealth.

A door a short way up opened into the chamber that housed the cathedral's gigantic bell, but the stairs carried on and so did we.

At the top there was another door.

Lady Hardcastle burst through, pistol raised, but it was another empty chamber with another spiral staircase on the opposite side.

We climbed again.

Surely we must be nearly there by now, I thought. My thighs were screaming, my heart hammering, and it felt as though I might never catch my breath again. The next time we tried to thwart an assassination attempt I wanted it to be at ground level. Preferably somewhere flat like Norfolk. Or Holland.

By now we could feel a breeze – fresh air from the outside world. One last twist of the stairs and we found ourselves in an arched opening with a high parapet before us, decorated at intervals with majestic stone eagles.

A quick look over the edge showed that we were on the north-east side of the tower, looking down at Ambrosden Avenue and the door through which we had entered. If the sniper was still there, he was on the other side, his eyes peeled for the arrival of the arch-duke's motor car on Ashley Place.

◆ ◆ ◆

We edged our way round the narrow platform, and I was only slightly distracted by the spectacular view across the city. I could see the Houses of Parliament and Westminster Abbey. Then there was St James's Park, where we had watched the pelicans. Queen Victoria's statue stood outside Buckingham Palace, looking down the Mall. Then the palace itself and its magnificent gardens.

And then there was a man with a rifle, though he was much closer.

He was leaning on the parapet, his arms braced on the stone lintel to steady the gun.

He was quite relaxed and was looking about as though he was just another sightseer. I was relieved to realize we weren't too late and that the archduke had yet to arrive.

Lady Hardcastle scuffed her heel on the floor and cleared her throat.

The man started and turned quickly towards us, his rifle still pointing towards the street.

'I'm so sorry,' said Lady Hardcastle. 'I didn't mean to make you jump, but are you by any chance the chap who's trying to start a war? We heard there was an assassination attempt up here. Have we come to the right place?' Her stolen pistol was aimed squarely at his head.

'Who the blistering blue blazes are you?'

'I'm Lady Hardcastle from the Secret Service Bureau, and this is Miss Armstrong. You're under arrest, dear.'

The man laughed. 'That's very funny. You know you have no powers of arrest, don't you? Isn't that why the SSB has its pet Special Branch thugs?'

'To be honest, I hoped you wouldn't know that. But the game's still up.' She waggled her pistol.

He laughed again. 'They send women to do the dirty work now?'

'They've found we do a better job. Not only do we take care of the nation's enemies, we clean up after ourselves and then make everyone a nice pot of tea. Now put down that handsome Russian rifle and put your hands up.'

He swung the rifle round and pointed it at her. 'How about you put down that dainty little pistol and put *your* hands up? Wait, is that one of ours?'

'It is, dear. But you seem to have overplayed your hand. You can't shoot me without alerting the people below to your presence. I'd wager you were relying on causing so much confusion that you and your confederate would be able to slip out into the crowd before anyone could work out where the shot had come from. By the time they'd fathomed it out, all that would be here would be a Mosin-Nagant and the *šajkača* that the assassin carelessly dropped as he fled.' She nodded towards the Serbian cap on the ground beside him. 'If you shoot us, there'll be no confusion, just a loud bang. And then your goose will be well and truly cooked.'

The man smiled and nodded. 'Touché. Or . . . perhaps not. I think you underestimate my employers' power. Gunshots from up here would alert everyone, it's true, but my comrades will ensure my escape. And when they find two dead SSB officers as well as the rifle and the cap at the top of the tower, Autumn Wind's poodles in the press will be able to paint a picture of a shocking assassination attempt by Serbian terrorists. It might not start the war as surely as the archduke's death, but Europe will march a step closer to it. And so, Lady . . . what was it? Hardacre?'

'Hardcastle.'

'Lady Hardcastle, yes, I'm so sorry. You must think me terribly rude.'

'Not at all, dear. You were saying?'

'Ah, yes, you can't shoot me, either. A bang, a hullabaloo, a dead Serbian with a rifle, and the press will still have their story.'

I wasn't sure if their logic held up, but I did have an idea for how to resolve things without anything having to go bang. It rather relied on his not having his finger on the trigger, but I decided to trust his obvious military training and assume that it would be safely out of the way.

I glanced quickly to my right as though I'd seen something startling coming towards the tower. Despite the absurdity of such a notion, it had the desired effect and the gunman instinctively turned himself and, crucially, his gun, to see what the danger was.

With one rapid but smooth movement, I drew my knife from the sheath on my forearm and threw it, catching his right hand and pinning it to the rifle stock.

He let out a bellow of pain and frustration and tried to bring the rifle to bear once more, but found that he couldn't move his trigger finger. I stepped in, lifted the barrel, and struck him firmly on the forehead, banging his head against one of the majestic stone eagles and rendering him, like his polite friend below, unconscious.

'I say, Flo,' said Lady Hardcastle. 'Well done you. I fear the poor chap's banjo-playing days might be behind him, but I believe war has been averted. For now, at least.'

'We still need to get downstairs in case they have a contingency plan,' I said. 'There are six of them, remember? There's one in custody, these two, and the two more on the cathedral doors. That only accounts for five.'

'You're right, of course.'

I retrieved my knife and bound his wounded hand with strips torn from his shirtsleeve.

Lady Hardcastle unloaded the rifle and pocketed the ammunition.

I checked the gunman's breathing and inspected the back of his head. The skin was split and he'd have a nasty lump, but he was otherwise in good enough shape for someone who was prepared to start a war for money.

Lady Hardcastle put down the rifle. 'Whose stockings are we using?'

'We'll tie this one with mine and we can use yours to restrain the gent on the stairs.'

'We ought to carry handcuffs, you know.'

'We probably ought, but where would we put them? It's hard enough finding somewhere for your gun and my knife without having to haul a couple of pairs of darbies about as well.'

Having checked him for further weapons, we hogtied the would-be assassin and left him on the platform.

His mate was still spark out, so he was similarly restrained and we hastened down the stairs.

Chapter Seventeen

Rather than run straight into the two Hats by the main door, we left the cathedral the way we had entered and hurried round to the front of the building from the outside.

The clergymen and church officials were standing proudly on the steps, waiting for the arrival of their special guest. The London Trade Confederation board member was chatting amiably to one of them, while the two Hats stood impassively behind them all, blocking the entrance and – or so they thought – keeping their comrades safe.

'What time is it now?' I said as we walked towards the cathedral door.

Lady Hardcastle checked her wristwatch. 'Coming up to a quarter past three. Speeches and introductions should be over by now, surely.'

'I pity the poor Austrians if they're not. Imagine trekking half-way across Europe, crossing the Channel, spending the morning on a train through Kent, and then having to listen to half an hour's worth of speeches of welcome from Sir Montague Windbag.'

'It's worked in our favour, though, dear. It gave us time to neutralize the sniper threat.'

'There's that, I suppose. But I'm still worried about the sixth man – what will the back-up plan be?'

'What would we do if it were us?'

'We'd make sure the first attempt didn't fail.'

'Well, everyone imagines they'll manage that. But the bombs have been disarmed and the sniper knocked unconscious by a giant stone eagle, so what next?'

I thought for a moment, looking round. 'There's no point in risking a man on the ground if the sniper succeeds, so nothing will happen until the car is safely past the killing zone and on its way here to the door. They want to make a splash for the newspapers. They need something horrifying they can blame on the Serbs. They need . . . they need that man standing over there on the corner, leaning oh-so-casually against that plane tree.'

'I say, well done you. You actually remembered the name of a tree.'

'Don't get too excited – it's the only one I know. Strange that I can remember the name of a Serbian cap like the one he has in his hand, but I can't tell a sycamore from an English elm.'

'The sycamore has—'

'Really? Now?'

'Sorry, dear. What does he have in his haversack, I wonder?'

'There's one way to find out. We'll split up. You approach him directly and engage his attention. I'll sneak up from behind and do what I do best.'

'Offer him a nice cup of tea?'

'And a delicious slice of cake. Ready?'

We set off.

The tree stood at a sort of triangular junction, where the road that led round the side of the cathedral grounds veered off from Ashley Place. I walked as though I was planning to go around the side of the cathedral, while Lady Hardcastle walked straight ahead towards the point where the archduke's car should be appearing at any moment.

When I was concealed from the man's view by the plane tree, I crossed the road and waited behind it.

Lady Hardcastle approached from the other side. 'Good afternoon.'

'Good afternoon,' said the man.

'I wonder if you might be able to help me – somehow I seem to have got myself lost. Obviously I'm at Westminster Cathedral, but I'm dashed if I can fathom out how to get from here to Buckingham Palace.'

'Not to worry, it's quite simple. Carry on along this road and turn right at the end. Then turn left on to— oof.'

He collapsed against the tree and we guided him gently to the ground.

'It never ceases to amaze me how someone so little can bring down men so big with so little fuss,' said Lady Hardcastle.

I curtseyed. 'It's just technique. What's in the haversack?'

She rummaged.

'A stick of dynamite with a fuse. Oh, and a box of Serbian matches. That's a clever touch. They've really thought this through.'

At that moment, a Rolls-Royce turned on to the road and came towards us. Sitting in the back seat was a man wearing a cocked hat and a white military tunic with a red and white sash. Next to him was a woman wearing a white dress and an enormous hat of her own. The Archduke Franz Ferdinand and Sophie, Duchess of Hohenberg. Two men in similarly ornate white military uniforms sat facing them.

The motor car rolled sedately past us and we gave them a little wave. The archduke didn't notice us, but the duchess smiled and offered a small wave in response.

Immediately behind the Rolls came a smaller government-issue car, with Harry in the back. He saw us and instructed his driver to stop. He hopped out and hurried over.

There were three more expensive-looking cars following Harry, these with their roofs up. They seemed to be carrying the LTC board. There was a moment's hesitation from the lead driver when he saw Harry's Austin stop, and that gave Sir Montague, sitting in the back, time to see us standing next to the unconscious Hat. He barked an instruction we couldn't hear and the car swerved around the Austin and accelerated down the road. The other two followed.

'What ho, sis,' said Harry. 'I say, is that man unconscious?'

'It seems to be happening a lot today,' I said. 'I think there must be an itis going round.'

'Must be. Is this the sniper you told me about?'

Lady Hardcastle showed him the inside of the haversack. 'No, dear. This is the back-up bomber. The sniper and his minder are up in the bell tower.'

'Are they unconscious, too?'

'They certainly were when we left them, but they're well secured even if they've come to. You seem oddly unconcerned that Autumn Wind are doing a bunk in their fancy motor cars.'

'All in hand, sis. All in hand.'

There was activity on the steps of the cathedral. The priests had stepped forward to greet the archduke and the duchess, who were being helped out of their car by the military officers accompanying them. There was a pause while both sides tried to decide on the correct protocol, and eventually it fell to the officers to make the formal introductions.

Some of the priests were looking behind them for the LTC man, so that they might include him in the welcome party, but at the sight of his colleagues speeding off back towards the main road, he and his bodyguards had bolted.

The Austrians regarded all this with baffled amusement, but something in their royal training told them to ignore the strange goings-on and concentrate on the reason for their visit. The priests led them inside.

'Properly in hand, dear?' said Lady Hardcastle. 'It really does look awfully as though they're getting away.'

The cars headed towards Victoria Street, but the men on foot tried to take the same route we'd taken down the side of the cathedral. I had no idea where that road might lead them, but I was reasonably certain they could easily lose themselves in the backstreets before anyone could round them up.

'Have a little faith, ladies. I'm not quite the duffer you always say I am.'

'Not always, dear. Only when you're being a duffer.'

Against our better judgement, we sat tight waiting for . . . we had no idea what we were waiting for, but we waited nonetheless. For all our teasing, Harry mostly did know what he was doing and we had to trust him.

It was a tense few moments, but to our astonishment the next thing we saw was the rearmost of the three LTC cars reversing back along Ashley Place towards us. Behind them – or perhaps that should be 'in front of them' – came the other two cars, both gingerly reversing along the street.

The reason for their panicked change of direction became clear when a column of Household Cavalry in full ceremonial uniform, breastplates gleaming, plumes bouncing and swishing on polished helmets, came trotting along the road, four abreast. Their dark blue tunics marked them as the Blues and Royals.

We could also hear the clopping of military hooves from the other direction, as another group of horsemen arrived, this time the Life Guards in their red tunics.

With both ends of the street blocked, the lead car – formerly the third car – attempted to turn on to Ambrosden Avenue, but it stopped abruptly as the LTC man and the two former Hats came running back up, pursued by a large group of policemen. Some of the police officers were still trying to button their tunics as they chased the fleeing men, and only a few were wearing their helmets.

In moments, the entire LTC group were bottled up in front of the cathedral, surrounded by policemen and cavalry troopers.

'You see?' said Harry with a grin. 'I told you we had it all in hand.'

'I never doubted you for a second, dear,' said Lady Hardcastle. 'Well, for a second or two, perhaps, but certainly no more than a minute.'

I nodded. 'Good work, Mr Feather-stone-huff. Just one thing, though: I know where you found the cavalry, but where did all the rozzers come from?'

'There's a police section house down at the end of the road there. One telephone call and the street was full of half-dressed, off-duty coppers, eager to do their duty and apprehend whatsoever miscreants and ne'er-do-wells they might encounter.'

'That was a stroke of luck.'

'Wasn't it just? I had no idea what to expect. All I had to go on was a scrawled note from Ems.'

'The lad found you all right, then?' said Lady Hardcastle.

'Cheeky little chap in a Grosvenor Hotel uniform? He did. I gave him half a crown for his trouble.'

'It's his lucky day. I already gave him five bob.'

'Five shillings? That's more than he earns in a week.'

'Then it really is his lucky day. I hope he spends it wisely.'

'I doubt it. It'll all be gone on humbugs, pop, and fine fancies for his sweetheart before the day's out.'

'Good for him.'

'Never mind that, though, I need to go and supervise the arrests. Meet me back at Whitehall Court – I'll need a full report.'

'*You* will?' I said. 'What about Valentine?'

'You mean the man in the army uniform up there being arrested by that eager young Peeler? I think he'll be doing some explaining of his own. Toodle-oo for now, ladies.'

The chaos looked fun, but I for one didn't fancy all the paperwork that would be involved in helping to sort it out, so we strolled off in the direction of Victoria station and our waiting motor car.

Back at the Basement we drank tea with the filing clerk and the duty officer while we waited for Harry's return. I liked to imagine that they were always pleased to see us, but they were especially glad that afternoon because we had stopped on the way to buy biscuits.

Harry eventually arrived, bearing a packet of biscuits of his own, and we retired to Colonel Valentine's empty office for our meeting.

'Are you the new boss, then?' I asked as Harry waved us into the visitor chairs.

'Who knows? All I can be certain of at the moment, both from my investigations and from today's events, is that Colonel Clifford Valentine has been a member of Autumn Wind for at least the past ten years and possibly longer.'

'How long have you known?' asked Lady Hardcastle.

'Well now, sis . . . "known" is quite a strong word. I've suspected for a while, but I didn't properly "know" until last week.'

'And you let him try to scupper our work?' I said.

'I certainly allowed him to think he was managing it, but I knew you two wouldn't be put off. I knew we'd be safe.'

Lady Hardcastle smiled. 'That's very flattering, dear. Thank you. But you could have told us.'

'I could, but where would be the fun in that? As I said, I knew we'd be safe in your hands. And I was right.'

'Infuriating but right, dear, yes. What happens now?'

'Now I have to report in person to the War Office. Tomorrow I shall have to show my face at the Home Office, and the Foreign Office. The Board of Trade will need to be brought up to speed at some point, and I fully anticipate having to speak to several parliamentary committees and perhaps even Number 10.'

'Busy boy. We ought to make sure you have all the facts at your disposal, then.'

'That's rather why we're here. I'll tell you what I know, you tell me what you know, then I can stitch it all together into a coherent narrative to explain the whole sorry mess to assorted government departments.'

'You first then, dear. What do you know?'

'I know that the London Trade Confederation is the current working name of Autumn Wind.'

Lady Hardcastle frowned. 'Is that it?'

'Well . . . yes.'

'We rather worked that out for ourselves,' I said. 'Presumably you need more than, "Well, Prime Minister, it's blindingly obvious."'

'Oh, I have contracts, title deeds, correspondence, surveillance reports – you name it. I've been working on this for months.'

'Did it have anything to do with those mysterious personal advertisements in *The Times*?'

'Not at all, no. Turns out that was just a couple of students having a lark.'

Lady Hardcastle laughed. 'Glad to see your instincts are still sound, dear. But I think you know everything we know already. Our East End contacts pointed us at suspicious activity in a Bermondsey warehouse. Which reminds me – we need to find out what happened to Benny Butcher.'

'And that reminds *me*: I need to smooth things over with Chief Inspector Whatnot—'

'Cromwell,' I said.

'Really? How on earth do you remember these things?'

'It's a gift and a curse.'

'It certainly seems to be. But Brownlow and Perlman ruffled some feathers when they took over the investigation of the shooting at Butcher's house, and we need the local rozzers on our side as much as possible.'

'You'll be charging one of the Hats for the murder?' I asked.

'It seems most likely that one of them is responsible, certainly, though we have no proof so I'm not entirely sure where we go from there.'

'That's annoying,' said Lady Hardcastle. 'What other information can we help you with, though, Harry? You know the results of our surveillance of the warehouse and our original presumption that six Serbians were planning a murderous attack on the trade delegation.'

Harry nodded. 'And obviously we now know that they were six British mercenaries hired by Autumn Wind to try to spark a war with Austria-Hungary. After some face-saving snarling they realized the jig was up and now they're singing like choirboys. They've already turned on their Autumn Wind paymasters.'

I frowned. 'But if the Hats are mercenaries – ex-army, presumably – why would they let the worst shot among them do all the killing?'

'To conceal their skill?' suggested Harry.

'That's not a bad idea,' said Lady Hardcastle. 'In fact, although Kovač's murder looked clumsy, it was a surprisingly effective shot. With one round, the killer managed to sever his spinal cord and clip a major artery. There's a level of diabolical artistry to that. And for all the apparently wild shots at Butcher's house, the deadly bullet went straight for the heart.'

I nodded. 'Cleverer than I supposed, then. I wondered for a moment if that might help to determine which of them killed Kovač and Tommy Adams. They might be happy to send Autumn Wind to gaol to save themselves, but I doubt they'll give up one of their own to the noose.'

'It's unlikely,' said Harry, 'but we'll question them carefully. They might let something slip, even if only by accident.'

A thought occurred to me. 'The bomb on the railway bridge and the one at the station. They were duds, weren't they?'

'They were indeed,' said Harry. 'The artillery chap said the detonators were just brass rods. How did you know?'

'Even before we found it, we'd decided that a bomb was a clumsy way to kill the archduke. There are too many "variables", as Herself likes to call them – too many things that could go wrong, too much uncertainty that he'd be killed even if it all worked perfectly. And even if they got him, it wouldn't be unequivocal that he was the target – it could have been anyone on the train. Either way, there were no guarantees that Austria would be sufficiently outraged that they'd go to war. He had to die, and it had to be unambiguously obvious that he was the target. A precision shot from the top of a bell tower in full view of a group of priests was a much better idea.'

'Sound logic. The artillery Johnnie also pointed out that, because of the design of the bridge and the amount of dynamite used, it might not have done anywhere near enough damage to kill the occupants of the train even if it were real. It would have closed the bridge for months while they repaired it, but there were no guarantees of fatalities.'

'So the whole thing was a diversion,' said Lady Hardcastle. 'With assistance from us. We were supposed to find the bombs and make everyone relax so that they could divert the car to the cathedral where the real murder attempt would take place.'

'Exactly so. Valentine has never been impressed by you two, but he was adamant that you should lead this case. I think he imagined he and Autumn Wind could lead you up the garden path and then lay the blame at your feet when it all went wrong. I'm so sorry.'

'Think nothing of it, dear. People have been underestimating me all my life, and it works to my advantage sufficiently often that I've stopped being bothered by it. To be fair, we *were* taken in by the *šajkačas*.'

'That was a nice touch,' agreed Harry. 'Flattering us into thinking we'd been clever by spotting a foreign hat. We'd have been more sceptical of flags or pro-Serbian leaflets, but a hat that only a few people from outside the region could identify was enough to fool us completely.'

I nodded. 'I wonder if poor Kovač wasn't so easily fooled. We'd assumed he was killed to stop him finding out that the Serbs were behind it all, but it's actually more likely he died because he knew they weren't. The ruse would never have worked if someone was able to tell the world it wasn't Balkan separatists but men hired by a shadowy British organization bent on starting a war for profit.'

'That might have started a war just the same,' said Harry. 'Whether it was us or Balkan separatists, we're still on the opposite side from Austria-Hungary in all the pacts and treaties.'

'It would have left Autumn Wind badly exposed, though,' said Lady Hardcastle. 'They'd not want that.'

'Nor would the mercenaries,' I added. 'It would have been much easier for them to disappear if we were all running around looking for Serbs. I'm still not entirely clear why Kovač ran for home rather than tell us, though.'

Harry shook his head. 'If he had it all worked out, perhaps he thought he needed to get back to make sure his own government was forewarned?'

'It would have been better to tell us and give us a chance to stop it,' said Lady Hardcastle. 'Unless . . .'

'Unless?' asked Harry.

'Unless he wasn't quite the loyal agent you took him for. Perhaps he was hoping the attempt would succeed and that his homeland would be finally free.'

Harry made a few more notes. 'We may never know.' He finally looked up. 'Is that everything?'

'It's enough to be getting on with,' said Lady Hardcastle. 'I'm not sure anyone can ask any questions you can't answer.'

'Oh, I have one,' I said. 'What did the Austrians make of it all?'

'They were a little baffled by the whole thing – especially the LTC chap legging it rather than coming over to greet them. The story we've fed them is that the LTC board were all arrested as part of a long-running fraud investigation. They were a little put out that we'd chosen the moment of their visit to the cathedral to arrest some fraudsters, but the priests were gracious hosts and showed them round their magnificent new building so it was soon forgotten. The advantage of Autumn Wind being so good at keeping secrets is that only we know what was really going on there. The archduke and his staff will never know how close he came to being shot, and an international incident has been averted.'

'What about the trade talks?'

'All going ahead, but without the LTC. The Board of Trade still has men ready to attend so I just have to have a discreet word with the minister. I'll stick with the fraud and embezzlement story. Embarrassing for all concerned, but no one ever started a war over dodgy accounting.'

'What do you want us to do now, dear?' asked Lady Hardcastle.

'I want you to take the rest of the day off and then join me and Jake for dinner at eight.'

I gave a sloppy salute. 'Aye-aye, Mr Feather-stone-huff.'

We left him to brief the War Office.

We waited as long as we could for Harry to come home, but eventually Lady Lavinia asked her staff to serve dinner without him. Both she and Helen pressed us for an account of the day and an explanation for Harry's lateness, but we held our nerve, saying that it wouldn't be proper to tell them anything without Harry's say-so.

He arrived during the fish course looking weary and dishevelled, but happy.

'Sorry I'm so late, ladies,' he said. 'But I'm glad you started without me – I feel a little less guilty. Is that turbot?'

Lady Lavinia rolled her eyes. 'It's Dover sole, you nitwit. It doesn't look anything like turbot.'

'So it is, so it is. Give me a few minutes to get dressed for dinner and I'll join you.'

'Don't be silly, darling – you can dine in your suit just this once, surely. Your shameful breach of etiquette will be our little secret.'

'Thank you. So, what have I missed?'

Lady Hardcastle took a sip of her Chablis. 'Nothing, dear. We've been fending these two off until we know what we're allowed to reveal.'

'Then top up your glasses and settle in, gels,' said Harry. 'For I am about to tell you a thrilling tale of intrigue and derring-do that will bedevil your shins and make your elbows quiver.'

And with that, he told them everything. From the murder in Bristol to the arrest of our SSB boss by members of the Household Cavalry – via fake Serbians, bombs, and a sniper in the campanile of Westminster Cathedral.

Lady Hardcastle raised her glass to Helen. 'We owe you an enormous debt of gratitude, dear. You deserve riches and honours.'

'Me?' said Helen. 'Whatever did I do?'

I raised my own glass in salute. 'If you hadn't shown us those stripper clips and told us about the smashed wig block, we'd never have been able to guess where the sniper might be hiding. It's all thanks to you and your photographic adventures.'

'Goodness gracious. Here's to me, then.' She raised her own glass and we drank to her health.

'That's all very well, darling,' said Lady Lavinia once the toasts were done, 'but why were you so late getting home? Surely all the hard work had been done. And mostly by Emily and Flo.'

'Oh,' said Harry. 'It was nothing important. I reported the incident to the War Office with Smith-Cumming and Kell in attendance. Lots of probing questions were asked and many minutes made on files marked "Top Secret". I thought I was for it, but then just as I was getting ready to leave, they offered me Valentine's job as head of Section G. With a pay rise.'

'I say,' said Lady Hardcastle, 'well done you. Do we have to call you "sir" now?'

'You do. And you should curtsey when I enter the room.'

'Oh, we do that anyway,' I said. 'Congratulations, Mr Feather-stone-huff.'

We toasted again, and turned to lighter matters.

It was gone midnight by the time we ventured out on to Bedford Square in search of a cab back to the flat.

Chapter Eighteen

Indian Clubs Man appeared on Fitzroy Square just as I was finishing my exercises the next morning. I gave him a cheery wave as I left and, to my surprise, he gave a nervous wave back.

'It's all yours now,' I called.

He gave me a confused shrug.

'We're heading home later. You can exercise in peace.'

I'm not sure what I expected, but I was hoping for more than him simply turning away and taking his clubs from his holdall before doing some limbering exercises. A 'nice to have met you', perhaps? 'Good luck with your future endeavours'? Even 'thank goodness for that – I find your Chinese garb and peculiar movements quite unsettling' would have been better than being ignored.

I made a slight detour to the baker's shop to get some bread, as well as some tasty iced buns for the journey home, and by the time I arrived at the flat, Lady Hardcastle was once more making breakfast.

'What ho, Flossie,' she said. 'Breakfast in five minutes. Did you get some bread?'

I gave her the loaf and went to get changed.

'I shall miss this little flat,' she said as we sat together for the last breakfast of the trip.

'You suggested on the way here that we buy somewhere. You said it would cut down on the amount of packing I have to do if we had some essentials and working outfits stored in our own little place in town.'

'I did, didn't I. I shall look into it. Talking of packing: do you need me to help?'

'Do you want to help?' I said.

'No, not really. I just thought it would be polite to offer.'

I laughed. 'I'll be fine, thank you. Remind me: how long do I have?'

'Harry has booked a porter for eleven, and the boy himself will be here shortly afterwards to take us to Paddington for the 12.05. We should be home by about six o'clock. I'd telephone the house to let Edna know but she still refuses to answer the blessed thing.'

'There's no guarantee we'd get a trunk call through before we leave anyway. Perhaps Harry could send a cable.'

'I'll ask him. It would be nice if Miss Jones could leave us a something for supper. I anticipate a decent lunch on the train, but some cold pie would be a very pleasant way to end the day. Perhaps with some chutney. And tomatoes.'

'I'm not sure the SSB's budget would stretch to that many words – I think you'll be lucky if he'll pay for "HOME BY SIX STOP PREPARE PIE",' I said. 'We'll just have to take our chances on what sort of pie and what accompaniments there might be. Miss Jones will see us right, though.'

'To be honest, as long as they've not drunk all the brandy while we've been away, I'm sure we can make do.'

'I'm sure we can. I presume the char will be coming here after we've gone? We don't have to clear up after ourselves?'

'Harry's problem,' said Lady Hardcastle. 'Or whoever he delegates that sort of thing to now that he's the gaffer. Either way, you should leave it, dear. We have averted an international crisis – I think the least they can do is to sweep up some crumbs and wash the crockery.'

It took me over an hour to get all our traps squared away, but there was time for another cup of coffee before the porters, and then Harry, arrived.

'What ho, ladies,' he said as we ushered him in. 'All set?'

'We are,' I said. 'We even have buns for later.'

'Don't trust the Great Western Railway to supply you with buns on the journey, then?'

Lady Hardcastle shook her head. 'They serve a fine lunch, but their cakes and pastries leave a lot to be desired.'

'Fair dos. Jake and Helen send their love and best wishes for a safe journey home, by the way, and hope to see you soon. Addie gabbled something unintelligible – some of it in Russian from what I could make out – but I think the gist was that she'll miss Aunt Emmy and "Fo".'

'Splendid,' said Lady Hardcastle. 'In that case, I think we're ready. Take us to Paddington, please, driver.'

The journey across town was a reasonably swift one, despite the traffic, and Harry waved us off on the Bristol train, having promised to send a telegram to Edna.

We were on our way home.

We fell back into our regular routines without any difficulty, and the rest of the week passed very pleasantly. Edna and Miss Jones expressed their relief that we had returned from another 'mission' unscathed – though there was some consternation at the sight of my bruised cheek.

I visited Daisy at the Dog and Duck. She pressed me for details of our time away, but this time I really couldn't tell her. Jokey, obliquely told stories about embassy balls and stolen documents were one thing, but I couldn't bring myself to tell her how close we had come to being drawn into all-out war. The country's mood on that score was already bleakly pessimistic, but at least war was still just a vague possibility – something that might happen at some unspecified time in the future. It felt as though I'd be doing everyone a disservice by turning it into an imminent and very real danger.

So I told her about our meeting with Queenie Pearce in her house of ill repute, and about asking one of the East End's senior villains for help, but I kept the story of Autumn Wind and the Fake Hats for another day. She seemed satisfied – Queenie's job offer amused her greatly – and an evening of gossip was planned with her, Cissy, and Blodwen Jones.

News of our return also reached Lady Farley-Stroud, who called on us on Friday morning while we were enjoying our elevenses in the garden. Edna answered the door and showed her through before bustling off to fetch another cup and saucer.

'Hello, Gertie dear,' said Lady Hardcastle. 'Join us, do.'

Lady Farley-Stroud chose the chair most shaded by the apple tree and eased herself into it with a sigh.

'Thank you, m'dear.'

'Miss Jones makes a marvellous Swiss roll – can we tempt you to a slice?'

'Just a small one . . . or perhaps a medium-sized one. I'm rather partial to your Miss Jones's cakes.'

I cut her a decent portion of cake, and Edna arrived just in time with a small plate and cake fork as well as the cup and saucer she'd gone in for.

'Good thinking,' I said as she put everything down.

Edna gave a satisfied nod of acknowledgement. 'Don't know of anyone who could refuse a bit of Miss Jones's Swiss roll.'

'There's plenty left. Help yourself.'

Edna grinned. 'It was much longer than that when she made it – we's already 'ad some. But I might take some for Bert if you don't mind.'

Lady Farley-Stroud's chauffeur was a familiar and welcome guest in our kitchen and we invited Edna to take the cake back inside so she could share it with him.

I poured Lady Farley-Stroud a cup of tea and she was silent for a few moments as she tucked in to her own piece of cake.

'Tell me then, m'dears,' she said after washing down her mouthful with a sip of tea, 'how stands the Empire?'

'It bumbles along,' said Lady Hardcastle.

'Safer now than it was before you left?'

'Marginally, yes. For now, at least.'

'Good show.'

'And how about you, dear? How are the preparations for the party?'

'It's mostly under control, I think. Mrs Brown and her kitchen staff have the catering well in hand. The marquee is up and the furniture arrives this afternoon. Hector has ordered enough booze to fill an ornamental lake. Oh, and we're thinking about digging an ornamental lake, by the way, but not in time for tomorrow. The only thing we haven't been able to organize is the orchestra. I've written letters, sent telegrams, made countless telephone calls, but no one has been able to help us at such short notice. I don't suppose . . . ?'

'We have that well in hand,' said Lady Hardcastle. 'I need to make one more telephone call of my own and all should be well.'

'It's not as though it's an essential part of the festivities, m'dear, but it would so add to the general jollity if we could have some entertainment.'

'Don't despair, Gertie dear. Leave it to me.'

I could tell from Lady Farley-Stroud's expression that she had hoped for something a little more concrete, but Lady Hardcastle took an infuriating delight in keeping secrets and springing surprises. It was obvious from the just-you-wait-and-see look on her face that it would be pointless for anyone to press her further. I could only imagine how much it must be bothering Lady Farley-Stroud – I knew exactly what Lady Hardcastle had planned, but even I found her smugness infuriating.

I was about to try to change the subject when Edna came bustling out with an envelope in her hand.

'I'm so sorry, Miss Armstrong,' she said. 'I meant to give you this when I come out with the cup and saucer. Postman called while I was inside, see?'

I took the letter and placed it on the table. 'Thank you, Edna. Most kind.'

She smiled and bustled off again.

Lady Hardcastle tapped the envelope. 'Well? Aren't you going to open it?'

'I thought it would be rude. We have a guest.'

'Don't mind me, m'dear,' said Lady Farley-Stroud. 'You open your letter. I'll busy meself with a bit more cake – this is delicious.'

I raised an irritated eyebrow at Lady Hardcastle.

'Oh, don't look like that, dear. It's from your sister. You know you want to read it.'

With a sigh, I opened the letter.

To her credit, Lady Hardcastle did manage to sit still for a few moments before her curiosity got the better of her. 'Well?'

'Well what?' I said, putting down the letter.

'What does she say? How is she? How's Dai? What are they up to? I want all the news.'

I picked up the letter again. 'Gwen's well. Dai's well. Gwen's had to buy a new pot after Dai destroyed their old one making his famous stew. Oh, and she's expecting a baby at the end of the year.'

Lady Hardcastle whooped with delight, and the sudden noise shocked Lady Farley-Stroud sufficiently that she almost choked on her Swiss roll.

'I say,' said Lady Hardcastle. 'Congratulations, Aunt Flossie. Good heavens, Gertie dear, are you all right?'

Lady Farley-Stroud took a sip of tea to get her coughing under control. 'Quite all right, thank you, m'dear. And yes, congratulations, Aunt Florence. Your sister is a good woman – we haven't forgotten how she took care of poor Agnes Bingle. She'll make a wonderful mother, and you'll make a splendid aunt.'

I thanked them both, and the conversation turned to granddaughters and nieces.

Later, with the tea drunk and the cake eaten, Lady Farley-Stroud wearily decided that she ought to be getting back, and we saw her out to her motor car.

'I'd better book that trunk call,' said Lady Hardcastle as Bert drove off.

I left her to it and returned to my mending.

Saturday dawned, warm but slightly overcast. There was a comfortable familiarity to exercising in the garden beneath the apple tree, but part of me missed the plane trees of Fitzroy Square. By the time I went back inside to change, Edna and Miss Jones had already arrived.

'Morning, ladies,' I said as I entered the kitchen. 'You're early.'

'We wants to get a start on the day,' said Edna. 'With it bein' the big party this afternoon, we thought we might try to get away early if you and the mistress don't mind.'

'I think it's a splendid idea, and Herself won't mind, I'm sure.'

'How long do you suppose it's goin' to last?'

'The party? I couldn't say. Lady Farley-Stroud didn't offer any details when we saw her yesterday and I neglected to ask, I'm afraid. Sorry. Knowing Sir Hector, he'll want the fun to carry on until the last person either leaves or passes out in the rhododendrons.'

'They doesn't 'ave no rhododendrons up at The Grange s'far as I knows.'

'Then the party may never end.'

'Good. Me and our Dan likes a "hooley", as his grandma used to call it.'

'I doubt it will be quite as raucous as that.'

'Oh, I don't know, my lover. They used to put on some wild parties in the old days, the Farley-Strouds.'

'Will there be music?' asked Miss Jones. 'I like a dance, but Daisy said they couldn't find no one to play for them.'

I tapped the side of my nose. 'Herself has a plan.'

Edna gave an emphatic nod of agreement and satisfaction. 'We's all right, then. We can rely on either you or Lady 'ardcastle to save the day.'

I only hoped her confidence wasn't misplaced.

◆ ◆ ◆

The party was due to start at three in the afternoon with, as Edna had observed, no finishing time advertised.

In a radical change from custom, Lady Hardcastle insisted that we arrive at three on the dot. She usually preferred to turn up an hour or more after the festivities were scheduled to begin, 'to give things a chance to get properly underway', but today she was adamant that we be there on time.

'I don't want Gertie to think we've forgotten her,' she said as we set off. 'She's been afraid that no one will turn up.'

Lady Farley-Stroud needn't have worried.

People were already crossing the village green in their summer finery as we emerged from the end of the lane, and we joined a procession of excited villagers climbing the hill towards The Grange.

Daisy, Cissy and Blodwen caught us up.

'All right, you two?' said Cissy. 'I 'ears you've been off savin' the country again.'

'Saving the world, Ciss,' I said. 'We're expanding the business.'

Cissy laughed. 'One day you'll tell us the truth about what you does.'

'When we're old and grey, dear,' said Lady Hardcastle. 'Although I think you'll be disappointed.'

'I doubts it,' said Cissy. 'Even the censored versions is excitin'.'

We walked on.

At The Grange, we were greeted by Sir Hector, who directed people to the rear of the house and the marquee.

'There's drinks and nibbles in the tent,' he said. 'There'll be a light buffet at five if you want to stay that long, and a decent buffet supper at eight for anyone who's still here. Or who's come back. I, for one, intend to keep goin' until I can't stand. Oh, and if anyone's interested in the story of the treasure, I've put together a little exhibition about Sir Teddy Elderkin in the ballroom.'

There were scattered groups of villagers and other friends on the lawn, and the marquee – home of the bar and buffet – was jammed. We found Reverend Bland and his wife Jagruti sitting in the shade of a large tree and asked if we could join them.

'We'd be delighted to have your company, ladies,' said the vicar. 'Lots of people stop to say hello, but no one lingers. Perils of being a vicar, I'm afraid.'

Lady Hardcastle sat with them, and I went off to the marquee to brave the crowds and see if I could find the promised drinks and nibbles.

By the time I returned, Mrs Bland was in the middle of a story about Hamlet, her enormous – and gormlessly mischievous – Great Dane.

'. . . with a whole ham in his mouth, pursued by the church flower committee and the ladies sewing circle.'

'He's for sale if you want him,' said the vicar. 'No reasonable offer refused. In fact, I'll pay you to take him off our hands. Our housekeeper threatens to resign every day if we don't do something about him.'

'You love him,' chided Mrs Bland. 'You'd be lost without him.'

'I'd have a lot more to eat, that's for sure. He's so huge he can sit down and rest his head on the dining table. Can you imagine it? It's like having an extra guest for dinner every evening. And those pleading eyes. And the drool.'

'He always seems absolutely adorable to me,' I said.

'He's yours,' said the vicar. 'Honestly. Take him. He could work with you on your secret missions.'

Mrs Bland smiled. 'They'd find it difficult to remain stealthily concealed with darling Hammy bouncing about.'

I was contemplating a diplomatic response when I noticed Sir Hector hurrying across the lawn towards us. I tapped Lady Hardcastle's arm and pointed.

'Hector dear,' she said. 'You look all of a pother. Is there something the matter?'

'Nothin' the matter, m'dear,' he said. 'I've been promoted to messenger boy. There's a Scottish lass at the gate, got a shower of lads with her. Says she knows you.'

'She does indeed. She's Jessie McKenzie, and the shower of lads are the Rip-Roaring Revellers. They're your band for the evening, dear.'

'I say, well done you. The memsahib's been havin' kittens over that all week. How did you . . . ?'

Lady Hardcastle tapped the side of her nose. 'We have a lot of influential contacts.'

'We know the drummer and the bass player,' I said. 'You've met them – Skins and Dunn. They were in Roland Richman's band. The ones who played at Clarissa's engagement party.'

'One of 'em got bumped off,' said Sir Hector.

'That's it. But these two survived and now they're in a new band.'

'And I asked them if they'd play for you,' said Lady Hardcastle.

'Splendid news. I'll get 'em set up on the stage. How much is it costin' me?'

'You'll have to sort that out with Mrs McKenzie, dear. But she's a canny lass, so don't expect to get away cheaply.'

A beaming Sir Hector scampered back towards the front of the house and the waiting band.

Acknowledgements

As always, I am indebted to the astonishingly wonderful team at Thomas & Mercer for their encouragement, guidance and support. Victoria Pepe kicked the whole thing off and Kasim Mohammed brought it home, but everyone pitched in. Thank you.

For some reason, Laura Gerrard still manages to tolerate working with me, and uses her editing skills to coax the best out of the books without making me feel like an idiot.

Whenever I need firearms expertise, I call on Andrew Rigsby, who recommended the Mosin-Nagant as a suitable sniper rifle for the period and reassured me that the 100-yard shot from the cathedral's bell tower was perfectly feasible.

Once again, I offered a named character in the 'Children In Read' auction in aid of BBC Children In Need. The extraordinarily generous winner chose not her own name, but that of her grandmother, Jessie McKenzie, a Glaswegian who emigrated to Australia with her four children. I made Jessie the singer in the Rip-Roaring Revellers so that she could sing with Skins and Dunn.

Author's Notes

The public mortuary overseen by Dr Simeon Gosling in the story is a fiction, created to give me control over its layout, location and administration.

The Belgian-made FN 1910 that Lady Hardcastle and Harry both mention was designed by the American gunsmith John Browning. It was the pistol used in 1914 by Gavrilo Princip to murder Archduke Franz Ferdinand and his wife, Duchess Sophie Chotek, in Sarajevo.

I mentioned the history of the Secret Service Bureau when they first appeared in *Death Beside the Seaside*, but it might be worth clarifying things a little once more. The SSB was founded in 1909 as a joint effort by the Admiralty and the War Office to coordinate British intelligence and counter-intelligence efforts at home and abroad. During its early years its work focused especially on the activities of Imperial Germany. In Lady Hardcastle's world it is better staffed and resourced than in reality, where, at its formation, it was run by just two men: a senior naval officer called Mansfield Smith-Cumming and an army officer by the name of Vernon Kell.

Even by the outbreak of World War One there were still only fourteen staff, so I invented roles for Harry Featherstonhaugh and his immediate superior, Colonel Valentine, as well as adding Lady

Hardcastle and Florence Armstrong (and unnamed others) to the payroll.

My use of Special Branch officers to undertake some of the legwork is more storytelling expedience. Special Branch had been formed in 1883 as a unit within the Metropolitan Police with responsibility for national security and intelligence, and was founded in response to the activities of the Irish Republican Brotherhood. By the time of our story, nearly thirty years later, it was a well-respected outfit responsible for all other aspects of counter-espionage, so its activities would have overlapped with those of the SSB. In our world I have imagined Special Branch sending their more annoying officers – whom Flo refers to as SBOs – to the SSB, to get them out of the way.

It's also true that the SSB – and its successors, MI5 and MI6 – had no power of arrest, just as the Hat in the tower points out. So the SBOs would always have been handy.

In *Death Beside the Seaside*, before being dragged back to the world of espionage by her brother, Lady Hardcastle refers to the SSB's offices being in 'some basement in Whitehall'. In fact they began life in Ashley Mansions on the Vauxhall Bridge Road. Mansfield Smith-Cumming established a fake address with the Post Office, so that the building appeared to be the home of Messrs Rasen, Falcon Limited, a firm of 'shippers and exporters'. Fans of James Bond might recall that the cover for the intelligence service in those stories is 'Universal Exports'. Ian Fleming was an officer in Naval Intelligence during World War Two.

In 1911, the SSB moved to 2 Whitehall Court, which is now a restaurant with an English Heritage blue plaque beside the doorway commemorating Sir Mansfield Smith-Cumming as 'the first chief of the Secret Service'. Since I have been cavalier in imagining the organization of the SSB in our story world, I felt justified in taking similar liberties with the layout of the offices. In for a penny, etc.

The name John Doe has been used in English law since the thirteenth century, originally to protect the identity of witnesses, and later to indicate an unnamed plaintiff in property disputes, where the defendant was referred to as Richard Roe. Since 1852 John Doe has been used to indicate any man whose name is unknown, though its use is now less common in England and Wales than in the US.

The travel times are approximated from old railway timetables, which are extremely hard to find and absurdly difficult to interpret. Although the story is set in 1912, I used a set from 1910 because it was all there was. Chipping Bevington is a fictional town, but it is fifteen imaginary miles from Bristol so I found another fifteen-mile route and used the travel time for that. In 1910, the journey from Bristol Temple Meads to London Paddington took four and a quarter hours. It now takes a shade over an hour and a half. The timetables are now much easier to read, but understanding the fare structure makes breaking the Enigma Code look childishly trivial by comparison.

The rented flat is on Southampton Street, off the north-west corner of Fitzroy Square. That part of the road began life as Upper Conway Street, with Lower Conway Street to the south of the square. At the time of our story it had become Southampton Street but has since been renamed again, with the whole length of the road from Euston Road to Maple Street now simply known as Conway Street.

The fictional version of the building has been converted into flats by an enterprising landlord solely to give Lady Hardcastle and Flo somewhere small, manageable and – most importantly of all – private from which to operate. At the time of the story it would, in reality, still have been a townhouse much like Harry's.

Non-UK readers probably don't need to be reminded that in Britain we number our floors ground, first, second, etc. This means that the second-floor flat is on what might elsewhere be known as the third floor.

There is no London Trade Confederation.

The Archduke Franz Ferdinand did, as Harry suggests he might, officially visit the UK in the autumn of 1913. There is no record of an unofficial visit in 1912.

Until 1909, the docks in London were owned and managed by a variety of private companies. The Port of London Authority was formed as part of the Port of London Act 1908 to streamline the operation of this essential part of the country's infrastructure. The PLA's original headquarters on Trinity Square is now a hotel.

There may have been one or more pie and mash shops on Cable Street in 1912, but Frankie's isn't one of them. From the middle of the nineteenth century, working-class restaurants sprang up across London – most especially in the East End and the corresponding area around the docks south of the river – selling simple meals of meat pie, mashed potato and 'liquor', as well as jellied eels. Liquor in this case is a silky, green parsley sauce made from the stewed eel stock the eels had been cooked in (i.e., the cooking liquor). Pie and mash shops, though now much less commonplace, are still popular in parts of London.

You already worked it out, of course, but 'Rosie' is Rosie Lee and is Cockney rhyming slang for tea, while 'satin' is satin and silk – milk. Young Billy mentions 'aris', where the link is harder to work out. 'Aris' is short for Aristotle, which is rhyming slang for bottle. Bottle and glass is 'arse' (which does rhyme in London, no matter what you might think).

It doesn't immediately sound generous, but adjusted for inflation, Lady Hardcastle's offer of £5 for Benny's help in 1912 would be worth over £700 in today's money. As I write this, that's about $910.

Farrand's Wharf was on Bermondsey Wall at the end of Cherry Garden Street, right next to the Cherry Garden Pier. The pier was controlled by the Port of London Authority as a lookout post. PLA staff on the pier would see vessels coming round the bend of the river at Limehouse and telephone the operators of Tower Bridge, so that they could raise the bridge to allow the ships through without making them wait. Many of the PLA piers along the Thames were removed when the docks were closed, but Cherry Garden Pier remains and has been used by a company offering river tours since the 1970s.

There were a number of warehouses and granaries near that section of the river, and in 1912 they were all busy. In Lady Hardcastle's world, though, at least one of them had been abandoned. The location I chose was a granary in 1912 and there's no evidence of an alleyway between that and the building next door – sometimes you just have to make stuff up.

Harry's claim of the number of named wharves on the Thames is almost certainly wrong, it being based on twenty-first-century information gathered by modern enthusiasts. A map from 1910 shows that even in just the tiny two-thirds-of-a-mile stretch between Tower Bridge and Cherry Garden Pier on the south side of the river, there were twenty-three. Harry's numbers feel far too low, but counting them 'by hand' for the sake of a throwaway comment by Mr Feather-stone-huff would probably not have been time well spent.

The advertisement for Sandow's Spring Grip Dumb-Bells really did take up the whole back page of the Saturday, 13 July 1912 edition of *Boxing*. Readers who took up the offer of a seven-day free trial would also receive a free gift: 'A fine photograph of Luis Hardt'. Hardt made a living as an artist's model and music hall performer, where he was billed as 'The Mighty Atom' several years before the American former wrestler Joe Greenstein famously used the name.

Betts Street no longer exists in its Edwardian form, and is now just a stub of a street off The Highway (originally Ratcliff Highway but known as George Street in Lady Hardcastle's time). It joined George Street to Cable Street and was, indeed, home to a public baths, a refuge (the Victorian/Edwardian equivalent of a homeless shelter) and a school, as well as a scattering of houses.

The modern trend for experimenting with the botanicals used to flavour gin has resulted in an accompanying trend for garnishing drinks with all manner of things to complement the flavours. But Lady Hardcastle would have to wait until 1999 – when Hendrick's Gin and Martin Miller's Gin, which both feature cucumber among their botanical flavourings, appeared on the market – before her cucumber garnish became properly fashionable.

The Order of Merit is a British honour established in 1902. When it was first mooted in the eighteenth century, it was originally intended to honour those distinguished in the arts. By the time it was eventually founded by Edward VII, it was expanded to include military service as well as contributions to art, literature and science. At the time of our story in 1912 it was one of the few honours open to women. It wasn't until George V founded the Most Excellent Order of the British Empire in 1917 that a 'knighthood' (a damehood, obviously) would have been available to Flo for the first time.

A 'standard' stick of dynamite weighed 1/2 a troy pound, which is 6.58 oz (or about 190 g). Thus seven sticks would be 46 oz, or 2 lb 14 oz. Lady Hardcastle rounds it up to three pounds.

The Grosvenor Railway Bridge (or Victoria Railway Bridge) has been widened and modified several times since it was originally built in 1860. Although the piers remain, the arched ironwork and deck have all been replaced so that it now looks slightly different from the way it would have in 1912.

The Grosvenor Hotel opened in 1861 next to the newly built Victoria station. The building is still a luxury hotel, but it's now called the Clermont.

In the initial planning stages of the story, I looked at the view of the Westminster Cathedral campanile from Victoria Street and determined that it would be an ideal spot for the planned assassination. It was only when I checked earlier maps that I learned that the Cathedral Piazza, which looks like such an integral part of the design, didn't exist in 1912 – there were buildings there. I was tempted not to let facts get in the way of a good yarn, but a little more poking around showed that the shot could just as easily be taken as the archduke's car turned on to Ashley Place from Carlisle Place. This would only work if the car were open-topped, but it was the height of summer and it echoed Gavrilo Princip's murder of Franz Ferdinand and Sophie two years later, so the plan was duly changed.

The landmark buildings around Victoria station are still much as described – even the Duke of York, which was demolished and rebuilt in the 2010s to make it look very much as it did when it was built in the late 1800s.

The stairs in the campanile of Westminster Cathedral still exist, but just as Flo predicted there is also a lift now, which takes visitors up to the public viewing gallery at 218 feet, almost at the top of the square part of the tower. I wasn't able to ascertain when the lift shaft was installed nor see any photographs of the tower before the installation, so my description of the staircase is based on a 3D scan of the tower which is available to view on the cathedral's website. It used to be possible for visitors to reach the much higher gallery used by the sniper, but that was closed some years ago for safety reasons. The small spiral staircases are visible on the 3D scan, so the route that Emily and Flo take is reasonably accurate.

There really was a police section house (a sort of police barracks) at 1 Ambrosden Avenue, opposite the end of the cathedral on the corner of Francis Street. The building is now an expensive apartment block.

As for the assassination attempt . . .

I've already mentioned Princip's pistol and the open-topped car, but those interested in World War One might recognize several other elements in the story from the real murder of Archduke Ferdinand and the Duchess Sophie in Sarajevo, Bosnia, in 1914. There were six main members of the real assassination team, who were intending to use bombs (grenades, in fact). Two men failed to throw theirs. The third man threw his grenade but it bounced off Archduke Franz Ferdinand's car and landed under the following vehicle. Members of the entourage in the car and several bystanders were injured, but the archduke carried on. After a reception at City Hall, the royal couple wanted to go to the hospital to visit the injured officers. There was some confusion and the drivers set off in the wrong direction, taking them past the waiting assassins. The royal cars entered a side street and realized their error. While attempting to reverse back out on to the main road, one of the cars stalled, and Gavrilo Princip stepped on to the running board and shot the archduke and duchess. Sophie died on the way to hospital and Franz Ferdinand shortly after.

About the Author

Photo © 2018 Clifton Photographic Company

T E Kinsey grew up in London and read history at Bristol University. *An Assassination on the Agenda* is the eleventh story in the Lady Hardcastle Mystery series, and he is also the author of the Dizzy Heights Mystery series. His website is at tekinsey.uk and you can follow him on Facebook: www.facebook.com/tekinsey.

Follow the Author on Amazon

If you enjoyed this book, follow T E Kinsey on Amazon to be notified when the author releases a new book!

To do this, please follow these instructions:

Desktop:

1) Search for the author's name on Amazon or in the Amazon App.
2) Click on the author's name to arrive on their Amazon page.
3) Click the 'Follow' button.

Mobile and Tablet:

1) Search for the author's name on Amazon or in the Amazon App.
2) Click on one of the author's books.
3) Click on the author's name to arrive on their Amazon page.
4) Click the 'Follow' button.

Kindle eReader and Kindle App:

If you enjoyed this book on a Kindle eReader or in the Kindle App, you will find the author 'Follow' button after the last page.